D0914048

# MODERN STORIES
# FROM MANY LANDS

*The Literary Review Book*

# MODERN

AUSTRIA
CZECHOSLOVAKIA
CHILE
ESTONIA
FINLAND
GREECE
HUNGARY
INDIA
INDONESIA
IRELAND
ISRAEL
ITALY
JAPAN
LATVIA
LITHUANIA
NETHERLANDS
NORWAY
PAKISTAN
PHILIPPINES
ROMANIA
SOVIET RUSSIA
SOUTH AFRICA
TURKEY
U.S.A.
YUGOSLAVIA

THE LITERARY REVIEW

LIBRARY
OKALOOSA - WALTON JUNIOR COLLEGE

# STORIES

## FROM
## MANY
## LANDS

Second Enlarged Edition

*Selected and Edited by*

CLARENCE R. DECKER

CHARLES ANGOFF

Revised Edition
*Edited by*
CHARLES ANGOFF

MANYLAND BOOKS • NEW YORK

PN
6014
D35
1972

SECOND EDITION

© Copyright, 1963, 1972, by The Literary Review

*All rights reserved. This book, or parts thereof, must not
be reproduced in any form without the permission of* The
Literary Review, *Fairleigh Dickinson University, Rutherford
New Jersey, U. S. A. Published by Manyland Books,
84-39 Ninetieth Street, Woodhaven, New York.*

*Library of Congress Catalogue Card Number:* 72-77856
ISBN 0-87141-040-0

MANUFACTURED IN THE UNITED STATES OF AMERICA

LIBRARY
OKALOOSA - WALTON JUNIOR COLLEGE

# Table of Contents

44749

# TABLE OF CONTENTS (continued)

# TABLE OF CONTENTS (continued)

# FOREWORD TO SECOND EDITION

The first edition of *Modern Stories From Many Lands* was published in 1963, under the co-editorship of Clarence R. Decker and Charles Angoff, who were co-founders and co-editors of *The Literary Review*. Dr. Decker ceased being associated with *The Literary Review* in the Fall of 1967, when Dr. Angoff became the sole editor. He alone is responsible for the present revised, enlarged edition.

The following stories have been added: "A Legend of Saintly Folly," by Vladimir Vondra (Czechoslovakia); "The Seventh Witness," by Karl Ristikivi (Estonia); "The Killer," by Veijo Meri (Finland); "Engagement," by Endre Fejes (Hungary); "The Vision From the Tower," by Margarita Kovalevska (Latvia); "He Wasn't Allowed to See," by Pulgis Andriušis (Lithuania); "The Actress," by Stepas Zobarskas (Lithuania); "Moment of Freedom," by Jens Björneboe (Norway); "Music from a Blue Well," by Torborg Nedreaas (Norway); "Grandma," by Iqbal Ahmad (Pakistan); "Encounter in the Fields," by Marin Preda (Romania); "The Prisoner," by Ahmed Essa (South Africa); "The Easy Life," by Yuri Kazakov (Soviet Russia); "Twilight Is Falling on the Earth," by Lojze Kovačič (Yugoslavia); and "The Steamer," by Charles Angoff (U.S.A.). More could have been added, so many and so varied have been the fine short stories that have come to us from so many lands, both large and small, but the matter of available space had to be considered.

ix

Again, thanks to the writers and translators who have made *Modern Stories From Many Lands* possible. One hopes that devotees of the art of the short story will find the present edition even more appealing than the first one. Perhaps a word of encouragement will be permitted: a period that can produce such lovely and perceptive and moving tales as are included in this book can hardly be called entirely hopeless.

A special word to scholars and translators. It has not always been possible to reach authors in foreign lands. This has been especially so in the case of those deceased whose representatives have moved. This will explain the gaps in the biographical notes. As we go to press, we still are trying to reach them, and we hope to fill in the informational gaps in a later edition.

CHARLES ANGOFF
*Fairleigh Dickinson*
*University*
*Rutherford, N. J., U.S.A.*

Spring, 1972

# FOREWORD TO FIRST EDITION

*The Literary Review* celebrates its fifth anniversary with the publication of its first book, *Modern Stories From Many Lands,* an anthology selected from its pages. It also commemorates the twentieth anniversary of Fairleigh Dickinson University, New Jersey, its sponsor and publisher. *The Literary Review,* in the words of its first editorial, is an "international quarterly of contemporary writing in the field of *belles lettres.* It seeks to encourage literary excellence and its appreciation by a wider audience and to further cultural exchange among the peoples of the world." From the beginning, it has stressed imaginative writing in all forms, though the purely critical essay, instinct with genuine insight, has not been neglected.

Seven entire numbers of *The Literary Review* have been devoted to the modern creative writing of individual countries—three of which are the first anthologies of the country concerned to be published in the United States—and more are in preparation. Our short fiction has perhaps given us the most satisfaction and it has evoked the most sympathetic response the world over. This short fiction has ranged across all lands, from India to Israel, and from Ireland to Japan. On rereading the 125 stories that we have published thus far, we have found it difficult to make a selection, so excellent they all seem to us, and our final choices have been made only after agonizing deliberation.

The history of European civilization from the decline and fall of the Roman Empire till the end of the Nineteenth Century and well into the Twentieth is largely a history of city states, small republics, modest kingdoms, mere principalities. The history of Italian culture is the history of such city states as Florence and Naples and such republics as Venice. A half dozen Popes referred to Michelangelo as the Florentine, and the Venetian school of painting is in a class by itself. Holland and Belgium and Switzerland and Sweden and Norway and Denmark, and the many kingdoms that in 1870 were "integrated" into the German Empire, offer more evidence of the love history has for small national communities: it seems often to prefer them to vaster lands when looking for a place to plant another of its seeds of genius.

This concept, of course, cannot be pushed too far. French culture was at its height when the French nation was at its height. Shakespeare and the whole Elizabethan galaxy of literary giants lived at exactly the time England leaped into the position of Ruler of the Waves. But it is a question whether mere size and military and commercial position are more conducive to cultural greatness, especially literary greatness, than a modest status in material power.

Ancient lands such as India and Austria and Greece and Italy are producing most creditable modern short fiction. We were happy, indeed, to print Heimito von Doderer's "The Magician's Art"—*The Literary Review* was the first to publish this fine Austrian writer in translation in the United States. We were happy to publish Elsa Morante's "The Sicilian Soldier" and Ennio Flaiano's "Armida and Reality" and Dino Buzzati's "A Siberian Shepherd's Report of the Atom Bomb" (among others) as representative short stories of Italy. We were delighted to publish excellent stories from India and Greece—and we are proud to reprint them in the present anthology.

Some of the greatest vitality, the loveliest lyrics, the most dazzling symbolism are found in the fiction of the smaller and

younger countries. *The Literary Review* printed a whole
Israeli number—on the occasion of the tenth anniversary
of the founding of that Republic—and our make-up problem
at the time was what we could afford to leave out since so
much excellent material was available. One story such as
Asher Barash's "Speed the Plow" is almost enough to justify
a decade's life in a nation.

The fiction the Netherlands is producing is truly remarkable. The issue of *The Literary Review* devoted entirely to that country's literature brought forth extraordinary
comment. There is no fiction in Europe now like it. It is
dark and brooding and startlingly honest. It leaps and sings
and burns. "Hijo de Puta," by Adriaan Morriën, shudders
with every mystical calling of blood: it is instinct with com-
mentary upon the cruelty of man toward man, and yet there
is a bizarre joyousness about it all. "The Stone Face," by
Simon Vestdijk, and "The Boslowits Family," by Gerard
Kornelis van het Reve, rival it in emotional impact.

Turkey has gone through one of the most historic up-
heavals in modern times, joining the Occident almost over
night. It still is little known to Western readers, yet it is
producing a literature of astonishing vigor and color. Its
melody comes from olden, mystic times, yet it is oriented
toward our own day. Yasar Kemal, who was proposed recently, at age thirty-eight, for the Nobel Prize in literature,
was first presented to the American reader in the Turkish
number of *The Literary Review*—a number which quickly
became a collector's item.

To jump across the other side of the world, there is the
Philippines, like Israel, a new nation, and like Israel blessed
with literary riches. In the Philippines number stories such
as "Love in the Cornhusks," by Aida Rivera, and "On the
Ferry," by N. V. M. Gonzales, are imbedded in the memories
of those who have read them.

Thirteen countries, including the United States—twenty-
four stories altogether for the entire volume—are repre-

sented in *Modern Stories From Many Lands*. We believe they offer ample evidence of the abiding vitality and marvelous potentialities of the short story as a literary art form. Further, they prove that small, new countries enjoy the favors of literary history at least as much as more ancient lands, with long and lofty traditions.

One paradox is worthy of comment. In Europe whole reputations have been made with the short story alone. There was Katherine Mansfield, there was Guy de Maupassant, there was Ivan Buin, whose classic, "The Gentleman From San Francisco," is really a longish short story. It seldom occurs to European critics to tell accomplished short story writers that they should write novels, thereby implying that somehow the writing of short stories is an inferior art. But that is exactly what is done in this country. Our short story writers are constantly being more or less bullied into writing fiction in the larger form. This is strange, indeed. The United States is the land par excellence of the short story. From Edgar Allan Poe to Willa Cather and Katherine Anne Porter, we have, in all truth, probably been more successful as short story writers than as novelists. Many of our novelists appear to suffer from what may be called literary asthma. They fill twenty, thirty pages, and then they get blue in the face, so to speak—which is why so many of our novels are, in effect, blown-up short stories, and why so many of our novelists do better work in the shorter space. Willa Cather's stories are better than her novels, good as some of the latter are. *My Antonia* is still readable, very much so, but "A Wagner Matinée" will probably live longer. Dreiser? *Sister Carrie* and *Jennie Gerhardt* are good, but *Twelve Men* is better. Hemingway? Aren't his stories, for all their limited insight, better than his novels, including *The Old Man and the Sea* and *A Farewell to Arms?* And Faulkner? Well, aren't "A Rose for Emily" and "The Evening Sun" more captivating than, even, *Light in August* and *The Bear?*

But what about less well-known writers, beginners or those on the way? We urge you to read "Lilli," by the American writer, Kaatje Hurlbut, which adds a special lustre of its own to this volume.

\*       \*       \*

The editors of *The Literary Review* are deeply indebted to the writers and translators who have made this anthology possible. We are also in debt to our publisher, Stepas Zobarskas, for whom this volume is a mission and a labor of love. And last but far from least, we are in debt to Dr. Peter Sammartino, president of Fairleigh Dickinson University, who inspired the founding of *The Literary Review* and who has taken a keen personal interest in the publication of this anthology.

We feel sure that modern readers from many lands will share our appreciation with the appearance of *Modern Stories From Many Lands,* a book which, we hope, will remind all of us that the short story, one of the oldest literary forms, is still a many-splendored thing, naturally subject to local influences but responsive to the universal and immortal in the human heart at all times and in all places. "Tell me a story" has rung down the ages, and the plea has not come from the young alone. The need is part of every heart, young and old alike.

Charles Angoff
Clarence R. Decker

# MODERN STORIES
# FROM MANY LANDS

*The Literary Review Book*

# AUSTRIA

# The Magician's Art

HEIMITO VON DODERER

Translated from the German by Astrid Ivask

TO PAN, the great god of summer, sacrificial offerings of camphor and naphthalene are brought by the city; the cool fragrance is pleasing to him in abandoned, half-darkened habitations, circling the shrouded furniture as a faintest whiff. Meanwhile the inhabitants of such rooms are walking in real woods, or standing in gardens on very narrow gravel paths between flower-beds adorned with glass globes of various colours. Dark woods encircle the foot of the distant mountain range like a discarded garment; rocks, already bare, shimmer milky and mild under the high summer skies, accented only here and there by a patch of snow.

The city has sunk below the horizon. In this heat she sinks into herself and becomes lonely, because so many have left her, and becomes lonelier still above the steaming asphalt, even though hundreds and thousands of people are still running and riding about. The city is in a meditative mood. She now has many hollow spaces for withdrawal, caverns and cavities, shaded and freshly camphorized. At long last furniture attains to a life of its own. But the city's meditations are not confined to sealed-off chambers alone. In front of a small inn, "To the City of Paris," tables with shiny beer-mugs are standing on the sidewalk of a by-street. A cool and cellary smell wafts from the vaults, a smell of barrels perhaps, of wine-casks and beer barrels. Only now does one notice that the moon has risen above the street. The evening stays very warm.

3

Summer in the hot streets of Vienna is not the best of
seasons for innkeepers, even though the heat makes beer flow
more abundantly, especially when the temperature reaches
six mugs in the shade, as a local saying has it. Daily a stream
of people leaves the city after working hours, not to mention
weekends, when the Vienna yard inns are favoured on account of their arbours, where moonlight transforms the
jagged grape-leaves into paper cut-outs or, on occasion, into
the metallic rigidity of tin.

A stream of people abandons the city, which then begins
to meditate in the forsaken inns and among the tables and
potted laurel trees on a sidewalk.

The young innkeeper of "The City of Paris" and his wife
were determined to get things going again after a succession
of hot days that were continuing obstinately, as if intending
to chase the very last customer into the verdure of the Prater
or to the "Heuriger"* in the suburb of Sievering. It would
certainly take some doing to counteract this pitiful state of
affairs! But since an innkeeper knows most of his customers
rather intimately, he also commands a wealth of personal
contacts, maybe more so than any other kind of businessman,
thus having connections with all sorts of professions and
walks of life, down to the very oddest. This is especially true
if the innkeeper himself has an attractive and pleasing personality, as was certainly the case with Franz Blauensteiner,
not to speak of his beautiful wife Elly, who in addition to a
typically Viennese plumpness displayed a pair of shapely
legs and thus, as a fair specimen of Viennese womanhood,
bounced busily and merrily about the inn.

They knew everyone. And more than that: they recognized, sooner or later, everybody's real worth. They recognized, for instance, the exact relationship of an engaged
couple whose feminine half had dyed her hair a fashionable

---

*Heuriger* is the new wine, traditionally enjoyed in the open at simple
inns and sold by the grower himself on the very spot of its origin.

Titian red, matching it with slacks and a loud shirt, while her partner, gentle and quiet, was always seen in one and the same respectable, though ill-fitting dress-suit. He was an employee of a private firm and devoted nearly all of his leisure hours to the peaceful art of bee-keeping, which is a fair indication that this young man was an introspective sort of character. She, on the other hand, would have much preferred riding a motorcycle, since she belonged, even in the absence of such a vehicle, basically to that group of people who keep up with the times, in other words, have a great capacity for making noise with whatever apparatus might best suit the case. "How in the world did she get hold of him, of all people?" "It's just the attraction of opposites," was Mrs. Elly's opinion, and furthermore: "She has bagged him safely, and it is evident who has the upper hand. She would not think of giving up that." "He probably has a lot of money and she knows it," said the innkeeper, whose opinions of the motives of human behavior were clearly down-to-earth. His wife, though no less outpsoken, proceeded with more consideration, and ultimately penetrated deeper. Only as a team did they make a first-rate psychologist.

Thus they soon knew all there was to know about their male and female customers, their sore spots as well as what they took most pride in, be it a photograph of one's aunt, because she had been the widow of an Imperial and Royal Captain or be it, as in the case of the old retired cloak-room attendant of the Vienna Court Opera, her intimacy with famous stage artists of her time ("such voices as in my time you just don't hear today"), this being documented by a vast number of photographs, complete with dedications. Through large, gold-rimmed spectacles the face of a bygone time seemed to be gazing at one, while reminiscences poured forth, the face of a time which, even while it lasted, was ultimately more preoccupied with the business of social appearances than with that of existence. . . . Then there was the fat little wife of a Civil Servant, her face all nose and looking exactly like a hoopoe. Her daughter appeared so satisfied with the world around her, her dachshund and, above all, herself, that the very world around her could hardly stand it; furthermore we must mention the civil engineer Anton Rieger, ever alone and ever a trifle sad, a truly handsome man, and head of a thriving business firm besides. The Blauensteiners knew him perhaps of all their customers most profoundly and could tell from slight indications, occurring toward midnight—certain gestures of his hands, maybe, and the recurrence of certain words—that his way home that night would be that of a straying star through the night and nightclubs of the city; this fate befell the inveterate bachelor from time to time.

We shall meet several other customers, but only after the magician's performance by which the Blauensteiners meant to awaken the place to life again in spite of the heat of July. They had, of course, connections even to this out-of-the-way profession, which is, nevertheless, a great favorite with the Viennese and has in that city a particularly venerable tradition. Around 1870 or '80 there lived in Vienna the famous Kratki-Baschik who, by changing the final vowel of his Bohemian name, Kratky, and by adding the incomprehensible "Baschik," had arrived at an Arabian or Turkish sounding name, in short, an Oriental one. There does exist in Turkish a word somewhat similar to "Baschik," but of vastly different meaning. . . . Well, what difference did it make! Everybody knew Kratki-Baschik in those days. He resided in the Wurstelprater, the beloved amusement park, and was a magician by profession and owner of a collection of curiosities besides. All kinds of rarely seen things, preserved in alcohol, were on view there. Down to this day any somewhat weird fellow is characterized by the saying: "He belongs in Kratki-Baschik's collection." His pupils and followers in the second and third generation have multiplied and increased in numbers manifold; they organize conventions and contests; few of them are magicians by profession and earn their living as prominent exponents of this art; most are amateurs, although some have developed their art to a high degree of excellence.

Mr. Blauensteiner had procured himself the services of one such amateur and on the appointed night there was only standing room left at the inn, since the magician charged no fee, obliging everyone by a free performance. One might have called him a Sunday magician, as we are used to talking about Sunday painters. This one was a Senior Secretary of the Magistrate by profession. The magician's art involves, by the way, considerable expense, for even a magician cannot get around money and conjure up something out of nothing. The required paraphernalia can, besides being expensive, also be rather complex and even bulky. The crowd watched them being brought in: coffers, tubular pipes, even an odd-looking piece shaped like an old-fashioned contraption for giving electrical treatment, complete with circular window and shining brass parts. The evening was a big success, not only for the innkeeper, but also for the gentleman who so obligingly displayed his art, wearing a detachable white goatee during the performance. Mr. Blauensteiner called this regular customer, whose name was a little difficult to remember, from now on only "Kratki-Baschik," having found out where the gentleman's sympathies lay.

Soon after the beginning of the presentation such feats of magic were performed by this rather important official of the Civil Service, that the audience had forcefully to remind itself of its being all the result of manual dexterity and a skillful display of tricks. Yet even this rational explanation seemed, for several moments, to be suspended. This happened when a beautiful, colored silk handkerchief of a young gentleman and a twenty-shilling bill of another were chopped and torn to bits in an apparatus—both men silently gave their possessions up for lost—only to be extracted, completely intact and under the very eyes of some spectators: the bill from the innkeeper's bushy hair and the handkerchief from the collar of his shirt. An enormous burst of laughter, applause, and many exclamations of surprise followed. The official of the Magistrate was profusely thanked for the very entertaining evening. The performance having lasted long enough, the consumption of drink keeping pace with the general enthusiasm, he could now pack up his curious and complicated equipment and call for a taxi. The crowd of patrons soon dispersed itself.

At the table of regular customers, only a few people remained with the host and hostess, some already known to us such as the ill-matched lovers and the civil engineer Rieger. Hoopoe, dachshund-daughter, and the member of the Vienna State Opera of the good old days were missing, and in view of the events that followed, we may call their absence a lucky coincidence. Not even the gold-rimmed spectacles of the *ancien régime* had accidentally been left at the inn, which circumstance often resulted in the lady's calling for them on the same evening. "Evening" would, in this case, hardly have done justice to the advanced hour of the night, for it was very late. Despite this hour, still present was a retired University Professor, Dr. Hugo Winkler, a gentleman commonly said to be seventy or more years of age, which seemed a correct assumption on account of his retirement; the gentleman himself, however, and especially his manner of speaking contradicted all evidence and made the above conjecture appear downright incredible: in his dialectics and willfullness he outdid a debating society, while in his capacity for enthusiasm he put a dozen secondary pupils to shame. Present was also a writer, a certain Dr. Döblinger. There is, admittedly, always a writer present. This one shared the whim of his profession: he did not much care to be addressed by his academic title; all writers evidently believe the splendor of their name sufficient to reduce to insignificance whatever titles they may possess.

"She is right, so very right!" cried the Professor emphatically, addressing the hostess, who in his particular case showed more forebearance than actual agreement with his views. "She is absolutely right!" (He was talking about the

Titian-dyed redhead in slacks.) "Extraordinary achievement is what makes a man! A woman must simply demand it of him. It matters not whether he be a boxer, a poet, or a magician. But achieve the extraordinary he must! For the object of every endeavor is woman, nothing but woman, nothing else, nothing at all. What other ideals are there? What are you trying to tell me, gentlemen? Am I not right, Mr. Rieger? Woman is the goal of all human endeavor, woman alone!"

"Permit me, Professor," said Dr. Döblinger cautiously. "I cannot go along here without voicing an objection and venturing a counter argument—"

"No objections, no arguments!" interrupted the Professor with animation, his smooth head popping up like that of an aquatic acrobat above water. "I do not tolerate arguments and objections! In this case truth is as clear as daylight. One must but make up one's mind to see it—"

While this kind of dialectics soon reduced the Doctor to silence, it was evident that the bridegroom and bee-keeper (in his respectable, though ill-fitting suit), who had continued in the lowest of spirits, was now sinking into quite a depression. We should not overlook here the implicit and by no means inconsiderable compliment to the Senior Secretary Kratki-Baschik, whose performance had touched off this conversation about things extraordinary in general and extraordinary achievement in particular. The Professor was, of course, always intent upon reducing everything to basic principles. Not so Anton Rieger. He had kept his wits about him during the performance, using his engineer's training to advantage, and had seen through and reconstructed for his own information three of the tricks down to the last detail. Yet he said nothing. Civil engineer Rieger hardly ever said anything at all.

The Professor had meanwhile digressed from his recent argument in favor of dithyrambic exuberance on the following subject: "Didn't you all notice her? During the performance, I mean. I tell you, Mr. Rieger, what a woman!

The most beautiful creature I ever saw. At the third table on the left—"

The conversation having reached this point, a silence ensued. The bee-keeper was by now completely wrapped up in his silent gloom. Poor fellow, who knows what imaginings were besetting him! His Titian-red bride took not the slightest notice of him, she did not glance at him once. She had been provoked (maybe by the Professor's speeches), she was in full sail, her bow high and erect, although not heaving with the waves. The bow of her future-bound vessel was, paradoxically, heaving all by itself.

The inn's wide-open doors admitted no coolness. The night continued very warm.

Not a drop of rain had fallen at the first stroke of lightning, and if a wind had arisen, it could not be felt indoors. Yet the blue flash outside was almost immediately followed by a violent clap of thunder. At that very moment a late customer entered the front room, occupied now only by the party at the table. He was a well-dressed gentleman, his face rather broad and smooth, with slightly slanting eyes. This became particularly evident after he had removed his hat, uncovering a highly domed forehead. He asked politely and in a low voice whether he could still get, in spite of the advanced hour, something to eat, even if it were but some cheese and butter. The innkeeper's wife bounced obligingly to the counter and the customer sat down at a neighboring table. He ordered only mineral water and apple juice to drink.

As it usually happens when one enters an inn at a late hour, where only a few people are still sitting together, one easily gets drawn into conversation. Meanwhile the talk had reverted again, by one accidental remark or another, to Kratki-Baschik. This topic seemed to hold some, even if incidental interest for the newcomer; it was at any rate evident that he followed the conversation in which now the Titian-dyed redhead also participated, after having observed the stranger for quite a while with interest and not very discretely; one had to admit that she watched him quite openly. Before he knew it, he was involved in the conversation, the innkeeper's wife herself providing him with some explanation of the evening's happenings, not forgetting to mention the excellence of the presentation they all had seen. The new customer was just getting ready to answer her, when he was asked by the innkeeper to join them. He accepted and carried his glass to their table. The innkeeper's wife continued her praises of the Senior Secretary's artistry, mentioning also his name and position.

"Yes," said the newcomer. "I know him. An excellent dilettante."

"Pardon me, dilettante—," laughed the innkeeper's wife. "Had I but a fraction of his ability!"

"Yes, indeed," said the stranger. "He is very good, this Mr. Blahoutek, and as amateurs go, one of the very best."

"Is the gentleman perhaps himself in this line of business?" inquired the innkeeper interestedly.

"Yes, indeed," was the reply.

"And what, if I may ask, is the difference, I mean: what distinguishes a professional from an amateur like Mr. Blahoutek?"

"Well, a dilettante may, in general, perform quite outstanding tricks, even of his own invention, but, naturally, he lacks the technique that only the most advanced professional training can give, he lacks real artistry."

"Well, then: is the gentleman himself such an artist?"

The answer was in the affirmative.

"What a pity that the Senior Secretary took all of his possessions along!" cried the innkeeper. "Otherwise we could borrow one of his gadgets and the gentleman could oblige us with a beautiful piece of magic!"

"One does not always need gadgets," remarked the stranger in a casual tone of voice.

"Did you just now come from another restaurant here in the vicinity?" inquired the friendly Mrs. Blauensteiner.

"No, I was alone at home until now."

"Why!" exclaimed the lady. "Then you first went out as late as eleven o'clock?"

"Yes, I did," was the reply. By this time it dawned upon Dr. Döblinger, and this by way of his nose (the nose of a writer is one of his tools and possesses a technique that only the most advanced professional training can give). From the very moment the stranger sat down at their table, the author had been besieged by a vision of his own quiet, empty flat in the vicinity of the inn. So vivid and persistent was this vision that it nearly haunted him, appearing before his inner eye, accompanied by a very subtly piercing longing: the easy chairs, heavily shrouded against the dangerous attacks of moths, and a large wardrobe with mirrors, its tightly closed doors hiding the rugs, yet emitting from time to time the faintest whiff of camphor and naphthalene into the relative coolness of the room.

It was the height of summer, there was no denying it.

This fragrance was everywhere, hovering in flats that had withdrawn into themselves and away from the hot and noisy street. The fragrance almost seemed to spread a gospel of gentle detachment, inviting one to withdraw deeper still.

The stranger, too, came from such a solitary flat. One could smell this loneliness.

Meanwhile two or three flashes of lightning had been seen, accompanied by thunder, though less intense than the first time; a short rain now descended, its splashing soon giving way to silence again. Yet coolness now wafted from the street.

Franz Blauensteiner, the innkeeper, was not one to give up an idea easily; tonight he had quite made up his mind to see for himself whether the unknown artist could really outdo the Senior Secretary, and yet, as he said, without equipment. So he proceeded to ask the gentleman what was needed for the performance of his trick. "It will probably be easiest for you to find some playing cards and a handful of nails, six to eight of them will do. The cards may just as well be old and dirty ones, they all fall to the floor in the end."

The requested items were brought. Suspense was mounting among the patrons. The stranger, sitting toward the end of the table and not very far from the panelled wall, handed the innkeeper and his wife the cards, casually requesting them to select one secretly, to keep it well in mind without removing it from the set, and to lay the whole pack of cards on the table in front of him.

This done, and the unknown customer having meanwhile paid his moderate bill, he seized the nails in his left hand, the cards in his right, and threw or rather hurled both simultaneously against the panelled wall. The flock of cards dispersed, falling and gliding everywhere, onto the table, into the laps of the onlookers, down to the floor, followed by a clatter of falling nails. The next moment the innkeeper's wife uttered a shriek: on the wall, directly across from her, hung, face toward the room and pierced by a nail, the card she and her husband had chosen by secret agreement: the ten of spades. A dead silence followed. The stranger smiled obligingly, reached for his hat, bowed slightly, and left the inn. The Titian-red bride now sat stiffly erect and stared with wide-open eyes, her bow heaving heavily in his wake, even after he had disappeared from sight.

Within a minute of the stranger's departure, however, an even more surprising event took place. The bee-keeper suddenly started up from his gloomy brooding and ran out of the room. He did not bother to pick up his hat.

As we were able to learn from himself at a later date, he had indeed succeeded in catching a last glimpse of the stranger in the street, and had overtaken him at a running pace. This had been the stranger's reply to his stammered address: "Young man, great art should not be studied with a purpose in mind; even less for the purpose of winning a girl over; purpose kills art. May you bear this in mind."

Well, for the time being we were all still sitting together, minus artist and bee-keeper, whose return was expected by everyone very shortly. Yet, he did not turn up. The first conjectures were brought forth along with attempts to console or rather appease the Titian-red bride, who was beginning to show distinct signs of the rage to which we all fall prey so easily when we glance off the fine, yet absolutely inexorable borderline of our dominion. "Of course he will come," said the Professor. "He will be here presently." Things did not, however, take quite as natural a course. Little by little the situation was getting out of hand, threatening to degenerate into a disgrace for the redhead. Civil engineer Rieger's eyes grew somber and sad, as they always did when somebody was caught in an embarrassing situation. Then, shortly after the Professor's words, the telephone rang. "It will be he," said Dr. Winkler. The innkeeper answered the call. It was he. The Titian-red bride disappeared into the booth. During their lengthy conversation not a word was said at the table; everything, including the Professor's pronouncements upon the natural course of human affairs, seemed to be hanging by a thread. The conversation went on forever. Finally she emerged. Her pallor escaped nobody's notice, nor did her altered looks: she was not a bit pretty now. She did not heave. Rather, her rage now burst the corset of respectability, she went to pieces before everybody's eyes. "What do you know," she cried—still by the booth, not even returned to the table. "That idiot has the nerve to tell me we are through, he never wants to see me again. . . ." Even the Professor could not get out his (though conceivably still possible) consolations, so he silently sank, smoothly shining head and all, below the surface of the conversation. The Titian-red bride left, not bothering about her bridegroom's hat. It was more a breaking with this circle (in which she was indeed never seen again) than leave-taking. After this the innkeeper tried again, unsuccessfully, to remove by hand the nail that still held the ten of spades. Everybody was pleasantly affected by this card on the wall. Finally Blauensteiner got a small pair of pliers. Now it worked. "It serves her right," said Elly Blauensteiner after the Titian-dyed redhead had left. "He will certainly come back to her again," reiterated the Professor, still submerged. "He will never come back to her," answered Rieger. His words, though few, were true.

During the next few days the ten of spades on the wall—which must have had something of a Menetekel about it and therefore was so often alluded to—this ten of spades was simply talked to death. This seems to be the way of all great art: it is gnawed by tiny teeth until it falls to pieces and can be argued away; it is the fate of miracles, reduced to a miniature scale. Art and miracles cannot be part of life; they would grow unbearable, only to end as hard clods of the beyond in this world, crushing everything. Late in the night, after the accursed playing card had finally disappeared from the wall, the innkeeper Franz Blauensteiner sat a long time in silence, staring straight in front of him, until he finally summed it up: "This one was, of course, a—a different magician's art."

# CHILE

# Cururo ... Sheep Dog

FRANCISCO A. COLOANE

Translated from the Spanish by Adèle Breaux

IN THE DARKNESS five horsemen were crossing the bleak plateau swept bare under the pounding hail and bruising winds. A driving snow lashed at their backs. Four pairs of dogs followed at the flying hooves of the sheepherder's shaggycoated ponies. Black ponchos flapped in rhythm with the gallop and scarcely protected the shivering bodies from the icy buffets. Breath froze as it met the air.

The men with their dogs and horses formed an eerie, fast moving shadow in the night. It glided past the many other mounds of shadows undulating with the rise and fall of the screeching wind.

Suddenly a portion of the shadow broke away. It was the horseman without dogs. He turned his pony into the wind, cleaving a way through the heaving waves of water, snow and darkness. He would be riding hard for three hours on the return trek over the highest plateau of Tierra del Fuego.

Subiabre felt compelled to return. He could not get out of his thoughts that he had failed to reach the dog that he had loved most in his life as a sheepherder. It had been lost that afternoon in an effort to rescue a herd of sheep.

A fresh gust of wind lashed his eyes but hurt less than the tightness which was squeezing his chest to the bursting point. He clenched his teeth to control the tears, gripped the reins tighter, and dug his spurs deeper into the horse's flanks. In spite of his efforts his anguish broke out in sobbing words,

"O Cururo! Not one of the flocks of sheep you herded on these great flat plains was worth as much as you! You were a great dog and now you are gone!"

Sheepherders are rough, lonely men, molded by the hard caress of frost. All softness is worn bare by the fierce *pampa* wind which can pick up a raveled string, knot it together, and use it as a weapon for bruising anything in its path. These men love their dogs as much as life itself. Closeness to an almost primitive existence has taught them at times a dog can be relied on more than a fellow man.

Cururo, companion in his work, had meant more than anything in his world. Now Subiabre had no one. Years before, his father had been discharged from the *Baja* ranch as old and useless. Thirty years of grueling work in the service of the foreign-owned company had burned away his vigor.

With his last wages in his pocket, the old chap had gathered together his wife and clutter of children, tied his miserable belongings together, and with a bitter sigh had looked out over familiar wide fields where he had endured so much hardship. Then he started down the trail, a road holding no promise, only bleak want.

Little Subiabre, child of the land, born and raised on those plains, huddled down beside the road. Choosing the right moment, he scurried to a dark thicket like a prairie rodent and carefully hid himself. The city meant the end of all things: he would not go there. Already he cared too much about the endless plains stretching away to the mysterious faraway mountain range.

By this maneuver he was saved one kind of death: life on the ranch would go on.

The cook looked after the child. At night he brought in the animals. With manhood, he began to work at the ranch as a new sheepherder, to repeat the cycle of his father's life.

In the gorge Tres Guachos, continuously razed by the clawing wind, he would probably find his other dog Partiera,

still howling and scratching a way into the snow in an effort
to get at Cururo. He, the human being, less grateful than the
beasts, had abandoned them both. That lash of wind and
snow at his eyes had come in time: now he was returning to
find them, to help in the fraternal task which Partiera had
begun on her own. He would not cross the plateau again
until Cururo was found. This time Cururo would not be left
forgotten for the birds of prey to hack at in the following
spring.

The springtime! The season when the plains of Tierra
del Fuego convert their thick hard shell of snow into fine
silver threads which weave their way down to the fertile valleys: the season when cadavers show up intact, to be gnawed
by eagles and buzzards who leave the bones to the sun for
bleaching. The springtime! It was in the spring that Cururo
had entered his life.

Zigzagging here and there in his memory as if in a dream,
Subiabre began to relive his life with the dog from the day
when he found Cururo, a tiny pup crawling through clumps
of the tough *coiron* pasture grass out in the field. He was
just like one of the little prairie dogs of Tierra del Fuego, the
*sururo* of southern Chile.

It had been a Sunday afternoon loaded with light and
languor. The land was teeming with signs of spring. On the
ranch it was the usual monotonous period following the midday meal. A group of men wearing loose, worn sandals played
cards. Some dozed on chests covered with ragged mats. Others
listened to moaning tangos played on accordions or ground
out on worn victrolas. Hearing the music, their imaginations
pictured the red-colored houses echoing with the shrill laughter of gaudily-dressed women, where the scrimpings of years
melted away in a few hours at the towns of Rio Grande or
Porvenir. The rest of the men spent the time gambling.

Subiabre, a somewhat reserved man, cared little about
mixing in the general afternoon routine. He set about sad-
dling his sorrel, fastened on a few bags which he had agreed

to deliver to Mac the gringo, and started off at an easy gallop on the road leading to the farthest post of the ranch.

Mac lived alone on that part of the plain designed as Twenty-Three, near the source of the Rio Chico at the foot of the Andes. He had taken part in the first World War, which had left its marks on him. There were times when Mac was unbalanced. From Saturday to Monday it was his custom to pour into his body several bottles of gin or whiskey and forget his loneliness. Except for this weekly interruption Mac was a good rancher for the post: he was undisturbed by ideas. Surrounded by his dogs, horses, and the sheep, he led the unvarying dull existence of the single ranchman who roams from one post to another in his care of the enormous flocks of "white gold" on the endless *pampas* of Tierra del Fuego and Patagonia, where the big ranches count from one to three million sheep. He was alone and would go on spending his whole life alone. And each week-end he would continue to keep company with a bottle of whisky in order to endure the never-ending lonely bleakness.

Subiabre, loping along, was already climbing the rolling hills whose long slopes led into the mountain range on the eastern part of Tierra de Fuego. The trail wound through black undergrowth as high as the horse itself. Suddenly the path opened onto a deep canyon whose walls reached to the tops of the mountain. In front of the sheer cut of rock spread miles of verdant valley walled off in the distance by the gigantic blue foothills of the Andes. On the mountain slopes rays of light revealed *guanacos* unaware, placidly crossing in caravans, majestic silhouettes that moved in cadenced rhythm.

Subiabre brought his horse to a halt in the mountain pass. Rider and pony let their eyes wander over the immense expanse of green, looking like a promise of peace and hope. They sniffed in the fragrant breeze exhaled by the valley which lay under a golden light. Its greenish-yellow *coiron* pasture grass rippled in rich fullness.

Loping easily, Subiabre and his horse began the descent

leading to Post Twenty-Three. The late afternoon sun
touched their bodies and caressed the fields. The waters of
Rio Chico, as if purposely quiet, left unbroken the deep stillness of the solitude. White swans were paddling upstream,
while farther on drowsing flamingoes studded a blue lake
with crimson patches. Off there, in that valley beside the
river where the sun embraced a merging sky and earth, he
would soon catch sight of the rose-tiled roof of the house on
Post Twenty-Three.

An odd movement near the ground suddenly caught his
attention. A dark object with white spots was crawling aimlessly on the uneven ground among the mound-like roots of
the tough *coiron* grass. It was a sheepdog puppy about a
month old, whimpering as it tried to hide in the pasture
grass just like the native *cururo* prairie dog. Surprised at
finding an almost helpless puppy some three miles from the
post house, Subiabre searched for the mother without success.
It was unknown for a dog to have its young so far away from
a dwelling. How had the puppy with its eyes scarcely opened
gotten to this spot? He picked up the tiny dog which nestled
quietly in the protective warmth of the rough hand.

Subiabre looked down on the dog and smiled. "Brave
pup! You've got to learn not to go so far without getting a
glimpse of the trail ahead! Adventure is pretty sure to bring
trouble. But you're going to be a fine dog! A sharp snout
and alert eyes tell me that you won't be found wanting. I'll
take you to Partierra for safe keeping. When your stilts are
strong enough, you can run with her and learn your job.
How about calling you *Cururo*? You don't like it! Well, I
agree it's an ugly name, but a few moments ago you looked
just like a *cururo*, one of those little furry creatures without
a tail. Anyway, with real people, names and prettiness don't
count. It's what you do!"

Beginning with that afternoon Subiabre and Cururo were
a part of each other's life.

Post Twenty-Three, like all lone posts on the Magellan

plains, sprouted out of the *pampa,* without color and without human touch. Beside the road rose a large pile of blackened, weather-beaten firewood, and the small horse-shed with its corral for housing the ranchman's personal horses. But nothing gave evidence of a human being. There were no footprints on the ground, no flattened path in the pasture grass, no piece of yellowed paper, no discarded can, no worn-out tin pan. A desolate quiet hovered over the surroundings.

A man's character is revealed by the handling of his dogs and horses. The gringo Mac would lock his animals in their enclosure when they were not working so that they would not use up their strength in useless running. He was neither kind nor mean to them. Their work reflected his attitude. They always had their meals on time, but an occasional caress does more for a sheep dog than a daily allotment of food measured out reluctantly.

Subiabre drew to a stop and dismounted. Now from the closed kennels behind the house came the barking of dogs. He fastened his pony to the hitching post, removed the bags, took off the saddle, and loosened the cinch. He placed little Cururo in the palms of his big hands and walked with long strides to the house. Abruptly he stopped. On the ground in front of him, near the mound of firewood crisscrossed in Indian fashion, he saw stretched out four puppies like Cururo. Their heads were split open. It looked as if they had been dashed against the sharp ends of the dried oak logs until killed. How strange! Now there could be no doubt: Cururo had miraculously escaped the death meted out to the rest of the litter.

The herdsman was completely bewildered. All of a sudden his head seemed to be swirling. His thoughts turned toward Mac as the perpetrator, and then rejected the idea. The gringo could never be so brutal! Mac knew the value of fine puppies. True, when drunk he suffered strange attacks, but the results were harmless. He usually rose from the bench where he was drinking and yelled, "Fire!" in a thick guttural voice, and then would fall to the floor croaking strange English words which ended in snores.

The heavy silence continued to close in on the house. Creeping shade, shoving out from the woodpile in the late afternoon sun, was slowly covering the small bodies. Dusk was about to fall. Heavy stillness hung in the air. No breeze came up to thin the dense atmosphere.

Mentally and physically upset, Subiabre got to the door, grabbed its worn handle and entered the living room which was also the kitchen. Mac was not there. Nothing. Everything within the brown walls was in order. The heavy crude table and the floor obviously received frequent scourings with sand and water.

The sheepherder, accustomed to picking up distant sounds on the far-reaching *pampa,* intuitively cupped his ear to catch any faint stirring. From the adjoining room came a labored breathing. "Mac!" Subiabre shouted. His voice fell flat like a falling board. There was no echo in the silence. With his ear against the door, he heard a scratchy intermittent breathing. He shoved. A soft resistance gave way. With the door opened he looked down at a body all in a heap on the floor.

The gringo Mac lay in the deepest of drunken stupors: his alcoholic face bestial, his square protruding jaw hanging open as it would later in death, his mouth set in a horrible grin, his yellowed teeth jutting out seal fashion, and one of his legs twisted grotesquely. A little beyond, but still near the door, there seemed to be an old sack, also in a heap. It turned out to be a female dog that had been savagely kicked and strangled.

Subiabre's habitual calm was profoundly shaken. His searching eyes traveled about the dark room partly in escape, but his glance like the penetrating ray of a lighthouse beam cutting through shadows over the sea on a stormy night, rested an instant on a single obscene picture nailed to the middle of the wall. The sheepherder turned his back and walked out of the house.

Night was now beginning to spread its dark cloak over the land.

With practiced touch Subiabre adjusted and tightened the trappings on his horse. Still holding Cururo in his arms, he mounted and bounded down the trail without once looking back. Only a few owls and night birds crossed the road on his return journey. When the moon had moved half its course through the thickly starred sky Subiabre unsaddled his sorrel in the horse corral of the main ranch.

For a while now Cururo took his place as one of the many unnoticed ranch puppies, but very much under the vigilance of his master, who looked after him daily. For a time he lodged with Partiera, but as soon as he was big enough he had his own kennel.

At the end of October, returning from a long trek with herds to Rio de Oro, Subiabre discovered that in his absence Cururo had become a herd guide. The man's eyes shone with pleasure at this sign of superior breed in his alert puppy. Cururo's rapid development could only be compared with foaming water. At meal time in the kitchen he listened to comments about his dog's uncanny cleverness.

"Why, Futre here found him one day rounding up a flock which he had taken upon himself to drive into Field Eighteen!"

The man to whom Subiabre had confided Cururo's care justified his decision to let the dog work, saying, "To think he was shut in with so much care to keep him from getting bad habits without his master's guidance! Well, it was just useless to lock him up! That dog is too smart! Why, even the Boss had noticed him. A few days ago on our way to a rodeo, he grinned and said the Subiabre's pup was going to be good. The other day while passing the enclosure of animals set aside for the meat plants, he noticed that the dog had herded them all. He had made them come and go along a line set by the wire fence and then enter the enclosure. That done, he started all over again, separating the animals and rounding them up, but always keeping them well in the open. A new dog working that way never allows a flock to hurt itself—not even when old age slows him down."

Subiabre, proud and satisfied, nevertheless felt he had to add, "That's fine, but a young dog shouldn't be sent to work so soon at a distance. He might become a mean animal and a nipper."

It was true. Cururo was of the keenest stock. His master and the herd were his great joys. At the sight of Subiabre he would come running in unrestrained leaps of happiness. Before a herd, however, the dog would check his impulses and use his strength intelligently. He would bound from one point to another like a rubber ball, grouping, pushing, and keeping in line the obedient mass of sheep. Isolated animals were of no interest to him: he looked at them passively. But with a herd he held himself triumphantly, like a general at the head of his armies.

He had another distinction which distinguished him from other dogs: he kept to himself. When his owner had to be away and the door of his kennel was left open, he disappeared on long wanderings. Possibly there was a strain of wild dog in him. The scouts had met him miles away at the far ends of the ranch. He had been seen crossing beaches, running into the wind, sniffing the air as it blew down from the high cold prairies towards the Atlantic.

At last came the day of his first rodeo, the ceremony which is the final consecration of a sheep dog to his work. The rodeo in Chile is neither a sport nor gala day, but a decisive test of physical endurance. Then the sheep dog must prove his real value and submit to a long, constant, exhaustive pull on his resources.

That day Cururo stood revealed before the astonished sheepherders.

The business in hand was to round up to a given field

seven thousand sheep over some four thousand acres of difficult terrain, broken up by ravines, crisscrossed by brooks and
small streams, and studded by great patches of dense black
thickets. Moreover, in the somber wooded gorges were often
treacherous drifts, thin coatings of snow concealing the water
underneath. These thin crusts were ready to give way at a
touch.

Subiabre with his two dogs was to work as *puntero*, a type
of guide. In a rodeo the *puntero's* job is the hardest and most
responsible. He is always working at a gallop, following endless miles of wire fences.

Partiera, the grown dog, not only did her work but kept
an eye on her fleet companion. She excused no imprudence;
she nipped and even shook Cururo in the difficult task of
getting small flocks together and guiding them through ravines to the central valleys where they were to be concentrated.

At nightfall the fertile valley plain was peopled with
thousands of sheep coming in droves, guided in the distance
by the herders' shouts and the barks of the dogs, whose
hanging tongues and heaving sides gave evidence of the wear
and tear of the day. Then and there, high praise was heaped
upon Cururo "come of age" and upon his fortunate master.

Subiabre, on foot, followed by his horse, came up to Cururo. Very much moved, he put his arms around his dog with
the tenderness shown by sheepherders to their dogs, so faith-
ful in sharing toil and hardship. The animal was panting.
Once again the man lifted him from the ground, mounted
his horse, and rode with Cururo across the saddle, as on that
afternoon when he found the pup crawling in his path, like
a prairie dog.

Cururo maintained his reputation. His days were full of
triumph until the afternoon of his disappearance. His strong
beautifully lined body, his lustrous black fur, his joyfulness
knew only a short span of time on the sheep plains of Tierra

del Fuego. His life did not fade out slowly in the usual way, but went like a sudden last flash of light.

It was a mid-winter day, sheeted with blue-white ice. The rancher overseeing the farthest northern section of the ranch reported that the entire flock had run northwestward, hunting shelter from the wind which had been blowing for hours with hurricane force. Great drifts of snow were piled high. That part of the ranch was seamed by gulches and ravines. The sheep searching shelter in them had been covered by mounds of snow. Unless taken out in time from the treacherous mass they would perish in those great soft caves.

A little before midafternoon four sheepherders with eight dogs from another part of the ranch had arrived to take part in the work on the slopes, beginning at the foot of the mountains which Subiabre was then crossing.

The herders advanced among the slippery hills, which were piling higher and higher under the drive of the snow-laden wind. Beneath the heavy tread of a hoof a hollow, deceitfully bridged over by fresh snow, would cause horse and rider to fall. The man would manage to get to his feet, hanging on to his poncho with one hand and pulling the horse with the other. The horse, assisted by the herder, would scramble out after many desperate gropings and slidings.

After a wearing struggle they all got to the hill near the flocks. From there on it was impossible to advance with horses.

In the distance they made out great mounds of snow, resembling colossal white whales cast up on a beach of snowy dunes, all formed and shaped by the milling gusts of wind.

The dogs were the heroes of the day. The men, hindered by the snow, were almost useless.

Cururo caught sight of a flock coralled at the end of a deep canyon. Skidding and rolling, he made off for the lower slope.

The sheep, sensing their danger, had squeezed together tightly in that mammoth pit for more warmth, and were munching their own wool. Some in the close center had fallen, some had died, and some had been trampled down.

The dog's intelligence, comprehending the situation, could find no possible exit from their location at that point, but he forced the sheep to change position. Then he started off reconnoitering from the other side of the ravine. After a long run, he returned to make the flock advance to where the hillsides were narrowed in the wind-swept gorge. Pushing the animals, even biting their haunches to make them move, he got almost all the sheep to file out by invisible paths to the upper part of the field free from drafts. A few sheep still remained in the gully. They had lost sight of the others and stopped blindly in their tracks. The dog had to work harder for them than for the entire flock. Harassed by their refusal to move, he finally abandoned them and went to guide the rescued herd.

It had been a feat. Cururo, all alone, had done the work. Partiera, on the other side of the hill, worked with more caution. Their master, useless, was yanking himself through the underbrush.

Strident whistles broke upon the quiet of the snow-covered slopes. Subiabre was calling his dogs. Farther away could be heard the deep "Yoh! yoh!" of the herders and the sharp barks of the dogs driving the sheep through the canyons.

Together Subiabre, Partiera, and Cururo went down to where the wind had heaped up snow over a fence at the foot of a small hill. The snow, having covered the fence, had steadily risen in smooth outline until it had topped the hill itself and filled in the hollow below. All was level to the casual glance.

Except to a sheepherder's practiced eye, that wind-raised hill could have no special significance. Subiabre recognized clues in the tiny openings scattered across the white covering. Partiera and Cururo together began sniffing at a black thicket, half-flattened out, which still resisted the weight of the snow. Its twisted branches wreathed a hole about the size of the entrance to a beaver's cave. That was exactly what it was—the entrance to a huge cave sheltering more than two hundred sheep.

By licking and eating their own wool, sheep are able to maintain themselves several days in the caverns made by the steadily falling flakes which pile up foot by foot on their backs. The hot breath of the animals pierces through the snow wall minute holes by which they get the necessary air. But after a while the sheep begin to fall and start rotting alive, or more often succumb to the crushing white cape, finally melted by their warm breaths, which avalanches upon them.

Subiabre examined again the tiny fissures made by the breathing, trying to estimate with certainty the resistance of the cavern, when he heard a bark like an echo from distant canyons coming out from the depths of the ground. Now he knew. The valiant Cururo, in search of the sheep, had bolted to the cave's interior by the beaver opening where he had been sniffing. Partiera, either through age or an instinct of caution, fortunately had not followed her impulsive companion.

Foreseeing the imminent danger, Subiabre ran to the thicket. Passing his head inside as far as he could, he placed his fingers in his mouth to give the characteristic whistle of sheepherders calling their dogs—one long and two short sounds followed by a cadence. Then with his knife he hacked at the opening to enlarge it. With the hard crust broken, his strong hands began desperately to shovel out snow.

He whistled his command again. It was answered. A hair-raising sound full of aloneness like the howl of a wolf pursuing a horseman in impenetrable darkness reached his ears. Then there was a sound of dulled thunder as if from hurtling clouds. The man's heart went tight in his chest. Partiera's ears stood up rigid.

The cavern of snow was crumbling in.

The two, Subiabre and Partiera, listened to blood-curd-

ling deep-toned murmurs, even, short, guttural, like those of
deaf mutes. It was the dying moan of the flock. Piercing
through that dull sound, prelude of death in the entrails of
the white cave, another howl cut into the bone and marrow
of the man. He became weak. Partiera gave an answering
cry, pressed her head to the ground and clawed through the
snow with fierce intensity, as if urged on by an invisible whip.

Everything had happened in a moment. Cururo the comrade had left them, lost, herding his last flock into eternity.
Perhaps his final howl had not been for himself but for the
flock being crushed by the avalanching snow.

The screeching wind kept on razing the plateau, passing
over it in hurricane gusts. No jutting ledge on the harrowed
land broke the tearing fury. Blasts of air and snow were un-
loaded upon the plain.

Subiabre calculated that by now the four other sheepherders had probably found lodging in one of the isolated
posts, or might even have arrived at the ranch headquarters.
There was no more time for reminiscing. He brought his
horse to a halt to examine the fastenings. Dismounting, he
rearranged the saddlebags and tightened the cinch loosened
by the hard galloping. Then he patted the horse's neck af-
fectionately and jumped into the saddle, again a shadow
advancing through the storm and the night until he arrived
at the edge of the plateau.

The descent in the treacherous darkness had to be made
carefully. He held the reins firm, every inch of him alert to
each shift in the position of the horses, nerves taut for a possible slip on the ice and a dangerous fall. Once below, he
hobbled the horse's legs and left him to cross the snow banks
again in a short-cut to the caved-in cavern.

There he located Partiera, still vigorously digging away
the snow and kicking it behind her. He took off his heavy
poncho and began to help the dog that had already made con-

siderable progress with the hole leading to the spot from where Cururo's last bark had been heard.

Their digging had probably been going on for an hour when Partiera's scenting warned him that the body was close. The dog redoubled her efforts, savagely clawing and heaping up the snow until her snout touched the lost companion. Partiera stopped abruptly and stood motionless with ears rigid. She eyed the body strangely. As if to bite into the air she opened her mouth. From throat and jaw escaped a peculiar bark, an unfamiliar sound, as though she were perplexed before the mystery of death.

The man was no different. He called too. "Cururo!" burst from his throat, but his voice was like that of the dog's: it knocked without answer on the closed doors of the unknown. Subiabre crept into the hollow and pulled out Cururo's body. Free from the hole, he threw the beloved burden over his shoulder and started in the direction of his horse.

In the east the first streaks of morning were clearing away the misty atmosphere. The wind seemed to be groaning less. The snowfall was thinning out and fell lightly on the odd procession, now outlined against the wide white *pampa*. Subiabre's hand was caressing the beautiful head which hung inert on his chest. Partiera, exhausted and subdued, marched behind.

The night was ending, and with it the storm.

# CZECHOSLOVAKIA

# A Legend of Saintly Folly

Vladimir Vondra

Translated by Marian Wilbraham

ON NEW YEAR'S EVE cars of every conceivable make, trolley-buses and clanking trams slid over the wet surface of Stone Square. Neon signs splashed their lights on to the street. Women in nylons, satins and silks clattered along the pavements on stiletto heels, enveloping their finery in coats, furs and glistening stoles. And they shone more brightly than the shop windows and the glowing entrances to wine parlors and bars as they hung on their men-folk to support their faltering footsteps. Accepting admiring glances without raising their eyes, they enjoyed being bounched like balls from one to another.

A plague monument stood in the square. It was in the nature of a little heaven in the midst of this New Year's Eve and in the middle of Stone Square. The Eye of the Lord kept kindly watch at the top, guarding three saints who stood above the waters of the fountain. Their shadows broke in ripples on the turbid surface and mixed with the dazzling reflections of the gay lights, competing with them for a bit of mirror space in a puddle. One of the shadows belonged to St. Sebastian, his androgynous body pierced by arrows, the other—representing a pilgrim with an ulcerous leg, accompanied by a dog with a crust of bread in its mouth— was that of St. Roch. The most imposing shadow, however, was cast by the ample bosom and comely hips of the pious anchoress Rosalia.

Now it will not be amiss to take a closer look at this graceful virgin, whose physical charms even the robes of a Basilian nun could not conceal. Spun into the sandstone by a masterly hand, they looked more like clinging muslin than rough, heavy wool. More noteworthy, however, was the fervent countenance of this Sicilian girl. A tender fire burned beneath her skin and the darkness of her hair harbored the slumbering winds, spilling its waves over the pleasant plain of her shoulders and back. Inclining her body towards the lights, she listened with rapt attention to the bustle of New Year's Eve.

The Eye of the Lord seeth all.

"Daughter," it said, "narrow and uncomfortable is the way of the saints. It is not like a wide boulevard to be trodden by cocktail shoes made for jive and twist."

"I know," Rosalia replied. "If I gaze at the boulevard, it is only because I am thinking about the unrighteous passers-by to whom abstention is grievous. And withal I delight in prayer and meditation."

"I see all," the Eye of the Lord continued. "I see how many young men should be accustoming themselves to purity and how many worldly women to a penitent life. But thou, my daughter Rosalia Sinibaldi, dwellest in our little heaven and thou hast found salvation.

"Yes," Rosalia said. "And therefore I am happy."

"What happiness," she said to herself bitterly, "what bliss to dwell with the heavenly host and rejoice!"

"How canst thou fail to be happy," the Eye of the Lord said, "for thou art my warrior girt with the armor of virginity, with the shield of modesty and with the spear of a strict anchoress's dedicated life. Nevertheless, I see at this moment that thou thinkest no more of the ascetic taste of mallow roots, nor of the refreshing rock-spring by the hermitage on Quisquina Mountain."

St. Sebastian was astonished and St. Roch dropped his staff in amazement.

But Rosalia rejoined, "My life is as a sweet scent, as the sacrificial roses in my basket. I lift up my voice in rejoicing."

"Oh, this rejoicing," she thought. "This bliss within the confines of the Ten Commandments!"

"Daughter," the Eye of the Lord wept, "the Devil is touching thee with the wing of folly. Thou speakest words of hypocrisy. Has not heaven itself had mercy upon thee that thou mayest lead a holy life and enter into Paradise?"

"Yes," Rosalia answered impatiently. "Eight centuries have I been holding a basket of roses in my hand and the honey of beatitude has been my fare. I've had enough. I'm bored."

"Daughter, daughter," the Eye of the Lord sobbed. "Did not the heavens place thee on this monument that thou shouldst comfort people in time of vile pestilence?"

"Where's the plague?" Rosalia asked. "I've only the municipality's care for ancient monuments to thank for the fact that I'm still standing here. I'm bored. I've had enough of that kind of heaven."

At this point Roch lifted his staff in amazement and smote the basin.

"Enough," he cried in virtuous wrath. "Have done with such backsliding talk! We are the Church triumphant and faint-hearts have no place in our ranks. May the Lord chastise thee with a heavy hand! Why dost thou not sit patiently and why doth thy tongue speak erring thoughts?"

"Virgin," St. Sebastian cried, swaying helplessly, "my beautiful virgin, how long have I been bound by fetters and pierced by arrows, and yet I have endured in humility."

"That," St. Rosalia said spitefully, "is because the Lord hath denied thee the lusts of the flesh, my dear. And our good sclerotic friend Roch is only a dogmatist because his memory no longer extends to the years of youth and folly."

"Thou hast cast off the mask of hypocrisy, my daughter," the Eye of the Lord said. "I see all, and I know full well that the lift boy from the Hotel Atlantic rests his back upon

thy knees every morning while he waits for the first tram. I
know full well how the fire rises within thee and how thou
holdest back thy hands from touching his temples."

"Of course," Rosalia replied. "His shoulders are broad
and firm and once he fell asleep on my lap and missed the
first number six tram in the morning."

"Sin is born of idleness," St. Sebastian said. "It is long
since the scourge of pestilence visited this town."

"What's this?" Patron Roch shouted so loudly that his
miserable dog cowered in fright beside the ulcerous leg.
"What does this crazy girl want here? Since when have we
had room in our little heaven for such follies? Where is
obedience, I'd like to know? What higher authorities have
given her permission to blather like this? What are we
coming to, I would like to know?"

"Well, maybe I'm right," St. Sebastian said. "A minor
plague epidemic would keep her busy enough so she would
have no time for such foolhardy ideas. Bubonic plague,
which settles in the glands and is especially addicted to visiting the groin, would be the best."

"Nonsense!" St. Roch cried, and his voice raised waves
in the fountain. "If there's to be a plague, let it be of the
skin as in Aquapendente and as in Cesena and in Rome and
in Piacenza in the days of my saintly youth! Ulcers which
burst and stink and leave deep scars, beneath which beauty
and desire for a life of lust fade away!"

"There's no plague and there'll never be one," St.
Rosalia declared. "And I've had enough of resting sweetly
in the Lord. I don't give a rap for any reward for services
rendered. I'm going to wash dishes at the Hotel Atlantic or
punch tickets in number six tram."

"Do you hear that?" St. Roch shouted, trembling with
rage, while his dog sent up a dismal howl. "Why is it in the
Atlantic Hotel she wants to wash dishes and why is it in
number six tram she wants to punch tickets? Look how she
mocks our little heaven, our fortress of order and our battle-

ment of upright living! Have we not stood here patiently until this very moment, united as statues of undying merit in the service of mankind?"

"What happiness!" St. Rosalia sighed. "What happiness! And all around people are being born and are dying and in between they manage to laugh and to cry and sleep beside each other in warm beds and in the grass beneath the stars, to drown their senses in wine and leave behind them traces of the sweetest follies."

"Make no mistake, my virgin!" St. Sebastian cried. "Thou livest in a calm harbor amidst the stormy seas of the world."

" I don't give a rap for a quiet harbor," St. Rosalia said. "I want to go out into the storm."

"Oh, wrath, do not afflict me!" St. Roch, cried and the tip of his staff was all frayed. "May thine eyes be struck blind and thy lips become dumb, may thy body be covered with unsightliness and may a millstone be hanged about thy neck that thou shalt not bring shame upon the command-ments, the law and the prophets!"

"Oh no, my son," the Eye of the Lord, wept "we must show forbearance. . . ."

At this moment the lift boy came across the square on his way to night duty at the Atlantic Hotel. He jumped over several puddles and stopped by the statues to lean on St. Rosalia's lap and look at the hotel. The massive 19th-century building towered above him, cafés and restaurants threw out a blaze of garish lights, cars drew up noiselessly at the en-trance and gay groups of guests, singers, artists, actors and musicians with their instruments stepped out, while the hotel buzzed with excitement and dilated like a paper lantern at a fête.

Our lift boy was fond of day-dreaming. Waking up alone in his bed, he would imagine a beautiful maiden at his side, for the simple reason that he had never yet spent a night with a girl. One of his dreams was that he met her at the dairy round the corner when he went to buy his morning cocoa, or he decided that he would meet her on the refuge and they would both by chance get into the same tram, and once he even had the temerity to imagine her as a foreign beauty whom he would take in the lift up to the fifth floor of the Atlantic Hotel.

He dreamt up other things, too. As a child he had decided to be a ship's captain, in the fifth form a bad report made him climb down to first mate and when he ended up as a lift boy he thought out quite a feasible career: he would go to hotel school and as a trained waiter he would sail the seas in a luxury liner. Some people might find these youthful dreams foolish, but they filled the happiest moments of the lift boy's life until he began to realize that it was not enough to dream. Moreover, they involved him in a certain absent-mindedness when this was least desirable.

Just now, for example. When he most needed to hurry to his night duty, he was calmly leaning against the statue and seein,g not the hotel, but a majestic liner moored at the dock-side in ink-black water, although in fact he had never seen either a liner nor any water other than the sluggish stream flowing in its narrow bed through the town. Look, he said to himself, today we are sailing through New Year's night and gay cormorants will clap their wings over the stern of the good ship *Atlantic*. That is what he said to himself and he had no thought for Matysek, the lift attendant who was waiting to be relieved, and he dreamt that he was braving the stormy seas in some distant clime. That is what he said to himself, and he never felt the tender quivering of the saint's knees nor their yearning pressure on his shoulders nor the light caress of a strange hand on his hair.

Then he came to with a start, ran like mad, rushed through the door and pulled up at the reception desk.

"Two minutes late," Matysek said and gave a meaningful tap with his long, thin forefinger to the glass of the watch on his long,thin wrist. At the desk Miss Gabrielle passed a comb through her yellow hair and yawned disgustedly. . . .

"But Matysek, after all, tonight. . . ."

Matysek drew his fingers down his long, thin neck round the thyroid gland and growled, "It makes no difference what night it is," and he thought of his long, thin wife sitting gloomily over a plate of sandwiches, watching the New Year television program and nervously tapping her long, thin finger on the table because she had not yet quarrelled with her husband that day.

"Two minutes," Matysek repeated doggedly in his thin voice. "Have you no sense of responsibility? Have you no idea what discipline means? Don't you know that there must be order in all human activity? This is the second time. Naturally, you realize that your frivolity will be discussed in the union branch and that I shall have a word to say about you in the appropriate quarters."

"But Matysek," Miss Gabrielle said, spitting on her finger to wipe the powder off the shiny freckles of her upper lip, then she winked encouragingly at the unhappy lift boy, put the finishing touches to the red bow of her lips and lit a cigarette.

"There's no but about it," Matysek said. "I'm a decent citizen and I've worked two minutes overtime for this parasite."

Whereupon he tied his scarf and scuttled to the door on his long,then legs.

"Do you hear his bones rattle?" Miss Gabrielle remarked. "He and his old woman in bed, what a racket they must make! Now he'll come properly home, have a proper row with his wife and then sit properly nibbling egg sandwiches and sipping lemonade and just before midnight he'll piously open a bottle of liqueur. So what, shall we have a drop?"

The unhappy lift boy was silent.

"Well, shall we? The head waiter fell for my hair tint

and brought me some Cinzano. I like sweet drinks. Don't you like sweet drinks?"

The lift boy was silent. So that's what he always got for his imagining. He wouldn't be surprised if they put something in his reference, and then what about the hotel school? He opened the lift door, the light went on inside—step in please, which floor please—only there was nobody there; after all, who would hurry to go to sleep under blankets embroidered with the monogram of the Hotel Atlantic?

"Like a lot of morons," Miss Gabrielle said. "It's always that way with you. And I used to think you were quite a boy. That bloody waiter has a head like a fat worm. For Pete's sake, go and take a nap, I'll pull you down if somebody comes."

The lift boy said nothing. He got into the lift, the cage rocked, a black hole yawned beyond the door. Miss Gabrielle drew the cork, poured herself some Cinzano into a coffee cup and sipped.

"Christ, what a New Year's Eve . . ." and she twisted the knob of the wired radio.

At that moment the hotel door opened and a visitor came in.

Miss Gabrielle was so taken aback, she put her cup down on the reception book.

For the visitor was wearing light sandals and from her shoulders flowed a flimsy evening dress, a bit ascetic and not unlike a nun's habit, but most elegant and in perfect harmony with the dusky face and the hair cascading down her back. Of course, Miss Gabrielle was quite used to foreign guests, but this lady was unaccompanied, she had no luggage except a basket of roses held in her slender hand. The things they go about in nowadays, thought Miss Gabrielle. Probably an opera singer, she's cut out for Wagner. Some people have all the luck, it's barely nine o'clock and she's got a bouquet already. . . .

The foreigner inclined her head.

"Your luggage is coming?"

The foreigner inclined her head.

"And your passport, if you please. I must register you."

"That's coming too," the visitor said.

"Then for the time being just your name and address, please," Miss Gabrielle said and took up her pen.

"Rosalia Sinibaldi of Quisquina a Rosis," the foreigner said. "Sicily."

"Oh yes," Miss Gabrielle said. "I'll note the passport number later. The lift boy will show you to your room."

And then she went and pressed the lift bell.

When the lift arrived the boy came out a new shock was in store for her. It provoked her a bit, and it moved her a bit, too. In fact, the lift boy stood stock still, he didn't say—if you please, which floor, please—he just stood and looked as if a flower had blossomed within him, or as if a spring had burst forth in him or as if a delicate ball of foam had fallen from a Christmas tree. He stood rooted to the ground amidst the white stucco, the gold cornices and the red carpets, rigid in his grey jacket with silver stripes on the collar and cuffs. And facing him stood the dusky Sicilian Rosalia Sinibaldi smiling faintly, and the scent of the roses in her basket was like unto that of no roses in this world.

"I've come to thee," she said. "I've come to thee after all."

The lift boy still held his peace, but a spark from some-where within him lit up a quiet, tender flame in his eyes.

"Shall we dance?" she asked. "I'm longing to dance. They've never allowed me to do anything like that, though the court of King William and Princess Margaret of Navarre excelled in gaiety."

She's escaped from an asylum, thought Miss Gabrielle. I wonder if I should call them up.

"I've had to care for the sick the whole time. And what sickness! All open wounds and pus! I've never been able to think of follies."

Miss Gabrielle was out of her depth. And that idiot didn't move an inch. He gaped like a dumb dog. But no, he wasn't gaping, he was looking deeper and deeper, the flame stole from his eyes to light up his face. Miss Gabrielle had never seen anyone blush so modestly, and it was infuriating because now he didn't know if he was on his head or his heels, and if that woman took him by the hand. . . .

She took him by the hand and all the stiffness left him and he said, "Of course, certainly, let's dance."

"Am I supposed to stick here by the lift?" screeched Miss Gabrielle, but they did not hear her, neither the lift boy nor the beautiful foreigner, because they were going hand in hand and the wonder of touch had drawn them into a soundless well and when the door closed behind them they left just the aroma of roses in all corners, and the deserted lift.

"Hell," Miss Gabrielle said and poured out some more Cinzano.

"You'll pay for this, my lad!" she added after taking a drink.

"Christ, what a New Year's night!" she muttered, wiping away a tear.

By now the lift boy and Rosalia were dancing and in the well of wonder they were seeking and finding one another.

"I have sought thee, long have I sought thee," Rosalia said, "among the deer in the mountains of Sicily, among the pigeons on the public squares. Oft has the plague sped by me, people have perished and nations have annihilated one another; among princes have I sought thee, on thrones and on scaffolds, among troops with pennants, and in the arms of the Lord."

"Who are you?" the lift boy asked.

"For thee I am pure as a dove and love slumbers within me as a song in the throat of a swan at nesting time."

"Are you from far away?" the lift boy asked.

"Far away," Rosalia said. "We would have to follow a

long road, and we would have to sail a long way, as we sail in the dance and to the music, till we should come to harbor in my homeland."

"I'd love to go a long, long way from here," the lift boy said. "To Egypt, to the Gold Coast and to Tierra del Fuego. But I don't know anything. That's why I want to go to the hotel school. And then I'll be a high-class steward on an ocean liner and I'll sail all the seas of the world."

"I have restrained all desire within me," Rosalia said, "and I have lived in my hermitage on Mount Quisquina like a hen on a dunghill."

"Today, while I was leaning against the monument," the lift boy said, "the Hotel Atlantic seemed like a great liner tied to the quay-side."

"Let's go on deck!" Rosalia said and they held hands and ran up the stairs until they stood breathless on the terrace high above the town. Above them billowed the clouds and below were the crests of roofs, but they were not crests of roofs, they were crests of waves as high as mountains and they tossed the Atlantic about like a toy. The lift boy and Rosalia clung to each other astern and albatrosses clapped their wings as they wheeled back to shore. The town receded, its lights melted into the darkness and the lift boy and Rosalia melted into each other with their eyes, hands, lips and their whole bodies.

Later the lift boy asked, "Who are you?", and he was not sure whether he was not sitting forgotten in the lift between floors, dreaming another foolish dream.

"I'm no longer a saint," Rosalia smiled, "though I used to live blissfully in paradise where rejoicing knew no end. But what's the use of heaven if you're not there? I'm not going back."

"You keep making fun of me," the lift boy said. "And tomorrow I'll be in a fix because of you. Matysek will go and complain that I came late to work and Miss Gabrielle will ring up the boss first thing. The hotel school? They'll say. If that's your attitude to work, then we've no use for you even on the lift. You are my first dream come true. But I have another. I really must go to sea."

"Do you want to go away now, when we've found each other at last?" Rosalia cried. "Isn't this the most wonderful voyage of all?"

She threw out her arms to the surrounding night. It was near midnight and the good ship *Atlantic* was ploughing through the towering waves.

"I won't let you go anywhere," she whispered. "What would I do without you?" I don't want to sit among those sage and unenterprising blockheads. I want to make my crazy escape to the end. I will be your wife and a dish washer in the hotel, or a conductor on number six tram."

The lift boy gazed at the waves and the sea sprayed salt tears into his eyes.

"I love you," he told her sadly, "but I won't be happy even with you if I don't see the Gold Coast and Tierra del Fuego."

"Yes," Rosalia smiled gently, "you are as foolish as I. What shall I do without you?"

They stood at the stern, they kissed and they wept and Rosalia threw her roses on the crests of the waves.

"Not saints, but statues of folly should stand in the public squares in every town," she said bitterly. "Folly conceals secrets one would blush to tell, though one's heart may faint at the wonder of them."

They shivered with cold and with the knowledge that love means to wish one another well. So the lift boy decided first:

"I don't want to sail the seas. I've finished with that. I want to open doors to hotel guests to my dying day. We'll get married, you'll be a dish washer and we'll live happily together in my little room at the terminus of number six tram."

"Oh no," Rosalia decided for her part. "What would I

do then with my conscience? Unfulfilled dreams hurt and the fulfilled ones are forgotten. Don't let's think about tomorrow."

And they thought not of the morrow and the *Atlantic* crossed the line of the year's last midnight and time flowed astonishingly with her until the first streaks of dawn showed in the heavens.

Then they joined hands and stepped wearily to the floor below, and then to the next, and down and down until all of a sudden they were by the reception desk on the ground floor with Miss Gabrielle's yellow hair behind it and Matysek beside her, because they had called him back when the lift boy got lost, and the manager was there, dying to get to bed, but he had to stay to put things in order.

"Look!" Miss Gabrielle squeaked, "here they are. The woman hasn't even got a passport, or luggage and she's in fancy dress and she must have escaped from an asylum!"

"You are an unconscientious, cheeky and lazy urchin," Matysek said in his long-winded, thin manner. "Because of a rascal like you, I, a married man, had to return to duty on New Year's Eve. I shall submit my complaint to the union committee. A fellow who dallies with a woman during working hours is not fit to be among honest toilers. Shame on you! You are a bad lot, a disgrace to the Hotel Atlantic."

"That's right," the Manager said, "I shall have something to say to you, my lad, when I have had a chance to sleep a bit. For the moment, let me tell you: the hotel school is off. I have no illusions about your character and you will be acquainted with my opinion in your reference. Yours is a heinous offense, for which there is no excuse. You have cut yourself off from your fellow workers by your disgraceful attitude to your duties."

"Mother of God!" Miss Gabrielle said as she gazed into the Cinzano bottle in the hope of finding a last drop. "Mother of God, what a happy New Year! And what about that woman? Shouldn't I call a policeman?"

Finally, they all looked at Rosalia.

She took fright and let go of the lift boy's hand. She ran along the red carpet to the door. It was open. Carrying her empty basket, she ran out on to the pavement and looked around in confusion. No one knew on the spur of the moment what to do, so they simply watched her crossing Stone Square. First her graceful figure hid everything, then the houses swung into sight, then the monument crowned by the Eye of the Lord appeared above her head, then she grew still smaller and St. Sebastian and St. Roch could be seen at each side—then suddenly she disappeared and the plague monument stood on the square as they had always known it.

For a while they stared disconcertedly, but then each of them thought to himself that after all he had passed a sleepless night and imbibed some wine.

"Where are thy roses?" St. Sebastian asked in the little heaven. "Thy sweet-scented roses for the glory of God?"

"The roses have faded," St. Roch said, leaning wearily on his staff. "What is the judgment of the Lord?"

"Judgment?" the Eye of the Lord said. "What judgment? Dost thou not see that she weeps?"

"Are they tears of repentance?" St. Roch asked.

"No, my son," the Eye of the Lord replied. " 'Tis the happiness of love and the grief of parting."

"But what about our little heaven, with its self-denial, enduring virtue and strict morals?"

"Yes, indeed," the Eye of the Lord said, "what about it?"

The lift boy was now crossing the square to wait for the first number six tram. He leant on the statue's knees and so tired and dejected was he, that he never felt the trembling of Rosalia's legs.

What a crazy thing to do! he was thinking. Whatever came over me?

Suddenly he felt two drops on his face. He glanced at the sky. Threatening grey clouds were scurrying overhead and the lift boy thought what a queer New Year it was to start by raining.

All the same, it's been the nicest dream I've ever dreamed, he decided as the tram approached.

Of course, it was not raining.

It was only that the patroness of those stricken by the plague, the blessed Rosalia Sinibaldi, was quietly weeping.

# ESTONIA

# The Seventh Witness

KARL RISTIKIVI

S O FAR, I believe, all witnesses have volunteered to testify.
What happens if I refuse?"

"The rule doesn't apply to you," said the Judge.

At this point Mr. X. interrupted.

"Under the law, the witness may not present his own
testimony. The Regulations require that the Court formu-
late and present it. He is permitted only to affix his signa-
ture."

Mr. Y. disagreed.

"The law doesn't empower the witness to offer his testimony, but I find nothing in it that prevents his being called
to testify. In this case it is distinctly preferable to allow him
to give his own evidence."

I was still in the dark. Which of these gentlemen spoke
for the prosecution? Which for the defense? I didn't know
which one was for me, and which against me. It didn't really
matter with which one I sided; I had no choice whether to
state my own case or whether someone else would speak
for me.

The Judge, apparently bored with the discussion, fin-
gered his pencil. He seemed to have reached his verdict, but
for form's sake he allowed them to talk.

"The fact is," said Mr. X., "this witness doesn't come
under the authority of this Court. He hasn't appeared before
any lower court."

"The judicial hierarchy does not apply to witnesses," insisted Mr. Y.

"Until the witness has testified, we cannot tell that he may not himself turn out to be the defendant."

"All the more reason to let him speak for himself."

"But this raises a purely practical problem. My point is, I don't think he can speak on his own. I believe he would muddle concepts and terms so badly as to confuse the people and create needless resentment."

This accusation or, more exactly, insinuation neither surprised nor offended me. I had always known I could not properly follow other people's trains of thought. The meanings of their words themselves seemed to me to blur, like the outlines of photographs retouched to show ghostly apparitions.

The debate between the prosecutor and the defense attorney went on, but I know too little about law to repeat it. At one moment, I gathered, they even discussed whether to declare the session secret—a suggestion Mr. Y. happened to make. During this long-winded, wandering talk, I was mainly regretting the loss of my wrist watch. I felt that time was running out quickly, and that soon I would really need a timepiece again.

At last the Court wrote on the blackboard—as it was announced through the loud-speaker—the word:

"Sloth."

I tried to put my mind into some order for my testimony, but without much success. I did recall a comment I had read or heard about the Seventh Deadly Sin. In Latin it has the sonorous name of Acedia; only through laziness or even negligence was it translated simply into "sloth." Here was an opportunity to grasp how the word had troubled its translators, for what it names is sluggishness of mind rather than bodily inertia; and even more aptly, mental and spiritual hopelessness, *taedium vitae*, recognition of the vanity of all things. (In an engraving by Goya, a hand rises from a tomb at dead of night and inscribes a cross, "Nada"—Nothing.)

I seemed to hear music, quite remote and faint. The Court premises were obviously close to the Concert Hall. I heard enough to recognize the piece—Beethoven's Seventh Symphony, especially the finale with its breakneck tempo, which to me, at least, expresses an exultation of despair, that of a thief, for example, who knows his pursuers are ready to seize him, yet who must still rush on and grab whatever he can.

By now darkness had fallen, the warm darkness of an August night. The sky over Stockholm was dark blue, a cloudy fringe at the edges completely black. The lamps were lit, and Solliden hovered above the August darkness of Skansen like a brightly illumined cloud.

The last notes, with their frisking, desperate tempo. . . . Soon I shall not see her again. Our ways that once met for a mutual glance are moving apart. . . . Now both of us have gone. Between the vacant benches the wind gambols with the first dead leaves. And then peace fills the heart once more.

. . . Excuse me for yielding to that vague, perhaps imagined music. For a moment it took me out of the Court to another place and time. Frankly, I was sick of that white, tiresome room. At first I hadn't even taken it seriously, until the Judge asked me sharply, without warning:

"Who are you? How on earth did you get here?"

"So far," I answered defensively," no one has ever asked me who I am." I knew that the decisive moment had come, and I felt calmer than during the whole period of uneasy waiting.

"How did you manage to get in? You have absolutely no right to be in this place."

"I went only where I was ordered to go."

"That is not an excuse," said the Judge.

And yet some people had acted as if they recognized me.

Bella, above all—and Olle, too. And Sixten, my old guide, not to mention Stanley. But none of them was here—I couldn't ask them questions. Who knows, even if they had been, could I have forced myself to ask them anything? It has happened that I could not talk to a person with whom I was in the same room!

Now it was clear that the Court had decided to forego my evidence, so that to call myself "the seventh witness" may seem out of place. But how could I have known this? I could argue that while the evidence had been dismissed, the witness had not. That is, not until the Court should decide to declare me non-existent.

No one in the Court showed disappointment that my evidence had been shelved. I found it difficult to account for the attitude of the public and the Jury. None had hidden their faces, and their clothes were quite ordinary, but I almost felt they were wearing masks—not only over their features but as if they were hidden in the kind of white cloak worn by members of the Ku Klux Klan at their secret sessions.

"Well, then—who are you?'

I was beginning to feel that everyone knew quite well who I was, and I told the truth. After all, the sixth witness had had to give the same information.

"How did you get into this place?"

"The door was open. I thought this was a sort of public spectacle—the kind of evening entertainment that one usually finds."

"And when you noticed your mistake, what did you do?"

"Nothing. Besides, the decision wasn't mine. The company accepted me—whether through oversight or not didn't bother me. It's always been that way with me. Kind people have never minded that I wasn't a member; they acted as if I had the same rights as everyone else. I went along, with the stream."

With the stream—wasn't that the very offense I was charged with?

"Then you state that it was simply a matter of curiosity?"

"Yes, partly. But not only of curiosity. I—I wanted to be with the others, even if only as a watcher."

"You had no other reason to enter this place?"

"That wasn't why I came in, but why I stayed."

"Then what made you come to this building?"

I had known it, all along I had sensed it. Now it could no longer be hidden. Maybe there wasn't even a reason to conceal it.

"Fear," I answered.

Mr. X. leaped up in triumph.

"Didn't I tell you? He is a coward!"

"Yes, but. . . ."

"Please, no remarks from you. Explanations are the court's prerogative. You came in because you were afraid to stay outside. And you stayed because you were afraid to go back outside. So, then—a refugee! Am I right or not?"

"And what do you fear?" asked Mr. Y. I couldn't tell whether his voice was ironic.

"I don't know."

"Cowardice should be listed as one of the Mortal Sins," remarked Mr. X.

"The issue here is not cowardice," the Judge corrected him. "Fear is no vice if there are good reasons to fear—if one is not afraid of what is not frightening."

"Some people fear life more than death," said Mr. X. "But why prolong the discussion? The man is a deserter— it's as simple as that."

"Not exactly," said Mr. Y. "As his papers show, this very person tried to enlist in the army by presenting forged documents."

"There are deserters and deserters," argued Mr. X. "Not all desert from the army, some desert into it. Just consider that refuge of criminals, the Foreign Legion. Desertion is cowardice, no matter what one deserts to."

"The Foreign Legion is not an army," said Mr. Y. "Genuine armies are those for which people are conscripted, not those they volunteer for. An army is a collection of men chosen by others; one cannot be authorized to choose oneself."

"Gentlemen," interrupted the Judge, "we are straying too far from the point. The defendant's motives are still unclear to me. Why didn't he simply stay at home?"

This was the first official use of the term "defendant," although the matter had already been obvious for some time.

"I have no home. I live in an apartment."

"What you mean is, you're a refugee, isn't that so? Aren't you suggesting that your real home is your homeland?"

"Not even that. There I didn't even have an apartment. I was only a subtenant."

"This way, we shall never get past the first question," the Judge interrupted with an impatient look. "All this talk leads us from the point at issue."

"If the defendant does not show sufficient cause to the contrary," said Mr. X., "he should be returned to where he came from. So far I have heard no such cause."

"He said he was afraid," Mr. Y. remarked. I couldn't tell whether he spoke for me or against me.

"Did anyone try to attack you?" asked Mr. X. "Or is it only that you yourself feel guilty? If so, you simply dread your own conscience."

"There is such a thing as a passive attack, the threat of attack," I replied. "Eviction. Arrest and deportation. Recently I heard the authorities were again considering this kind of attack. That is enough to make people afraid."

"Afraid of what?"

"Emptiness."

Why didn't anyone try to help me? Why, if only for the sport of it, wouldn't anyone stand up for me? That would have offered splendid opportunities for more paradoxes in this room, which was already so paradox-ridden. Were there no sportsmen here?

"You are contradicting yourself," said Mr. X. "How can you speak of emptiness, with the streets so crowded—far more than usually?"

"That's true. But I don't belong there."

"How is that? Did anyone order you to leave?"

"No. But it could have happened at any moment, as easily as here. A new law—no loitering in the streets without cause. A court verdict—you went one step too far, away with you! What a peculiar law court!"

"This is not a court of law," said the Judge. "This is a committee. We do not judge. We merely decide."

"But then, why did you call me the defendant?"

"Has anyone? You must be mistaken. You simply haven't listened closely!"

"I was also called a deserter. . . ."

"Ah, so you object to that, too? Why didn't you stay at the front, then? Why did you escape?"

I offered an apology that sounded idiotic, even to me:

"I wasn't the only one to go. What else could I do against such tremendous odds?"

"Let yourself be killed," said the Judge.

"That's easy to say! Every general does. But generals die in their beds."

"You aren't a general. What right have you to die in your bed? Where is your bed?"

"You're right—I have no bed. But I am not a soldier. As a private individual I am allowed to die where I wish."

The Judge did not lose his temper, as I had hoped. He burst out laughing. It was a new and unexpected turn in this court procedure, yet no one showed surprise.

"Just listen to that, everybody! This man claims the right

to die wherever he likes. But he can't make up his mind whether to die!"

"In a way, he's right," observed Mr. X. "In his case death has little importance. He has never lived. The word 'death' means no more to him than to an infant learning to speak, who ignorantly parrots the word."

"Please keep to the point," said the Judge.

Mr. Y. intervened. "I feel that we're attacking the problem from but a single angle. We assume that the defend . . . the examiner is a deserter who should have fought. But isn't there another solution—adjustment? Why not ask his reasons for not adjusting himself to the circumstances?"

"I refer the question to the defendant," said the Judge.

There was no doubt this time. I had been distinctly called the defendant. But I saw no sense in dwelling on the point. Even though I could only expect an unfavorable verdict, I wanted at any cost to pull out of this dilemma, to see the issue clearly, to reach some kind of conclusion. As things stood, what could have helped my case? Any change would be for the worse, but to prolong the situation was intolerable.

"I could not adjust myself to the circumstances."

"Why?"

"I reject communism."

"Why?"

I don't know who asked the question. It seemed to hit me out of the blue, to come from some impersonal entity, probably at the same time from everyone in the Court.

Now, suddenly, I stood there tongue-tied, unable to reply. An old question, yet one that paralyzed. What could I say? Was it the theory I rejected, or the practice? Many support the theory and deplore only the practice. I reject the theory itself, and I don't believe any improvement could make the practice acceptable. People often attribute its failure to man's imperfections. But if man were perfect, what would any system of government matter? If you can use freedom well, why throw freedom overboard? But this was not the question they had asked. A black wall seemed to rise before me, impenetrable, unscalable—as if I were to answer in a language of which I didn't know one word.

Mr. X., I believe, went on: "Do you base your rejection on personal grounds, or on principle?"

I stood silent. Whatever my reply, it would not in the least affect these people's views.

"On personal grounds, then," Mr. X. concluded as he would have, even if I had replied. "You fled merely for reasons of personal convenience; you refused to make sacrifices for others. You are an utterly asocial type."

Of this, too, I have often read and heard. To demand sacrifices from others is to be social. To refuse to sacrifice oneself is asocial. I had no argument in my defense. I stood silent before the Court.

A thief before a judge once tried the hackneyed excuse: "But I must live."

"That," said the judge, "is precisely what you must not."

I remained silent, quite sure that my examiners felt no interest in communism or even in my views about it. Their questions were no more than tiny links in a chain on which they would draw up the answer whether I had the right to live. I have often glimpsed this in such innocent queries as, for instance, whether we in Estonia had curtains on our windows or whether we drank coffee. I was tired of answering queries.

Others, too, have sometimes asked me what it was I had been escaping from. I, who had nothing to lose but freedom. What was my freedom? Freedom can be only a spoon for eating soup. But what use has a spoon, when there is no soup.

I stood there, silent and humiliated, as I once stood before my godfather when I longed so much to see the city and had begged him to take me there. All my schoolmates had seen it. "What business do you have in the city?" my godfather asked. And I stood wordless—I had no business there.

I waited for the verdict and hoped it would come soon. I might have attempted some kind of answer, if I had been less alone—but in that case they would not have questioned me.

I had not resigned myself to the circumstances, and was now obliged to face the Court, to stand before it a long time, the whole time—perhaps forever, with no end in prospect except my own.

"You want to tell me that, unlike the others, unlike yourselves, I came in without permission. Yet I entered through the same door. None of you were born in this building. Probably none of you will die here. Why must I be the exception? I have the same right to judge you as you have to judge me."

"You are completely wrong," said Mr. X. "The problem is not through what door you came. The crucial point is: who are you? The fact of being is no crime; we do not claim to sit here in judgment of you. None of us wishes to judge; crimes may be forgiven. What a person *is*, however, cannot be changed."

"Don't frighten the patient," said Mr. Y. ". . . We mean you no harm. You will simply be sent back in the most humane way. The car is already waiting outside."

"Will the gentlemen of the committee please get on," the Judge urged. "A few formalities still remain, and—"

"Suppose I refuse to enter your car? I came here on my own and am quite able to leave on my own."

"You won't do that," said Mr. X. "You could have done that some time ago. But you were too great a coward."

"But may I not appeal?"

"You can always appeal. But the higher Court never interferes in our actions, as you may have noticed. Otherwise, you wouldn't be here. Where you are going, you may be awarded damages."

"And is there no chance of a suspension?"

"You were granted a suspension," said the Judge. He riffled his papers and raised one close to his eyes. "You were given an extension on January 27, 1943. Now we can do no more."

Mr. X. quickly supplemented this remark, triumphantly.

"Here, time does not count. Our decisions transcend time, they include both the future and the past. We are no more than your conscience."

"It may be just the opposite—that I am your own conscience, which you are trying to suppress."

My remark gave rise to general laughter. The atmosphere seemed to have eased; a verdict, it appeared, had been reached. I no longer existed. The car waited to take me where it was thought I belonged. The rest was only a minor matter of form.

"You haven't lost your sense of humor, I admit," said Mr. Y. "But it won't help you now, for we have none. We never indulge in the superfluous."

"I do," I stated, not sure what I was saying. "Perhaps you are no more than my own invention. If I cease to exist, so will you."

"Do not threaten the Court!" the Judge warned. "That will help you least of all."

He was right. What could I gain? Why shake off one nightmare only to find oneself in another—the nightmare of emptiness? I was a prisoner unable to escape, because he would long for his bars and walls.

Mr. X. seemed to read my thoughts. "You cannot escape," he said. "You've never been here, really you're still there. And this means nothing, for there and here are the same—space, like time, is an illusion."

"That's not my affair," I replied. "I'm not a native of this place, and your laws don't apply to me. You can't do away with me, since without me you don't exist."

"That only proves how closely you're bound to us and how completely subject to our laws."

"It proves nothing," I said, and I turned my back on the Court. No policemen were there to stop me, no guard stood at the exit as I walked out. I found myself in the same old passage, but could see nothing distinctly, for it blazed with light. But from farther down the corridor I heard something like the tread of marching soldiers.

I knew I had not escaped; the car was waiting, and the steps were moving nearer and nearer. The verdict stood. I had but one problem—would I be able to face it?

# FINLAND

# The Killer

VEIJO MERI

Translated by John R. Pitkin

HE LAY MOTIONLESS in the marshland on the river's shore from dawn to dusk and then vanished. He had been there for about a week without his position being discovered.

His bulky cloth garb was shaggy and shredded. In it he was like an alder shrub rustling in the wind, opening and shutting, but never quite letting you see through.

Now through, now around his telescopic sight, his open eye relentlessly scanned the river's opposite shore, and sand bank thirty yards high. He was particularly interested in the sinuous crest that separated the brilliant sky from the bleak earth. Occasionally he let his wide-eyed gaze slide down the slope for a change of scenery—grey sand and mounds of grey stones of various sizes—until suddenly the log jam which filled the river seemed to be falling over him. Then he slowly raised his wide-eyed gaze, which saw very little but was all the more far-reaching, up to where the earth ended and the sky spread out. So slowly that it didn't seem to move, he raised his weapon, which was dressed in the same kind of shaggy and shredded garb as its master.

So that his body wouldn't grow numb he changed his position every so often—he bent his knees and simultaneously arched his back and then straightened himself while spreading his legs, but so slowly that he didn't seem to move. This

58

movement might consume half an hour, but afterwards he could lie a couple of hours without stirring.

He didn't pay any attention to the rolling fire of the artillery, because the targets were far away from him, to the front and rear. The third day however the enemy had attempted to eradicate him with mortarfire by directing a fierce concentration into the cluster of young spruce right on the shore of the river. The enemy fired supersensitives, which exploded in the air, but he had foreseen this and shifted to the open swamp. He turned over his camouflage and lay there like a yellow swamp pool dappled with blue.

The front was quiet, too quiet. Many times he would stare an enemy soldier straight in the eyes, which seemed to look knowingly through him, but his finger wouldn't press the trigger. He could have been pinpointed on the basis of a shot.

They tried to coax him into firing. They arranged decoys for him: a helmet would creep along the top of the bank like a turtle. When a man moves, his head slightly rises and falls. When his feet are apart he is shorter than when they are near each other. The contrivers of the decoy didn't seem ever to have learned how to arrange even such a simple matter as this. He had been taught all possible tricks. Besides, he wouldn't shoot a man in the helmet, but always in the face, in the center of the face. He aimed at the intersection of the axes of the nose and eyes, the origin of the face. He scarcely ever shot when a head was turned sideways, because the target was diffuse then and it was rather difficult to find a fixed point of aim in a tenth of a second. The only possibility was the ear, but to attain a conclusive result it was best to shoot just behind it. Then, however, the target-area was narrow. Furthermore the helmet had a long neck plate. If a man had a helmet he wouldn't shoot from the side or rear unless the range was very short. Because of its curved structure a helmet would deflect a shot from practically any angle.

A man is considered competent for this profession when he is capable of hitting a head-sized object at a distance of 650 yards with one hundred per-cent certainty. But that's not enough. You can shoot the face out from under a man's eyes and it's nothing but a squandering of gunpowder. Even in the head there are places where a hit is not fatal. But he knew all the fine points of his field—the structure of the human head through and through. If his bullet didn't immediately prove fatal, he had failed and his whole day was spoiled. A prolonged cry of pain was a blot on his reputation. Nothing less than perfect results were demanded of him. Even a blunderer could disable a man with a shot in a limb or ogan. Indisputably instantaneous death is very rare, so rare, that many believe there is no such thing. A man who dies in an instant doesn't even utter a sound; his limbs freeze in mid-motion.

The fifth day he didn't get anybody. The enemy had become too cautious. His mission in this sector had been completed. Ahead was the transfer to somewhere else. He was hardly ever in the same sector for longer than a week. He was on tour to wherever he was needed, which might be as far as fifty miles away.

Without firing a shot he left the swamp after nightfall. Mist rose from the river as from a deep ravine and rolled over the opening into the forest. Like a puff of bluish smoke in the white smoke of a straw fire he drifted there at the same slow speed as the mist.

The soldiers living in foxholes saw him go past. They didn't venture to pose him questions and their conversation broke off as if tacks had been driven into their hard palates. Only a Second Lieutenant in the infantry joined him on the path and offered him a cigarette, but he never smoked. Then the Second Lieutenant began to talk about a machine gun nest which had inflicted heavy casualties on his unit with enfilade fire. Repeating every sentence, he rattled on the whole time. The enemy was on the other shore on top of a high bank. His men were in a flat swamp below. The western shore of all rivers is high like a mountain, but the eastern shore is swampland. God had intended the nation to be born facing the other direction. . . .

They came to the forest road. The Second Lieutenant's pale face and flickering eyes were discernible in the light. His mouth and eyes were continuously in motion. He explained that at the age of seven he had fallen through the ice. After that his eyes had always fluttered. He didn't know for sure what had caused it, but thought that the icy water had damaged them. He was night blind—couldn't see a thing.

The Second Lieutenant offered him some chocolate when they got to the motorcycle, but the sniper got onto the rear seat with his back towards him and placed the butt of the rifle on his foot. The rifle had no sling. He had found that it caused nothing but trouble, even though it and a tight leather jacket are thought by marksmen to noticeably steady one's aim. But this business was more like shooting on the wing. He couldn't put his rifle on his back but had to carry it in his hand. When the driver started the motorcycle with a kick the din of a hundred motorcycles reverberated in the forest and drove along beside them in the brush like a huge escort.

The sniper was quartered in a village ten miles away. Every morning before daylight he was taken from there to the front by motorcycle and after dark every evening he was brought back. He had his own room in the officer's club next to the rooms reserved for the regiment's staff. He spent his nights there in a proper bed and the motorcycle driver brought his food there. He was entitled to supplemented officer's rations.

When he telephoned his daily report to the commander of the batallion the commander began to talk about a machine gun nest that had inflicted heavy casualties on him. He didn't consider himself able to make it an order, but asked the sniper to destroy it or keep a lookout on it.

The sniper said he had noticed the machine gun. It was right opposite the junction of the river and a small tributary which flowed from the east, and its assignment was apparently to prevent lateral troop movements across the marshy tributary. There was a bridge further up, but it couldn't even be used at night because it was plainly visible against the surface of the water. Even in total darkness the machine gun's fire could be directed towards the bridge. He couldn't shoot at the nest from his own territory because the shore of the tributary was bottomless swamp that wouldn't support his weight. Besides, his rifle couldn't destroy a machine gun and it was not worth the risk of going into no-man's land with an anti-tank gun.

He went to his room, ate, and cleaned his rifle carefully, even though he hadn't fired it. Then he put new cartridges into the clip. They had been specially prepared; the grains of powder had been counted exactly. They and the rifle might have absorbed moisture in the swamp. He took just as conscientious care of himself as he did of his weapon. He saw to it that his regimen was consistent. When he thoroughly emptied himself in the morning he could spend his day without having to think about satisfying his appetite or the demands of nature.

When a private woke him before daybreak he put on his camouflage and dressed his rifle. He had decided to take on the machine gun nest. The solution seemed self-evident— as if his brain had solved the problem in his sleep, even though it was a difficult equation with many unknowns. Not once did he think of his decision to move to another sector, to which he had already been ordered and where they were heavily counting on him. But he also had a task waiting for him here and he knew just how it was to be accomplished.

He took the map from his map case on the wall and checked that it actually showed the road he needed to skirt the tributary to the Second Regiment's sector. He hadn't known that such a road existed, but it had been a given factor in his calculations.

In passing he noted that the Second Lieutenant had been lying the night before about the menace of the machine gun. If he couldn't shoot into the machine gun nest from his territory, how was it possible then to shoot from there into the Second Lieutenant's sector! But the Second Lieutenant had to account for his company's losses somehow. The battalion commander had in turn believed the Second Lieutenant's fabrication. They had to make a detour of over twenty miles before they arrived at their destination. He dispatched the motorcycle driver and ordered him to pick him up at the same place that evening. Then he crawled along parallel to the tributary until he was at its mouth, facing the nest. This short of the tributary was firmer than the other. In the evening the last thing the Second Lieutenant had mentioned was these "miserable" banks.

He directed his rifle toward the nest and stared at it through the scope. At daybreak the form of a watercooled machine gun appeared in the black aperture. He couldn't destroy the weapon itself, but its crew, yes. Even at this point he could inflict such casualties on the enemy that its desires and capabilities would be stemmed for a long time. Occasional stray bullets gave off shrill, whinning noises.

It seemed that the day would be very quiet. The faint rumbling of artillery could be heard only far off to the north.

The piping yell from beyond the tributary did not draw his attention—nor did the nascent, sporadic rifle fire, which ultimately crescendoed to a deafening crackle, as if an enemy patrol were being repulsed. He noticed the man swimming beneath the surface of the river only when the current had propelled the man almost even with him. The bullets smacked against the water and ricocheted into the opposite bank, where they punched white indentations in the dark logs right in front of him. He saw an arm wrapped around a log, but it disappeared right after he had seen it.

The current was stronger and swifter than might have been inferred from the movements of the logs. Although the Second Lieutenant had dashed into the river at the northern limit of his company's sector, it had carried him almost to the machine gun. With unbelievably long and swift dives he threaded through the water. Between dives he rested behind a log, keeping only his face above the surface. Actually a hand remained in view and divulged his hiding place, but when the bullets began to whistle in his ears he dove out of sight again. Despite the daylight you could distinguish the paths of some tracer bullets. Because of their low trajectory the bullets couldn't penetrate the water's surface, but ricocheted back into the air.

Only when he saw the swimmer dashing to the shore did the sniper recognize the long blond hair—the enlisted men were shaved bald—and the over-all build—the man was naked. The Second Lieutenant hid in the long reeds so quickly that the sniper didn't have time to note the spot where he disappeared. Desultory bullets kicked up small, scarcely visible puffs of dust from the bank.

The Lieutenant seemed to have calculated nicely. Only when the sniper didn't come to his sector did he make his attempt, confidently and at once.

The sniper was the only one to notice the deserter start up the slope. He was only a couple of hundred yards from the man. The nearest infantrymen were three or four hundred yards back and slightly to the side. The Second Lieutenant took long bounds like a mountain goat. He so nearly matched the color of the sand that at times only the steadily advancing wake of white dust betrayed his presence. The sniper reacted quickly. In anticipation he raised his sight straight to the top of the bank. Beyond the sight three enemy soldiers and the machine gun nest were visible in the scope. One of the enemy's faces was cut by the cross hairs.

They were all exposed from the waist up! Further along the bank some more men popped up to follow the course of events. The deserter worked himself into a frenzy—when he began to tire, the sniper's ears could pick up his rhythmical wheezing. When the man reached the summit of the steep bank and lunged over the top, it was the sniper's move. In spite of his frantic speed, the deserter froze for a perceptible instant in his tracks and stood out plainly against the sky.

The baffled men instinctively looked along the top of the bank for the source of the bullet. Who shot the deserter? Was the rat one of their own? Judging from its sound, the shot came from someplace nearby. Their impression of the noise prompted them to scrutinize the swamp down in front of them, but it was empty. It was wrong that the man should not be allowed to live the life he had offered for sale in broad daylight. For ten minutes the man had splashed around in the river and scampered along the shores and just when he leapt to shelter so that he dropped to the bottom of the trench, reached his goal. . . .

Huttunen got hit in the forehead and fell to the bottom of the trench. The others stared at the swamp from which the shot reverberated. There in the vicinity of some clumps of tall grass the stentorian noise still seemed to linger. They dove down headlong as soon as they could. Somebody said, "Sniper." But Huttunen was still alive.

"I'm going to die," he moaned and lay motionless with his eyes open. "Damn it, I'm *not* going to die," he moaned then and probed his forehead. "See if there's a hole in the back of his head."

"I can't see any hole," somebody said.

Huttunen sat up. Huttunen stood up.

"I'm going to the dressing station," he said quietly, not believing his own words.

Huttunen went into the connecting trench and was seen to disappear around a bend.

An enemy sniper was right opposite them in the swamp, because "The bullet got Huttunen right in the middle of the face."

Maenpaa the machine-gunner already envisioned himself as the destroyer of this abominable creature. Unhesitatingly, so that the others wouldn't have a chance, he seized the grips and began to fire a burst into the swamp. He did this so suddenly and reflexively, that fear, which had been tranquilized by a feeling of security, didn't have time to raise a finger. A bullet snapped into his forehead. Its exit from the neck went unnoticed because of his long hair. Maenpaa lifted himself as if trying to fall upwards and pulled up on the machine gun as the burst continued uninterrupted. The moving parts of the machine rattled as they repeated the same, very monotonous movements. When Maenpaa finished and began to drop, he stooped to see the ground where he fell without uttering a sound or even bending a finger.

When the men dared to look beyond the river after a long time, there had appeared a strangely twisted heap, which there hadn't been a while ago.

No one noticed when Maenpaa started to whimper, but he was still alive and two men took him away.

"I'm not going to die in action," he claimed. He had always made this claim, so it wasn't astonishing in itself, but at the same time he wrenched himself from the arms of his escorters. However he lost consciousness while stooping through the doorway of the dressing station. A medic verified that he had received a bullet through the head and dragged him behind the tent into a detachment of fallen men. There lay four men, of whom three had received bullets between the eyes: the sniper's prey.

Meanwhile the surgeon examined Huttunen and refused to believe the impossible. Huttunen was dying only because he was not yet dead. Ultimate death could come at any moment, quietly and unobtrusively. Maenpaa crawled back into the tent.

"What are you crawling here for?" asked the surgeon.

"I'm going to die when I bow my head," said Maenpaa, groggy from his lapses into unconsciousness. "If I don't bow my head I'm going to die."

The surgeon left Huttunen and ordered the medic to put some dressing on his head. He set about to examine Maenpaa. He shook his head. Yes, this man too was certainly going to die at any moment.

Soon it was afternoon. There were no others in the tent besides Huttunen and Maenpaa. It was the kind of peaceful afternoon that makes you believe there will always be such afternoons. They lay side by side on mattresses. The light of day filtered through the walls of the tent. They waited. Little by little Huttunen's head began to ache and he remarked it to Maenpaa. Soon Maenpaa's head began to ache too.

Only after a month did Huttunen and Maenpaa rejoin their units. They had been examined by an erudite doctor who knew why they had not died. Occasionally in the past— in the First World War—it had happened that a man had been shot through the head at the most vulnerable point and survived. The brain must have had a passage for the bullets—a zone, through which a bullet could pass without doing damage. It had to.

"He was too sharp a shooter. He missed Huttunen and Maenpaa in the head."

# GREECE

## TWO PARABLES

KOSTES PALAMAS

Translated from the Greek by Helen E. Farmakis

# A Man from Afar to a Village Came

A MAN FROM AFAR once came upon a village. Sunken, it was in a deep ravine. Round it, like steep prison walls of thick green verdure, rose the mountains that hemmed it in.

The man spoke to the villagers who came and gathered around him, "How beautiful and how large seems this world of yours!"

"That is so!" replied one of the villagers.

"Look," said another, "how rich is the verdure that encloses our village."

Still another said, "Ours are the olive groves too. We gain our livelihood from them."

The first one spoke again, "Further up, yonder, by the foot of the mountain, there we hold our feasts and revels twice and three times yearly. We lay our spread in the shade of the great pine. We carouse and adorn our brows with the myrtle wreaths we ourselves twine together. The broad green belt of the ravine wraps us close through the seasons of the year, summers and winters. When we are not at our plowing or sowing we have the joy of looking upon it from our windows."

The man from afar then said to them:

"Even so, let me tell you something else, too. This world of yours, this world you have all round you which is so beautiful and so large, dear people, is something you cannot know in all its true beauty when you only peer at it as you do from your windows down below. Climb up the mountainside, climb farther up than the feast grounds by the foot of the mountain. Climb and climb, till you reach the very peak of the mountain. After you reach the top of the mountain, cast your glance far and wide about you, into the depths and into the distance far, to the very horizons that you cannot sight from your windows.

"Skies, oceans, all the coloring and all the different shadings of light, all of creation will lie before you in one solid piece all round you. Then you will look and see below, a little to the side and very far below, one small whitish speck tightly ringed in by a slim belt of verdure. That speck will be your village in its velvet green cradle.

"But when you first see it from so far away, it will seem so paltry small and so strange a place, so different from the village as you know it living in the midst of it here, that seeing it from afar you will see it as a whole, neatly gathered together, like something live and moving, like a masterpiece enframed, which loses nothing of its charm by being small.

"Then, my dear people, at the very moment when you will realize the tininess of your village, if you will let the entire world see it in all its tininess and all its humbleness, you will come to love your village much more deeply than you do now. It will happen that way because you will realize that your homeland is not the entire world and because you will also realize that your homeland is only one of many other precious stones on the ring of the cosmos.

"You will then come to love your village in a new way. The love you now have for your village neither sees nor knows of horizons; it is a love that distinguishes no beauty of distances. The new love you will have for your village will be a more significant and more fruitful love. You will be able to realize a larger love that does not cut itself off from the whole. You will love your village not simply for the way it looks from your windows below; you will love your village for the way it looks from the mountain peaks, as a part of all creation."

The man's words swept through the village. As his words were difficult for the simple peasant people to understand, at each telling his words were changed and interpolated till all the meaning of his words was lost. Thus carried round from mouth to mouth, his words reached the ears of the overlord who like a feudal lord held the village as his own and the peasants as his serfs. The thoughts of the overlord ran thus through his mind:

"This wanderer has come to sow unrest among my people. He will fire their minds with yearnings for wanderings and for high places. His words will lure them from their labors, he will take them from their daily chores, he will turn them into shiftless insolent braggarts. He will make them indifferent to the care of their homes and their day's labor. They will raise their heads and turn against me. My labor hands will become fewer and my possessions will be endangered."

He thundered at his serfs:

"Drive out this evil man! This wanderer! This gypsy! This bedeviled man! He will contaminate our village! He has no home of his own. He comes to preach against the most precious of God's gifts, our Homeland!"

And he set his serfs upon the man and they stoned him.

# Digging for the Statue

I CLIMBED to the top of the hill guided by the words of the world traveler of old. Out of the book I held—while I bent over the passage reading and rereading—poured a voice, as if it came from inside a deep well, revealing lost treasures.

On the spot I stood, once rose the temple to the Great Mother. Here stood the statue, the great and miraculous statue of the Universal Mother, the goddess of the godly, mounted upon an awesome fierce lion. But no tempest, no lion's fierceness was ever so awesome as the calmness of absolute serenity that she radiated.

Over her brow towered her crown; the sky and the earth and the sea harmoniously blended in her stole. And the populace, storm-tossed, night and day scoured for gifts both the entire mainland and the depths of the sea, and brought to the feet of the goddess altar gifts of the most precious of precious stones.

Here stood the temple, a cyclopean structure, a creation of wonder. And the world traveler of old drew me to dig, arduously and unswerving by day and by night, till my pick axe should strike on that tremendous unresisting essence of all, the world renowned unseen statue.

I started to dig and dig and dig. And I tried to envision what it will be like to watch the Great Mother reborn out of the efforts of my own hands. A shiver ran through me. I felt it will be like watching the first morning star rise over the horizon after that first of all sunsets at the beginning of time.

And the summer sun rose high. And came the blazing heat of the noon hour. And far and wide dry heat blazed forth from the drought-hit land and every last vestige of dewy freshness was gone.

Through every month the earth had been yearning for the freshness of sweet water. And, where the one spring by the wayside gave water, water came slow as teardrops. Here people came from far and wide, and ever more pressed in daily, and daily fought tooth and nail for the yield of one drop of precious moisture.

And I, as if untouched from need of water, sought only the supreme thirst-quenching and went on with my digging. I stayed on at my digging to no avail. I went on digging among the ruins and at my lonely task I kept my thoughts immersed in the guiding words of the ancient world traveler. Still to no avail.

There passed another day, and came another night, and followed another dawn. And the third day, sharply upon the hour of twilight, my pick axe suddenly struck not on resisting rock, but on a thrust of deep-sprung water. My thrust burst forth a spring, a rich flowing spring of water that rushed forth unresisting, overflowing, as if it would flood all the land.

And now I see reflected on the surface of the spreading waters a whole populace thirst-freed, in a world of plenteous verdure, a world of liberated dawns and clear horizons.

To you, unearthed, unfound statue, I have this to say:

"Follow your deep mystic ways in the dark unknown. I am only a mortal. I am not the superhuman being meant to bring upon the earth the supreme unthirsting.

"Enough for me is this blessed sight that lies before me of so many lips, so many hands, so many brows refreshed and restored by the waters of this spring—arrested in their kneeling postures, as if they stayed to kneel before me in homage."

# HUNGARY

# Engagement

ENDRE FEJES

H E WAS a taciturn, stingy, rude man; everybody knew it
and so no one cared for him. During the day he hud-
duled diligently under the cars, bent over the engines and,
if they let him, worked overtime until midnight. For years
he had no lunch. While the others spooned their food from
small dishes, he stretched his thin body along a plank and
brooded with a frown.

Only the "norm-man," the payclerk, could make him
talk. This was good fun. At such times they all watched
how the blood drained from his face.

"Bloody robbers! I won't be treated like dirt!" and he
tore up the pay slip. "I'd rather work for nothing! Blast
you all, you filthy crooks!"

"He's in top gear now!" laughed the mechanics and
perched on the radiators.

His tools fell with a dull clatter on the concrete floor as
he threw them down. His blue eyes glittered and he swore
cruelly.

The payclerk, hiding his amusement, kept on arguing with
him, teasing him; then he had enough and made out another,
correct pay slip. He looked at the adjusted figures and grinned broadly as if he had won a battle.

One winter he found a blackbird in the snow. For a
long time he warmed it at the radiator, made a cage for it
and, to save it from petrol fumes, hung the cage on the wall
in the locker room.

73

The bird fluttered inside; after work, he pushed his oily finger through the bars for a peck or two.

Then, as the spring sunshine divested the outside workers of their wool-lined waistcoats, he let it go.

He watched his blackbird, rising with slow wing-beats above the chimneys, towards the silver clouds and said angrily:

"Go to hell. You'd have perished alone, anyhow. . . ."

He was certainly a strange man.

When he met priests, he greeted them with respect; passing a church, he raised his hat, but during work he cursed God incessantly. On Sundays he put on his striped brown best suit, knotted a purple tie and went to church. This was a tradition he acquired during the years he had spent in the orphanage and he kept it up. He listened to the organ, stared at the women, then crossed himself and began his usual window-shopping tour. Around noon he lunched on goulash and a lot of bread, standing at the counter of a place called the Beer Sanatorium. Then he went home and slept without stirring until Monday morning.

So the years passed.

But one November afternoon something wonderful happened.

He was buying some sausage for his supper at the Lehel Market when a parcel dropped on his boots.

"Holy Virgin!" cried a girl and just stared at the salami scattered in the mud.

He gave an embarrassed cough and said:

"Oh well, no use crying over spilled milk. . . ."

"It's not milk and I'm not crying, pal," the girl crossly replied. "It's my supper—or it would have been. . . ."

They started to walk in the drizzle and he couldn't take his eyes off her because he had never seen such a beautiful thing in his life. He said suddenly:

"If you'd let me invite you to Ilkovics . . ." then, startled by his own daring, he added timidly: "that is, if you don't take it amiss. . . ."

"Tell me—are you married?" she asked.

"Me?" he protested happily. "How can you imagine such a thing?"

They had veal stew with pickled cucumbers and some jam tarts afterwards.

He opened the top button of his fly and put his elbows on the table.

"D'you know the sort of man I am? You can enquire about me, if you like. When I start work, I carry half a dozen others. . . ."

"What's your job?" she smiled.

He leaned back on the chair.

"Universal mechanic." But as the girl said nothing, he added nonchalantly: "Petrol, Diesel, any bloody engine— makes no difference to me."

"And the pay?"

"I take home a fat envelope. And the norm-man's no bogey for me."

After the third glass of rum, he ploughed his fingers through her hair.

"Ever been in love?"

"Once every week," the girl laughed.

For a long time they were silent. The waiter brought another couple of rums.

"Love isn't a joking matter," he said, severely.

"How d'you know?"

Again there was silence.

"Nor are children . . . a family . . ."

"That's right," the girl agreed.

"When I go home in the evening, I fill up the tiled stove until it's real hot. Then you lean against it. . . ."

"That must be fine. . . ."

"In the summer cherries, strawberries and plums. . . .

You can make jam—twenty jars or more. . . . Later you just take it from the shelf to eat. . . ."

"If you got money," the girl held out her glass and clinked it against his. They drank.

"One knows how to save. . . ."

"Let's drink some more," her eyes brightened. "You're a very decent man. . . ."

And she gently caressed his broad hand.

The waiter, as he put down the glasses, smiled at his clumsy handkiss.

"You got somebody?"

"Not a soul—in heaven or earth. I'm just drifting alone," said the girl softly and lifted her glass. "To us!"

"Two people are never alone. God always knows what He's doing. . . ."

"But a place to live—that's very difficult," she sighed.

"Where do you live?"

"Far . . . very far out," she replied vaguely. "Alone in a room. . . ."

"You can buy a flat to share, they say, for two thousand forints. . . ."

"Two thousand forints!" the girl bubbled with laughter.

"I've got it!" and he slapped his chest, adding modestly: "One knows how to save. . . ."

"You need a ring and a little furniture, bed linen. . . ."

He gazed dizzily into the girl's big brown eyes.

"There's a little chapel, we can hire a white dress and a bouquet. . . ."

"And you?" she nestled against him.

"I . . . in my brown Sunday suit . . . then we'll buy a big cake and eat it at home. . . ."

"Is that how you want to save money?"

He laughed, too, and in his mighty happiness tipped the waiter five forints.

Arm-in-arm they walked slowly along Lehel Street. Near the Stakhanovite Bridge, behind the tiny stone house of the instant photographer, where not even the light of the pale lamplight could penetrate, the girl stopped. She cradled his thin face in her hands, stared at him for a long time, then put her arms around his neck and gave him a lingering kiss.

He pressed her to himself, trembling, and she, like a bird that had found a nest, clung to him and laughed like a child. Then she freed herself from his embrace and caressed his hair.

"Go now, it's late . . . we must get up early to-morrow. . . . Sleep well and have fine dreams. . . . There, near the movie," she pointed to the other side, "I'll wait for you in that small pastry shop tomorrow afternoon. . . ."

He stood watching her as she ran across the road. As her footsteps died among the fruit stands, he set out for home.

It was only at the Western Terminus that he noticed— his wallet had disappeared. He turned out every pocket, searched every inch of his jacket—it was gone.

He roamed the streets through the filthy, grey November dawn. His soaked loden coat was mud-heavy, his thin hair hung into his face and, with terrified eyes, he searched in the comfortless sky and the puddles for his lost happiness.

For two weeks he sat in the pastry shop through endless afternoons.

Then he no longer went there.

Nowadays he is often drunk when he gets to the workshop. Everybody knows that he is a taciturn, rude man, and no one pays any attention to him.

They only miss the old fun.

Whatever appears on his pay slip, he goes on huddling under the cars, bending over the engines and doesn't say a word.

And this is something the mechanics do not understand at all.

# INDIA

# The Letter

DHUMKETU

Translated from the Gujerati by the author

IN THE GREY SKY of early dawn stars still glowed, as happy memories light up a life that is nearing its close. An old man was walking through the town, now and again drawing his tattered cloak tighter to shield his body from the cold and biting wind. From some houses standing apart came the sound of grinding mills and the sweet voices of women singing at their work, and these sounds helped him along his lonely way. Except for the occasional bark of a dog, the distant steps of a workman going early to work or the screech of a bird disturbed before its time, the whole town was wrapped in deathly silence. Most of its inhabitants were still in the arms of sleep, a sleep which grew more and more profound on account of the intense winter cold; for the cold used sleep to extend its sway over all things even as a false friend lulls his chosen victim with caressing smiles. The old man, shivering at times but fixed of purpose, plodded on till he came out of the town gate to a straight road. Along this he now went at a somewhat slower pace, supporting himself on his old staff.

On one side of the road was a row of trees, on the other the town's public garden. The night was darker now and the cold more intense, for the wind was blowing straight along the road and on it there only fell, like frozen snow, the faint light of the morning star. At the end of the garden stood a handsome building of the newest style, and light gleamed through the crevices of its closed doors and windows.

Beholding the wooden arch of this building, the old man was filled with the joy that the pilgrim feels when he first sees the goal of his journey. On the arch hung an old board with the newly painted letters: POST OFFICE. The old man went in quietly and squatted on the veranda. The voices of the two or three people busy at their routine work could be heard faintly through the wall.

"Police Superintendent," a voice inside called sharply. The old man started at the sound, but composed himself again to wait. But for the faith and love that warmed him he could not have borne the bitter cold.

Name after name rang out from within as the clerk read out the English addresses on the letters and flung them to the waiting postmen. From long practice he had acquired great speed in reading out the titles—Commissioner, Superintendent, Diwan Sahib, Librarian—and in flinging out the letters.

In the midst of this procedure a jesting voice from inside called, "Coachman Ali!"

The old man got up, raised his eyes to Heaven in gratitude and, stepping forward, put his hand on the door.

"Godul Bhai!"

"Yes. Who's there?"

"You called out Coachman Ali's name, didn't you? Here I am. I have come for my letter."

"It is a mad man, sir, who worries us by calling every day for letters that never come," said the clerk to the postmaster.

The old man went back slowly to the bench on which he had been accustomed to sit for five long years.

Ali had once been a clever shikari. As his skill increased so did his love for the hunt, till at last it was as impossible for him to pass a day without it as it is for the opium eater to forego his daily portion. When Ali sighted the earth-brown partridge, almost invisible to other eyes, the poor bird, they said, was as good as in his bag. His sharp eyes would see the hare crouching in its form. When even the dogs failed to see the creature cunningly hidden in the yellow-brown scrub, Ali's eagle eyes would catch sight of its ears; and in another moment it was dead. Besides this, he would often go with his friends, the fishermen.

But when the evening of his life was drawing in, he left his old ways and suddenly took a new turn. His only child, Miriam, married and left him. She went off with a soldier to his regiment in the Punjab, and for the last five years he had had no news of this daughter for whose sake alone he dragged on a cheerless existence. Now he understood the meaning of love and separation. He could no longer enjoy the sportsman's pleasure and laugh at the bewildered terror of the young partridges bereft of their parents.

Although the hunter's instinct was in his very blood and bones, such a loneliness had come into his life since the day Miriam had gone away that now, forgetting his sport, he would become lost in admiration of the green corn fields. He reflected deeply and came to the conclusion that the whole universe is built up through love and that the grief of separation is inescapable. And seeing this, he sat down under a tree and wept bitterly. From that day he had risen each morning at four o'clock to walk to the post office. In his whole life he had never received a letter, but with a devout serenity born of hope and faith he continued and was always the first to arrive.

The post office, one of the most uninteresting buildings in the world, became his place of pilgrimage. He always occupied a particular seat in a particular corner of the building, and when people got to know his habit they laughed at him. The postmen began to make a game of him. Even though there was no letter for him, they would call out his name for the fun of seeing him jump and come to the door.

But with boundless faith and infinite patience he came every day—and went away empty-handed.

While Ali waited, peons would come for their firms' letters and he would hear them discussing their masters' scandals. These smart young peons in their spotless turbans and creaking shoes were always eager to express themselves. Meanwhile the door would be thrown open and the postmaster, a man with a head as sad and inexpressive as a pumpkin, would be seen sitting on his chair inside. There was no glimmer of animation in his features; and such men usually prove to be village schoolmasters, office clerks or postmasters.

One day he was there as usual and did not move from his seat when the door was opened.

"Police Commissioner!" the clerk called out, and a fellow stepped forward briskly for the letters.

"Superintendent!" Another peon came; and so the clerk, like a worshipper of Vishnu, repeated his customary thousand names.

At last they had all gone. Ali too got up and, saluting the post office as though it housed some precious relic, went off, a pitiable figure, a century behind his time.

"That fellow," asked the postmaster, "is he mad?"

"Who, sir? Oh yes," answered the clerk. "No matter what sort of weather, he has been here every day for the last five years. But he doesn't get many letters."

"I can well understand that! Who does he think will have time to write to him every day?"

"But he's a bit touched, sir. In the old days he committed many sins; and maybe he shed blood within some sacred precincts and is paying for it now," the postman added in support to his statement.

"Madmen are strange people," the postmaster said.

"Yes. Once I saw a madman in Ahmedabad who did absolutely nothing but make little heaps of dust. Another had a habit of going every day to the river in order to pour water on a certain stone!"

"Oh, that's nothing," chimed in another. "I knew one madman who paced up and down all day long, another who never ceased declaiming poetry, and a third who would slap himself on the cheek and then begin to cry out because he was being beaten."

And everyone in the post office began talking of lunacy. All working-class people have a habit of taking periodic rests by joining in general discussion for a few minutes. After listening a little, the postmaster got up and said:

"It seems as though the mad live in a world of their own making. To them, perhaps, we too appear mad. The madman's world is rather like the poet's, I should think!"

He laughed as he spoke the last words, looking at one of the clerks who wrote indifferent verse. Then he went out and the office became still again.

For several days Ali had not come to the post office. There was no one with enough sympathy or understanding to guess the reason, but all were curious to know what had stopped the old man. At last he came again; but it was a struggle for him to breathe, and on his face were clear signs of his approaching end. That day he could not contain his impatience.

"Master Sahib," he begged the postmaster, "have you a letter from my Miriam?"

The postmaster was in a hurry to get out to the country.

"What a pest you are, brother!" he exclaimed.

"My name is Ali," answered Ali, absent-mindedly.

"I know! I know! But do you think we've got your Miriam's name registered?"

"Then please note it down, brother. It will be useful if a letter should come when I am not here." For how should the villager who had spent three-quarters of his life hunting know that Miriam's name was not worth a pice to anyone but her father?

The postmaster was beginning to lose his temper. "Have you no sense?" he cried. "Get away! Do you think we are going to eat your letter when it comes?" And he walked off hastily. Ali came out very slowly, turning after every few steps to gaze at the post office. His eyes were filling with tears of helplessness, for his patience was exhausted, even though he still had faith. Yet how could he still hope to hear from Miriam?

Ali heard one of the clerks coming up behind him and turned to him.

"Brother!" he said.

The clerk was surprised, but being a decent fellow he said, "Well?"

"Here, look at this!" and Ali produced an old tin box and emptied five golden guineas into the surprised clerk's hands. "Do not look so startled," he continued, "they will be useful to you, and they can never be so to me. But will you do one thing?"

"What?"

"What do you see up there?" said Ali, pointing to the sky.

"Heaven."

"Allah is there, and in His presence I am giving you this money. When it comes, you must forward my Miriam's letter to me."

"But where—where am I to send it?" asked the utterly bewildered clerk.

"To my grave."

"What?"

"Yes. It is true. Today is my last day: my very last, alas! And I have not seen Miriam, I have had no letter from her." Tears were in Ali's eyes as the clerk slowly left him and went on his way with the five golden guineas in his pocket.

Ali was never seen again and no one troubled to inquire after him.

One day, however, trouble came to the postmaster. His daughter lay ill in another town and he was anxiously waiting for news from her. The post was brought in and the letters piled on the table. Seeing an envelope of the color and shape he expected, the postmaster eagerly snatched it up. It was addressed to coachman Ali, and he dropped it as though it had given him an electric shock. The haughty temper of the official had quite left him in his sorrow and anxiety and had laid bare his human heart. He knew at once that this was the letter the old man had been waiting for: it must be from his daughter Miriam.

"Lakshmi Das!" called the postmaster, for such was the name of the clerk to whom Ali had given his money.

"Yes, sir?"

"This is for your old coachman Ali. Where is he now?"

"I will find out, sir."

The postmaster did not receive his own letter all that day.

He worried all night and, getting up at three, went to sit in the office. "When Ali comes at four o'clock," he mused, "I will give him the letter myself."

For now the postmaster understood all Ali's heart, and his very soul. After spending but a single night in suspense, anxiously waiting for news of his daughter, his heart was brimming with sympathy for the poor old man who had spent his nights for the last five years in the same suspense. At the stroke of five he heard a soft knock on the door: he felt sure it was Ali. He rose quickly from his chair, his suffering father's heart recognizing another, and flung the door wide open.

"Come in, brother Ali," he cried, handing the letter to the meek old man, bent double with age, who was standing outside. Ali was leaning on a stick and the tears were wet on his face as they had been when the clerk left him. But his features had been hard then and now they were softened by lines of kindliness. He lifted his eyes and in them was a light so unearthly that the postmaster shrank in fear and astonishment.

Lakshmi Das had heard the postmaster's words as he came towards the office from another quarter. "Who was that, sir?

Old Ali?" he asked. But the postmaster took no notice of him. He was staring with wide-open eyes at the doorway from which Ali had disappeared. Where could he have gone? At last he turned to Lakshmi Das. "Yes, I was speaking to Ali," he said.

"Old Ali is dead, sir. But give me his letter."

"What! But when? Are you sure, Lakshmi Das?"

"Yes, it is so," broke in a postman who had just arrived. "Ali died three months ago."

The postmaster was bewildered. Miriam's letter was still lying near the door; Ali's image was still before his eyes. He listened to Lakshmi Das' recital of the last interview, but he could still not doubt the reality of the knock on the door and the tears in Ali's eyes. He was perplexed. Had he really seen Ali? Had his imagination deceived him? Or had it perhaps been Lakshmi Das?

The daily routine began. The clerk read out the addresses —Police Commissioner, Superintendent, Librarian—and flung the letters deftly.

But the postmaster now watched them as though each contained a warm, beating heart. He no longer thought of them in terms of envelopes and postcards. He saw the essential, human worth of a letter.

That evening you might have seen Lakshmi Das and the postmaster walking with slow steps to Ali's grave. They laid the letter on it and turned back.

"Lakshmi Das, were you indeed the first to come to the office this morning?"

"Yes, sir, I was the first."

"Then how. . . . No, I don't understand. . . ."

"What, sir?"

"Oh, never mind," the postmaster said shortly. At the office he parted from Lakshmi Das and went in. The newly-waked father's heart in him was reproaching him for having failed to understand Ali's anxiety. Tortured by doubt and remorse, he sat down in the glow of the charcoal sigri to wait.

# The Gold Watch

## Mulk Raj Anand

THERE WAS SOMETHING about the smile of Mr. Acton when he came over to Srijut Sudarshan Sharma's table which betokened disaster. But as the Sahib had only said, "Mr. Sharma, I have brought something specially for you from London—you must come into my office on Monday and take it . . . ," the poor old despatch clerk could not surmise the real meaning of the General Manager's remark. The fact that Mr. Acton should come over to his table at all, fawn upon him and say what he had said was, of course, most flattering, for very rarely did the head of the firm condescend to move down the corridor where the Indian staff of the distribution department of the great Marmalade Empire of Henry King & Co. worked.

But that smile on Mr. Acton's face! Specially as Mr. Acton was not known to smile too much, being a morose old Sahib, hard working, conscientious, and a slave driver, famous as a shrewd businessman, so devoted to the job of spreading the monopoly of King's Marmalade and sundry other products that his wife had left him after a three months' spell of marriage and never returned to India, though no one quite knew whether she was separated or divorced from him or merely preferred to stay away. So the fact that Acton Sahib should smile was enough to give Srijut Sharma cause for thought. But then Srijut Sharma was, in spite of his nobility of soul and fundamental innocence, experienced

enough in his study of the vague, detached faces of the white
Sahibs by now and had clearly noticed the slight awkward
curl of the upper lip, behind which the determined tobacco-
stained long teeth showed for the briefest moment a snarl
suppressed by the deliberation which Acton Sahib had
brought to the whole operation of coming over and pronouncing those kind words. And what could be the reason for his
having been singled out from among the twenty-five odd
members of the distribution department? In the usual way,
he, the despatch clerk, only received an occasional greeting:
"Hello, Sharma—how you getting on?" from the head of his
own department, Mr. West Sahib, for a reprimand because
some letters or packets had gone astray; otherwise, he himself being the incarnation of clockwork efficiency and well-
versed in the routine of his job, there was no occasion for any
break in the monotony of that anonymous, smooth working
Empire, so far at least as he was concerned.

To be sure, there was the continual gossip of the clerks
and the accountants, the bickerings and jealousies of the people above him for grades and promotions and pay, but he,
Sharma, had been employed twenty years ago as a special
favor, was not even a matriculate, but had picked up the
work somehow and, though unwanted and constantly repri-
manded by West Sahib in the first few years, had been
retained in his job because of the general legend of saintli-
ness which he had acquired. . . . He had five more years of
service to do, because then he would be fifty-five and the
family-raising, *grhst* portion of his life in the fourfold
scheme, prescribed by religion, finished. He hoped to retire
to his home town, Jullundhur, where his father still ran the
confectioner's shop off the Mall Road.

"And what did Acton Sahib have to say to you, Mr.
Sharma?" asked Miss Violet Dixon, the plain snub-nosed
Anglo-Indian typist in her sing-song.

Since he was an old family man of fifty who had greyed
prematurely, she considered her virginity safe enough with

this "gentleman" and freely conversed with him, specially during the lunch hour, while she considered almost everyone else as having only one goal in life—to sleep with her.

"Han," he said, "he has brought something for me from England," Srijut Sharma answered.

"There are such pretty things in U.K.," she said. "My! I wish I could go there! . . . My sister is there, you know! Married! . . ."

She had told Sharma all these things before. So he was not interested. Specially today, because all his thoughts were concentrated on the inner meaning of Mr. Acton's sudden visitation and the ambivalent smile.

"Well, half day today, I am off," said Violet and moved away with the peculiar snobbish agility of the Mem Sahib she affected to be.

Srijut Sharma stared at her blankly, though taking her regular form into his subconscious with more than the old uncle's interest he had always pretended. It was only her snub nose, like that of Sarup-naka, the sister of the demon king, Ravana, that stood in the way of her being married, he felt sure, for otherwise she had a tolerable figure. But he lowered his eyes as soon as the thought of Miss Dixon's body began to simmer in the cauldron of his inner life because, as a good Hindu, every woman, apart from the wife, was to him a mother or a sister. And his obsession about the meaning of Acton Sahib's words returned, from the pent-up curiosity, with greater force now that he realized the vastness of the space of time during which he would have to wait in suspense before knowing what the boss had brought for him and why.

He took up his faded sola topee, which was, apart from the bush shirt and trousers, one of the few concessions to modernity which he had made throughout his life as a good Brahmin, got up from his chair, beckoned Dugdu from the verandah on his way out and asked: "Has Acton Sahib gone you know?"

"Abhi-Sahib in lift, going down," Dugdu said.

Srijut Sharma made quickly for the stairs and, throwing all caution about slipping on the polished marble steps to the winds, hurtled down. There were three floors below him and he began to sweat, both through fear of missing the Sahib and the heat of mid-April. As he got to the ground floor he saw Acton Sahib already going out of the door.

It was now or never.

Srijut Sharma rushed out. But he was conscious that quite a few employees of the firm would be coming out of the two lifts and he might be seen talking to the Sahib. And that was not done—outside the office. The Sahibs belonged to their private world where no intrusion was tolerated, for they refused to listen to pleas for advancement through improper channels.

Mr. Acton's uniformed driver opened the door of the polished Buick and the Sahib sat down, spreading the shadow of grimness all around him.

Srijut Sharma hesitated, for the demeanor of the Goanese chauffeur was frightening.

By now the driver had smartly shut the back door of the car and was proceeding to his seat.

That was his only chance.

Taking off his hat, he rushed up to the window of the car and rudely thrust his face into the presence of Mr. Acton.

Luckily for him the Sahib did not brush him aside, but smiled a broader smile than that of a few minutes ago and said: "You want to know what I have brought for you—well, it is a gold watch with an inscription on it. See me Monday morning. . . ." The Sahib's initiative in anticipating his question threw Srijut Sharma further off his balance. The sweat just poured down from his forehead, even as he mumbled, "Thank you, Sir, thank you. . . ."

"Chalo, driver!" the Sahib ordered.

And the chauffeur turned and looked hard at Srijut Sharma.

The despatch clerk withdrew with a sheepish, abject smile on his face and stood, hat in left hand, the right hand raised to his forehead in the attitude of a nearly military salute.

The motor car moved off.

But Srijut Sharma stood still, as though he had been struck dumb. He was neither happy nor sad at this moment —only numbed by the shock of surprise. Why should he be singled out from the whole distribution department of Henry King & Co. for the privilege of the gift of a gold watch! . . . He had done nothing brave that he could remember. "A gold watch, with an inscription on it!" Oh, he knew now—the intuitive truth rose inside him—the Sahib wanted him to retire. . . .

The revelation rose to the surface of his awareness from the deep obsessive fear which had possessed him for nearly half an hour, and his heart began to palpitate against his will, and the sweat sozzled his body. He reeled a little, then adjusted himself and got onto the pavement, looking after the car which had already turned the corner into Nicol Road.

He turned and began to walk towards Victoria Terminus Station to take his train to Thana, thirty miles out, where he had resided for cheapness almost all the years he had been in Bombay. His steps were heavy, for he was reasonably sure now that he would get notice of retirement on Monday. He tried to think of some other possible reason why the Sahib may have decided to give him the gift of a gold watch with an inscription. There was no other explanation. His doom was sealed. What would he say to his wife? And his son had still not passed his Matric. How would he support the family? The provident fund would not amount to very much, specially in these days of rising prices. . . .

He felt a pull at his heart. He paused for breath and tried to calm himself. The old blood pressure! Or was it merely wind? . . . He must not get into a panic at any cost.

He steadied his gait and walked along muttering to himself, "Shanti! Shanti! Shanti!" as though the very incantation of the formula of peace would restore him to calm and equanimity.

During the weekend, Srijut Sharma was able to conceal his panic and confusion behind the façade of an exaggerated *bonhomie* with the skill of an accomplished actor. On Saturday night he went with his wife and son to see Professor Ram's circus which was performing opposite the Portuguese Church. He spent a little longer on his prayers, but otherwise seemed normal enough on the surface. Only he ate very little of the gala meal of the rice kichri put before him by his wife and seemed lost in thought for a few moments at a time. And his illiterate but shrewd wife noticed that there was something on his mind.

"Thou has not eaten at all today," she said as he left the tasty papadum and the mango pickle untouched. "Look at Hari! He has left nothing in his thali!"

"Hoon," he answered abstractedly. And then, realizing that he might be found out for the worried, unhappy man he was, he tried to bluff her. "As a matter of fact, I was thinking of some happy news that the Sahib gave me yesterday: he said he had brought a gold watch as a gift for me from Vilayat. . . ."

"Then, Papaji, give me the silver watch you are using now," said Hari, his young son, impetuously. "I have no watch at all and am always late everywhere."

"Not so impatient, son!" counseled Hari's mother. "Let your father get the gold watch first and then . . . he will surely give you his silver watch!"

In the ordinary way, Srijut Sharma would have endorsed his wife's sentiments. But today he felt that, on the face of it, his son's demand was justified. How should Hari know that the silver watch, the gold watch and a gold ring would be all the jewelry he, the father, would have for security against hard days if the gold watch was, as he prognosticated, only a token being offered by the firm to sugarcoat the bitter pill they would ask him to swallow—retirement five years before the appointed time! He hesitated, then lifted his head, smiled at his son and said:

"Acha, Kaka, you can have my silver watch. . . ."

"Can I have it really, Papaji, hurry!" the boy said, getting up to fetch it from his father's pocket. "Give it to me now, today!"

"Vay, son, you are so selfish!" his mother exclaimed. For, with the peculiar sensitiveness of the woman, she had surmised from the manner in which her husband had hung his head and then tried to smile as he lifted his face to his son that the father of Hari was upset inside him or at least not in his usual mood of accepting life evenly, accompanying this acceptance with the pious invocation, "Shanti! Shanti! Shanti!"

Hari brought the silver watch, adjusted it to his left ear to see if it ticked and, happy in the possession of it, capered a little caper.

Srijut Sharma did not say anything, but pushing his thali away got up to wash his hands.

The next day it happened as Srijut Sharma had anticipated.

He went in to see Mr. Acton as soon as the Sahib came in, for the suspense of the weekend had mounted to a crescendo by Monday morning and he had been trembling with trepidation, pale and completely unsure of himself. The General Manager called him in immediately and the peon Dugdu presented the little slip with the despatch clerk's name on it.

"Please sit down," said Mr. Acton, lifting his grey-haired head from the papers before him. And then, pulling his keys from his trousers pocket by the gold chain to which they were adjusted, he opened a drawer and fetched out what Sharma thought was a beautiful red case.

"Mr. Sharma, you have been a loyal friend of this firm

for many years . . . and . . . you know, your loyalty has been your greatest asset here . . . because . . . er . . . otherwise, we could have got someone with better qualifications to do your work! Now . . . we are thinking of increasing the efficiency of the business all around! And, well, we feel that you would also like, at your age, to retire to your native Punjab. . . . So, as a token of our appreciation for your loyalty to Henry King & Co., we are presenting you this gold watch. . . ." And he pushed the red case towards him.

"Sahib! . . ." Srijut Sharma began to speak, but though his mouth opened, he could not go on. "I am only fifty years old," he wanted to say, "and I still have five years to go." His facial muscles seemed to contract, his eyes were dimmed with the fumes of frustration and bitterness, his forehead was covered with sweat. At least they might have made a little ceremony of the presentation. He could not even utter the words, "Thank you, Sir."

"Of course, you will also have your provident fund and one month's leave with pay before you retire. . . ."

Again Srijut Sharma tried to voice his inner protest in words which would convey his meaning without seeming to be disloyal, for he did not want to obliterate the one concession the Sahib had made to the whole record of his service with his firm. It was just likely that Mr. Acton might remind him of his failings as a despatch clerk if he should as much as indicate that he was unamenable to the suggestion made by the Sahib on behalf of Henry King & Co.

"Look at the watch—it has an inscription on it which will please you," said Mr. Action to get over the embarrassment created by the silence of the despatch clerk.

These words hypnotized Sharma and, stretching his hands across the large table, he reached out heavily for the gift.

Mr. Action noticed the unsureness of his hand and pushed it gently forward.

Srijut Sharma picked up the red box, but, in his eagerness

to follow the Sahib's behests, dropped it even as he had held it aloft and tried to open it.

The Sahib's face was livid as he picked up the box and hurriedly opened it. Then, lifting the watch from its socket, he wound it and applied it to his ear. It was ticking. He turned it round and showed the inscription to the despatch clerk.

Srijut Sharma put both his hands out, more steadily this time, and took the gift in the manner in which a beggar receives alms. He brought the glistening object within the orbit of his eyes, but they were dimmed with tears and he could not read anything. He tried to smile, however, and then, with a great heave of his will which rocked his body from side to side, pronounced the words, "Thank you, Sir. . . ."

Mr. Acton got up, took the gold watch from Srijut Sharma's hands and put it back in the socket of the red case. Then he stretched his right hand towards the despatch clerk with a brisk shake-hand gesture and offered the case to him with his left hand.

Srijut Sharma instinctively took the Sahib's right hand gratefully in his two sweating hands and then opened the palms out to receive the case.

"Good luck, Sharma," Mr. Acton said. "Come and see me after your leave is over. And when your son matriculates let me know if I can do something for him. . . ."

Dumb and with bent head, the fumes of his violent emotions rising above the mouth which could have expressed them, he withdrew in the abject manner of his ancestors going out of the presence of a feudal lord.

Mr. Acton saw the danger to the watch and went ahead to open the door so that the clerk could go out without knocking his head against the door or falling down.

As Srijut Sharma emerged from the General Manager's office, tears involuntarily flowed from his eyes and his lower lip fell in a pout that somehow controlled him from breaking down completely.

The eyes of the whole office staff were on him. In a moment, a few of the men clustered around his person. One of
them took the case from his hands, opened it and read the
inscription out loud: "In appreciation of the loyal service of
Mr. Sharma to Henry King & Co. on his retirement."

The curiosity of his colleagues became a little less enthusiastic though the watch passed from hand to hand.

Unable to stand because of the waves of dizziness that
swirled in his head, Srijut Sudarshan Sharma sat down on
his chair with his head hidden in his hands and allowed the
tears to roll down. One of his colleagues, Mr. Banaji, the
accountant, patted his back understandingly. But the pity
was too much for him.

"To be sure, Seth Makanji, the new partner, has a relation
to fill Sharma's position," one said.

"No, no," another refuted him. "No one is required to
kill himself with work in our big concern. . . . We are given
the Sunday off! And a fat pension years before it is due. The
bosses are full of love for us! . . ."

"Damn fine gold watch, but it does not go!" said Shri
Raman the typist.

Mr. Banaji took the watch from Srijut Raman and, putting it in the case, placed it before Srijut Sharma as he signed
the others to move away.

As Srijut Sharma realized that his colleagues had drifted
away, he lifted his morose head, took the case, as well as his
hat, and began to walk away. Mr. Banaji saw him off to the
door, his hand on Sharma's back. "Sahibji," the parsi accountant said as the lift came up and the liftman took Sharma
in.

On the way home he found that the gold watch only went
when it was shaken. Obviously some delicate part had broken
when he had dropped it on Mr. Acton's table. He would get
it mended, but he must save all the cash he could get hold
of and not go spending it on the luxury of having a watch

repaired now. He shouldn't have been weak with his son and given him his old silver watch. But as there would be no office to attend, he would not need to look at the time very much, specially in Jullundhur where time just stood still and no one bothered about keeping appointments.

# INDONESIA

# All Our Yesterdays

BEB VUYK

Translated from the Dutch by Estelle Debrot

DURING THAT MONTH it rained every day, but before evening fell it was dry again. Then the damp
garden smelled of leaves and grass. The hospital was a rebuilt
country house, surrounded by a park-like garden, where a
famous painter had lived a hundred years ago in royal splendor. In spite of all the changes made by the scores of altera-
tions for different purposes, it had retained much of the old
in its sphere, a composure which is not of today and a naïve
rusticity. It lay just outside the centrum on a busy highway,
an enclave of rest in the town and in time.

Groves were cleared away and ponds were filled up, but
the old driveway of royal palms had been spared, was· as-
phalted, and led from the modern entrance building to the
nurses' quarters, the former main building, bombastically
ugly and yet with a gesture of grandeur. Though small courts
had been formed by additions to the side wings, adequate
lawns remained, partly overshadowed by trees, to preserve a
feeling of space, of coolness and rusticity. Deer grazed there
in the afternoons under tall trees.

She always lay alone in this white room. During the day
the shutters remained closed, to open an hour before sundown, when the light had lost its glare and a grey shadow rose
on the white of the walls, not cast and not directed, as if
coming from inside. There are places where temporary things
become lasting. From the tandem, through the dark tunnel

97

of unconsciousness, she had been flung in this place, no longer in life and not yet in death. At night the door to the wide rear gallery stood open. From the dark room she could see into the gallery where some twenty meters from her bed, in the middle, a low-hanging lamp spread a soft yellow circle over the table of the night nurses.

One night she had dreamed aloud, but when she wakened she could not remember what the dream was about. The night nurse was standing over her bed offering her something to drink.

"Are you afraid?" she asked. "There is no reason to be, everything is going to be all right. You have only to lie flat in the dark a few weeks longer."

"No, no, I am not afraid," she said hastily and was surprised about the feeling of guilt that she recognized from her youth, when she had fibbed without being caught.

"Shall I give you something to make you sleep?"

"Oh, no" she answered almost offended and closed her eyes. "Thank you just the same, I'll fall asleep again."

But she did not go to sleep again. The nurse finished her rounds and sat down at the table under the lamp. She knitted for a while, went to help one of the patients in another room, and then put her knitting away and took up a newspaper.

The yellow light from a low-hanging lamp, under it a policeman reading the newspaper. She lay on a mat on the dirty floor and dreamed, screaming in the dream. She was sentenced and the judge was the Kempaitai captain with the pale face and the immobile eyes of a reptile. She told her story with Ann and Chris sitting next to her, they knew her lies and would bear her out.

Then Bennie was brought in. He did not wear a uniform any longer but the old khaki shirt and trousers which he always had on when he went in the gardens. He looked calm and unsuspecting and greeted the judge unconstrainedly with a nod of his head. She had not been able to warn him, he was not taken prisoner together with them and had never been confronted with them. Now they had taken him from the prison camp and brought him here to testify.

She thought with dismay, he does not know the story I made up, he will betray us. His evidence will show that we are lying.

His face came nearer like a close-up in a film, a friendly trustworthy face, the face of an honest and simple person. In his guilelessness he will betray us, she thought, he will tell the truth and his truth will be our death.

Then she saw his face begin to decay. The eyes sank deeper, the cheeks fell away, the teeth became bare. The image fell backwards, she saw him from feet to head. His shirt was open, she could see his chest and how the flesh was already rotting, that the ribs were visible, that only a few shreds of dark flesh hung between the bars of the thorax.

She screamed, she heard herself screaming.

Someone touched her hand and said: "Are you afraid, do you want something to drink?"

The little policeman gave her the glass of water with trembling hands. Two others stood behind him.

"You frightened us," he said. "Were you dreaming?"

"Yes, about the Kempaitai."

She could see their faces, she nodded to both and repeated: "About the Kempaitai."

"Did they torture you?" asked the tallest one.

"Yes, with electricity, but it was not about that."

"You must not frighten us," said the small one earnestly.

She sat up straight on her mat and looked in their faces and recognized their fear. One of them squatted down next to her, took a little box from his pocket and rubbed some salve on her forehead.

"What is it?" she asked.

"*Obat matjan.*" The other offered some aspirin and got more water.

LIBRARY
OKALOOSA - WALTON JUNIOR COLLEGE

"Go to sleep again," said the tall one and added comfortingly as to a child, "tomorrow you will not be interrogated."

She lay down again and closed her eyes. Then they spoke Javanese to one another; a little later she heard the door close. When she looked up again the little policeman sat at the table under the low lamp—like a nurse who is watching a patient, she had thought then.

She was taken to the Roentgen room for an examination on a stretcher that was wheeled along the gallery. It was still early, but the light there outside her room was already unmercifully dazzling. Babus were mopping the long tiled gallery; nurses were moving swiftly from one section to the other; convalescing patients, their faces still sunken from illness, were walking with care in the garden. She closed her eyes and covered her face with her hands.

"That is better," said the nurse, "the light is too sharp for you."

She always made remarks that were intended to be friendly and were correct but which, for some reason or other, were not suited to the situation. After this trip the Roentgen room was dim, cool and mercifully quiet. They left her lying on the stretcher because the doctor had not yet arrived. She kept her eyes closed, especially when they gave her the injection, and she remained for a time in a state between the border of consciousness and moments of unconsciousness. Afterwards the things around her became clearer again, though farther away and slightly shifted. The doctor stood next to her, before she was aware that he had come in.

"She has already had the shot," she heard the nurse saying, "but we did not know if we should shave off her hair or not."

He laid his hand on her neck. His fingers were as cold as the blade of a sword. Deathly cold like a sword, she thought. There was one word that expressed it exactly, but she could no longer remember it.

Now there was nothing left but to die with dignity. This was the last command, die with dignity. At the same time she knew that she did not have to die, not at this moment in any case. The strain of fear was insupportable, though she knew with certainty that she was not going to die. More direct and more urgent than the fear of death was the fear to be lacking in dignity, to go to pieces, deteriorate under the torture, to shrink from the pain, to give in to a complaint, to beg with indignity.

They had not closed her up in a cell, but in the *gudang* where the confiscated goods were kept. One evening a woman in one of the cells began to scream. She hardly knew her, only that she was the wife of the former mayor. On the way to the water closet, she had to pass the woman's cell; in the beginning a policeman always walked in back of her, later not, at least if there were no Japanese. Sometimes they exchanged a few words. The woman always stood in back of the observation hole, a white face, framed by tangled reddish hair that was completely shaved away on one side of her head. "They did that right away at the first interrogation," the woman had whispered to her. In the afternoon the woman's niece came to bring her food, the prisoners who were pending trial were allowed to receive their food from outside. Sometimes her little son came along, a cute, fat fellow of about four. One afternoon Pak Ateng, the oldest policeman, opened the cell door, the woman came out and opened her arms and the little boy ran to her.

She had seen it all from the window in the *gudang* and she had thought of her own children.

"Who will take care of your little boys when we have beheaded you?" the Japanese captain had inquired a couple of days ago.

It was nearly dark when she heard the screaming and she knew at once who it was. She had looked out of the window without seeing anything, her body rigid with the effort not to scream too. The inspector carried the woman out of the cell and laid her on a camp bed in the *gudang* and gave her a bromide. Then she wasn't screaming any more, but lay cramped, sobbing out loud. Later a doctor came with a Japanese lieutenant and they took her to the hospital. She was calm by then. She had sat on a bench and combed the long part of her hair over the shaved skull.

"Whoever is accused of a capital crime gets his head shaven," the woman had said, "but they cannot prove anything on me. I took the radio to pieces and threw the broken parts in the river. Every afternoon I walked past the river with my little boy."

"You are sentenced to death," screamed the Japanese captain at her.

He threw the revolver on the table and pulled out his sword.

"The way you would like to be executed you may choose yourself, revolver or sword." And when she did not answer, she was more surprised than afraid at that moment, he had pulled her hair up in back and laid the blade of his sword on her neck. She felt the ice-cold of its thin edge penetrate her body.

"Then the coldness of death penetrated his body." It was a line from a poem, but she no longer knew of whom. It is not true, she thought, he is acting, that belongs to the nerve treatment. Nothing is going to happen!

She was not afraid and could think clearly. It was the coldness of the metal that penetrated to her spine and was reverberated from there that made her tremble. He brushed the sword upwards along the back of her head and then pulled it away, holding it loosely in his hand.

"She has not been shaven yet," he said to the lieutenant. "I cannot cut off her head like that. Tomorrow. Then I'll call for her and take her to Bogor. It is really too difficult here—in Bogor we have all the necessary arrangements for it."

He won't come, she had thought. This is a case in the

stage of inquiry, no judgment has been pronounced. But he did come, in a light-yellow, open car with red upholstery inside that smelled like new leather. She had to sit next to him. He himself drove. They rode in the direction of Bogor. Acting, she thought, acting. She was not trembling any longer, but sat straight up, her body rigid, with a fixed smile. After ten minutes he turned into a side street, then she knew that they were going back.

He stopped near the guard.

"I'll give you one more chance tomorrow. We will interrogate you and then you must tell the truth."

She stood next to the car and he put out his arm and laid his fingers between two cervical vertebrae. "Watch out, here is where the cut comes," he had said.

The sun was shining, it was a warm day, but his fingers were as cold as his sword.

The doctor took his hand away. "We do not have to shave her hair for this roentgen photo," he said. "Is everything ready, nurse? We will make the puncture first."

They had put her in a sitting position on the table. She had not sat up for days and it made her dizzy and still more unsure. The contours of things shifted, but the voices remained clear and close. She felt his fingers between the vertebrae, but lower, much lower than then.

"Bend further forward," he had commanded and she obeyed.

She heard the needle push the cartilage and it was as if she felt the pain only much later that began to spread from the top of her skull, through thousands of little cells, like water seeping through sinter. She sat still, gripped in an icy rigidity from head to hips. She knew where she was, she knew the doctor and the assistant; if she had been asked she could have said their names without faltering. She knew what was happening to her and why and yet her reactions were only indirectly determined because of that.

"Don't you feel anything yet?" asked the doctor.

"No," she answered vaguely.

"No," repeated the doctor and it was the surprise in his voice that helped her gather the enormous exertion to bring up an answer against those other forces.

"Yes, now I do." This time she spoke calmly and clearly. The clarity only lasted a moment, for when the pain began to stream through her in full strength, she repeated several times: "It is terrible, terrible." Stammering, not about the pain, but about the indignity of this confession.

# Mr. Satterthwaite's Conversion

OLIVER ST. JOHN GOGARTY

SOME FAMOUS MEN, Oliver Cromwell and Dr. Johnson for instance, had an inordinate fear of death. Naturally, we all fear death. Fear of death is a measure of the relish for life. Think of the reverse—what failures suicides are!

Mr. Satterthwaite, though not as famous as the men mentioned above, easily outdid them in their obsession. I will admit that he was helped in this by living in the age of advertisements. Cromwell was unaware of the respectability of funeral "parlors"; and Dr. Johnson was not coaxed into cremation by the cheerful glow of an open furnace. Mr. Satterthwaite suffered from both. One day inadvertently he took a bus. What did he see above the heads of the passengers opposite to him—an advertisement for vaults! That they were in a bank does not matter. The effect on Mr. Satterthwaite does. Beside it was another for Planter's cooking oil; and then, unabashed, one for a funeral parlor. So bad was Mr. Satterthwaite's obsession that he could not bear any hint of his last end. "Vault" suggested interment; and as for planter, he recognized in that (for he was a well-read man) a slang word for burial as in the song, "When we plant Matt Hannigan's aunt, we won't be too put out." To him the word "cooking" was less associated with domesticity than with cremation. And as for the last advertisement, we won't go into that. Suffice to say, he never entered a bus again.

Mr. Satterthwaite had purchased his apartment in a co-operative building. In it he kept books and bric-à-brac. It was his home. He began to fear that the district was not as fashionable as when he took up residence in it some years ago. His daily stroll to the avenue where he could hail a taxi gave him some visual evidence of some slight falling off in the social amenities of the place. The last straw or, to be exact, the second last straw was provided by the office of a mortician who had established himself right in front of the building in which Mr. Satterthwaite dwelt. He could not take his daily walk nor at night could he rest because of a pink neon light which blinked in and out and admonished all and sundry to "Get Dead!" The pink glare pierced his window shades.

What could be done? Of course, he could move to another part of the city; but he had bought his apartment and was loath to leave. To pack all his bric-à-brac and perhaps to lose some in the moving was not to be thought of; it would be nothing less than an upheaval.

Mr. Satterthwaite had a brain wave: he would send his man of business, Mr. Shattock, to interview the mortician and prevail on him to remove the sign and, better still, himself to a less salubrious neighborhood.

Mr. Shattock was a shrewd man but, though he was shrewd, Mr. Satterthwaite always found him reliable and he regarded him as a Mentor, for his advice was sound and left no room for regret if it were followed.

Before calling, Mr. Shattuck went to considerable trouble to find out the mortician's name. That of the firm was written in large letters, "Loam Inc.," but the mortician's name was moot. At last, from a woman who worked in the building on the ground floor of which the funeral parlor was situated, Mr. Shattock learned that there were two partners one of whom was a Mr. Tuck. The name of the other was unknown to her; he was usually away at funerals or, rather, interments.

He called on the mortician by appointment. He met a suave little man with an extremely unctuous voice. His pro-

fessional pose was touched by melancholy for his outlook on
life appeared overcast. This was to be expected because life
is the enemy of the mortician; and, though we are assured
that in the midst of life we are in death, the latter is not as
frequent as those who live by death wish. This is becoming
somewhat confusing. It is likely to end in a paradox, so let
us drop the subject and turn to Mr. Shattock's interview with
Mr. Tuck.

When Mr. Shattock entered the office Mr. Tuck offered
him a chair. He regretted that, owing to a temporary absence
in the course of duty, his partner could not share the pleasure of making Mr. Shattock's acquaintance. He inquired
what he could do for Mr. Shattock and assured him that all
the resources of the firm would be gladly put at his disposal.
Mr. Shattock said, "I have come to see you about a friend."

Mr. Tuck bowed as one who would say "naturally" and
sighed gently. "I am glad that it is not a relative."

Mr. Shattock, sensing cross purposes, hastened to say,
"Not about a dead friend; but one who is alive. In fact, I
have been instructed by him to call on you and to discuss
this business of yours."

At the word "business" the manner of the mortician became sensibly cold. You would think that a spot of *rigor
mortis* had set in so chilly was his reply:

"Before you go any further, I would have you know that
ours is not a business—it is a profession."

Mr. Shattock was not slow to recognize that here was an
Achilles heel. He decided to humor Mr. Tuck. "I beg your
pardon." Mr. Tuck bowed. Mr. Shattock took the bow for an
acceptance of his apology. He continued, "Surely in this profession of yours you must have had many moving experi-
ences?" He was sorry that he had said "moving." Mr. Tuck
might think that he was making his profession a butt for ridi-
cule. It was too late to change it and it would never do to
apologize twice.

Evidently Mr. Tuck, over-sensitive though he was, saw no

concealed sarcasm in the word "moving," for he adopted it: "Moving," he exclaimed, "I should say I have had. I can give you an instance that occurred only the day before yesterday. You remember that accident on the Elevated? Well, we had a basket case. All I had was a few photographs of the poor fellow and 168 pounds of wax. He was well-known to my partner who unfortunately was away in the country, so I had to rebuild him all alone. I worked for 35 hours on end without a let-up. The relations and friends were already filling up the parlor. You know how diffident an artist feels before an exhibition? I was about to admit the relatives when in comes my partner—and this I consider the peak point of my artistic career—I turned to my partner and pointed to my handiwork. 'What do you think of that?' I asked. My partner went over to the casket and stretched out a hand, 'Speak to me, George!' My heart leapt up! Art, as the poet said, is its own exceeding great reward."

At that moment the door opened and a tall, merry-eyed, red-faced man in a black frock coat, black kid gloves and a tall silk hat entered the room. He took no notice of Mr. Shattock. "That's that," he said and went over to the window breathing relief. Mr. Tuck called, "Let me introduce you to Mr. Shattock. Mr. Shattock, this is my partner, Mr. Ashe."

"Pleased to meet you," said Mr. Ashe, "excuse my gloves," as he extended his hand. "I'll be out of uniform in a moment."

He left the room and returned quickly without hat, gloves or frock coat. Instead he wore a light alpaca sports' coat of grayish blue. He had doffed his manner with his "uniform." He was in a merry mood.

"The $250 at Woodlawn and the $600 with canopy. The one at Trinity is still to be checked—well over a thousand bucks a day. I could do with a boiler-maker. Where's the bourbon?"

Apparently the question was not rhetorical, for Mr. Ashe returned to the window and, lifting the window seat, produced a bottle and two glasses which he placed on a table. "Tuck, we'll want a third tumbler."

When Mr. Tuck found a third tumbler, Mr. Ashe proceeded to pour the bourbon into the glasses with an experienced hand. At the third glass he turned to Mr. Shattock and asked solicitously, "Say when." When the glass was about half full Mr. Shattock nodded. Mr. Ashe handed him the glass, "Neat or on the rocks?" Mr. Shattock asked if there were a chaser. Mr. Ashe went to the window and produced a can of beer. He tossed off his liquor while his partner was toying with his.

"We are giving a dinner on Saturday with a client in the chair. Perhaps you could join us. Couldn't Mr. Shattock join us, Tuck?"

"By all means, by all means. Nothing could give us greater pleasure." Then he added seemingly as an afterthought, "I am sure."

There must have been an ice box under the window for when Mr. Ashe politely opened the can for Mr. Shattock the beer in it was cold.

"That's settled then. Here's mud in your eye."

Mr. Shattock winced at the toast. While the mood was cheerful he thought he would broach the subject of his visit:

"I am representing a Mr. Satterthwaite," he said.

"Bring him along; bring him along! The more the merrier, eh, Tuck?" Mr. Tuck inclined his head until it reached the rim of his glass.

"Does your friend play or sing?" Mr. Ashe inquired. Mr. Shattock shook his head.

"A pity, a pity. Perhaps he can recite?"

The thought of Mr. Satterthwaite reciting at a mortician's musicale was overwhelming. Caution fell from Mr. Shattock. He laughed immoderately.

Mr. Ashe took the laughter for an assurance of Mr. Satterthwaite's power as a reciter: "I suppose he can give us 'I learned about women from her'? Talking about women, you should have seen the blonde at the second interment. None of your jokes, Tuck, about an Ashe blonde. She was all in black. She must have been the daughter of the dear departed. She was too young to have been his wife. She was under the canopy nearest the grave. I'll check on her when I get through with my arrears of home work," Mr. Ashe announced.

When Mr. Shattock entered the large cellar under the mortuary parlor the "band" was in full swing. Every musician played on some sort of bottle, jar or jug which he used as a wind instrument by blowing into it. One or two used ash trays for cymbals. The din was terrific. Mr. Ashe stood behind an improvised bar and kept the musicians lubricated. He hailed Mr. Shattock with "Where's your friend?" Mr. Shattock explained that owing to a slight indisposition his friend was unable to attend. The fact was that Mr. Shattock had resolved not to inform Mr. Satterthwaite of the result of his interview until he had something definite to report.

"Indisposition? That's bad. What height is your friend?" Mr. Ashe asked.

Mr. Shattock, who failed to see the connection, said, "About your height."

"That would be six feet and half an inch in my stockinged feet. Weight 210 pounds."

The place continued to fill. Mr. Ashe was kept busy behind the bar. An old gentleman entered. One or two of the musicians began to cheer. Mr. Shattock found Mr. Tuck and asked who the newcomer was.

"That's our chairman tonight. He is well over seventy. He had a lot of money at one time but he spent it all on mink and nylons. Now he is reduced to travelling for a stocking factory. He says that he does not regret it one bit. If he had his money back, he'd spend it the same way again. He insured himself long ago for a $3,000 funeral and he is engaging us. Ashe is presenting him with a gold pencil at the dinner. You must meet Mr. Kinsey."

The band blared again. Mr. Kinsey greeted his host behind the bar. He was handed something in a glass.

Mr. Shattock sat beside Mr. Ashe. Mr. Kinsey had the place of honor at the first table-head. Mr. Shattock looked at the second table but not too closely for he wished to smother the suspicion that it was a trestle. On Mr. Shattock's left were two policemen in plain clothes, one of whom invited Mr. Shattock to a pistol competition which would be held at the barracks in the following week.

"If my book is out next week we'll all go," Mr. Ashe announced. Mr. Shattock was interested. He inquired what was the subject of the book.

"What do you think?" Mr. Ashe asked winking. "I call it *After Death . . . What?* If that isn't an intriguing title, I'll eat my hat."

Mr. Shattock ventured to say that there might be some misunderstanding—the religiously inclined might buy it for curiosity. When the contents, which he took to deal with interments, were disclosed, Mr. Ashe might find himself in trouble.

*"After Death . . . What?* Why a decent funeral, of course! I have no religious scruples. Anyhow, I don't want to take sides. I have my job to do, ain't that enough?"

"I don't know how you find time to write," Mr. Shattock said impressed.

"Write?" said Mr. Ashe. "I only provided the title. My publishers do the rest." Somebody, probably Mr. Tuck, rapped on the table; Mr. Kinsey was about to speak.

The old gentleman at the head of the first table rose. His voice was feeble, but as he spoke it gathered volume. He raised his champagne glass:

"Don't take my toast amiss. I know that I am in the eyes of Loam, Inc. a case of delayed burial. Nevertheless, here's to our next merry meeting. Then, ashes to Ashe."

Prolonged cheers and laughter followed Mr. Kinsey's speech. The musicians who were assembled at the second table cheered loudest.

Mr. Ashe, still laughing, rose and struck his glass for silence. He held a gold pencil in its case.

"Gentlemen, my friends, I have here a present from our firm to one of its firmest supporters. I have known Mr. Kinsey these many years. As you are aware, it is not often that we have the opportunity to talk to one of our customers beforehand; and I am sure that none of you would like to talk to one of them afterwards. Mr. Kinsey, I am glad to say, though I say it myself, is far from being a ghost. Mr. Kinsey, on behalf of Loam, Inc., I present you with this gold pencil with the hope that you will not use it to write your memoirs which are known to us all (more or less) and which are the envy of the old and a caution to the young—Mr. Kinsey!"

With raised glasses all stood and drank to the oldest man in the room.

When Mr. Shattock saw Mr. Satterthwaite he had more than a missionary's task to accomplish. He had not only to cure him of his obsession but to convert him. No easy thing to do, but it would not be said of him that he had failed because of lack of enterprise.

"Not only did I see the two partners of the firm but I dined with them." Mr. Shattock decided that shock tactics were the best approach.

Mr. Satterthwaite regarded his agent with suspicion. Had he betrayed him? Fraternization with the enemy looked very like it.

"I dined with them," Mr. Shattock continued, "and I came to this conclusion: they have found a means of making the common enemy work for them. They make death pay. They have as it were blunted his scythe—or what have you? Behind the black glass of their office window there is revelry and joy. I never had a more amusing time than when I went under the parlor to an extensive cellar, to a dinner that was given in honor of a valued and prospective customer. I am bold enough to suggest that you put some money into the firm, obtain if possible a controlling interest, become a partner and get out once and for all of the state of fear which every suggestion of mortality puts you into. Take your courage in both hands. I have asked the partners if they required capital; what money they have invested is increasing a hundred fold. I am joining them. I advise you to do likewise. Put your money into a mortuary and make death pay. Get behind it, drive it in front of you. And as for your art—your artistic nature will not be blighted. There is wax to be sculpted into the resemblance of flesh. There is death to be made likelike—what more is the aim of art?"

And that is why if you care to cross the city, you can read on a discrete pane of dark glass, "Ashe, Tuck, Satterthwaite and Shattock, Morticians." There is no neon light, only the words "After Death . . . What?" in golden letters on a background of black.

# ISRAEL

# A Passover Courting

## S. J. AGNON

THERE ARE MANY who have heard the tale of Reb Mechel, the beadle, and the wealthy Sarah Leah. At the same time there are as many who have not heard it; and for those who have not heard it, it is worth the telling.

This is the tale of Mechel, the beadle. When Mechel, the beadle, left the House of Study on the first night of Passover his mood was cheerful. Blessed be Thy Name, said he to himself, that the Eve of Passover is over and done with so that I too can rejoice this night like other folk. But when he had locked the doors and found himself proceeding homeward his good mood left him. He knew that he went to no royal feasting hall but to a tumble-down dwelling; that he would be sitting not on a fine handsome couch but on a torn cushion unmended by woman's hand; and that he must trouble himself a great deal to warm his food. For at the time, Mechel, the beadle, was a widower; there was no woman in his home to prepare his table, make his bed or cook his meals. Truth to tell, many householders had wished to invite him to celebrate the Passover feast with them. Reb Mechel, they said, tonight the whole world is rejoicing and all Israel feasts with their households, so why should you celebrate on your own? Be happy, Reb Mechel, that the demons have no power on this night; but even so there is a peril of sadness, which is as much prohibited on the Passover as leaven, the Merciful One deliver us. Yet Mechel refused all offers of hospitality, for he did not wish to burden another's table at the festival.

The streets had emptied, and all the houses of the town shone with Passover light. The moon was bright and gracious, and a spring breeze blew. Mechel began to turn his mind away from himself and enjoy the wonders of the Creation, jingling the keys of the synagogue like a bell. But hearing the sound of the keys he grew sorrowful and began to remind himself bitterly how he was the beadle of the House of Study, toiling hard and doing all sorts of work; and how, when he had completed his work and returned home, he remained cramped and lonely between the walls, never even tasting cooked food; since if he put food on to warm he would be asleep before it was cooked. So he would stay his hunger with an onion roll or some bread and radish, or the potato a woman might bring to the House of Study so that he would pray for the souls of her dear ones to rest in peace. But what you may do all the year round, and rest satisfied, you may not do on a festival when we are bidden to rejoice.

On the way home he noticed that one house had a window open; looking again, he saw that it was a window in the house of Sarah Leah, the widow. She herself was standing at the window looking out. Mechel bowed to her with the greeting, "Festivals for joy, Sarah Leah."

"Holidays and appointed times for gladness, Reb Mechel," responded Sarah Leah. "Whence and whither, Reb Mechel?"

"I am coming from the House of Study," said Mechel, "on my way home to prepare my table and sit and celebrate."

Sarah Leah nodded her head and sighed. I see she would like to say something to me, said Mechel to himself, and stood waiting.

Seeing Mechel standing waiting, she said, "I just opened my window to see if it were time to leave, for I am celebrating at my neighbor's. I've prepared all sorts of good things, by your life, and I'm short of nothing in order to celebrate the Passover down to the last detail, and all the same I have to go leave my own home and burden myself on others. It is not enough that I go burdening them every Sabbath and festival, when I suddenly appear among them for the Hallowing and the Havdala; I have to go bothering them on Passover as well."

"Well, it may be a bother in your eyes," said Mechel, "but others regard it as fulfilling a commandment."

"A commandment, d'you say, Reb Mechel?" responded Sarah Leah. "Do you suppose such commandments come easily to those who perform them? Here's a man who's busy all day long and never sees his wife and children; Passover comes, a time of rest, he wishes to sit quiet with his family when in jumps that widow all of a sudden and sits down among them. May it be His Will that I shouldn't sin with my words, the years grow less and the world grows wearier and weaker. In times gone by a Jew would bring any number of guests home with him and there'd be room enough; and nowadays there's no room even for a lonely widow like me. I remember Passover at Father's, may he rest in peace, when we'd have ten Jews and more there. And was my husband, may he rest in peace, accustomed to celebrate Passover without a guest? And I have to leave my home now. And am I short of anything here? If it's wine a body wants, here's wine and enough to spare for an extra glass; and if it's matzoth, here are the extra special matzoth; if it's meat, here's a turkey cock whose wings were absolutely hidden by fat.

"Why, what did the neighbors say, 'Sarah Leah, don't tie him to the foot of your bed or he'll drag you across Sambayton River.' That's no bird, that's an aurochs. But as long as a woman's in her husband's home, it's all worth while; and once he's dead even the whole of the world isn't worth while. At first I thought of inviting a guest only folks would say, 'That old woman's a fiend from Hell, wants a man for to serve her well'."

Mechel smiled, sighed and quoted the Talmud, " 'Tis better to dwell in trouble than to dwell in widowhood."

And although the saying was in Aramaic, a tongue Sarah

Leah did not understand, she nodded her head like a person saying, "You said it well and true." Mechel's an upright man and assuredly has some good thought in mind. And she added, "There's everything here, but if there's no master in the house what is there in the house? I often ask myself, Sarah Leah, what are you doing here and whom have you here? I have reared children to their full size and they forsook me, so now I am bereft and forsaken, as a table after a feast. I thought of ascending to the Land of Israel to be near the holy places, and not be thinking all the time of my loneliness; but then how can a woman go alone to a place where she is not known? All Israel are brethren, but nevertheless my heart troubles me at the thought of ascending alone."

Mechel felt full of pity for her. He took hold of his right earlock and wished to say words of comfort to her. Yet he could get nothing out, began stammering and at last said, "Woman, is my luck any greater than yours? You, God be praised, are adorned as a bride and eat fine food, while I am chidden and mourning as a widower. But no man in Israel has other to depend on than the loving kindness of the Holy and Blest One. What has any living person to grumble at? The festival should not be degraded."

And from seeking to comfort her he began to feel sorry for himself and he said, "And what is a man? Something bare in the waste. Blessed be He that did not make me a woman. Blessed be His Name that I know how to hallow the wine and prepare for the Passover according to the law. But now go to a tumbledown dwelling and warm up half-cooked food and sit on a broken bed, and then sit on a torn cushion and think you're like a king. It was with good reason that the *Yalkut says,* 'All sufferings are hard to bear, but those of poverty are hardest of all; all sufferings come, and once they are gone leave things as they were; but poverty dims the eyes of a man.' I'm only saying this to balance your saying, 'I'm a woman.' And what's more, the Holy and Blest One has brought a bad cough upon me, may you never know its like, which takes away my breath and steals the life from me and will drive me out of the world." Before he finished speaking he had begun coughing.

"Reb Mechel," said Sarah Leah to him, "don't stand out in the cold; winter may have gone but it's still chilly. Better come into the house and not stand about in the open."

Mechel bowed his head between his shoulders, entered and found himself in a fine dwelling with handsomely decked cushions to recline upon, and a table covered with silverware in the middle of the room, and a bottle of wine on the table, candles burning in all the candlesticks and every corner of the room gleaming and shining with festival. His first words were in honor of the place, for he said, "How fine this room is, where the hands of a woman have been employed." Sarah Leah at once rushed to show him all she had ready for the table. Matzoth and bitter herbs lay there, parsley and haroseth, eggs and a sheepshank and flesh and fish and a fat pudding and borsht, red as wine.

"And who," said Sarah Leah to Mechel, "needs all this array? I'm just about to go off and bother somebody else, but it's hard for me to forget that I'm a housewife, so I prepared a Passover for myself as though my husband were still here and he and I were celebrating like all other folk."

Mechel's heart warmed within him, and he wished to say something, but a furious fit of coughing overcame him. Sarah Leah stared at him with her two eyes and said, "Don't eat too much bitter herbs and don't eat sharp foods, Reb Mechel; you cough too badly. You know what you need? It's a glass of hot tea you need. But who have you at home to make something hot? Wait a few minutes and I'll put the kettle on for you."

But scarce had she finished her sentence when she struck herself on the mouth, crying, "What a silly head I have, to forget that we have to hallow the festival first. Maybe you'll celebrate here?" And since the thought had found expression in the words she repeated, "Maybe you'll celebrate here?"

Mechel saw all the goodness of the housewife and could not move, as though his limb were fastened to the spot where he stood. He began stammering and swallowed his indistinct answer. And Sarah Leah began preparing the feast as had been her wont when her husband was still with her.

So Mechel took the keys of the House of Study and put them away somewhere, staring meanwhile at the white cushions that Sarah Leah had prepared for reclining on during the celebration as though the High Light shone from them. Within a few moments he had let himself down among them, by reason of the thought that the woman would again ask him to celebrate with her. When she saw him at his ease she filled a glass of wine. With one eye on the wine and one on the household ware, he thought to himself, "What a fine spot this is, where a woman's hands do the tending." While thinking, he found the glass of wine at his hand, and his lips of themselves began repeating the hallowing of the wine.

Sarah Leah sighed with satisfaction; her face grew bright; her clothes were suddenly filled with her body, as happens with a rejoicing person; and she thought to herself, "How fine is a Jew's voice when he utters holy words." And within a moment she had brought him a ewer of water. He washed his hands, took a leaf of greenstuff, dipped it in salt water, broke the matzoth in half, put one half in a cloth and hid it away for dessert, lifted up the dish and began reciting, "This is the bread of affliction, that which our fathers ate in the Land of Egypt."

And Sarah Leah wondered at herself, saying, "Just a little while ago I was preparing to leave my house, and now here am I sitting at home?" And she watched Mechel's hand, observing how accustomed his hands were in holy things, until her face grew red and she lowered her eyes in shame. Then she filled the glasses afresh and uncovered the matzoth. Mechel made her a sign. Sarah Leah blushed, dropped her eyes to the prayer book and recited the Four Questions to their close, "This night we all do recline."

Thereupon Mechel set the dishes back in place and repeated in a loud and joyful voice, "We were the slaves of
Pharaoh in Egypt"; and he continued reciting the Relation
of the Departure from Egypt as far as the feast, interpreting
to her in Yiddish all that required interpretation and season-
ing the entire Relations with parables and tales of wonder.
His sufferings and troubles far from him, his head resting
on the cushion, sweat caressing his earlocks and the cushion
growing deeper beneath him, he continued. His blood beat
through his limbs and his heart might have leapt forth; a
single hour here was preferable to his whole life in This
World.

The Order of Passover came to its appointed end. The
whole town was silent; the moon spread a canopy of light over
the house of Sarah Leah. Mechel tunefully sang, "May His
House soon be built," and Sarah Leah responded, "Speedily,
speedily, in our own day soon." From the other houses of the
street came the chorus, "God rebuild, God rebuild Thy
House soon." And the fantasy that is root and branch of Man
led them to imagine that here was a strip of the Land of
Israel, and they were calmly and happily singing the Song of
Songs.

The night passed. The morning birds rose to repeat their
portions of song. In the home of Sarah Leah could be heard
the voice of a man chanting the Song of Songs.

*"Here ends the tale of Mechel,*
*On whom God did bestow*
*The wealthy lady Mistress*
*Sarah Leah, the widow."*

# Speed the Plough

ASHER BARASH

YAIR, himself of farming stock and a member of the youthful Moshav in the Emek, went out at dawn to plough his portion of field. He had stood on guard with his rifle in the trench under the starry skies until the third watch. When he had handed over the rifle to his relief, he dashed off for his horse and plough.

He proposed to plough for a couple of hours, since his portion was small. By the time morning was well advanced he would have finished the work and could return to his shack and his wife Hemda, as though he were just coming back to rest from his night on duty.

Bowed between the two handles of the plough, pressing down with the full weight of his body, Yair plodded along the furrow, and as he went a straight course he could not turn his eyes away from the rising sun. It rose high in the distance over the mountains. As it mounted it dispersed the rose-colored mists as though by a wave of the hand; and clear and hot it came forth to give light to the world. Swarms of birds all wet with dew descended to the overturned heaps of earth, whirled and danced along the waves of air and welcomed the ascendant day with joyful song. Myriads of tiny eyes of light gleamed and glistened from the unopened wild flowers. The wild grasses began to thaw after the frozen night, and gave off a faint incense.

121

Yair felt that the darkness which had been gathering in his heart during the days of bloodshed was also being swept away, that the sun of a vast happiness was rising within him. The wife he had wedded eight months earlier was now sleeping on their bed, and within her the tracery of his living seed was taking final shape. Strong arms she had, an upright heart and much experience of toil and poverty. He had taken her from Upper Galilee, from a poor peasant home, and had brought her to the village he was helping to build. Yesterday the eldest of her sisters had come to stay with her until after the birth, so that she no longer needed to do anything but light work about the house and the yard. When Hemda went to the hospital her sister would take charge of everything. This sister was a widow whose husband had been killed in the field during the first month after their marriage. She was a widow and childless, but very brave of heart. Whether the child would be a son or daughter, a name had already been decided upon by the three of them; a name that would be fresh and musical as the song of yonder birds to the rising sun. It was only another month.

As Yair ploughed straight towards the rising sun, with only a third of his portion left, an echoing shot burst from ambush, and a bullet pierced his back, coming out through his chest and hitting against the iron plough. He fell forward upon the plough between its two handles. And the horse stopped, pricked up its little ears and stood frozen and immobile like a statue.

The sound of the shot brought the men of the village running to the spot. Among them were the four guards of the night watch. One of these was the man who had taken the rifle over from Yair at the end of the third watch.

They lifted him up and laid him flat on the earth. Then they kneeled down and listened to his heart. One of them pulled out a fine thread of wool from his coat, and set it under the nostrils of the murdered man. The thread did not stir. Then the men rose and stood to attention on either side of their dead comrade. Their faces were stony, tears froze in their eyes and their lips were tight.

They turned the plough over, cut green branches from the neighboring oak, set the branches along the plough and placed the dead body on the living green. The horse jerked forward and made for the village, his head bowed, dragging the burden of his master.

The funeral was held at sunset as the evening breezes blew. Many came from the surrounding villages to do the last kindness for Yair, who had fallen at his plough. Never had so silent a procession been seen. The whole of the Emek seemed to be holding its breath. The fields wore a scarlet prayer-shawl. That day the first grave had been dug in what was to become the gathering-place for all who live. A few furious words were said, a few words of pain were whispered. Hemda gave one brief scream but no more, for her sister's hand stopped her mouth from utterance.

Silent and bent they returned to their places. But the four guards marched at the roadside with firm stride and heads erect, as they had been taught.

The setting sun kissed the moist and solitary grave and a wing of the evening breeze caressed it lovingly. A small stir lit up, in memory of the soul.

That night the two sisters lay on the bed in the room of mourning. They fell asleep only after midnight; and when the first ray of light edged through the window Hemda roused herself suddenly and awakened her sister.

"Did you hear anything? It seemed to me that the horse went out of the courtyard pulling the plough. . . ."

"Hemda my love, what ails you? Calm yourself. You must have been dreaming."

And the weary woman turned over and fell asleep again. But in a little while Hemda shook her by the shoulder a second time. "What, did you not hear it this time either? The horse has come back. . . ."

The light of dawn shone grey through the window-space against the wall of the shack. The sister got out of bed.

"It's dawn already. Time to milk the cow and feed the chickens."

Hemda remained lying on her back, her gaze turned to the ceiling where the shadows were forming themselves into the visions of her dreaming eyes.

When the sister passed through the yard she saw the plough in its proper place. But her heart, despite all her bravery, hammered strongly within her; and she could not refrain from going to look at the horse. So before proceeding to the byre she went into the stable. In the light of the rising sun which reddened the entrance she saw, aghast, that a white foam covered the horse, which quivered and panted as it stood. She passed her hand over its flank. Her hand came away wet with the warm lather.

In the morning the field of Yair was found entirely ploughed.

And to this day no man knows whose hand it was that sped the plough.

# ITALY

# The Sicilian Soldier

ELSA MORANTE

Translated from the Italian by John Fisher

DURING THE DAYS when the Allied Armies, because of winter weather, were encamped beyond the Garigliano, I had found shelter on a mountain top on our side of the river. One day, in order to save some people I loved, I had to make the trip to Rome. It would be a bitter journey, for Rome, the city where I was born and had always lived, was at that time an enemy city.

The train was to leave early in the morning. I came down from the mountain during the afternoon of the preceding day in order to be on level ground before nightfall. I was supposed to spend the night on the plain and to make my way to the railroad station at dawn.

I found refuge for the night with the family of a cart driver whose name was Giuseppe. Giuseppe's residence consisted of three huts; one served as a shelter for the cart and donkey; Giuseppe, his wife Marietta, and his three daughters slept in the second; in the third meals were prepared over an open wood fire.

It was decided that I would sleep in the bed of the two older little girls—they would sleep with their mother and baby sister in the double bed. Giuseppe was quite willing to sleep on a pile of straw in the kitchen.

Those were nights of danger and fear. More than a thousand German soldiers, waiting to move to the front lines, had set up camp in the surrounding area. Noisy military vehicles traveled endlessly over the nearby roads. One could see the lights go on in the tents in the lowlands. The shouts and cries of foreign voices were audible.

When the door of the hut had been closed, Marietta, the girls and I got ready to go to bed.

"Why don't you undress?" Marietta asked me while untying the corners of her kerchief. "We're all women here, and I've changed the sheets for you." But I was not used to sleeping among strangers, so I lay down on the blankets without undressing.

The older little girls, happy to sleep in the double bed, continued to laugh and play with their baby sister even after the light had been turned out. Their mother warned them to be quiet. A short time later, I could tell they were asleep by their regular breathing.

I prepared myself for a sleepless night. I imagined the crowd of fellow passengers on the train, the stops in the midst of barren countrysides—and the slaughter. I thought what I'd answer if a voice suddenly ordered me to show my identification papers and baggage. Considering the fact that the railroads were being bombed every day, I wondered whether I'd ever be able to reach Rome.

At that moment, I heard a heavy beating of the branches on the roof. It had begun to rain, but since bad weather made it difficult to bombard, I felt that my journey would be quieter.

In the middle of the night, the baby began to cry. I could hear a whisper and movement in the double bed. It was Marietta nursing her baby and speaking to her in a very low voice. Then everything was quiet again. The rumble of military vehicles, as well as the shouts and cries of the patrols, had ceased a while ago.

I thought how much I would have liked to cross the Garigliano River and find myself in Sicily. It was nostalgically

beautiful at this season. I had never been to my father's
homeland, where now I could live free.

At that moment, the double rafter door was pushed in,
and a ray of white light filtered through the opening. I sat
up on the bed, for I feared a visit from the Germans. A tall,
ragged soldier of our own army appeared. His uniform was
still recognizable, although it was faded by bad weather and
covered with mud.

"Don't come in! There are only women in here," I cried
out. He said he wanted only to rest a while, and entered the
hut. He was a middle aged man with thick eyebrows and a
black, curly beard. His hair, protruding from beneath his
cap, was curly and wild and partly gray. His strong legs were
noticeable through the tears in his uniform. He was carrying
a miner's lamp.

I told him he would awaken everyone with his blinding
light. His only reply was that my hosts were too sound asleep
to be aware of his presence. He placed the lamp on the floor,
sat down on a case near the door. He seemed feverish.

"If you want to rest, ask Giuseppe to let you sleep in the
other hut," I replied.

He said he didn't want to rest. "And why don't you go to
sleep?" he asked.

I told him I was afraid the bed was not clean.

"Well, what does that matter!" he said. "Look at my coat,
it's full of lice."

He then told me he had fought in the army but that now
he was a member of the Italian maquis, fighting the Germans.
Later he intended to join the English and continue to fight.
By fighting, he explained, he hoped to reach a certain goal
of his.

I had immediately recognized the Sicilian accent in his
strong, somewhat monotonous voice.

"Are you a Sicilian?" I asked.

"Yes," he answered, "I'm from Santa Margherita."

"Just as you were coming in," I mentioned, "I was thinking that I'd like to go to Sicily."

"So far as I'm concerned," he said, "I shall never return to Sicily alive."

I asked him why, and he told me the following story in Sicilian:

"My name is Gabriele. I was a miner in Santa Margherita and had a wife and daughter. Two years after our marriage, my wife went astray, ran away from home to lead a life of shame, leaving me along with our baby daughter who was as yet unable to walk. The baby was called Assunta. When I went to work in the mine, I'd leave her in bed. She was a well-behaved child and didn't cry. I had tied a brass ring from an old lantern with a string to the iron bars of a bed. It would swing back and forth and make her laugh. It was the only toy she had.

"We lived in an isolated house in the middle of an arid plain, not far from the mines. A peddler friend, who passed by regularly, would come in for a while, dress the baby, and seat her on the floor. When I'd return in the evening, I'd prepare some *minestra,* which Assunta would eat seated on my knee. At times I'd fall asleep before finishing my meal. Perhaps I'd wake up after an hour and find Assunta asleep in my arms or staring at me in bewilderment. One day, when she was home alone, she fell from the bed and broke a joint in her wrist. My friend, who came in later in the morning, found her where she had fallen, almost suffocated by pain. From that day on, she was never able to do any heavy work because of her misshapen hand. In spite of this, she grew up to become a truly beautiful Sicilian girl. She was rather slender and had a fair complexion, jet-black eyes, and long, black, curly hair which she used to tie together with a red ribbon at the nape of her neck.

"Shortly afterward, my peddler friend moved to another town, and we were left friendless in this desolate valley. A little later, the mine was shut down and I could find no other

work. I would spend my days out in the sun doing nothing.
Idleness made me ill-tempered. Since there was no one else
around, I would give vent to my rage. Although no one was
more innocent than she, I struck her, insulted her, screamed
at her: 'What are you doing here? Why don't you follow in
your mother's footsteps?' Assunta gradually began to hate me.
She did not speak because she was used to being alone and
never was very talkative. She continued to look at me with
her flaming dark eyes, as though she were the devil's daughter herself.

"I was still unable to find work. The Marshal of Santa
Margherita suggested that Assunta come to work for him as
a maid and we accepted. She was now fifteen years old and
her work was not very heavy because the Marshal lived alone
with a teen-age son. Assunta had a tiny room near the kitchen.
She received board and a salary which was given to me. Most
of Assunta's work was in the kitchen beneath the stairs.

"It wasn't long before the Marshal's son, a dark, wild
youth, hardly older than Assunta, began to annoy her. She
would repulse him, but he, in order to frighten her, would
jump down from the window beneath the staircase like an
evil spirit. Looking at her with burning eyes, he would seize
her hair, embrace her, and try to seduce her with kisses. He
too was little more than a child and had never been with a
woman. Her repulses infuriated him and he tried to overcome her by violence. She would get away from him by fighting with all her strength, screaming and crying. She dared
say nothing to the Marshal, let alone to me. She could not
leave her job because it was very difficult for her to find work
with her crippled hand. Besides, how could she return home
to a father she hated and who was unable to feed her? No
matter what happened, she did not want to end up like her
mother.

"This continued for about a month. One night, when the
Marshal had returned home later than usual, he found the
household completely silent, his well-prepared supper on the

table. His son was already sound asleep. After he had eaten, the Marshal got ready to sleep beside his son. As he looked out before closing the window (it was a clear night), he caught sight of Assunta in the courtyard seated on the edge of the well. She was nervously braiding her hair and talking to herself. He was about to call her when he realized that perhaps she was outdoors in order to enjoy the night air, for the weather was sultry, and her little room beneath the stairs must have been stifling. Without saying anything to her, he leaned out to close the shutters. At that moment, he thought he saw her winding her braid across her forehead and fastening it above her ears with hairpins, like a headband covering her eyes. Though he scarcely noticed what she was doing at the time, he was to remember it all later. Assunta had blindfolded her eyes that way so as not to have to look and to be more courageous. When she did not appear the following morning, they searched the house and the whole town and countryside—they found her at the bottom of the well.

"Because she had died by her own hand, she was not blessed by the church or buried within the cemetery. Instead she was buried outside, near the entrance. The Marshal, out of pity, had a tombstone engraved for her. As you know, those who suicide cannot rest, like the other dead, in their graves or anywhere else, but continue to circle around the cemetery and the house, from which they tore themselves so violently, without ever finding peace.

"That's why I no longer wish to sleep. How can I ever rest in peace knowing that my daughter cannot sleep? After they buried her, I could no longer remain in our house in Santa Margherita, knowing that she was walking around in torment and trying to make herself understood. And I could not understand my own flesh and blood. That's why I enlisted in the army and came to the mainland. I shall continue to fight until I have reached my goal."

I asked the Sicilian what goal he was talking about.

"I want to be killed some day or other. I don't have the

courage to die the way Assunta did. But if I am killed, I'll become one like her, and I'll be able to return to Sicily, to Santa Margherita. I'll search for my daughter wandering around the house and I'll make her understand. I'll be with her always and perhaps she will be able to sleep in my arms, just as she did when she was a baby."

When dawn came and the light was turned out, Gabriele finished his story and bade me goodbye. I got up with a start, since I too was supposed to leave. I could still hear the rain —it had not stopped all night long.

A short time later, traveling along the muddy road, I began to wonder whether the Sicilian soldier had been real or a figment of the imagination caused by insomnia.

I still wonder. There are many things that lead me to believe he was not of our world. Still, I cannot help thinking of that soldier and of what became of him. I wonder if he returned to Sicily and whether Asunta finally found a little rest in her father's arms.

# Armida and Reality

ENNIO FLAIANO

Translated from the Italian by John Fisher

ARMIDA has been a grandmother for several years. In the belief that she would be pleased, her two small grandchildren are sent to spend a whole afternoon with her once a week. Armida is still young; that is, she is not more than fifty. She carries her years well, smokes strong tobacco, drinks dry liquor, looks at men and is always happy. She is also a widow and quite blandly believes she will find another husband. This thought, however, does not cause her any real concern. She spends her days in bed or playing solitaire, which she wins on an average of one out of four games.

Armida's great shortcoming—which everyone always finds fault with—is this: she has no imagination. She lives with no notion of what she wants to do the next hour, the next day, or the next month. Her life is a succession of unrelated moments, each lived as if it were the first and the last. With great elegance, she goes to a cigar store and buys only *one* cigarette—she is not sure she will still care to smoke later on. Even when she was a little young girl, she had no imagination. When told to write a descriptive essay on the subject, "A Pleasant Outing in the Country," she would write: "We left at eight o'clock, arrived at nine and came home about seven. Everything went well, thank God." It was impossible to get her to describe anything, not even the scenery, the sky, the flowers, her friends, the hospitable peasants who welcome picnickers by slicing bread and salami for them. "Armida, your composition is poor in ideas." Armida

132

would smile sorrowfully. She did not have any ideas and she did not feel the need of any.

For this reason she never reads books. The one time she had to read a book—*The Betrothed*, I believe—she read only the last few pages; it did not seem right to her to read a book to find out something that was already past and done with. At the theater Armida always avoids looking at the stage— other people's affairs do not interest her. At the movies she either falls asleep or confuses the main feature with the news-reel. "I do not understand," she once said, "why, after they are married, they go to New York with our Foreign Minister, then take the grand tour of Italy."

During an entire season of concerts, she counted at every performance the number of rows and the number of seats in each row, then mentally multiplied the two numbers until she got the total number of seats. She multiplied the price of each ticket and got the gross receipts; she then subtracted the federal tax plus a certain amount for overhead, finally obtaining the net profit. The music of Beethoven, Brahms, Stravinsky—or even our modern composers, Petrassi, Tuchi, Dallapiccola—assisted her mental calculations. She clearly preferred Bach. "He is wonderful for multiplication," she once said. Thus we came to understand the mystery of her ecstatic concentration.

And yet Armida is not bored, since she is always busy wondering about everything. She once had a strange experi-ence. An acquaintance she met at a party invited her to his bachelor apartment to see some prints. The visit ended with the usual results. A year later she was still reproaching him for not having shown her the prints. When she finally con-vinced herself that the prints did not even exist, her comment was: "I would never have been able to think up such a scheme." And she admired the man all the more.

Well, now that Armida is a grandmother, her two grand-sons are sent to visit her once a week—in the belief that she will be amused. That is why she has to get out of bed, treat the children to nice things to eat, and take an interest in what they have to say. Of course she loves them, but she does not know what to say to them. She has no ideas.

One day, because she did not want the conversation to lag (because she was well-mannered), she asked her younger grandson, "Do you think there will be a war?" After a pause the boy broke into tears, because he too did not have any ideas and the question upset him. "Silly child," she said, trying to console him, "I don't really want to know. If you know, all right; if not, it does not matter."

At any rate, such a complete lack of imagination must have its compensations—patience, continual gaiety that nothing can dim (for sorrow is imagination), the wish to be helpful to others, a sense of one's proper duty. And now she has discovered that one of her duties, as a grandmother, is to tell fairy tales to her grandchildren. Since the beginning of time, grandmothers have had this duty—a duty that has become, thanks to the fantasy of grandmothers, the pleasant privilege of old age—to introduce the young to the world of dreams, the spelling-book of our symbology. But Armida has no ideas. Which fairy stories should she tell?

She remembers one they always used to tell when she was a little girl—but to her, since she had no imagination, it was always incredible and boring. She makes an attempt to tell it anyway. It is the story of a little girl who has to take something to eat to her grandmother who lives in a forest. "Why does grandmother live in a forest?" the older grandson asks immediately. This is the first stumbling block. Armida really does not know, nor does she know which forest all this takes place in. She promises to find out and then goes on to describe the meeting of the little girl and the wolf as well as their conversation. "Do wolves talk?" her other grandson asks. "Of course they don't," Armida replies, astonished at the nonsense she is telling them. She does not go on.

One day she finally gets an idea. It is the first one she has ever had and the effect is slightly intoxicating. She opens a newspaper and begins to read a news item. "I shall now tell you the story of a man who kills his family while they are asleep. Once upon a time there was a man called Pamponi Ruggero who was forty-eight years old and was born in. . . ." The children are delighted. In this story everything is precise, nothing is hazy. When she describes the murder they clap hands. It seems to them that they are present at the scene. After a while they want to know whether Pamponi Ruggero has been put in jail. Armida rereads the article rapidly and announces: "They are looking for him, and if they catch him, he will certainly go to jail, because it is not right to treat one's family, which makes so many sacrifices for us, like that."

"More, more!" the children cry. Armida, who has made her début with this first triumph, announces: "We continue with the mystery of the woman who has been cut to pieces." The children become very attentive. They want to hear the story repeated; they want their grandmother to show them a trunk so that they can see what it is like. Armida takes them to a clothes closet and shows them a trunk. The children become quiet, they touch the trunk without being able to hide their uneasiness. When Armida starts to open the trunk, the younger boy runs away and then laughs awkwardly to give the impression that he was only pretending. They return to the room and continue the fairy tales. The crimes committed in the country all take place at night; those that are committed in the cities take place preferably during the day. Someone kills his fiancée because she no longer wants to marry him, another kills his wife after being married only one day, a third kills his wife after thirty years of matrimony and also kills a passer-by. Many kill one another because of disputes over money. "How much money?" her grandsons ask. "It depends," Armida answers. In order to give them an idea of the money that would justify a crime, she opens her purse and spills its contents on the table. She then counts the

money and tells them how much it is. The children look at
the money and touch it.

When the governess comes to take them home, they are
stubborn, want to stay. The following week they insist that
the governess buy a newspaper, fearing that Armida may
have forgotten to do so. They hand it to her all folded, with
the air of accomplices. Even before they sit down at the table
they say, "Come on, tell us some fairy tales." "Ah," says
Armida as she opens the newspaper, "today is a good day.
There are lots of stories to tell."

Armida has become so good at this game that she now
reads every news item, even those of a few lines, and she is
becoming vain and really believes she invents the stories and
is proud of it. If she knew how to write (and why not try,
since she has so much free time?), how many fine stories she
could write, stories that are in the newspapers and are
thrown away. She thinks to herself (because now she even
thinks) that one should never tell lies to children. "Reality,"
she says, "reality is sufficient."

# A Siberian Shepherd's Report
# of the Atom Bomb

DINO BUZZATI

Translated from the Italian by John Fisher

A MONG US SHEPHERDS of the tribe there is a very old legend that says when Noah gathered all the animals of creation in his ark, the animals from the mountains and from the valleys made a truce among themselves and with man, recognizing Noah as their master for the time they were to remain in the ark—all, that is, except Moma, the huge tigress that snarled when Noah approached her and the only animal Noah feared. That was why the tigress found no room in the ark and why the flood caught her in her cave. But she was extremely strong. She remained afloat by sheer strength, swimming for forty days and forty nights and more until the waters subsided, the trees rose out of the sea and the earth reappeared. The tigress Moma was then so tired she fell asleep. She is still asleep in the depths of the great forests of Amga, Ghoi, Tepotorgo and Urakancha.

The legend also says that when the great tigress wakes up, all the other animals will flee from the forest, for man there will be a good hunting season, and Moma will reign in the great forests until the god Beyal descends from the sky to devour her.

Who among us believes this legend? Since our solitude is so great, so many stories are told around camp fires and all of us are accustomed to believing and not believing. Rare and most uncertain is the news that comes to us from distant lands, for our wandering life is entrusted to the will of heaven. What, for example, do we shepherds of the steppe know of the measureless realm that stretches toward the setting sun? Old laws forbid us to go beyond the boundary line, and even if we were to cross it, we should have to travel endless distances through great dangers before reaching the nearest inhabited regions. It is beyond the boundary line that lie the forests of Amga, Ghoi, Tepotorgo and Urakancha, where the tigress Moma fell asleep at the end of the flood.

Sometimes troops of armed horsemen gallop by along the boundary line. Once in a while they stop, look toward us, make measurements, and drive red poles with strange signs into the ground. After a few days the wind of the steppe uproots the poles and carries them God knows where. Sometimes even airplanes, those strange flying machines, fly over us. Nothing else happens.

But what is the use telling all this if not to explain our uneasiness? Recently strange and dreadful things have happened. No serious harm has come to us, but we feel fearful forebodings.

We noticed the first unusual happening last Spring. The soldiers galloped by more frequently and they drove heavier poles, which the wind would not be able to uproot, into the ground. The poles are still there.

In the middle of June, two large snakes were killed near our camp. Creatures like these had never been seen before. The following day hundreds were seen. They did not bother us or our flocks—they were all moving toward the East. They were of different kinds and of every size. This strange happening astonished us.

Then we noticed that the snakes were not alone. Rats, moles, skunks, worms, and numberless kinds of insects began to cross the plain, all moving in the same direction. They were strangely mixed together, but they showed no hostility toward each other, even though they belonged to species that are ordinarily enemies.

We saw even rabbits, wild goats and quite a number of small, four-footed creatures of whose very existence we had not known. Some of them were really very beautiful, with fur that is highly prized. Then came the birds. They, too, were fleeing toward the East, abandoning their old homeland. But what were they running away from? What danger hung over them? Instinct does not easily deceive animals. Even we men were uneasy. Yet what good reason did we have to abandon the region which this year was so good for pasture? No matter how much we wondered, we could not imagine a plausible explanation for this great emigration. An earthquake? How could birds fear an earthquake? A plague? What disease could strike so many different species at the same time, the beetle as well as the marmot, the serpent as well as the wildcat? A fire? No smoke could be seen on the horizon nor did the wind smell of smoke. Someone among us jokingly mentioned the old legend of Moma the tigress. I did not like that joke at all.

Finally, it seemed that the whole forest on the other side of the boundary was empty. The last to come through were the wood pigeons and swarming columns of ants that continued for miles and miles. Some stragglers followed, a few at a time. Then the flow stopped completely. The echo of our guns ceased (these had been days of triumph for the hunters), and a sepulchral silence settled over the Siberian steppe. At night, we would foolishly strain our ears. Could it be that we expected the roar of Moma the tigress?

One day this great uneasiness even took hold of our flocks. It was clear that the goats, sheep and rams were becoming excited, that they, too, were trying to escape to the East. We had to chase some of our fleeing livestock for a long time on horseback. It was necessary to build heavy enclosures.

Many of us were afraid. For no good reason, many wanted to move camp to the East. There were bitter arguments. We finally agreed to take the advice of the elders. They met and decided—we would depart with the next dawn.

It was a hot July evening. The sun had just set and the refreshing breath of night was descending when the dogs suddenly began to bark. Just after sunset, from the direction of the forest and at a great distance, an extraordinary light was seen. It semed as if the sun had turned back, as if its burning face had become swollen on the rim of the horizon. The mass wavered a few moments, then burst, shooting forth a whirl of frightful flames—red, white, violet, green, yellow. The sun had blown up!

How long did it last? Instinctively I thought it was the end of the world. But it was not. When it was dark again, I raised my dazzled eyes to the zenith. No, the stars were still there.

Then the thunder came. And with the thunder—so frightful a noise was never heard—came the wind, a hot, suffocating wind that took our breath away and razed everything to the ground. I thought I would not be able to stand it, but the wind, too, passed on.

When we recovered our senses, we again kindled the fires the burning wind had blown out, and set forth in search of our livestock, which were fleeing crazily in every direction because the enclosure had been broken to pieces. At that moment, the necessity of the chase prevailed over every other fear. But suddenly we stopped and stood motionless—even the goats, the sheep, the old people. We were all paralyzed together.

Above the bellowing and bleating, above our excited shouts, another voice was heard. No, it was not so powerful as the thunder of a little while before. Yet in a way it was even worse. Once, twice, three times, mournful and cold, it filled the night and froze our hearts. It was the roar of the tigress.

The fires, the fires! Leaving the flock to its fate, we rushed to gather twigs and weeds to increase the number of our fires. Soon there was an almost unbroken chain of flames to protect us. At last the great tigress Moma had awakened and was coming toward us.

At that very moment a long, deep roar rose on the other side of the fires. In the darkness we could see something move. Suddenly it appeared, illuminated by the red shadows. It was she, Moma. She was not an ordinary tiger. She was a monster of gigantic proportions.

Not one of us fired. We saw that the huge beast hardly moved any longer—she was about to die. Her eyes had turned to shapeless lumps of black pulp. Her hide was scorched. On her right side was an open gash as deep as a cave, from which blood flowed.

Moma the tigress, right in front of our eyes, hunched her back to the height of two horses one standing on top of the other and let out a hellish shriek. I felt that I was done for. I fired my rifle without even aiming. The others did the same.

Her huge body fell with a crash. Was she dead? We continued to fire shot after shot, senselessly. The tigress no longer moved.

These are the strange facts referred to at the beginning of this report. The legendary tigress really existed—and even though we immediately burned her carcass because of its horrible stench, the immense skeleton has remained right there on the spot and anyone can come and measure it. But who awakened her? Who took away her life and her promised reign? What was the terrifying explosion that night? The sun had notihng to do with it—in a few hours it was born again at just the right time and in its usual place. What had happened? Could some infernal power have taken over the forests? And if its flames devoured mighty Moma, could it not capriciously reduce us to ashes too? How then can we live calmly? No one sleeps at night and in the morning we wake up tired.

# JAPAN

# A Red Moon in Her Face

Hiroshi Noma

Translated from the Japanese by Kinya Tsuruta

KURAKO HORIKAWA, a widow, had a kind of painful expression on her face. Her face did not have that unapproachable elegant beauty, a beauty possessed by some Japanese women who conceal mellow sensuousness within their somewhat cold features. Nor had it that appeal which is often created when either the eyes or nose or mouth upsets the balance of the whole face. The face, one might say, had the usual, accepted classical features. However, her face gave an impression of a slight distortion, for something had robbed it of the full and natural growth of life. This distortion gave the face a beauty filled with an almost abnormal amount of energy. And this something painful in her face radiated from her fair and broad forehead and around her rather thin lips which responded sensitively to the changes of the outside.

Toshio Kitayama had to admit that the expression of that face gradually stole into the depths of his heart the more he saw her. He had come back from the South Seas about a year ago. He was now working for a firm run by an acquaintance on the fifth floor of a building near the Tokyo Station. He often saw Kurako in the elevator or around the rest rooms. Each time he found that mysterious, painful expression in her face. He then became aware that some pain in his heart reacted to her face and that the reaction left at the same time a sweetness and an ache in his soul.

He could not judge her age. Perhaps it is better to say

that there was never any question of her age in his mind, for her beauty hid her age from him from the beginning. This may have been partly due to the fact that he had not seen Japanese women for a long time, but particularly because he had lived determined to stay away from women as a result of his unpleasant experience with one in the past. He did not have the slightest idea that she had once been married. He judged her to have been far younger, so he could not see how, since this was rare among Japanese women, such a young person's face could maintain an expression of its own qualities as hers did.

She worked at the New Yachiyo Industrial Company across the hall facing his office. The long hallway lined by similar offices was dark and he could never observe her face too well since the moments when he came across her or passed her were very brief. But, when he saw her face approaching him as if floating in the dark air of the hall, or when he turned and saw her face caught between people's backs in the elevator, he felt that some energy of beauty was being released toward him. It was as if the distinct lines of hill-tops or the horizon suddenly gleamed with the last rays of extraordinary brilliance that were to fade into the tranquility of the air as at sunset.

It was her face which had attracted his attention at first, but he had perceived recently that the same element of pain radiated from her entire body, clad in quiet, dark suits, forming a contrast to her face. He felt that her figure, which seemed drenched in pain, drew out and revived his bitter memories of the past. He sensed that her face had a kind of beauty that was in accord with his inner suffering, but he could not discover why it nestled in his heart. In any case her face touched a wound in his heart. He sometimes felt that something was pressing his heart. He did not know just what it was at first, but he discovered that it was the image of that painful expression which had sunk to the depths of his being. He felt her face in the center of that something which choked his heart. He stared at the face within his breast, then he felt his heart ache and was seized by a vague apprehension which somehow gave him the sensation that his own feet were refusing to accept his will. A lightning of dark, unexplainable emotion suddenly flashed through his being. It came up quickly from his innermost memory and exerted over him a power that he could hardly suppress. It knocked him down. Oh, no! He staggered a moment. Oh, I can't stand this. He shook his head. Confounded, not knowing what to do, he stood trembling. He felt negative words for life and humanity rushing up from within him, words that he could never acknowledge himself. It was an unbearable moment. He was certain that his body was illumined to the tips of his fingers by the dark lightning that pierced through him. Oh, you are wrong. You are not thinking that way. You would never deny humility. You are more trusting. You are a simple man and you have more faith than that in men, he tried to persuade himself. But an impression which he had received on the battle field revived in him. It was an impression that men in war are vastly different from men in everyday life. He felt that the animal which lived in man was falling on him, baring its teeth. He recognized that the cruel tooth marks which his fellow-soldiers had made on his flesh in battle were not erased. He realized when he thought about it that he must have made the same tooth marks on his comrades. He chilled at those self-seeking scenes they performed when their lives were threatened in battle.

The reason that her image reminded him of the negation of humanity and of the battle field in the past was that there existed in his memory of the war a painful tormenting figure of a woman who corresponded to the image of Kurako Horikawa. Kurako always conjured up vividly in him those miserable days of war when soldier Kitayama trod on the battle field, embracing the image of a woman.

Toshio Kitayama once had a lover whom he could not love with all his heart. She was, one might say, a substitute for his last love. The woman he had loved had left him a long time before. This woman he had loved was not endowed with any outstanding characteristics but it was his ill fortune to have met her in his youth, full of uncontrollable passions. He idealized her as many young people do in such a state. He thrilled himself with virtues that never existed in her, adored her blindly. He naturally hated the woman when she wanted to dissolve the affair for she could not ignore the opposition of her family and felt insecure of his ability to earn a living. However, he chose to keep her image warm in his heart for a long time. It was under such circumstances that the next woman appeared before him. She was a clerk in a munitions company where he was working. She loved him. Unlike his former lover she handed everything to him immediately. She was a fragile but intelligent woman with a slender face, a narrow neck and small hips. She possessed something that drew close to his mental make-up and culture. He was then barely sustaining himself in the face of his painful failure in the previous affair, but he was not the sort of man who could stand solitude forever. Besides, he had no will power to give up that feeling of vanity satisfied when he had around him a woman who loved him. He naturally lacked the determination to reject her love. She believed in him thoroughly, and her love gave him everything. He did not know the value of love given so easily. It was something that he would not come across twice throughout his life. He treated her as something of a substitute and loved her accordingly. His eyes looking at her were cool and critical. He felt his heart growing cold as he touched her inelastic breast. His eyes were comparing hers with the former lover's breasts full of supple flesh. He was somehow unsatisfied and felt his heart shrinking. He would become irritated as he saw her pale face with its slightly prominent cheek bones, barren of any vigor which could drag him into a sexual passion. Her face might be said to have modern features. And as he drew her face close, he would find an insult in her clumsy makeup. Of course, he did not feel cold this way all the time, but as this happened again and again, he felt himself being crushed under the heavy burden of her devotion. He felt the thin thread of her passion coiling unbearably around him.

While he was still at the army camp in Japan he learned that she had died. With her death he admitted for the first time his crime of falsehood against her love. Amidst the torturing daily life of a raw recruit he was finally made to realize the value of love. Draftees used to say, "You will never appreciate your mother until you get into the army." Lying in bed at the camp, he, too, thought about his mother and his lover. He thought about the nobleness of one loving another. This in a way was sugar-sweet and even comical; a man over thirty, in tears, munching hardtack under a blanket. He thought, nothing is necessary in life any more, the only valuable thing is love. This he deduced from his daily life in the army, tightly occupied by drills and punishments. As his cold hand touched his swollen cheeks that had turned purple after having been hit by the sole of a combat boot, he remembered the soft hands of his mother and the tender palms of his lover. This kind of sentimentalism grew increasingly violent in him as he got out to actual field operations.

There was still mutual sympathy, pity and some room for understanding among the new conscripts who underwent the same kind of tortures together in Japan. They would exchange short phrases loaded with feeling and lament their fate beside the dark latrines. However, such an exchange of hearts was lost even among the first year soldiers, not to mention the higher officers and senior soldiers, in the life of the front, always visited by the enemy's bullets and a dearth of food. He learned that when one was in a fierce battle one had to protect his life by his own hands, to heal his own sufferings and to watch his own death. Each man must preserve his own life in a skin bag, himself, as water in a flask. Neither man would give the water to others, nor would he give his life for them. If his physical strength was a little bit weaker than that of his fellowman, he immediately became a straggler and death would assail him. When the whole unit was starving, giving one's food to another meant death. Comrades would look blackly at each other before a scrap of food.

While he was at close combat which demanded tremendous nervous tension, he would suddenly look back on his past. He found that those who had loved him truly were not among his many acquaintances, his close friends and fellow workers, but were only his mother and that woman. When in a battle an enemy skirmish line curiously stopped shooting, a suffocating silence began to cloak the front. He looked through the telescopic sight of his 4.1 mountain gun, seeking in a plain spreading before him some tree that would serve as a firing target. He then saw the two figures who had loved him truly whirl up and rush toward him. In a scene unfolded in the gun sight his dead lover approached with that gait of hers turning her longer left leg to the outside. It was a walk she could never cure no matter how hard she tried. While he recreated her gait in his mind, he felt her marching right into his painful inner being. Her clumsy walk shook his heart which had already been exhausted by both heat and fatigue. He had walked with her when she was alive; he had scorned and cursed in his mind her left leg, and treated her bitterly.

I am sorry, sorry, he said in his heart as he faced the enemy line. He endured the sufferings of battle by always embracing the image of his lover who had withheld nothing from him.

He was transferred to the front in the South Seas. To him, as a new conscript, it was not a battle against the enemy. It was a fight against Japanese soldiers. Heat developed saddle-galls on the horses' backs. The skin peeled and slipped from their backs, and saddle blankets were of no use. Raw recruits instead of horses dragged the gun carriages. Heat was so intense that marches were out of the question in daytime, so the troops marched mainly at night. One a.m., reveille; one-thirty, departure; eleven a.m., billeting. But the raw recruits had to groom horses, to check ammunition, to repair guns and to prepare provisions, so they ended up with only two hours of sleep a day. The gun carriages towed by the exhausted soldiers did not advance much. Superior privates who had been four or five years in the army cruelly abused those who served as horses. They barely managed to survive the attacks of their senior soldiers. The real enemies of the new conscripts were not the foreign soldiers ahead of them; they were the fourth and fifth year soldiers, noncoms, and officers.

While being goaded and beaten by the senior soldiers, Toshio, harnessed by the shoulders, pulled a gun-carriage through thickets but kept the image of his lover in his heart.

"What are you thinking? You are thinking about that again, aren't you?" the woman would plaintively ask Toshio who would lie still without a word after making love. She was aware that he was not satisfied with her. She thought that he must be remembering the other woman. "No, nothing," he would immediately deny, but his tone negated nothing, rather it somehow hinted acknowledgement.

"I have no other way to live except to love you, and I cannot afford to care what you think of me," she used to write to him. "I am positive that you will understand my heart some day, but then I will be dead." Whenever he thought about her, her heart behind those words thrust into his breast, and then he felt that he deserved any kind of suffering. He told himself, "Suffer more!" and walked dragging the gun-carriage under fifth year soldiers' whips. Sweet potato fields burned up black by Filipino soldiers stretched murkily far below. A large red tropical moon was up over the horizon, obscured by the dust that the soldiers raised. Yellowish cheeks of fevered soldiers and their sweat-stained uniforms reflected the moonlight and looked as if they had been dyed crimson. The unit, extended thin and long without much order, proceeded along a mountain path that gradually became narrow.

"Numbers two and three, relieve!" a squad leader's husky voice came from behind. The relief, with gas masks dangling, came up from the middle of the line breathing heavily without saying a single word. Their tunics were covered with mingled sweat and dust like black moss. Toshio handed his second rope to a relief and left the line with Private Nakagawa, of the third rope, who had been a fishmonger. Toshio did not know when he gave up the rope nor how he left the line. His neck was hot; his eyes were swimming in his head; and his heart leaped and crashed against the walls of his chest. He was rooted to the ground with Nakagawa for a while, but finally followed at the end of the line. They took the bridle of a horse with jutting bones and began to walk, but they had lost the energy to keep up with the horse's pace. The feeling was gone from their legs which had not been ungaitered for the past two days. They felt that a single step on a slope took blood from their bodies. A lance corporal, an acting squad leader, came down and said, "What the hell are you doing?" and whipped their hands which were holding the bridle. "Hanging on a horse like that! Can't you see the horse is just about done in? We got a lot of replacements for you guys but none for the horses. Don't bother me when it's so damn hot." They looked up at the lance corporal wordlessly, gave up, and slackened the rein. They walked away from the horse. No matter how deeply they breathed, it seemed the dirty air still stayed in their lungs. They were almost out of breath. Finally, the straps of the gas masks which were pressing their right shoulders seemed to give the finishing stroke. The surface of mountains, which sucked in the heat of the sun in daytime, breathed it out at night and wrapped the soldiers' bodies, whose pores were clogged with sweat and dust. They kept on walking merely because their marching unit dragged their bodies forward.

Toshio heard Private Nakagawa say over the horse, "I

can't walk any more." Nakagawa had already repeated the phrase a number of times, and every time it pierced Toshio's weakened heart. Utterly exhausted, Nakagawa had no energy to carry his large boned body. "This time I really mean it. I can't walk any more," said Nakawaga. However, he managed to be dragged by the horse for about half an hour.

The unit came near Mt. Samat. A quick march became obviously necessary. Otherwise the unit would surely receive a fatal blow from the well provisioned and munitioned enemy advancing from the right. So the unit marched on without even a short halt. "I, I'm going to let my hands go. I've got to." Nakagawa's voice told Toshio that his friend was completely exhausted. The end of the sentence died away. At first the tone of his voice seemed to call Toshio, but the calling faded before it was finished. It then began to sound as if he were making himself hear or as if his consciousness was running through his entire past life. These touching words reached the bottom of Toshio's heart, but he had no energy to help his comrade, not even to pat him on the shoulder or to offer encouragement. Indeed, if Toshio had started to do anything, he would have lost the balancing force to support himself, and would have perished. He remained mute and walked on, hardening his heart which was on the verge of being drawn by Nakagawa's voice. "I'm going to let go," gasped Nakagawa, and his hands were off the line. He fell to his knees, and became motionless. He chose this road covered with a thick layer of dust for his burial place. He stirred his head a little as if to demonstrate that death had finally released his body which had been dragged by the rope of slavery. Then he was completely down on the ground. The life of Private Nakagawa, who was slow in action and poor in memory and often beaten by senior soldier,s ended on the side of Mt. Samat. Thus, Toshio let a comrade die before his eyes in order to save his own life. When he came home he discovered that his own mother had passed away also.

\*  \*  \*

One day in the early spring, Toshio left the office with Yoshiko Yugami who worked for the same firm. The entrance in front of the elevator was crowded with office workers who were through work for the day. There was a large crowd of people before piles of sundries on a table in a trading company's special bargain section near the tobacco stand. When they elbowed their way through the crowd near the exit, Yoshiko practically shouted, oblivious to the presence of others, "Kurako!" Then a woman's face turned around among the crowd in front of a newsstand on the left. The face somehow floated in the reflected light of the building outside and faintly smiled amidst the people. "Are you going home now? Let's go home together, shall we?" Yoshiko said to the approaching Kurako. They walked side by side towards Tokyo Station among people who were hurrying home. Yoshiko Yugami who was between the two had a child left by her husband who died in the war, but was the most cheerful of the three. She seemed to have been walking through her life with the same firm step as that she was taking now. Her hair, which hung a little tangled over the dark blue half coat, hid her broad shoulders.

Toshio on the left was past his mid-thirties but looked old for his age. One could easily observe in his carriage traces of the indifference and fatigue of a vagabond, which were naturally acquired by those who had been long in the army. But at the same time one could sense a certain strength, a kind often hidden in a man who had experienced and overcome the sufferings of war and military life. And he walked dragging his long legs as in the army.

Kurako on the right had on a bright spring suit with sky-blue stripes, which appeared to melt softly into the square in front of the station, still in the light of dusk. She was reserved and did not say much even to the open-hearted Yoshiko, and she walked with somewhat downcast eyes and mincing steps. When they came to the line of people before the ticket window, Yoshiko thrust out before their eyes a large bundle that she had been carrying in her right hand, but apparently she did so with no intention of showing it to any particular person. "I'm going to take care of this today," said Yoshiko.

"What is it, may I ask?" Kurako inquired. "I am going to sell this, it's a fur, bear skin," Yoshiko replied and pulled out a paw with black claws from a corner of the bundle. She waved it michievously a couple of times and then broke into laughter, which led Kurako to smile. "Oh, a skin, is it?" said Toshio. He was startled that this humorous bear hand would support her.

"Yes, they told me that they would give me four thousand yen for this. If it were a little bigger the price would go up quite a lot. Because they pressed me so much to sell this I finally gave in. I really don't have anything to sell any more," said Yoshiko.

"I am in the same boat, you know," Kurako responded turning to Toshio and smiling.

Yoshiko said, "Everybody is the same. Isn't it awful?"

"But you are better off because you have something to sell," said Toshio. It sounded indifferent, but that was because he did not know what to say since he was embarrassed suddenly to find himself being introduced to the inner lives of these women.

"Well, this can't go on forever, not even another year. How about you?" Yoshiko turned to Kurako seeking agreement.

"No," Kurako shook her head, "I don't have much left either." Toshio saw on her face, when she nodded, a shadow of uneasiness.

The train was quite crowded. They were pushed apart from each other. Toshio was thinking, pressed by many human bodies, that what was threatening these women's lives was also darkening his future. Toshio's company, run by his acquaintance, dealt in many things from ironware and tableware down to children's tricycles, but it was running out of supply material. The company was finding itself in financial difficulties. Although he had worked for an ammunition company once, his military life of the past six years had completely robbed him of clerical ability.

Kurako got off at Yotsuya. The train became less crowded. Toshio and Yoshiko stood at the center door facing each other.

"She is pretty, isn't she?" said Yoshiko.

"Umm," Toshio's voice suggested that he was lost in thought.

"Don't you think so?" she pressed.

"Yes, she is pretty, very pretty," he said unhurriedly. But he did not have words to express amply that painful feeling which he received from Kurako. Neither "pretty" nor "beautiful" was the term for it. It choked his heart strangely or rather shook him violently as it choked.

"I always wish that I had seen her when she was younger. As for me handsome men don't interest me much these days, but I never get tired of looking at beautiful women," said Yoshiko.

"Is that right?" Toshio responded.

Yoshiko then said to him, "You know, she is like me."

"Like you?"

"Yes, she lost her husband in the war."

"I see," said Toshio rather indifferently, but he could not continue. He thought that Kurako's image flashed in front of his eyes. He recreated her face. Then he felt that beauty loaded with extraordinary energy straight towards his heart from her face. For the first time he clearly understood the source of that anguish in her face.

According to Yoshiko, Kurako fell in love, got married and lost her husband after three years. They loved each other and could not have been happier. War destroyed their happiness. Recently, they were trying to get her to marry again, but she had been reluctant about it.

Toshio parted from Yoshiko at Shinjuku and went on

walking alone up a back alley that led from the station. He did not feel like going home for he knew that a near-by transformer was burnt out and that he would be depressed by his gloomy room in the lightless apartment house. He went into a small cafe and ordered some croquettes and a cup of coffee. He ate rice that he had steamed on a hot plate at his office. He asked for a refill of coffee and lighted a cigarette. He had been thinking about the two widows. The agony of those who had received the blows of war was what he felt closest and understood best at present. He recalled the bear's paw with black claws. He smiled only vaguely, then felt a pain in his heart. His smile disappeared before it spread over his face. He thought that her husband must have loved her passionately and that she must have responded equally. What was she living for now that her husband was dead? Where would her love that had lost its object flow? Would it try to burn the air of the sky as the afterglow of the setting sun does even more violently than the midday sun? This unfulfilled love must have made that strain in her face. That distorted beauty which seemed to radiate from her face must come from this lonely burning of love.

He went out of the cafe and rejoined the bustle along the stalls in front of the station. An offensive odor of cheap frying oil filled the area. Electric lamps threw a dim light on people's faces as they munched things. He happened to see a man who was holding a dish close to his mouth at a slanted stall where stew was sold. He looked at the lean face of the man who wore a cotton military uniform which was tight at the ankles.

The guy must be hungry. Looks like a day laborer, Toshio thought. He remembered recruiting bills of a ward office posted on electric poles that said: "—— yen a day, room and board, etc." How in the world is he supporting himself? He hasn't got anything to sell. Besides, they surely don't pay much for a guy of that kind. . . . But. . . . Oh, well, what do you think you can do to help him? Toshio was staring at the man's mouth which was mechanically munching on something. The mouth had thick lips which were wet and shone red over the dish. Suddenly the mouth was transformed into the mouth of a pig that Toshio had beaten to death on the battle field. He felt an unbearable emotion accompanied with heat rising out of a corner of his body.

Oh no, I can't stand this, he denied as he walked.

Swine! Swine! he kept crying. A hot lump came boiling up from the depths of his body. The lips of the pig's mouth went on slimily squirming in Toshio's head. That son of a bitch, superior private Matsusaka stole the water from my flask at Lingayen Gulf, and I clung to food so desperately. . . . This is terrible. . . . The wet lips of the swine were still wriggling in his head. Matsazuka's mouth is a swine's mouth and mine is too. They all squirm and wriggle, Oh God! He was horror-stricken for a while, closed his eyes tightly and shook his head. After the pig's mouth had disappeared, he saw a black flame in the deep black boundary. He opened his eyes; the burning emotion rising from his body had vanished like an ebb tide.

He kept on walking, staring at his heart where that emotion had surged up, and where some spots of the emotion were left like a black flame. He thought, no matter how strong this emotion, this disavowal of humanity, it is merely momentary. At other times I vaguely affirm humanity as usual and I eat my meals, walk and breathe. But he now saw clearly that those people who were eating and walking had never known what love was. Placed in that battle field, they would have done nothing but protect themselves as I did. They would glare at each other before a small bit of food. They would let a comrade die before their very eyes. . . . He started to think about his mother who was reported to have died during an air raid. They say that a mother's love is blind. What human being can love another except a mother? If anybody would share his own food with others, it could be only a mother. Wait, I don't even know about a mother either. The image that came to his mind gradually changed into the image of the woman who had loved him. He recalled her who had died. He was then reminded that she did not exist for him. He needed only her love. Was the war that robbed millions of lives necessary in order for him to realize the value of her love? He got through the throng of people and then came fighting his way back again. About the time when his body became cold to its core, he reached his dark apartment.

Toshio sometimes drank tea with Yoshiko and Kurako, stopping on their way home. Then it happened that he began to spend time with Kurako alone. He never positively entertained a fancy that his feelings towards her were that of love. However, he had to admit that he was attracted to her beauty. Probably attraction would not be the term for it. On the contrary, her existence kept reminding him of his past and demanded that he see his miserable past life. He did suffer from seeing her, but he needed the pain. If somebody had pointed out that love was mixed in his feeling towards her, Toshio might have admitted it but he did not want her in that sense. Besides he was well aware that she still loved her dead husband.

"I hear that you were very happy," he remarked to her one day.

"Yes, I was happy, indeed," she answered. Then she added in a clear tone, "I know I made him happy. In that respect alone I had nothing to regret after he died, because I did everything I could for him, and of course I could not have been happier when he was with me."

"I did not know that a person like you still existed," he said.

"My husband was very fortunate in having suffered from a lot of problems with his family. But I believe that he must have been happy during our three years together."

"Then he went into the army, didn't he?"

"Yes."

"He was an officer, wasn't he?"

"No, he was a private."

"Did he go to the South Seas?"

"Yes, he died from a disease there."

"It must have been agony to leave you behind."

Kurako looked slightly embarrassed but answered boldly, "Yes. He said that it would be a trip at government expense, but I knew exactly how he felt."

"I suppose so."

"People frequently expressed their sympathy for me after my husband died, but I think he deserved their sympathy more. Nobody thinks about the dead that way, you know. I can't think otherwise. . . ."

"———"

"After all, if one dies, everything is over. Everything is over."

"Um."

"My husband would have been satisfied if he had chosen to die."

"There are many in your situation around us, aren't there?"

"You mean Yoshiko?"

"Yes."

"I really admire her for the way she is making her own living." He related his past love to her who had opened her heart to him and had told him about her past.

"I was thinking that you must have experienced something unfortunate," she responded. They left the coffee house. She said she had to do some shopping and walked toward the station.

He stood there for awhile and watched her go. She disappeared and appeared again in the bustling square in front of the station. He was thinking as he looked at her, I wonder how she can live. There are no longer arms to embrace her, are there? Why is it that her face had to be made beautiful by such grief? He kept watching her without realizing how odd his question was. He did not know whether it came from inside his heart or from her appearance, but a lonely feeling flowed out and covered the square. Together with the soft color of the dusk that descended from the sky, widened after the destruction of the tall buildings, that feeling seemed quietly to permeate the breasts of those who had experienced that unfortunate war.

One of his friends who had been demobilized from the South Seas with Toshio came to visit him one day. He was a college graduate and a first year soldier who had been among the last replacements sent to his unit from Japan. When he had got there he had been quite fat. The intense heat, however, had reduced him to a bag of bones within a month. Toshio used to look after him. It was because he was not a hypocrite who would curry the favor of senior soldiers with money or other things when threatened by their punishments. After he got back to Japan he got a job at a small firm near Hamamatsu Cho through a college friend. He occasionally visited Toshio and got his complaints off his chest by talking with him.

"Oh, boy, I have caught you now! How many times do you think I came to see you in the past few days? When I got to the corner by that fruit shop and saw your room with no light on, was I ever discouraged! Just imagine the way I went home dragging my heavy feet," said Saburo Kataoka in his usual tone, leaning his back against the wall.

"Hum! your big fat body can hardly evoke any sympathy, no matter how hard you try, Saburo."

"You never understand your old friend's feelings, do you? And every time he comes you are not here."

"You mean the 'feeling of no money' as Taisetsu Suzuki would say?"

"Yeah, I've been penniless and mindless recently. But

seem rather mindful. You must be in love, judging from the
fact that you haven't been in any night lately."

"Humm, love?" Toshio stammered a little but said, "Is
there any woman in Japan who can love?"

"That should not make any difference. It is a natural
law that man loves woman. Even though we lost the war, a
man needs a woman and she needs him."

"Are you going to make love with that impressive phys-
ique?"

"Why sure! If I'm in love, I will lose some weight." They
began to eat sweet potatoes which they had baked on a hot
plate.

"I'm finding it harder and harder to feed myself," said
Saburo, "and so I decided to take a side job this coming
month."

"Yeah?"

"Do you want to take one too?"

"Translation or something?"

"What? No, it's the black market."

"Yeah?"

"I mean a sort of salesman, selling medicine. You can do
it in your spare time. Aren't you ready to scream for help
too?"

"Yeah. I've just about reached the limit, but a salesman
is something I can't be."

"Well, you may be right." There was silence for a while.
Then Saburo resumed the conversation, "I bumped into
Yamanaka the other day when I went back home. Everybody
in our group is miserable." Yamanaka was one of their demobilized comrades.

"What's he doing?"

"Oh, he is selling chocolates. You know those chocolate
bars. He buys them and peddles them around villages."

"Humh! You mean Yamanaka does?"

"Sure, but don't let a chocolate bar fool you. He is doing
a lot better with chocolates than we are. He pays seven yen

fifty sen a bar and sells it for eight yen and fifty sen to village grocery stores. He says he clears three thousand five hundred yen. Oh, I've got to tell you this, Toshio. Where do you think he went on the first day he turned himself into a chocolate peddler? He figured on the easy money at Atami because it was flooded with the new yen, you know. But he couldn't sell a single bar as he had hoped to. When he climbed the hill in front of the station with the package on his back, he said that he was reminded of Yoshinaka Kiso's death."

"Yoshinaka?"

"Remember the scene where at the end Yoshinaka is wounded and says to his men that he feels his armor too hard, where he thought nothing of it before? Yamanaka said that he felt each chocolate bar on his back was an iron bar. You would think you would break your teeth on it, wouldn't you? No wonder he couldn't sell any."

"Oh?"

"You didn't laugh. My joke is no good, eh? Anyway—things are no good for any of us, are they? When you came back, your own house was burnt down, you had nothing to wear. What's more, your landlord is trying to get rid of you. Besides, jobs are all filled up. What can you do? The other day, for instance, they distributed mosquito nets in the middle of February. That's all right, but you haven't got money for that sort of thing. If you bought one, it would be handed to a black marketeer right away. And oh, those damn black marketeers, they have it all figured out and try to buy up special rationed goods for the war victims. What do you think I got in yesterday's distribution? A military pillow case and children's shoes!"

"———"

"You know what I thought I would do? Fall in love with somebody."

"I don't think you can make it, Saburo."

"Maybe not———. Then I may stay fat forever———."

"What have you been eating anyway?"

"Potato croquettes at a stall."

"Croquettes? I like them, but I never put on any weight."

"You know why? Because you are in love." They laughed.

Toshio did not particularly think that he was in love. But he needed her. He had never felt that any other person suffered as he did until he was with her. When he was watching her face he was reminded that he had been living very loosely, already forgetting the agony of the battle field. When he first came back to Japan, the deformed homeland really touched him, but the impression began to fade. He now thought nothing of burned down buildings, lines of street stalls along the sides of roads and squirming people. But the painful suffering in her face always brought back memories.

They often visited Ginza together on their way home. She was with her family, but she said that her life was not too free, for some of her relatives were living with her family. She always insisted on returning home after eight. He did not attempt to dissuade her from it. He wanted to take a new step in his life, but did not know how. The new step meant to him lifting up the weight of his past which had suppressed him. He did not know how to go about it. He attempted a question one day, "Can you go on living?"

"Yes," she answered.

"Are you sure?"

"Yes, I am sure."

After a short silence, Toshio continued, "Maybe that is because you have lived more straightforwardly than I."

"You think so?"

"It really is a job for a person to make another happy. I have never yet come across one who could. Of course, I couldn't but you could and probably that's what's supporting you."

It was evening. Spread over the town was a transparent spring sky tinted yellow. They sat close to an upstairs window of a coffee house and were deep in conversation. He told her that in college he ignored his mother's wishes and changed from law to esthetics. He said that his mother accepted this willingly, although she felt a little insecure of his getting a job after college. He said his mother sacrificed all her life for him. "I so wanted to see her again," he said. Kurako did not say anything and he realized that what he had said reminded her of her late husband.

"I think that I won't ever be able to get out of this mess because my six years in the army completely destroyed my life. I will find something soon. I'll regain my strength again. I intend to do anything. Fortunately, the army made over my body so I can." He talked a little about battle and said that what kept him together in the sufferings of the battle field was not his learning, but the agony in his heart.

"When I am with you, I feel like doing something for you, but I understand clearly that it is far beyond my power. I wish I could," she said in a broken voice as if holding her breath. Toshio did not know what to say to that. They stared at each other for a while without uttering a word.

One day Toshio was climbing the stairs to the third floor when he saw Kurako stooping in the middle of the stairs. "What happened?" Toshio asked.

She turned around and recognized him and replied, "I just stumbled over here," and she added, "I was thinking." Toshio caught something very sad which flashed on her face.

They met on their way home. They went on walking aimlessly toward Gofukubashi. Kurako seemed unusually melancholy. As he walked with her he sensed that her heart was not with him but had slipped down into the depths of her being. It was a windy evening. White dust whirled up over the street and the boards of the wooden bridge squeaked. They walked along the river. "Is your foot all right?" he inquired after a while.

"Oh, the foot?" As she turned, her hair fell over her face.

"Yes, you stumbled on the stairs and you were limping."

"Oh, I am all right now. Somehow I have been in the

dumps these days. I was thinking about something else then and was absent-minded."

"_____"

"I've begun to feel forlorn all of a sudden these days. I don't know why. It's never happened before."

"Oh, you have?"

"Yes, I have. Do you think it's strange?" They passed by a crowd of people in a park and came out to Ginza.

"I have let you pay all the time so please let me pay tonight."

"You say 'all the time' but it is only coffee."

"Oh, well. Anyway, would you let me? Because I have some money tonight." They had a simple dinner and went into the coffee house next door for coffee. They thought that they had something they wanted to talk about and that they must talk about, but they remained silent. Finally Kurako, avoiding his eager eyes, as usual broke the silence.

"Toshio," she said, "remember you said that you would find something? Does it look like you can find it?"

"No, not so easily as that. But I've started studying again. I began to feel like studying while working. Some day I shall become a decent human being. I think I want to die after I become a decent man."

"_____"

"I managed to live through that war, so if I cannot live that way now I might as well have died."

"I am sure that better days will come."

"To whom? To the Japanese?"

"Well. . . ." she stammered.

"_____"

"I've been thinking that I should find you somebody really nice."

"Oh," Toshio stopped there, and thought about the meaning of her statement and then said indifferently, "Thank you, but how about you?"

"Oh me?" she pulled her face back slightly.

"I mean, I heard that somebody was interested in you," Toshio remarked maintaining the same indifference.

"Oh, you did?" Kurako said as if being crushed by his cold tone.

"Yes, I did."

"But," she stuttered, "but I couldn't be enthusiastic about it even if I tried. Toshio, do you think it's better to get married again?"

"Of course it is better."

"I see." They held their hearts far apart and kept on sitting without a word to each other. It was quite late when they got to the Yurakucho station. It was long past eight. There was a flock of cabaret women with heavy make-up at the platform. They were laughing gayly under the dim lights. Toshio and Kurako stood apart from the women at the end of the platform and looked down at the black town spreading before their eyes.

Outer trains of the loop came one after another but it seemed that the inner train which they were waiting for would never come.

How long is she going to last? She said that she was living by selling her things. What will she do after running out of possessions to sell? He began to think about Kurako who stood by him, looking at the dim lights of the streets at night.

What on earth am I trying to do and to look for? he went on thinking. Am I looking for love from her? A woman who lost her husband in war is united with a man who was made to appreciate in war the feeling of his dead lover. This sounds like a novel alright. Suddenly he became aware of the small life stirring beside him, a life that carried suffering everywhere, deep in Kurako's body. Then here was that suffering quietly deep inside the life like some animal. No, what I am looking for is not her and what she is looking for is not me either. She said that she couldn't do anything about my suffering and I too stand helpless before hers. Now I can't do a thing about that single soul that is near me, so I can't help but think that my life is my life and her life is, after all, her life. Again an outer train came. Suddenly she stood up and walked to the train saying, "Let's get on it."

"Why?" said Toshio as he followed her as if being drawn by her small back.

"Let's ride. We could go by this anyway." She gave him a quick look and went into the train, paying no attention to him. He followed her as if throwing himself against her body, seeing a young temptation moving in her face. Once in, there was not much to talk about.

"What happened? How come we are on this train?"

"Nothing, but somehow I couldn't wait any longer," and then the conversation was over. There persisted a suffocating tension between them. He sensed an air of temptation flowing from her as she held to a strap. "Our place is far from the station, isn't it?" he said after a while.

"Yes," she replied, looking ahead.

"How long does it take you?"

"It takes about fifteen minutes."

"That's dangerous, isn't it?"

"Yes," she nodded and said, "a few nights ago a woman was attacked. It cost her only a parasol, though."

"Shall I see you home?" said he. She did not answer but he saw her shaking her head quietly and forlornly. Again they stood with their hearts far apart. After Meguro and Shibuya the train arrived at Shinjuku. Toshio was still debating whether he should take her home and walked to the platform of the Chuo line. "Shall I see you home?" he repeated but she remained silent.

The train was almost empty but they stood at a door facing each other. He watched the wind blowing in through a window fondling her hair that came down around her neck. And he also looked at her small body tilted a little to the left which gave a forlorn impression. He sensed that she would not be able to live on in this defeated country. Pretty soon she won't be able to keep on. There will be a small raise this month but that won't be much help in buying food. I think her company's much the same. . . . He imagined that her body before his eyes would grow thinner, would lose the radiance of its life and would disperse like dust.

He did not have any more to say to her. He was aware that his words, whatever they might be, could not reach her heart. . . . There is great agony in her, and it is about to crush her, but I can't even touch it, and I don't know a thing about her. I know only my own suffering and that's all I care about . . . that is all. . . .

Toshio saw her turn and look at him. Before him her fair face floated into the dusky space. He was staring straight into the face. He thought he saw there the agony of war and wanted to enter it. He thought that if there was truth or sincerity left in a person like him, he wanted to let it come in touch with her agony . . . if two hearts can exchange their sufferings, if they can hand to each other the secrets of their existence, and if a man and a woman can show truth to each other, their lives will come to have a new significance . . . but he thought it impossible.

The train was approaching her stop, Yotsuya. His eyes continued fixed on her face. Suddenly he recognized a small spot in a corner of her fair face. The spot curiously threw his mind into disorder. It was such a small speck that people would not have noticed. It might have been a spot caused by dust or soot and smoke. Or it was perhaps a mole faintly visible beneath face powder. Anyway it transmitted a short vibration to his heart. Feeling an urge to see what it was, he concentrated on the spot above her left eye. He looked at it intently. What distracted him, however, was not the spot. He felt that there was a spot somewhere in a corner of his heart. He knew already what the spot signified. He fixed his eyes on the spot in his heart. Presently he noticed the spot start swelling and becoming larger and larger. As it grew it approached his eyes. It came near his eyes from inside them. It

drew closer to his eyes. Oh! he cried out in his heart. Then he
saw the spot spreading rapidly in Kurako's fair face. A large
red round thing appeared in her face. A large, red, round,
tropical moon rose in her face. The yellowish cheeks of soldiers' faces afflicted with fever came into sight. Then, the
long shadow of the disorderly unit trailed far behind.

A roar of vehicles struck his body. He heard Private
Nakagawa the fishmonger say, "I can't walk any more!" and
mixed with the roar, he heard again, "I'm going to let
this go—I, I—." The roar of the vehicles came out of the
depths of his body. Something boiling hot came gushing
forth out of him. "I will let go, I will." He felt Nakagawa's
body leaving him and plunging toward death. He saw himself pushing Nakagawa away to death. The train left a tunnel
rumbling. He suffered his gloomy thoughts arising from
within his body. I couldn't help, I couldn't. I had to watch
him die to protect my own life. To protect my life. To protect my own life. There was no other way, he tried to persuade himself. There was no other way, and I am exactly as
I was then. Placed in a similar situation, I am the kind who
would do the same, letting a friend die before my eyes. I
am merely protecting my own life. I can't do anything to
help her and her suffering.

He felt the breath of her heart being blown to him from
her faint face. I cannot be in her life. I am in my own. He
felt that he could not come in touch with what was within
the breath of her heart. I can't. I can't do anything about
other people's lives. How can I protect other people's lives
when I protect only my own? . . .

The train arrived at the Yotsuya Station. The train
stopped. The door opened. He saw Kurako look at him. He
saw her small right shoulder inviting his heart. Shall I see her
home? What shall I do? . . . No, I can't, I can't.

"Goodbye," he said, lowering his head.

"Uh-huh," she said drawing back her face as in reflex
action. A wan smile appeared on her face. She got off the

train and the door closed. The train started. Through a sheet of glass he saw her face looking for him in the train. Her face on the platform moved further and further away. He saw the cracked door glass scraping her face. He saw his life scraping hers. He felt that a sheet of transparent glass had passed between their lives with infinite speed.

# LATVIA

# The Vision from the Tower*

MARGARITA KOVALEVSKA

Translated by Astrid Ivask

LIZBETH stepped into a silence strangely suffused with
loneliness and felt coolness waft all around her. Closing
her eyes, she took a deep, greedy breath. She had been
climbing for a long time, her skirts sweeping dust and
pigeon drippings from the narrow winding stairs. Lizbeth
had strained herself and stood now with trembling knees
and ringing ears. Wide, unglassed windows surrounded her
with their gaping stare. What business do you have standing
here, black candle? the belfry walls seemed to ask. This
place is for the sexton alone, to set God's tidings swinging.

Lizbeth straightened herself. Not a faltering movement
showed that her head was swimming. She knew very well
why she was here. Pulling her kerchief back from her ears,
she stepped forward. Lizbeth will listen to the silence. Yes,
to a silence free from all earthly noise. Not once will she
glance around, standing high up, as if on the edge of a
cloud, without a roof over her head.

But her ears would not be deceived. They heard her
heart beating in her breast, the hum of blood in her veins,
heard pigeon-wings swish and the carts of market-folk rumble
in the streets down below. And just above her head she
sensed the mute bell's presence, dangling from a thread like

---

* From *Flower of Disaster* (1962).

an empty, yet heavy jug. The gentlest touch of a pigeon's wing or the church clock striking and lopping another hour off the day, and the huge bell would come crashing down upon her.

Lizbeth moved one step aside. What good was a steeple no longer than a goose's neck! Were masons' hands afraid to pile stones higher into the sky? Lizbeth heard the organ's grumbling roar creep up the stairs behind her, interwoven with the melody, "If thou but suffer God to guide thee," lulled as if by shepherds' pipes. She stood for a while listening with knitted brows. Her mouth opened as if to speak the words that followed, "Who trusts in God's unchanging love, builds on the rock that nought can move."

No, no, she shook her head, I will not be caught in the net of these sounds! And she lifted her face to the sun. How would it be when one's eyes were shut forever, when one's vision was finally freed from colors and all the other delusions that blind man and titillate his lust for life? Lizbeth wanted to know what it would feel like to be an angel or, as her friend Augusta put it, a soul, fluttering like a near-nothing between the sun and the moon. But the sun penetrated her eyelids as a pale, purple light, and Lizbeth saw her own blood purl in the delicate net of veins within her lids. Her blood was still fermenting strongly. It sparkled through coil after coil, the years she had lived rolled past her gaze, rolled like green and yellow wheels, pivoting in the very center of the eye, tempting her with still more restless swarms of years that stung her sight like needles.

Lizbeth passed her hand over her forehead. Such transparent gates of darkness suit only the sleeping hours of this earthly life. But Lizbeth was not one to give up easily. And she pulled her kerchief tightly over her ears and covered her eyes with the palms of her hands. Now it should be possible for her to catch it, this nothingness, up there in the air so high, it made one dizzy. . . .

But alas, no coffin-lid cut her off yet from the sun's

warmth. With the joy of life fluttering in every pigeon's wings, the day laughed her straight in the face. Lizbeth looked up into the sky without a trace of shyness or humility. She was no hypocrite, no holier-than-thou, she certainly prayed for nothing, asked nothing; all she desired was to find a truth of her own. But the sun made her hide her eyes behind the narrow slits of her lids. Wasn't that the way only near-sighted people looked, who could not see beyond the end of their noses? Lizbeth again raised her arm and shaded her eyes. She gazed long and hard, with wide open eyes into the blue of the sky, as if she expected something. Light breezes drew the low hum of the organ out of the belfry windows and up into the skies. They seemed to draw Lizbeth skyward, too. Yet she saw clearly the roof of the sky rise higher and higher and recede farther and farther away. No river whirlpools churned there, nor was there lure of sinister deeps of lakes and the sea. The sky had neither shallowness nor depth. Pitiless infinity surrounded her. These were the empty skies of late fall and nothing else. She nearly had to laugh, remembering Augusta's words, "Fred is in heaven." The last sigh uttered by the germ-eaten young man was ridiculous, "Thank you, Mother!" In Augusta alone, who was still unravelling under her feet the roads of this earth, only in her was her son's last sigh still alive, together with his image. Augusta gone, Fred's soul will vanish too. Oblivion will cover them both. And the grave of Augusta's late husband, now decked out in flowers and soft sod, will become overgrown, then slowly sink back into the earth.

All that Lizbeth could hear and see was a figment of her own imagination and nothing else. And if she could trample underfoot the hum of the organ, she would have certainly done so. It hummed now in a man's deep voice, somewhat like her sick son's question on a dark autumn evening of yonder year. Lizbeth leaned against the wall. But it was not that, it was a song of praise heard long ago, "Oh for a thousand tongues to sing." Lizbeth had forgotten how to

praise, she could not even sing the Song of Songs any more—
it brought only bitterness and wrath into her heart. Why
did God need such songs when everything was so different in
life, bespattered with the vile spittle of a curse?

Lizbeth glanced down into the garden encircling the
church. It seemed to be warmer down there than up here.
The sun had melted in places the covering of hoar-frost.
Damp patches shimmered darkly through silver-tipped
branches, looking up and straight into Lizbeth's eyes. A man
clad in black was walking the garden paths. Looking down
from the belfry, Lizbeth could see only the hump of his
back and the hatted button of his head; she was reminded
of moles, ravagers of gardens. They were forever uprooting
plants, ruining meadows—and unwillingly, as if turning into
a mole herself, she fastened her eyes to the earth.

At this very moment, the sound of clocks striking the
hour was obliterated by a tinkling of graveyard bells; the
neighing of horses at the market was pierced by the drawn-
out whinny of the railroad station's long-maned voice. Lizbeth's shoulders slumped, she felt that she might faint at any
moment. It grew dark around her as her glance penetrated
deeper and deeper into the earth's layers. Now she saw centuries that had long ago sunk into oblivion. All that remained of man's ages of glory and chaos was slowly rotting
down there, and turning into crumbly soil. A rich man's
remains nestled in the pelvis of a poor devil. A single finger,
still sporting a ring, was all that was left of a wealthy man.
It lay now in a poor man's gaping toothless mouth. The rich
man's gold-filled purse shone through the poor devil's crumbling fist. Not even money could buy immortality, nor
could one take another's life by force. And there, farther
away, the pale shimmer among the crooked pitchforks of
rib-cages and the sad flutes of leg-bones—they were not
blown-out, empty eggshells, they were skulls void of thought
and the active brains of minds once alive. But did not skeleton lie across skeleton in the deepest layers of the earth,

mowed down as with one single swath of a scythe? And were not the spears and breast-plates of the Teutonic knights rusting there?

When her glance had extricated itself from this pile of skeletons and climbed but one layer higher up, did not the terrifying ghosts from the eimes of the Duchy of Kurland grin in their lead coffins, clad in silk and velvet, yet without eyes or noses, only jewelled bracelets around their yellow arm-bones? A golden pin gleamed through somebody's rib-cage; and, probably, that was a string of pearls around a collar-bone. Higher up, layer after layer was strewn with epaulettes, buttons, and silver-spurred boots belonging to the men of the Russian Czar. Beside the German Baron's crumbling meerschaum pipe rotted the overseer's whips like snakes crushed underfoot. And those? Lizbeth knitted her brows. Were they not the damp layers of the war years? Sharp needles of barbed wire wove through a porridge of torn-off-legs, half-rotted organs, grenade splinters, and burned chunks of flesh. Heads, which had been exploded sky-high and rolled off into the distance, still bore on their faces the petrified features of horror. In the heart-lumps, torn out and hacked to pieces by scavenger birds, still steamed remnants of the will to live; and the unspent love of young men was drying up, as hostility grew dull and wore out. And the girl there, protecting with her arms a grey, tattered soldier as if warding off the specter of death—was she not Susan, the lost daughter of Mathilda and Michael? And the soldier pressing his blind-eyed face into a clod of earth, guarded by Susan's arms, wasn't that George Bird? Certainly it was Lizbeth's broad-shouldered, fair-haired George. *My proud, sharp-eyed falcon!* "I love our country, Mother. I shall look vigilantly in every direction; I shall spit fire, I shall protect every inch of soil over which I have trod!" Did he say that once?

"But you were stupid, my handsome son, you shouldn't have died for a mere crust of earth. It is green above, bright with flowers; it gladdens the eye and draws the heart. You might still be alive, hiding like an animal in the forest thicket, lying in ambush for the enemy. You might have lived and blossomed above the crust. . . ."

Probably the sun was already melting the belfry walls as well—a warm drop of water rolled off Lizbeth's cheek and fell heavily down, straight into the radiance of the church garden. And invisible shepherds' pipes, the bees from the fields, the horse-flies from the green pastures of the Birds' homestead, were calling through the power thunder of the organ, "Wake, awake, for night is flying." Yes, indeed, Lizbeth felt her head swaying along, "Your lamps with gladness take; Alleluja, Alleluja!"—Let them toll, blow, play, ring all the bells. . . . But then she blinked, and continued to burrow with a steady glance in the blackness of the earth. Above this layer, saturated with sweet blood avid for life, and with salty blood as well, the crowd of those who follow in the footsteps of war—driven by hunger, despair, and want —slept the long sleep wherever they had happened to fall. Neither were they tormented by worries about their tomorrow, nor did hunger gnaw at them. In vain their hands clutched empty tin vessels, horses' bones, in vain their faces reflected the smiles of the humble, the same smiles that had sickened her when she saw them on the faces of refugee mothers and troubled and perplexed her on the children's emaciated features.

In shallower spots, where even the sun found a crack for a bright beam and the ant discovered a path for a walk, slept those in their coffins with thankfully crossed hands who had been lamented yesterday in the crypt. What right did the living have to cross the hands of the dead who had fought so hard over the to be or not to be! They slept in flower-filled coffins, their faces still damp with the sweat of their death agony and the tears of their loved ones. The victorious germs crept dazed around their mouths. And worms approached.

Nauseated, her face a waxen yellow, Lizbeth straightened her back. These dark layers of the earth received everything with open arms: the fly-covered carcass from the roadside or Augusta's beautiful lady, bedded amidst the fragrance of flowers. They received everything and ground it between grains of sand that were their teeth. Ground everything down and filled at summertime the canals of Jelgava with the stench of the earth's belches.

Lizbeth held on to the wall and swallowed a mouthful of bitter saliva. She wanted to vomit.

When she was feeling a bit better, the church clock struck the half-hour. Lizbeth dragged herself to the window which opened towards the blue shadows of the north. Here, watching the town bask in the benevolent rays of the sun below, she felt the turmoil of her thoughts grow calm and her mind regain its balance. Her eyes found their own way in the streets, which seemed narrow and crooked from above. One could roam and get lost, could flee the terror of darkness and destruction. Her glance travelled over the bridge across the river Driksna. Skirting treetops, it stopped at the reddish ruins of Duke Biron's castle and then glided downstream, following the river's course. Smoke from a small steamer was curling into the air. Lizbeth had taken several short trips on that same steamer, but now it seemed ages ago. Her eyes traversed the larger bridge across the river Lielupe, glanced to the right where, farther upstream, the Riga-bound train was just crossing the railroad bridge, glanced left at the low-lying meadows of the river-bank, and again glided over bridges and along the road, past a tree-sheltered, shabby manor-house and on to the horizon. Beyond that hazy line of woods, the road should run on through Dalbe and Olaine and, with the clatter of well-shod horses, enter Riga itself, where smokestacks blacken the skies.

Below, the market was in full swing. Carts with firewood attracted few townspeople. They appraised and scoffed at the source of warmth for the coming winter months. Here and there, men stood with saws and axes dangling from their shoulders, hoping to earn a day's wages chopping and stacking the purchase. Just behind the silvery streaks of carts filled with birchwood and gray-skinned alders, the faded sunlight fell on the hunched backs of mushroom-mongers. But at this time of year hardly any mushrooms sprouted in the woods, nor did berries redden any more. Surely by now the women were squatting behind crocks of pickled mushrooms, bending over them and in the same breath offering for sale bags of caraway, poppyseed, and freckled runner beans. They also displayed their harvest from summer meadows—herbs and teas, neatly bunched and carefully dried at home. During this chilly season of coughs and sneezes, there were few indeed who wouldn't care to buy a bunch of yarrow and camomile, of bitter wormwood, peppermint, and catnip. Here and there women offered baskets abloom with bright everlasting flowers. These emptily rustling blossoms had been dipped into dye-vats like skeins of wool to please the eye, their own paler color thus heightened to deep red or blue. Townspeople liked to use them to make their windows more cheerful. Between double panes, they covered the sills with moss or white cottonwood, and added a small bag of salt to absorb moisture and prevent the windows from steaming up. For a touch of luxury they studded the moss with such stars of everlasting flowers.

Farther down the market place, the wives of gardeners sat with much dignity in their green canopied carts. They squatted like blustering brooding hens among huge yellow pumpkins, firm heads of cabbage, pungent winter radishes, slender-fingered roots of horseradish, garlands of onions, bunches of beet and carrot. With their reddened, weatherbitten hands they fished around in barrels for cucumbers, pickled with dill, garlic, and horseradish leaves, or lifted full measures of juicy sauerkraut, shaved fine and sprinkled with caraway. At least one customer, basket in hand, circled each of them. But a few rows down, by the horse-carts from farther

out in the country, they crowded more eagerly, milling
around in a constant flux. These carts certainly belonged to
the smaller farmers whose land surrounded the town. Like
the gardeners, they displayed cabbages and other vegetables.
From her perch in the belfry, Lizbeth knew quite well what
every one had brought in his load. Some, no doubt, also had
potatoes for sale, with rough skin and many eyes. Cans
concealed milk and cream, carefully skimmed with a spoon.

Farther down in the market, behind those rows of carts,
how often had not Lizbeth herself been sitting together with
Big Bird, her husband, atop a mountain of fiery red apples,
while a cartload of moon-bright ones from the neighboring
Gauri orchard had shimmered close beside her. The towns-
women jostled each other as they reached their bags up to
be filled. Big Bird would feverishly weigh out their ware,
his brow damp. Lizbeth herself did nothing but grab, count,
and shove the money into her skirt pockets. In the left one
it rustled, in the right one it rang. . . . Farmers from other
distant parishes sat in their carts beside the fragrant loads of
the Birds and their neighbors, the Gauri. They, too, had
rumbled late into the marketplace, where local small farmers had already taken the choicest spots. But what did it
matter? In their carts, sacks of flour and pearled barley lay
like well-fed pigs, and pound packages of butter, wrapped
neatly in transparent paper, were laid out on a white cloth,
tempting the eyes of townsfolk. Rich butter, without a drop
of buttermilk or salt water! And cottage cheese, yellow caraway cheese, eggs. From buckets thick cream flowed slowly
like honey and tasted of almonds.

When one's legs grew numb from sitting in the cart, one
could stretch them in the streets of Jelgava, run to Augusta's,
chat for an hour or so, try on new hats with flower-laden
brims, and admire one's own face. One could step into this
store or that and like a wealthy farmer's spendthrift wife
buy silken kerchiefs to satisfy the craving for luxury. A
flower sports the splendor of but one color all summer long,

but Lizbeth covered her head different each day. Once her face hid from the sun in a rosy strawberry shade, then again in the deep green of a garden; or it glowed, well in sight of the Gauri windows, in a kerchief of dazzling white. And in church she never once stepped over the threshold without lifting her skirts a bit higher than necessary and putting forward a foot like the silver-spangled stem of a flower.

Lizbeth stood smiling for a while, staring with glassy eyes through the whirl of the marketplace at those bygone days. There had been other times, too, when Big Bird himself wanted to walk beside his portly wife. Then they stopped at the nearby fish market, bought a few dozen smoked sprats, and acquired a good-sized barrel of salt herring. This would do for the whole year, both for themselves and the hired help. Herring tasted so very good with cream, sour milk, and potatoes, especially during the hot summer season, when pork stuck in one's throat and one craved something leaner. Big Bird loved baked herring. Wrapped in a newspaper, thrown on the glowing embers, it was put in front of the giant Bird—charred, black strips of paper still sticking to it; he ate, moaned, and threw the fish-bones under the table. In that remote summer, when at nightfall a shadow would steal into the Birds' orchard from the neighboring Gauri homestead and the clock showed the approaching hour of love, Lizbeth herself had baked herring on the embers, had served them herself on the largest platter. . . . Now Lizbeth's mouth began to water. She remembered Augusta, who by this time was waiting below, and she leaned forward to get a better look at the corner of Castle Street. But at that very moment, as if it had collieded with the posts guarding the entrance to the church garden, her glance stopped and remained fixed. It spread in terror over a beggar who had fallen and now sprawled full length exactly across from the gates. His cane had jumped sideways across the gutter, the discs of small change scurried along the sloping sidewalk, past the doors of the parsonage, disappearing in cracks between cobblestones, rolling around among horse dung in the street. A crowd of curious onlookers rushed toward him from every direction. The beggar lay, arms flung wide, head bald, completely motionless. Someone stooped and felt for his hand, his head. Lizbeth grimaced in disgust. This hairless head, round and smooth, reminded her of the blown-out, empty eggshells deep in the earth. Such a negligible fall, and not one thought left in the pot of the head; in a few days it too will be buried.

Suddenly a strange gurgling sound of joy welled up in her throat. *Lizbeth was alive!* But how close she had come to being the one around whom the crowd of onlookers was thronging. Very likely Augusta, too, was standing there, adding some excitement to her day. And not long ago, quite recently, Lizbeth herself had walked along this sloping sidewalk, unaware of death lying in ambush behind the church gates. Her thoughts turned now to the money she had in a bank and at home, in a tin can, tucked away in a mousehole, as well as right here deep in her skirt pocket. Doubly eager to seize with both hands all that life might still offer, she quickly turned her glances back into the whirl of the marketplace. A horse, its head raised high and teeth bared, was neighing out to the world its animal joy; a feeding bag full of oats dangled from its neck. Lizbeth laughed, the piercing and spiteful sound throwing her own being like a dart into the very center of the living world. She felt a sudden desire to squander money, to attract attention, to be needed by those down below. With what playful lightness they all rolled and crawled about, stooped and straightened themselves, those tiny bug-sized people! Houses like matchboxes with roofs made of shells, the streets—narrow meadow brooks that one could easily cross with a jump. A real city of insects! Country roads wound from all four sides of the horizon like thin threads unravelled from balls of wool. The thinnest one of all, almost worn through in the middle, wound its way across the viaduct. . . . And while the world at the foot of the church shrank in size and grew more and more insignificant, Lizbeth atop her belfry expanded both in size and power.

"I must hurry," she reminded herself, fearful of seeing the world disappear altogether. Her head tilted back a little, a grimace rather than a smile in the wrinkles around her mouth, she descended the stairs. Along with the dust stirred up by her skirts, the triumphant roar of the organ rushed up and past her, but little did Lizbeth care now; she was carrying a new vision down with her. A very unusual vision, and yet as easy to realize as child's play. She laughed —softly, slyly, passing her tongue over these honey-sweet thoughts, savoring them again and again in her mind.

At the foot of the stairs, by the exit, stood a hump-backed man, very likely the same black mole that had burrowed in the church garden, the one with whom her thoughts had penetrated those dark layers of earth. He jumped aside, pressed himself against the wall and let the triumphant Lizbeth glide past undisturbed.

It was the sexton with his bunch of keys. "God forgive us our trespasses, there goes a fortunate one even in her misfortune." And he closed the door very slowly and with awe. The pastor's own son, Gottfried, was playing the organ for the third straight hour—as on no other morning.

# LITHUANIA

# He Wasn't Allowed to See

PULGIS ANDRIUŠIS

Translated by the Author with the editorial assistance of
Clark Mills

UNCLE MYKOLA was already retired, if thus you could
describe the bachelor farmer who, after long toilsome
years, afflicted with asthma and stomach troubles, could now
only shift his horse in the pasture or chop brushwood behind
the house. Mykola would say to himself:

—Behold, now I'm almost eighty. Who knows if I'll ever
see into the nineties?

On fine autumn days, strolling about the orchard, or offering a succulent apple to a random visitor, he would sigh:

—It's true. I'm like an over-ripe apple, myself. Just one
drop more of the night dew, and there it lies, quite still on
the ground!

As he chopped kindling in the back woodyard, separated
from the outer world by a dark wall of nettles and mugworts,
Mykola surely knew little of what was happening beyond.
Sometimes a woman would trudge by, her yoke over her
shoulders, carrying her laundry to the village pond. Or a
neighbor's urchin would run past, chasing a gadfly.

Yet after a walk to Ožkašlaité to move his horse in the
pasture and then back home, Mykola's sitting room would
fill up to the ceiling with the latest news, so that you had to
open the door, through which filtered broken fragments of
the mild tales he told:

—By the gush of the spring! I think to myself . . .

—And then, behold, click! And it turned off . . .

—End of the world! I say to myself . . .

You could guess easily that Mykola had finished his long day's journey, and was recounting his adventures since early morning to a neighbor who has come to borrow his steelyard.

—Then I think I'll just sit down behind the hawthorn bushes at the edge of the loampit, to have a peaceful smoke on that boulder, you know the one I mean, the one that's hollowed out on top.

—I turn my head, and behold, above the birch grave of Skriaudakalnis stands a fairly tall cloud. Mykola, Mykola, old friend, you walk out to move your horse, and as soon as you pass the barn you walk straight under a rain-cloud, I think to myself!

—Look, the round cloud has stretched, and's now hanging a sleeve over Čečergis' *sauna* bath by Devil's Footbridge, and has another sleeve pointing straight at my own collar. But what do I care? The barn and a good shelter are right here. And I think, well, now we'll see if thou'lst make rain, or if all thy efforts come to nothing!

—Near the little bath-house, right at Devil's Footbridge, a frog's croaking, oh, it's calling, trying to draw the cloud. Good, thou canst croak on and burst! I think to myself. Not for thy sake do the clouds wander up in the sky, they can bring rain to good Catholics without thy help. Under the willows, hast some water covered with duckweed, just enough to wet thy belly, make the best of it. Thou hast no reason, none at all, to draw a cloud! It has its own ideas where to pour down a shower. Just think of my own barley field, gasping for water like Lenten fish—and not a drop falls.

—Well, my thoughts were running on like that, when the dark-edged cloud pauses just above the thornbushes by the loampits, casting a faint shadow across Devil's Footbridge, and here are my barleys, their beards gaping wide with thirst. All right, come on, I say. As for me, I've plenty of time to run to the barn for shelter. But we'll see—what willst thou do now, thyself?

—And while I was watching the cloud, up springs a whirlwind from Devil's Footbridge and hurls it to the other side of the barn. All at once the cloud swelled out like the sheepskin coat behind Tilindis' knees. And I was right not to rush back into the barn.

—My guess was right! How could such a skinny, shriveled cloud ever make rain? You could even move over it on your knees, squeezing and wringing it dry like wet trousers after a day casting the nets.

—And so I walk on through a narrow patch of meadow, and I think how we get teased and annoyed at every step. Then, all at once, my heel's bogged down, sunk into the earth. That's the end! I say. What's pulling me down?

—I turn around, and what do I see but a mole busily at work, lifting my own good meadow with his shoulders. Turn sour, will you? I think. Couldn't it move away, farther down, past Skriaudakalnis, into the fallow fields? —As if the soil wasn't just as good over there! And still the dirty beast raids my own meadow, my soul, not a poor patch of chickweed or thistles, but all clover and sorrel. When it's time for hay-mowing, those molehills can wrench the scythe out of your hands, and you have to go all the way home and hammer its edge straight against the front of the granary, because a whetstone wouldn't help when the edge has gone crooked as Čečergis' wooden plough.

—As I was thinking all this, the mole kept churning my dear clover, just as heartburn sometimes upsets your guts. And in your very presence, Mykola! And what can you do about it? With your heel you can trample in the molehill, that's sure. But who can promise you'll ever find your dear clover safe tomorrow? If the mole had any sense, you could ask him a straight question: Think, man, what do you imagine you're up to in these parts? Of course, you could pull him out of the earth by his ears, but alas, one of his brothers would finish what he left undone, and probably do still more harm—much more, to get even with you for wringing his neck. Still, you can't afford to stand a man with a cudgel by each molehill. Where would you find so many helpers, with such work to be finished: trips to the mill, welding your ploughshares, and hurrying to plough, again and again and again?

—So here I am, walking along the boundary ridge of Verstakis' barley field. Though a couple of days ago I didn't think much of his plants, they did find a good rooting—I was wrong when I thought they'd hardly crowd their beards up out of the mustard weeds. Even my own barley can't be compared to Verstakis'—mine has managed to push down the mustard and couch weeds, but they've obviously been athirst for rain since St. Peter's day, their ears caved in like people with asthma, their beards spread out helter-skelter like Tartilas' whiskers, our bailiff of blessed memory, as he lay in state after his calamitous ailment.

—And I walk on down the ridge, thinking all this to myself, and behold! A flock of sparrows flies up from my feet, and in a while they settle at the edge of Darymas' meadow, all around the stone with the lightning-cleft hollow that holds water for two days after a downpour and gives drink to the ravens. And suddenly my hat bobs up on my head, it could easily have come down, because, God, how can anyone control matters in such an emergency?

—Here, Mykola, I tell myself, you labor and sow, you even try to pull the rain-cloud down with your own hands, and already the sparrows flock to your barley field with its unripe grains melting on the tip of your tongue, if you wanted to taste them!

—By gush of a spring! What brings such disorder into the world? If somebody's horse strays into your oat-field you lead it home and lock it in your stable to hold for ransom; or let a piebald pig get into your potato patch—you just

smack it with a stick. At its first squeal, who should come
running but Čečergis' wife with tears in her eyes!

—And I ask myself, all alone, who could be held responsible for the sparrows, if you injured one? It has no master
to come running, that's sure, swearing with tears in his
eyes never to let it happen again.

—A sparrow must live, too, that's clear, if God has
breathed life into it and given it a crop. My faith, who minds
a grain or two? But when it scatters more than it eats, that
*is* something to make you sad.

—Before, I was about to throw a stone to the meadow's
edge, but I was right to hold back. Because, you know, by
the time you pick up a rock and move it into full swing,
ready to throw, the sparrows are too far away and your target's lost. And anyway, they'd already flown into the tanner's
wheatpatch.

—Well! I say to myself, I'll just sit down on the black
boundary stone with the reminder of the plague years carved
on its north side. It's a fact, I wanted to relax a little before
I went into the fallow field near the gates. Because as I
jumped over the ditch I felt a little "crack" in the hollows
of my knees, and a pain went through me when I coughed.
And that's no joke, you with your shoulders carrying the
weight of eighty years!

—While I roll a cigarette with the tobacco from last
year's crop, my eyes fall on Meldaikis' pea-patch. The peapod
wonders if it should add one more pea—maybe it has enough.
And while it was arguing with itself—click!—The sun finished the pod. —Enough! the sun said.

This is the way Mykola would talk when he was back
home, after his great journey to shift his horse in the pasture
just outside the fields. This trip usually took him the whole
morning. For, slowed by his asthma and the fitful pains in
his stomach, he had to stop often to rest on a stone or a
stump by the lake, taking some soda powder or smoking some
of his good yellow tobacco.

One year followed another, and his trips became less and less frequent. He was almost too weak even to chop the brushwood, and one day, as he was strolling in the orchard around the tobacco patch, he fell into the seedlings and had to be carried home, gasping for every breath.

—Now I'm like a perch tossed up onto the lake shore, my mouth agape for air. I'm afraid I won't breathe on into my nineties!

One spring, Mykola's condition improved. He planted some tobacco himself, pruned the apple-trees, and went to Bruzgakalnis Hill to cut a new supply of birch twigs for his *sauna* baths—he did enjoy using them, especially during the first three steams in the bath-house.

Just after Whitsuntide, when the fields were flowering in all their splendor and the primroses were in full blossom, Mykola felt safer in himself and walked out to Ožkašlaite, near Lake Gilys.

And that was his last walk. They found him lying near a large stone, his tobacco scattered all around him.

When his nephew closed Mykola's dead eyes, the image of Lake Gilys still seemed to shine in the pupils.

—Well! I'm walking along the edge of the Degimai Bog, and the peewits hop from one stump to another and greet me: How are you? . . . How? I'm in good health, but for how long? I wonder. I'm glad you remember me, you crested ones, back after your winter of troubles. Ah, it hasn't been easy for me, either, wearing out my thigh-bones over the stove. Welcome! Welcome back to these parts!

—The breeze, warm as a human breath, blows lightly around the bend of my knees. I'd even loosened the belt on my sheepskin jacket. Let it shake the winter staleness out of my seams!

—And then I straddled my way over the plank bridge, farther down into the narrow meadow, filled to the brim with marsh marigolds. The frogs were croaking in unison, the brook purled, singing away the marks of winter straight into Lake Gilys. As I turned from the meadow toward the crab-apple tree I had a good mind to roll a cigarette, and I said to myself, when I get to the top of the hillock I'll sit down on that veined stone from where you can see all Lake Gilys, as flat as your palm.

—But as soon as I'd gotten halfway up the rise, by gush of a stream! A kind of darkness falls over my cycs. Just a moment ago everything seemed to be sunlight, and bright green carpets were laid over the fields. Now, all at once, everything looks drab, as if it were covered with smoked glass. And then I feel a stitch somewhere under my heart. It takes my breath away. Ah, I think to myself, this time it has you for sure, Mykola!

—I crawl toward the stone, my blue veins bursting; I didn't have a chance to roll that cigarette, I drop my tobacco-box, and my fine-cut yellow tobacco from last year scatters all over.

—And I fell so softly onto the stone, and Lake Gilys glittered a short moment through the alders, and my ears were full of the sweet warblings of the Ožkašlaite nightingales. Oh, God! The lake's getting bigger, the riverbank blurs and then it's gone, and at last all begins to fall in on me. I grope for the stone, I can't reach it. End of the world, I'm falling, falling into a pit, and still I reach for the stone, the songs of the nightingales deepen into rich organ music, the peewits are still calling me back to Degimai Bog, and the wild ducks soar up from the bulrush thickets, enshrouding me with their black wings.

—And now, again, I see such radiance! The marsh marigolds glitter everywhere, my heart is light, light, a greater music plays in it, louder and louder.

Thus may Mykola have spoken to the saints in heaven, after his long journey back to the eternal home, where he was brought before he was allowed to see into his nineties.

# The Actress

## Stepas Zobarskas

MILDA WAS NOT a striking beauty of the type to make a man's heart dance at a mere touch of her hand, although her full, sensual lips made her appear extremely feminine. Her cheeks were hollow, her face was covered with freckles, and her shining oriental dark eyes gave the impression that she was constantly in a trance.

Milda had come to New York from Vilnius, Lithuanian capital, at the end of the World War II and had married a fellow countryman, who worked as a supervisor in a large bank.

She had studied literature and dramatics in her own country and in Germany, and had also played some minor roles in a Munich theatre.

Milda admitted to me more than once that her marriage was not a happy one. Her husband was a cool, stern and domineering man. He had divorced his first wife and had taken custody of their only child, a son. He and Milda had no children themselves—not because she didn't want any, but because he had decided that one child in the family was enough. His decision made Milda suffer a great deal.

"Some people think that I'm sterile," she remarked once, when the two of us happened to meet for lunch. "What's more, I don't feel like a wife without a child: I feel more like a mistress."

"But you have normal sexual relations, don't you?" I asked.

"Yes, but he's so careful!"

One Saturday afternoon Milda invited me to her home. She lived in a pleasant one-family brick house which was spacious and comfortable. She happened to be alone that day. Her husband had taken his son to visit some relatives in Pennsylvania.

"I didn't go with them because I'm expecting a very important telephone call," Milda explained.

After she had brought out the coffee and a couple of drinks for us, she sat down beside me on the sofa with a copy of Ibsen's *Hedda Gabler* in her lap and began to talk with great animation.

"People haven't understood the real spirit of this play," she said. "Just look at Hedda! She's a woman very close to my own heart. To play the leading role in this drama is my life-long ambition."

Milda's face flushed as she spoke. Her narrow eyes widened, and I could see the spark of genuine inspiration in their shining darkness. I couldn't help staring at her with awe. She was dressed in a black and white striped dress which was extremely becoming to her. I found it impossible to sit so close to her and remain a mere listener. She seemed to me to be growing more beautiful with every phrase she uttered, with each movement of her lips and each flutter of her eyelids.

I listened to her low, soft voice and I felt that our thoughts were beginning to flow like two parallel rivers. She saw herself as the leading lady in the play; I saw her as a lady in my arms.

When she stopped talking, I embraced her. Milda looked at me for a long time. Her lips were partly open. Then she gently removed my hand.

"I like you very much, Darius," she said. "But we are not in love. Let's remain the way we have always been— just good friends."

I made no reply. Milda started talking again, this time

about the theatre of the absurd in which she saw a transition to something more meaningful.

The telephone rang. Milda leaped to her feet and picked up the receiver. Her eyes warned me to remain silent, as she listened with growing interest. The color of her face deepened, her eyes widened, and her lips broke into a smile. At one point she covered the microphone with her palm and whispered: "This is the happiest moment of my life. I have been offered the lead in *Hedda Gabler* by the manager of the North American Repertory Theatre." Then she resumed listening, saying a few words now and then, or bursting into exclamation of enthusiasm.

I stood up, paced the floor for a while, then I came back and sat beside her again. Milda lay comfortably on the sofa with a pillow behind her back. She seemed so completely absorbed that I began to wonder whether she would notice if I leaned over her and kissed her lips. Milda did not respond. This was more than I could bear, and I walked out the door without even looking back at her.

I did not hear from Milda again until five or six months later, when I received an invitation to attend *the* play, which was being produced in a small off-Broadway theatre.

A seat had been reserved for me in the first row of the mezzanine. The actors were good, but Milda surpassed them all. Her portrait of Hedda was superb, and she was cheered repeatedly by the audience during curtain call. Bouquets of flowers were brought to the stage when the curtain came up again, and I noticed that Milda had picked up and was holding the one I had ordered.

When the performance was over, I met Milda backstage and invited her to a restaurant across the street for a drink, to celebrate her success.

"For a short while only," she said. "I can't stay away from the rest of the cast."

We sat in a secluded corner and drank champagne. Milda

looked exalted. She wanted to know my frank opinion, and I told her that she was far better than anyone I had seen so far. She talked about the company's future repertoire. One of the plays would be by Ionesco, and one by Eugene O'Neil was already in rehearsal.

"It looks like you're on your way to stardom," I said. "I wish you all the success in the world."

Suddenly Milda raised her head and I was surprised to see tears in her eyes.

"What's the matter, Milda? Aren't you happy?"

"He didn't come to see my performance," she said. "He ignored me completely."

"Who ignored you?"

"My husband."

"I'm glad he did," I said laughing. "We wouldn't be sitting here if he had come."

"All three of us would be sitting here. I would have introduced you."

She dried her tears and finished her drink. I did the same. What else could I do? Milda had to rush back to a cast party at the theatre. She thanked me for the flowers and gave me a peck on the cheek before she left.

After successful performances in New York, the North American Repertory Company toured Boston, Philadelphia, Chicago, Detroit, and Cleveland. They even put on several performances in Los Angeles, Toronto, and Montreal. And every time that Milda returned from one of the trips, she would call me and I would join her for a drink.

"My husband thinks I'm wasting my time," she said to me one day. "If he would come to see me only once, I know that he would change his mind. But he absolutely refuses to attend. He wants me to stay home. If I had a child, it would be a different story, but the way things are now, what is there for me at home?"

She gave me a searching look, as though she were trying to discover some solution to her problem in my eyes.

"Do you think I'm being foolish and only wasting my time, too?"

"Of course not!" I assured. "You're perfectly marvelous. But I must admit that if you were my wife, I'd like to keep you home, too."

"You mean you wouldn't let me act?"

"Oh, no. I would let you act, and I would send you huge bouquets of flowers after every performance. But at the end of the evening I would take you home and lock you up."

"I couldn't want anything better!" Milda exclaimed, laughing. She took my hand in hers and pressed it against her face. "I'm so glad that you are my friend. I'd cry if I ever lost you."

The repertory company shut down for the summer, and the actors scattered throughout New York and its suburbs. Milda went to the Catskills for a few weeks. She needed the peace, calm and the clean air of the mountains, she said. Although her husband agreed to her plan, he remained behind.

I did not hear from Milda for the rest of the season. She didn't write to me—not even a post card. But in the fall, she called me again, wanting to meet me in a small coffee shop near Columbia University where she was doing some research on a play.

She looked healthy and tan, although her eyes showed signs of fatigue. She talked about her vacation for a while, then she suddenly pressed her face against my shoulder and began to cry.

"I'm pregnant," she whispered through her tears. "And not by my husband."

I was slightly taken aback. My eyes turned automatically towards her stomach—but there was no sign of pregnancy yet.

"I've only found out it recently," she explained.

"Who's the father, then?"

"You couldn't believe it." She spoke slowly, as though

she were searching for the proper words. "It's all so crazy.
A man whom I hardly knew and whom I didn't love then
and certainly don't love now."

"What's his name?"

"Oh, that's not important. He was just a man who came
to spend a week-end in the Catskills."

"He must have been young and terribly handsome to
make you lose your head."

"He wasn't young and he wasn't handsome—just a plain,
ordinary middle-aged man. Although I must admit that he
was rather intelligent and pleasant to be with. And he
knew so much about the theatre."

"Where did you meet him?"

"At the resort hotel where I was staying. One evening
he invited me to go for a drive. We stopped at a small restaurant for a drink. We danced to juke box music. I wasn't
drunk at all. Then we went for a walk. . . ."

"And then he seduced you?"

"That's the strangest part of all—I practically seduced
him. I don't know what came over me. Maybe I wanted to
get even with my husband . . . or maybe my desire for mother-
hood was so strong that I couldn't control myself. Anyway,
whatever it was, here I am, crying over spilt milk."

"Does your husband know about it?"

"Heavens, no! You're the only one in the world who
knows."

"What else did you do up there?" I asked just to keep
the conversation going.

"I did practically nothing for the first three weeks except
rest and read scripts. After that, I took a waitress job in the
restaurant of the hotel in which I was staying."

"A waitress! What on earth for?"

"I ran out of money, and I didn't want to ask my husband for it or go back home."

For some reason, I suddenly felt myself getting very angry
with her.

"So you spent the summer taking rides into the mountains with your customers," I snapped, scarcely able to control my trembling voice.

"I've done nothing of the sort!" Milda retorted. Her face blushed scarlet. "That was the one and only time."

A moment of uneasy silence folowed her outburst. Then she raised her eyes and whispered: "Of all people to accuse me of immorality. Just because I took a job as a waitress doesn't mean that I automatically hopped into bed with any man who came along!"

I began to regret that I had been so abrupt with her.

"Instead of quarreling," I murmured, "we'd better think of something to do under the circumstances. Do you know a doctor who could. . . ."

Milda cut me short:

"I'm not going to have an abortion! I'm not going to kill my baby."

"Then why not tell your husband that the baby is his?"

Milda smiled ironically.

"He hasn't touched me since before I left, and he has been sleeping in his study since I've been back."

"In that case why not tell him the truth and see what his reaction is."

"I was considering it, but I wanted to talk it over with you first."

"If he makes your life impossible, I'll find a place for you to live. Just don't panic. You're not the first woman in the world to carry a baby that is not her husband's in her womb. And you won't be the last."

I must have sounded like an actor in some melodrama, because Milda threw her arms about my neck and squealed: "Oh my dearest, dearest friend! I knew I could count on you."

When I was alone again I began to think about Milda's predicament. What a hell of a situation to be in. She had told me once that her husband had very high moral standards. Would he be able to forgive his wife's indiscretion? And would he realize that, in a way, he was more to be blamed for it than she?

Every day after that I waited for Milda to call, but she never did, until finally I dialed her number myself.

Her voice sounded relaxed and cheerful.

"Forgive me for not having called you," she said, "but I've been so busy around the house these days."

"Did you tell your husband?"

"Yes, I told him," she answered after a moment of hesitation. "I had to. There was no choice."

"How did he take it?"

"You know, Darius, I never thought he would be such a good sport. At first, he didn't believe me, but after a while I managed to convince him that it was really true. He was annoyed, of course. He asked me who the baby's father was and whether I was in love with him. I said no, that he meant absolutely nothing to me. Then he asked me whether I wasn't afraid of child bearing. I replied that I was prepared to pay the price for having the baby. Then he asked me whether anyone else knew about it. Here I had to lie. I couldn't possibly admit that I revealed my secret to you. He paced the floor for a long time, then he turned to me (he looked so solemn and dignified!) and pronounced in a slow, deliberate tone of voice: 'Listen now, Milda. It will be *our* baby, yours and mine.' I was so moved that I wanted to shower him with kisses, but he walked straight back to his study and locked the door behind him."

"Does he still stay away from you?"

"No, no! He's changed quite a bit. The following morning, before he left to work, he brought me breakfast in bed. He's forbidden me to lift anything heavy. He has become so terribly solicitous!"

"So now, of course, you sleep together again?"

"Of course."

We seemed to be stuck for words after that.

"Sorry, Darius, but I must go now," Milda finally said. "The washing machine is full of clothes. One of these days when I'm not so busy I'll call you and we'll have a drink together. Bye now!"

And she hung up. I remained seated beside the telephone feeling somewhat disappointed at the news that Milda's husband had forgiven her so quickly. At the same time, I was relieved to know that I wouldn't have to worry about her, after all.

Milda did not keep her promise to call, and as time went by I forgot her almost completely. But after three years or so, she sent a note asking to meet me at the off-Broadway theatre where she had made her debut as Hedda Gabler. She enclosed a couple of complimentary tickets for her next play.

Milda was not alone this time. A man and a small boy were with her. She introduced me to her husband and son, and the four of us proceeded to the restaurant across the street from the theatre.

"Mr. Darius helped me to celebrate my first performance here," Milda explained.

"Some celebration!" I laughed. "The prima donna barely finished one drink and then ran off to join her friends, leaving me all alone."

"Sorry I missed that play," said her husband.

"You should be sorry, indeed. Your wife gave a fine performance. Her portrayal of Hedda Gabler was one of the most impressive I've ever seen—either here or abroad."

Milda blushed. She looked over at me and smiled gratefully.

"I won't miss this next play, that's for sure," remarked her husband.

He was tall, slim and handsome—self-reliant tennis player type with a clergyman's head. I could almost feel his brown eyes piercing uncomfortably through me, but when I looked up to parry his thrust, he looked down abruptly, picked up his glass and toasted the success of the future performance.

The little boy imitated him by raising his own glass of milk and smiled broadly. His features resembled Milda's. He was to all appearances a strong, healthy, slightly overfed and very likely badly spoiled child. After a while he grew restless, and Milda's husband took him out to look for a candy stand. We were left all alone.

"Well, it looks like the baby has changed a lot of things," I said.

"Oh yes! My husband simply adores him. And do you know something, the little rascal is beginning to look like him? Of course, he looks a lot more like me."

The following day Milda phoned me and said that she would like to see me again, that is, if I had the time.

"I always have the time for you," I said. "Come over whenever you wish."

"To your place?"

"Why not? Unless you'd rather meet me somewhere else."

"I was only thinking of how much time it would take to get there by car. You see, I have to be back by five o'clock if I'm to make supper."

"It's only ten o'clock now."

"I'll be there by noon."

"I'll be waiting for you."

She came late, a few minutes before one. The phone had rung just as she was locking the door. She had to answer the phone.

"Don't tell me it was the president of the North American Repertory Theatre?"

Milda laughed. "No. It was my husband."

She wore a minidress and a pair of light sandals. Her long hair fell over her shoulders in unrully strands.

"Today, you look like a fully-liberated woman," I teased.

"Does that mean I look sloppy?"

"You look fine, mamma! Just fine!"

I gave her a friendly kiss and led her inside.

"You know this is the first time I've been in a bachelor's apartment."

"Is there much difference between a bachelor's apartment and a married man's?"

Milda looked around rapidly.

"Well, I don't see any nylons or panties drying in the bathroom. Otherwise it looks the same."

"I'm glad we pass inspection," I replied. "Now what would you like to drink? Scotch, bourbon, whiskey?"

"Whatever you have on hand."

I brought out a bottle of scotch and some soda.

Milda removed her sandals and curled up on the sofa. I sat beside her. I could feel that she had come to tell me something important, but that she did not know how to begin.

"How did you like my men?" she asked.

"Both looked fine to me."

"You know, Darius, the whole atmosphere of the house changed for the better after the baby was born."

"It's too bad your husband didn't realize sooner how much you needed a child. Had he done so, he would now have a son of his own flesh and blood."

Milda's lips curled into an enigmatic smile at my words. She pulled back her hair, and began to fuss with her necklace.

"Darius, will you promise never to reveal what I'm about to tell you to anybody as long as you live?"

"What's this, more secrets?"

"Will you swear?"

"Look, if it's so very important, why let it out at all?"

"But I want to tell you. I have to. You must know about it."

"All right, tell me then. I'll keep the secret."

"I know that you don't think much of me because of that Catskill story."

"That's not true, Milda. What happened there is really none of my business."

"Oh, but I could see the look in your eyes when I told you—although you tried to conceal it. I believe at that moment you actually hated me. Don't deny it."

"Maybe I felt slightly irritated, but that's long since over and done with."

"In a way I was glad that you didn't take it lightly because it showed that you had some feelings for me."

"Whatever it was, forget it."

"Well, Darius, what I want to tell you now is that. . . ."

Milda hesitated and looked into my eyes for a moment before continuing.

"It was all lie, Darius. Nobody ever took me for a ride or for a walk or anything."

"Then how did you get pregnant? Who was responsible for that?"

"Nobody."

"Well now, Milda, babies don't grow on the trees."

"I only said I was pregnant because I wanted to have a child so badly. I lied to you because I wished to test your friendship; and then I told my husband the same lie. . . ."

Suddenly I began to comprehend.

"You lied to your husband because you wanted to set a trap for him, to put before him the accomplished fact, so to speak."

"Darius, darling! You should write plays! You understand the workings of a woman's mind so well!"

She flung her arms about my neck and gave me a tremendous kiss.

"Amazing, amazing," I murmured. "Don't you think you risked a great deal? Let's suppose your husband hadn't been so very noble and forgiving? What would you have done then?"

"My life was so empty without a child that I didn't care

what happened to me. Besides, you had promised to look after me, remember?"

She smiled again.

"But didn't your husband begin to suspect the truth when the baby took so long in coming?"

"No. There was no problem there. After the initial shock, he came back to me . . . even sooner than I had anticipated. And naturally he took no precautions whatsoever. I suppose he wanted to make the best of bad situation."

I chuckled at the vision thus evoked and proposed a toast to Milda's ingenuity. We emptied our glasses in one gulp. Then I placed my arm around her shoulders and said:

"Why not tell your husband the truth now? Why not make him really happy?"

"Oh no! No! If I told him the truth I might lose him again."

"But why?"

"Because knowing the truth would deprive him of the opportunity to exercise all this Christian charity and spirit of forgiveness he's been enjoying so much all these years."

"You're a terrific woman, Hedda Gabler!" I exclaimed, and doubled up with laughter on the sofa.

# NETHERLANDS

# The Stone Face

SIMON VESTDIJK

Translated from the Dutch by Roy Edwards

THE THIRD HOUSE, which came forward out of the
night and at the same time, as though with a gesture of
reserve, allowed the light of any torch to skim untouched
along its façade, was larger than either of the other two. A
hatlike roof rose in the livid darkness; some low outbuild-
ings stood at the side. The house lay fairly close to the road,
and when my eyes had become somewhat accustomed to the
scanty light I perceived that the entrance was in a side road
—or perhaps that road, into which mine must come out, was
the main road, for it was difficult to judge their relative
width.

For a while the problem of those two roads took the place
of that which should by rights have concerned me so much
more; but then, tearing myself with an effort out of the vain
reverie, I began to think hard about my situation. I must
have lost my way. If it came to that, my host had warned me
about this part of the road . . . how I wished I was back in
his villa in the dunes, with the two shaded lamps, under
which our red wine had sparkled! But he had warned me
about vigilant watchdogs, not about what I was going to
experience now. Experience: with a certain foretaste already
of mysteries, which seemed to come from the night wind and
couch on my tongue over which my own winy breath blew to
meet me. . . .

Let's say I recognized the region. Not as any identifiable

201

part of this dune area, where I might therefore have been before, but as something about which one's read long ago, or dreamt about, and of which one's always carried the vaguely outlined sketch around with one. Every landscape numbers some of those road systems which, like Gordian knots in a harmless-looking net, wait for years, for centuries even, for the traveller who is to get entangled in them. As often as not there stands in such districts an old mill whose sails are missing, looking like a guide who's given up and stands in the act of drawing in his arm dejectedly. Cats prowl around there. Those places ought to be indicated on the map by a special color, but no! . . . Since they must not look like each other—that would make it only too easy!—each of them, again, differs in other minor details, in the present case in possessing those big, isolated houses which, well-nigh feudal, have annexed whole chunks of their surroundings and registered them as dark and inaccessible demesnes, or as that deserted garden—one knows it's there, even though one doesn't see it—with the two broken plaster figures in it and many gusts of wind where of old the arbor used to stand. . . .

And I asked myself *why,* in the dark and in such equivocal places, the world has to be so different, so much deeper, more despairing, and with that certain dissimulation which constitutes the candor of night. . . . Let me go on dreaming for a bit, I thought, until I'm past this house, for it can't bode much good to me. . . . Two plaster figures, broken, but of the same workmanship? . . . Let's suppose so. Let's believe that the wind actually did go back into the garden and create from nothing a life which was lost again and yet is still there, even though one doesn't see it by day. . . Once more I tore myself out of musings which could be of no possible use— the prolix, free translation of four glasses of wine and wild conversations. . . .

Close in front of me the road seemed suddenly to break off short; the line where it ended glimmered there, widely separated paving stones gave place to a little wilderness of thistles and refuse. There the cats must be prowling, there the mill had stood, or the burnt-down farmhouse, or what have you. And perhaps the center was there too—the nodal point, the solitude of solitudes, where all threads came together; I had expected to get there, but still could not get there, even though I was there now . . . my thoughts ran into confusion afresh.

The torch, my Alexander's sword, would now have to find everything for me, and liberate me from this confusion. For a few moments, it distracted me: a circular patch, which became elliptical, stuck out an arm, took in the night in a wide embrace, and hesitating, hovering, almost throbbing with the throbbing of my pulse, returned, halfway, then disintegrated in a rain of livid light on leaves and pebbles, or groped along planks over which splinters, knots, and nailheads came running to meet it like mad. But then the house attracted my attention again, standing there so tall and isolated. Long, straight walls—the kind of walls to walk past after a nocturnal conversation that asks from us no anguish but only apathy. . . . I could not at first make out in what way the façade was ornamented or overgrown. But my light soon discovered the fantastic, caressing climbing plants which writhed their way upwards in arcs as though seeking a window or a hand—each branch, each leaf swiftly provided with a Chinese silhouette behind it, which moved a short distance away from it, crept back and then instantly grew sharper. I distinguished stone frames round the windows, in front of which shutters had been closed. I made my cone of light rise and fall several times more, meanwhile forming the resolution to walk on and look for the road in accordance with my friend's directions, when the light fastened on to something above me—and fastened me with it, as if I were directed by a power in or on the house, which had seized the torch. I looked more closely: *there*, a solemn stone head! I was amazed. I was even overcome by a certain hilarity—a series of fits of laughter somewhere in my body which, however, could not penetrate to my still fuddled wits. That doesn't alter the fact that I immediately felt linked with that stone head as with a companion in distress: he too had gone astray, one might assume; he too—

I suddenly saw the ivy as vine tendrils—must be intoxicated, lost, an outcast from life, even though it would not be easy to determine whether he was all those things by day, when walls, plants and stone ornaments lead an existence so totally different from the one they lead at night. No . . . little could be said about that. Did he, for instance, like living in the light, or was he a born solitary, a dweller in shadow? By day he remained almost invisible, behind that tangle of branches which sprouted from his skull in all directions like rather too luxuriant antlers. Thus he lived as in a cool cave. But now, at this hour in the night, my light caught him in the right place, unclosed his eyelids, dilated his nostrils and at last, when my hand had ceased to termble quite so much, showed his forehead, exalted high above the broad shadows of the eyebrows, which it bestrode like weary thoughts. The direction in which the eyes were looking was indeterminate, but their expression distinctly voiced satisfaction at having below them someone who wished to set in light the forgotten one of that house! A serene smile, a few little lines in the corners of the eyes; and I had already ceased to regret my night journey. Steadily I trained the torch on him, in order in this way to awaken new life in one who, through chill communion with leaf and stem, could no longer be used to anything but the color of green mould— who had enjoyed no accentuation of relief for years, and now tasted the light as though from behind vines. I had been drinking: *he* had to drink too; I gave him plenty. The twigs thrashed to and fro in the wind, but I would not be driven away, no matter how much they whipped and waved. I had found a confidant. Who was he? Had this house more of such heads? But no—that I refused to believe; how could it be so, anyway, now that I had found him and wanted to

stay with him till morning, and go away before all loneliness
and privation had been shone out of his face! . . .

But my light cone slipped off, suddenly, through an in-
voluntary movement of my hand. Now I had to look for him!
High and low, left and right, of course he must still be there.
. . . *There,* I caught him full in the face, as with a snowball;
he laughed. That face looked young now, younger than it had
a few minutes before, and the ivy tendrils suited it better.
And even though my hand trembled unconscionably, I
wanted to keep on as long as possible, for it really seemed
as if he changed under the light, became more and more
youthful under my hand, pristine and revivified as an antique god. Was I creating him myself, out of nothing? Was it
possible to make statues of marble or stone assume any age
by shining any light on them? But anyway, I was the creator,
he owed everything to me—everything, to the very vines
which, red-translucent, grew up contrastingly out of the
green, under the magic power of my circle of light. And,
although the night wind grew colder, making me shiver and
button my clothes up more, over and over again I lost myself
in contemplating the stone face, which glowed with inviolable youth.

Inviolable? Arrived at a climax which seemed not easy
to surpass, he nevertheless appeared to be rebelling against
something, to be trying to overcome something, in doing
which my torch would have to help him. Carefully I directed
the beam in such a way that as few branches as possible cast
shadows; but there was always one which would not be put
aside—a thick, hairy one. I could distinguish it clearly from
below. Then, when I lowered the torch a little, he suddenly
looked like a drowned man, ashen and bloated, among seaweed and polyps; but how quickly that image was banished!
My stone face lived and re-lived, over and over again, feverishly and unquenchably; he drank my light, he shone out in
all directions, though I could never rout that high shadow
out of his eyebrows and send it in retreat over his forehead,

because I was standing too far below. So I walked back in order to try from a greater distance. In the twinkling of an eye he had disappeared. It's not surprising that he's rarely to be seen by day, I thought; what wouldn't he give, always to have such a life as he's having now! From time to time it seemed again as if a smile was playing round his lips, but now it remained a smile of youth, matter-of-course and effortless. Youth hasn't acquired enough wrinkles to be able really to smile; it was the natural smile of sleep and innocence, which I had conjured up there with a single turn of the hand.

But the night wore on, and with that an insidious change came into his face—a change which had already announced itself before for odd moments, when the shadows played over his features. Wrinkles returned, crystallized, first hid themselves in the corners of mouth and eyes, then shot across cheeks and forehead. Painful furrows clashed with each other; they cancelled each other out for a spell, but then everything slid irresistibly towards old age. How was I to preserve him from it? I kept my hand as steady as possible; no condensed moisture dulled the glass of the torch; no chill mist drove past. For a moment he gazed at me as if reproachfully, before subsiding still deeper in his own dissolution, corroded by a fatal decay which I so desperately wanted to arrest, for I felt that now everything was at stake, that within a few minutes he would be past saving. . . . All about me was complete solitude, no dog barked, there was no light anywhere, the house seemed unoccupied. Every chance was in my favor, if only my will remained equal to the task! I continued to hope—nay, I believed, I insisted, that the process of rejuvenation would begin again. But it was not only age from which he was suffering now; it was also pain, sorrow, despair, fear of death. . . . That night I saw every possible expression of human woe glide across stone, faint but unmistakable and not susceptible of any explanation other than the painful emotions they evoked in myself.

Then, again, it was as if he was on the point of coming

down to whisper his secret to me, a secret which would rob me of all peace of mind forever; he begged, he prayed, his cheeks fell in, stubble sprouted swiftly on them, growing grey under the light; if he had had a body he would have knelt, or writhed in pain, but his body wasn't there, after all, his body was the house, the ground on which the house was built, the fields round it, the night . . . and how ancient and far-off and elusive is the night! . . . And then I suddenly realized that *he* must be the one condemned to unrest who ruled this landscape and who had lured me thither to assert his wretchedness! I was seized by a feeling of impotence. I wanted to go, but could not. Scraps, fragments of my first thoughts, flashed across my mind, and behind them a new thought loomed up, not yet to be put into words—a thought for which I was not yet ready because all my attention was occupied. . . . My arm grew stiff; with muscles that were already losing their strength, I trained the light on the same spot. And his eyes just stared, stared—and sucked me slowly towards them. . . .

At that moment I heard the crunching of gravel: footsteps! Instinctively I dropped the beam of my torch. I expected a cry, as if I had wounded him or torn a bandage from his face. But the first change initiated by those sounds took place in myself. It was the rudimentary thought of just now which came to the fore, as though round a corner of my consciousness, in its full shape and accompanied by all the symptoms of sobering-up after my slight intoxication. In three seconds I knew everything again, in three seconds I had fallen back thirteen years, back through the night, through time. Hurriedly the thought suffered itself to be examined from all sides, like a beggar who shows his wounds, who becomes one with the giver of alms, cleaves to him, and would like nothing better than to pass on to him all the diseases ravaging his carcass in order to be sure of getting the compassion he asks for. . . . Sickness, death, a deathbed? . . . Yes, I had watched beside him, my father, for a whole night, struggling against sleep and ennui. A long night of emptiness, and one in which no thoughts of any importance could have touched my mind. Towards morning he called me to him, with his feeble voice, and then I saw that he had become young again, like the stone image just now, unwrinkled and carefree before he died, as if he wanted to recover a long-past fragment of his youth and in doing so was not content merely with thinking and dreaming, but had also adapted his outward appearance accordingly. Even then he had almost lost the power of speech, and half an hour later it was all over. But who can tell what childlike game occupied him a few minutes before his death—in what childlike difficulties he was still entangled? Who knows how much labor it cost him to go back so far in his life, which had already almost ceased to be life? How strange and inexplicable, this return into oneself, this completion of the circle, in which life, by throwing youth out like an extreme loop round the farthest point of old age and drawing it tight, ties itself in a knot which can never be untied. . . . And I? To think that I saw it and didn't understand! To think that it was my father and yet someone else—an ordinary, untragic deathbed without grand gestures, which I had thought about very little in those thirteen years—and that I understood it only now that it was too late, even after this warning, this notification—too late for the one who had stirred that memory awake again . . .!

Sounds . . . outside me again now!

A door was opened, words were spoken: a woman's voice. At the same time blinding light blazed up, evoking an unreally hard garden, such as I could not have expected to find there. Close-cropped yew hedges cut through the night in horribly straight lines, their leaves like little chisels crowded viciously and densely together; each small gravel pebble seemed to glitter separately, without joining up with the one next to it. Before me lay the beginning of an entrance drive for machines, white, smooth and soul-less. When I moved a little to the left, I saw the electric lamp above the door, which was standing half open; on the top step lay an iron scraper mat. The figure of a man was moving down the drive in my direction, youthful and slender but almost staggering as he walked. Behind, at a slower pace, came a woman, much older than he, with grey hair through which the light shone silver, who now called for the second time a name I could not catch. . . . But the young man had already reached me, and seized me tightly by the arm:

"He's dead, and you could have saved him! If you'd only come sooner! He's dead, he's dead. . . ."

His voice was hoarse and trembling. I looked him straight in the face, which still caught some reflected light—a distorted, confused face, pale as death, with eyes like abysses; and everything framed in long, black hair. With his unformed features, from which the nose, isolated and helpless, seemed to detach itself, he looked like a boy not yet out of his teens. And now the old woman was with us; my presence had not penetrated to her, evidently:

"Come now, come home, you musn't. . . . That's the last thing, you're not that far yet, you can't go back yet. . . ." Half peremptorily, half soothingly, she put her arm round his shoulders. But again he turned to me:

"You could have saved him, you're too late, why didn't you carry on longer, why . . . ?"

Hungering, full of reproach, his eyes looked at me, his hands clasped as if to pray to me or simply to give me strength, even though it did seem too late for anything. . . .

What could I answer? I felt there was nothing out of the ordinary in what he said. I *was* too late, I knew. Once again I thought of the stone face; the transition had taken place too rapidly for me to be able to banish him from my thoughts already. And in a flash the young man's question echoed on in my mind in another form: why had I not continued to shine my torch on him longer, why had I let my attention be diverted? And—especially since the memory of that death bed of thirteen years before loomed up again, more ominously than a short while ago—I felt only too keenly the extent of my failure, now, and earlier as well. For I realized for the first time why my father had become young again during his death agony. It had been in order to spare *me,* in order not to load on my shoulders the burden which everyone has to carry who feels guilty and tormented by remorse when he sees his father die, even if there has never really been anything to justify such feelings. Everything had taken place imperceptibly and soothingly through the alteration in my father's outward appearance, through the support given by that singularly rejuvenated face, although he was really older than one can ever become in this life. But across the gulf of time that other, real deathbed, of which he had not deemed me worthy, had gone along with me, suddenly to manifest itself poignantly to me now, as poignantly as a reproach, more poignantly than self-reproach, and nevertheless akin to self-reproach. For I could have checked it, just as I had done with the stone face! I could have made him live on, even if it had been for but five seconds longer; and, who knows, if I had done that, Death might have retreated in discouragement, scared off by that short-lived resistance. No . . . no, it had *not* been in order to spare me: it had been a chance which he had given me, and which I had not known how to use. It had not been for me that he had made himself young, but for his own sake—with my help, for which he had hoped! Who knows the fluctuations of the heart-beat, the vitality of dying brains? I should have spoken to him, not stood idle with my hand on my chin and thoughts of a tiresome funeral in my head. I should have responded to that strange rejuvenation, laughing, stimulating, and bringing to bear all our joint self-confidence. I should have drawn his attention to old portraits, to memories which are eternal, to a childhood which constantly returns, to the enormous vital force which transcends all that and death too. . . . The reality of that staring boy's face brought me to myself again. A question pushed itself to the fore, gained power over me. I had to utter it. I went a step closer to him, so that we stood looking into each other's eyes.

"Is it your father who's died?" I asked gently.

He backed away; no reply came from his lips.

Now he was leaning sideways, against the woman, who could have been nurse or mother, and who had held her arms outstretched as if to receive him. His face fascinated me like a mirror. What was the meaning of that strange smile? I no longer expected an answer. Behind them I saw the hard white garden recede far back into the distance, grow blurred, fade away. . . . It was as if the young man's face came very close to mine—still closer. . . . But how long did that last? . . . Years? . . . How dark it was now, as dark as if nothing had happened and nothing would ever happen. Could I still hear footsteps? The light had gone out all too suddenly, and the night wind had taken possession of me again so irresistibly with its whisperings that I was not able to make out whether the young man walked back along the gravel drive to the house or disappeared in another way. Blinded as I was by that swift transition from light to darkness, dazed by nameless emotions, it was only after some minutes that I felt in a condition to take a step forward, like a convalescent putting his feet to the ground for the first time. I did not look for the stone face. I knew I could not be able to make contact with him any more, nor he with me. I wandered round until morning in that inhospitable landscape, whose like is not to be found on any map. Poplar trees whispered at my side, interminable board fences fled distractedly away from me, bent round, seemed about to return to the same point; constellations of stars twinkled which I did not recognize. Never have I seen that house since, nor have I ever known what, of all that, can have been true—whether a father actually did die there that night.

# Hijo De Puta

Adriaan Morriën

Translated from the Dutch by James S. Holmes
and Hans van Marle

MY MOTHER was one of those prostitutes of the old sort: once a year she had a child whose father remained unknown. All the races of the earth fraternized in the bosom of our family. Even the children who were quite brown and showed all the traits of my mother's and my stepfather's race could lay claim to her parenthood alone with certainty, for my father's countrymen, too, crossed our threshold with dishonorable intentions. Only my big brother, a few years older than I, was in all probability my stepfather's. He had been born in the days when my mother's conjugal fidelity still held the upper hand over poverty. Soon after that she set to earning a bit of extra money, just as other women go out washing or let themselves be pent up in a shed to sort fruit or process tobacco leaves.

My mother liked the open air and the company of men. Every evening after she had finished her work in the household and had got the youngest children to sleep she would set out in her nicest frock, with a flower in her hair and a smile wreathing her mouth, and walk to the harbor where the ships lay at anchor and the foreign sailors came ashore, their bodies tense with desire. Not long after she had left, we would see her coming back with a man on her arm, her white frock standing out in the shadows of the evening, and talking and laughing as though she had known her friend for years. Sometimes when it was raining she would surprise us

—that is, my stepfather and the older children who were allowed to be up still—sitting inside the house because it was raining. Then, with the wave of an arm, but not unkindly, she would shoo us outside, while the sailor turned his head away as if shamed at such visible consequences of so rash a deed.

Sitting together on the bench under the tall trees, we could hear mother talking inside with the sailor while the two of them undressed. She could call him all sorts of endearing names, names that she repeated in the daytime to my father and us children. Her voice was flattering; through the fall of the rain her kisses had a sweet and peaceful sound. Then it grew still, as they lay down to make love. The windows were closed off with a kind of rolling curtains or shutters of bamboo slats that let the light shine through in thin strips. After my mother had finished her work and the man had gone away, she would pull the bamboo curtains up and lean laughing out of the window, her body naked to the waist, although that was hardly visible against the light of the kerosene lamp. That was the sign for us to come in again. She would show us the piece of money she had got, and we children would admire the effigy of a foreign king or queen on the silver of the coin.

While the piece of money was going from hand to hand, my mother would already be busy making her toilet. She was a beautiful woman, in the autumn of her youth, with a full, hard bosom, smooth, well-rounded shoulders, and a mouth that had become extraordinarily agile, no doubt the result of the business of love. Later when I thought of her I often compared her mouth to a hand. It gave the impression of being loose from her face, as if it was always slipping off her teeth. It would catch the words, as though to caress them before letting them loose. With a fresh flower in her hair, my mother would set off down the path once again, while we stayed behind in the odor of the sailor's tobacco and my mother's perfume.

Sometimes when business was good it would grow quite late. Then we would take refuge with each other in the house even when it wasn't raining, and often we'd have to be wakened to go sit on the bench outside again. For the one room in our house, or rather hut, didn't offer a great deal of space. And the delicacy of the client had to be taken into consideration.

Outside, we could feel the cool of the night passing over our sleepy heads. Beyond the rustle of the trees was the drone of the sea. I remember the night sky, with the stars above the treetops. I was amazed that one's gaze could reach so far. While sleep was making my consciousness small and hard, my senses sent long festoons through the tenuous space. My father would sit with two sleeping children on his lap, time after time working a hand free to take his cigaret out of his mouth. The other children leaned up against him, all contributing something of their warmth. Our breaths formed a thick clump of shrubbery together.

At last my father and mother would carry us inside the house and lay us down beside each other, careful not to disturb our sleep. Sometimes I woke up, and saw my parents having a bite to eat—rice or a piece of cold chicken. They wouldn't talk, but it was as though my mother's mouth was forming words even when she chewed. Afterwards they would lie down on the mat where my mother had lain with the sailors. Through a veil of sleep I could see their bodies moving, as though there was something of a shame that had to be erased. My mother would sigh, or laugh—a last deep-resounding laugh my father had a right to.

Now and then my mother would come home with some young lad, a white ship's boy with new leather shoes and a dagger in his waistband. I would feel just as nervous as he, and in my mind I would take just as big steps and make just as angular gestures. At other times I was never jealous, but now I would feel my heart pounding in envy. Though usually I hardly imagined what happened, in such cases I would think of the warm nakedness of my mother. The mother image would grow vague and detach itself from this woman for whom the desire to please had become a habit. I would watch her let down the bamboo curtains in front of the windows and hear her say: Is your mother at home this kind to you, too? Does she have such nice breasts? And though I had never seen it, I would know she was taking her breasts in her hand and pressing the nipples to the boy's mouth, one after the other, while she caressed his body with her free hand. His white body would yield itself to her brown one as to its negation. He would lose himself in her lap, far from his country and his white family. The butt of his cigaret lay beside the door, still smoking, with the affability of an offering. Otherwise I picked up butts that sailors threw away before they stooped over and went inside the house, but in this case I would circumvent it in abhorrence. Inside, it had grown silent, a silence that begged me to forget her.

After a while my mother's voice would sound again, and this time also the voice of the boy, who had earned his right to speak. He would come out of the house with a fresh cigaret in his mouth, his movements lighter, almost free of the stiffness that kept him from talking with us. His warm piece of money would already be going from hand to hand. He's fourteen years old, my mother would say. He has the love of a missionary priest, she'd laugh.

Sometimes she brought home some old man who would stop to look us over and offer my father a cigaret. It would last a long while. He needed a lot of time to undress, and it never grew completely still. I could hear him groaning, as if what he did distressed him. My mother consoled him with the cheeriness of her profession, which cannot go deeply into another's sorrow. If her body could not give happiness she had failed, and was brought face to face with her own despair. At such times everything would serve to cut her off from the caller: the smaller children sleeping in a corner of the room, her husband and the larger ones whose voices she could hear outside as she peered along the client's head toward the ceiling. She was good-natured, and had a great deal of patience with an impotent body twisting above hers and pouring its sweat out over her. She would forget herself, but the man could not forget, attempting to perform by sheer force of mind and will what he had earlier been able to do without thought or effort. Even in the decisive moments there was a gap between enjoyment and awareness. The old man would crown his labors with a long spell of coughing. His fulfillment was a mixture of relief and fatigue. He grew friendly, genial, ordinary. I would have a feeling of sympathy for him, as though we had robbed him. And I could never keep from gazing after such clients as they walked down the path beneath the dark trees, toward the city and the ships. The thing that mattered to them was to prove to themselves that they were still alive. But everything about them spoke of destruction: the heels of their shoes, the patches of sweat on their shirts, the brittle nails, and the skin that hung loosely over the bones of their faces. When I held their pieces of money in my hand, I felt the longing to engross myself in their unknown lives. Even though they took nothing of my mother's that I myself valued, they left a great emptiness behind in me.

My mother washed off the memory of them with the tip of a towel that she dipped in water and rubbed along her armpits, her thighs, and the entrance to her womb. She would stand with her legs spread apart, big, gleaming, with busy hands whose innocence had changed into mechanicalness. Her full, round breasts would dance up and down as though she wanted to shake them off her. Her smile ran in advance of her thoughts.

My mother was the real head of the family. She had cast off all vestiges of submissiveness, and in everything that happened her sacred work had to be taken into consideration. My father put up a show of resistance now and then, and sometimes he would take the lead in the most nonsensical

way. When my parents went into town with the larger children to buy things, he carried the money and did the talking.
On such occasions he would be extraordinarily loquacious,
while my mother would keep silent, basking in her aloofness.
She would gaze at the men in the streets with the candor of
a woman for whom love no longer holds any secrets, a woman
whom no amount of unfaithfulness could lead into temptation. She must have had the feeling that no man white or
brown could escape her, that for every man her hut was a
prerequisite to further living. In lovemaking she radiated
self-assurance, satiety, the gentle vanity lent by power and
prestige. In other things she was childlike, stupid, a woman
who could neither read nor write. My father's vaniety, though,
was not warranted by anything at all except a strong body
and an outward handsomeness that did not become him.

One day my father brought an old sewing machine home
from the market. My mother didn't know how to operate it,
but it was set on a chest to remain there as a symbol of progress. Sometimes, visitors would give the wheel a surprised
turn before they undressed. And my mother would laugh,
more flattered than when a sailor took her buttocks in his
hard hands or pressed his thirsty tongue into her mouth.

The sewing machine was never repaired, but it was oiled
and polished from time to time. The clothes we needed my
parents bought in town, where they were gypped by the
white and yellow dealers. They didn't defend themselves,
because to them money no longer meant subjection. They
had set themselves free, free of the grim sheds where women
sat sorting fruit or processing tobacco leaves, free of the hot
wharves where men worked as coolies.

The last months of my mother's pregnancies were always
the most difficult; out of sheer necessity she would go with
her heavy belly and report to the overseer for work in one
of his packing houses, and my father, too, would be absent
for days at a stretch. In the evenings only a few visitors willing to be careful enough to respect the pregnancy of a whore

came home with my mother. Often she satisfied them in another way than the customary, but the pieces of money did not get any the bigger for it. Usually they were only coppers. The birth of the child would reunite and strengthen the whole family. And as soon as it got dark my mother would gaily go to the harbor to entice the men with her breasts full of milk.—He suckles like a child, she would laugh when the sailor had left.

Later, after everything was over, I understood that it could never have gone on that way. One day the foreign police appeared at our hut—heavily perspiring men in white uniforms, with sun helmets on their heads. They forbade my mother to leave the vicinity of our house. A few days later she and my father were taken to the hospital with two of the younger children who were the worst off. I myself, my elder brother, and the other younger brothers and sisters went to a mission home where our sores were cleaned and dressed. I was terrified of the needle the doctor used to prick me in the arm.

We never saw my father and my mother again. They died soon after they were taken into the hospital. They were buried in the graveyard for non-whites outside the city, where space had been cleared in the woods, a peaceful place as long at the monkeys were not screechng. We were allowed to go along to the burial, early in the morning while it was still cool. We had been dressed in white clothes, under which I could feel the scar of my nakedness. We began to sweat, just like the white people, but without the justification they derive from the memory of their cool motherland.

We had been told that there was a heaven, with angels, where all the people went who had lived good lives. The brown and black people would become white there, and night would never fall. I remember my curiosity about that heaven where all the races would be reconciled, just as once in my mother's lap. The everlasting light seemed to me a shortcoming. I thought of our fine evenings outside the hut, the moonglow dripping through the trees, the stars that made my gaze reach infinitely far, my mother's laughter behind the bamboo curtains while the light fell outside in thin strips so that we never felt lonely. I have never liked white bodies, although I was called into the bedrooms of white women even when I was very young. I couldn't forget my mother's nakedness, which I was afterwards required to consider a sin. I never learned to believe it. I would see her brown breasts dancing, her body twisting in a careless voluptuousness that was her undoing. The sight of a shiny, well-oiled sewing machine still sends a quiver through me.

When I grew up and was turned free, I went down to the harbor. I saw the sailors coming from the ships as if nothing had changed in all those years: coughing old men and boys with new leather shoes, a dagger in their belts, a cigaret between their lips. I could smell the Virginia tobacco. I hated those men, not because they were white, but because they went to the women standing and waiting for them at the end of the wharf, young women with flowers in their hair and smiles wreathing their mouths.

# The Decline and Fall of the Boslowits Family

GERARD KORNELIS VAN HET REVE

Translated from the Dutch by James S. Holmes
and Hans van Marle

M Y FIRST CONTACT with the Boslowits family was at
a children's Christmas party at some friends'. There
were paper napkins on the table, with gay little red-and-
green figures printed on them. In front of each plate burnt
a candle in a socket carved from a half potato turned cut-
edge down and covered neatly with dull green paper. The
flowerpot holding the Christmas tree was covered the same
way.

Near me, holding a slice of bread over the flame of his
candle, sat Hansie Boslowits. "I'm making toast," he said.
There was also a boy with a violin; while he was playing I
almost had to cry, and I thought for a moment of giving him
a kiss. I was seven years old then.

Hansie, who was two years older, began wiggling the
branches of the Christmas tree with seeming nonchalance,
until a branch above a candleflame began to sputter and emit
a sharp scorching smell. People shouted, mothers came scurrying, and everyone near the tree was forced to sit down
at the table or go to the other room, where a few children
were playing dominoes on the floor.

The two Willink boys were there, too. They were the
sons of a learned couple who let them go about with close-
cropped heads because they were of the opinion that man's
appearance is not the essential thing; this way it was easy

to keep the boys' hair clean, and no valuable time had to be spent combing it. The cutting was done monthly by their mother with the family clippers—an important financial saving.

It was fine having the Willink boys around, because they would dare to do anything. Sometimes on Sundays they came with their parents to visit us. Then I would go out with them to wander around the neighborhood and follow their example by throwing stones, rotten potatoes, or pieces of horse-dung through every open window. A wonderful fever of friendship would liberate me from all my fears.

At the Christmas party they amused themselves by holding a burning candle at an angle over someone's hand or arm until the hot tallow dripped on the victim's skin and he jumped up with a scream.

Hans Boslowits' mother saw it and said, "I don't think that's nice of you at all." But his father smiled: he admired the ingeniousness of it, and he didn't have to be afraid that anyone would try to joke on him, since he was an invalid, his whole lower body crippled by disease. After that evening I was to call them Aunt Jaanne and Uncle Hans.

I was very anxious to watch Uncle Hans leave, because I had seen him carried in by two other guests and the spectacle had fascinated me. But at half past eight, already, I had to go home with my parents.

Four days later, it was still Christmas vacation, I went with my mother on a visit to the Boslowits family. The street had a long, narrow stretch of grass down the middle, and we had to walk round to it. "Well, big boy Simon," Uncle Hans said, "Hansie is in his room. Go play with him."

When I entered the room Hans asked, "What do you want?"

"To play with you, that's what your father said," I answered, taken aback.

He had on a pair of knickers and a green sweater, he was wearing glasses, and his black hair was plastered down and parted sharply. I looked around the room and caught sight of a small statue on the shelf above the convertible bed; on touching and smelling it, I found it to be a little dog made of soap.

"I made that," he said.

"Oh?" I asked. "At school?"

"By myself," he claimed, "at home, out of soap from the store." But I had already stopped believing him, because he had been confused for a moment by my question.

On his desk was an object that he kept looking at and picking up in a way designed to arouse my utmost curiosity. It was a metal box in the shape of a writing tablet, two fingers thick and a bit slanting, with a push button at the top. The cover was surrounded by a frame with a transparent celluloid window in it. You could write words on the plate. Not only with a pencil, but with a stylus that wouldn't write otherwise, or with a stick; the words appeared in purple beneath the little window. If you pushed the little button everything that had been written disappeared. The possibility that such a thing could exist had never entered my mind.

I myself was given the opportunity to write on it and make what had been written go away with a push on the button. Sometimes, though, the apparatus refused to work, and the text remained wholly or partially visible.

"I'm going to throw it away," said Hans. "It's broken."

"It's a nice thing you can write on and it goes away when you push on it," I said to Aunt Jaanne, who came in just then. "Hans say's he's going to throw it away."

"Now he's being bad again," Aunt Jaanne said. "He's going to throw it away because he doesn't want to give it away." All afternoon I kept hoping to possess the apparatus, but I didn't dare make any reference to it.

In the living room, too, were interesting objects. For example there was an armchair that was six feet long, covered with leather and resting on one round metal foot. Because of its easy-to-damage construction I was only allowed to lower myself into it sideways; then I could use my right arm to turn a wheel underneath, whose position determined the angle of the seat.

On the mantelpiece stood two old delft tiles, one depicting a fisherman, the other a skater. Potted plants in little antique copper pails lined the windowsill—there was a small indoor palm, and any number of cactus plants, including a ball-shaped one covered with rope-like growths that Aunt Jaanne called "the plant with grey hair."

We sat down to lunch, and we had knives with yellow ivory handles. The blades bore an elegantly engraved trademark with the letters H.B.L. "What do these letters stand for?" I asked, but my mother, Aunt Jaanne, and Uncle Hans were so engrossed in conversation that only Hansie heard the question.

"The H is for Hans," he said loudly, "and the B is for Boslowits."

"And the last letter?" I asked, waiting.

"But the L," he went on, "yes, the L!" He ticked on the knifeblade with his fork. "What that is for is known only to my father, me, and a few other people." I didn't want to bear the responsibility of asking something that there were weighty reasons for keeping secret, so I held my tongue.

After the meal there was something new: a woman came with Hans' brother Otto. I had already been instructed about him by my mother: "The boy is a little backward, so if you dare tease him . . ." she had said.

"Here we are again!" the woman called out, and turned the boy loose like a dog given the liberty to jump up on his master for a moment. He stooped forward when he walked, and he was wearing extraordinarily high shoes with toes that pointed in towards each other. He had on knickers, like his brother, and he was perspiring so heavily that strands of his colorless hair were plastered to his forehead. His face was strangely wrinkled, and his eyes didn't match.

"Well, are you here again, my little fellow?" his father said.

"Yeah," he called, "yeah, yeah father mother!" He kissed them both, and Hans. Then, standing still, he suddenly jumped into the air so hard that everything rumbled.

The violence frightened me, but he appeared to be harmless, as my mother had already told me.

"Go shake hands with Aunt Jettie," he was ordered, and after the words had been repeated for him several times he succeeded in bringing out "Aunt Jettie" and "Hello Aunt," until they finally got him to say the combination, "Hello Aunt Jettie."

"And this is Simon," said Aunt Jaanne.

"Hello, Otto," I said, and shook his sopping-wet hand.

He jumped into the air again and got a piece of candy, a bonbon Aunt Jaanne stuffed into his mouth. Every time anyone asked him something—in the usual way, without expecting an answer—he would shout "Yeah yeah," "Yeah mother," driving the words out forcibly. Someone put a portable phonograph on the table, and the woman who had come with Otto wound it up.

"He stayed dry last night," she said.

"Oh, that's good, what a good boy, Otto; you stayed completely dry, didn't you?" his mother asked. "Isn't he a good boy, Annie?"

"Yes, he's been a good boy, haven't you, Otto?" the nurse answered.

"What do you say now?" his mother asked. "Yes, Nurse Annie."

"Yes Nurse Annie." After an endless struggle he got it out, all in one breath.

He was busy sorting out phonograph records from a box. He held each one up close to his face with both hands, as though he were smelling it. His nose was read and damp, with a small yellow pimple at the end of it.

"He smells which ones they are," explained Uncle Hans, helping to sort from where he sat in his chair.

"This one," he said, and handed one to Otto.

The boy took the record, inspected it, sighed, and leaned on the table with his elbow for a moment; unluckily he happened to lean on a record, and with a quick little sound it snapped into thirds. I shouted something, but Uncle Hans took the pieces and looked at the label, then said, "A very old one, Otto."

"Old one!" Otto forced out, and put the record that his father had indicated on the turntable.

It was not like the other records: it was brown and thin and looked as if it was manufactured of cardboard or paper. Only one side was playable. Hans put a rubber piece on the turntable rod, because the record bulged upward a bit. When it started to play, a flat voice said, "The Loriton Record, to which you are now listening, is suitable for recordings of every sort. It is light in weight and flexible, and it is three times as durable as the ordinary record."

Then the speaker introduced a dance orchestra. When it had finished playing the voice said, "The Loriton Record can only be played on one side, but if you will check with your watch you will see that it plays twice as long on one side as an ordinary record. And, ladies and gentlemen, the price is no more than half."

Otto was jumping up and down with impatience. His mother quickly chose another record, a small one with a pink label. Two voices sang a song about the three little children.

Outside the windows, a fine, drizzly rain was falling. I sneaked to Hans' room, where I looked at the little dog and felt and wrote on the writing apparatus until I was called to go home.

On the way I asked my mother, "How old is Otto?" "A bit older than you are, pet," she answered, "but remember you must never ask at Uncle Hans' how old Otto is." It seemed to me that the rain suddenly blew a bit harder against us.

I was lost in my thoughts, but I heard my mother add, "They're afraid that Otto won't be taken care of after they're gone." These two bits of information gave me food for days of thought.

Only with the second visit did it become clear to me from the conversation that Otto didn't live there, but at a children's home, and that the woman who brought him was a friend of Aunt Jaane's who was a nurse at the institution.

It was on a Sunday, and my father went along. When we came in Otto was being talked about in a reprimanding tone. Hans was standing in front of the window and Otto by the antique cabinet with glass doors; Uncle Hans was sitting in a chair beside the table.

"Yes," Aunt Jaanne said, going into the room ahead of us, "we were just talking about Otto."

"Yeah," Otto shouted, "yeah mother!"

"There was a bowl of grapes in the next room, in the office," said Uncle Hans—what he meant was his small study on the street side. "I wondered why he was coming in all the time. And each time he picked off a grape from the bowl, and now they're all gone."

Otto laughed and jumped into the air. His face was glistening with sweat. "Mother doesn't think it's funny at all," Aunt Jaanne said. "You've been very naughty, Otto."

"Otto naughty!" he yelled, his face twisted anxiously.

The phonograph was playing busily most of the time, and the talking grew still more noisy when the Fonteins appeared. I had never seen Mrs. Fontein before, but I had heard at home that whenever she came upon an acquaintance carrying a shopping bag she would hide behind a fence or in a doorway so she wouldn't have to say hello to someone who went out for her own groceries. I had also heard that whenever she was somewhere visiting in the evening she would leave for an hour to go back home and see whether her nine-

teen-year-old-son had gone to sleep. She was called Aunt
Ellie, but grown-ups made fun of her as "crazy Ellie."

Once my mother had gone to see her at home, and she
had talked to my mother in the hall, saying that the chirop-
odist was there; but she had stuffed a gigantic bonbon in my
mother's mouth, with the words, "Actually it's one for high
society, but I'll let you have it." At home my mother had
given only a feeble imitation of her nasal tonsilitis-sufferer's
voice, but now I heard the sound unadulterated.

Aunt Ellie's husband, my father, and Uncle Hans went
to the study, uncle Hans propelling himself forward in an
extraordinary way, first searching for support with his hands,
hunching over, and then letting his frail legs swing forward
with a jerk, one after the other.

I followed them through the hall and went into the room
behind Uncle Hans. "Was that crazy Ellie there?" I asked
Uncle Hans, pointing back in the direction of the living
room. Later I comprehended that this question, asked in her
husband's presence, must have embarrassed Uncle Hans extremely. He fumbled in his vest pocket till he found a quarter
and gave it to me, saying, "You go buy yourself an ice-cream
cone."

I went outside just as an ice-cream man was passing. I
put the quarter on the cart and said, "An ice-cream cone."

"A five-cent one?" he asked.

"That's all right," I said.

"Or a ten-cent one?"

"That's all right. An ice-cream cone," I said.

"For five or ten cents?" he asked then. There was no
definite decision reached, but he made a very large one, and
I was taking it from him just as my mother came outside.

"He's been naughty," she said to the man. "He's been
begging for it." I kept hold of the ice-cream cone. My mother
pulled me along with her. "He still has some change coming!" the ice-cream man called out, but we were already inside
and the door banged shut. The ice-cream cone didn't taste

good, and I was allowed to put it on a plate in the kitchen.

After that, visits were exchanged regularly. On my birthday my new aunt and uncle gave me a metal toy car that wound up, and I tried not to let them know that I was really too old for it.

Usually they spent New Year's Eve with us, and my father would carry Uncle Hans upstairs with the help of the taxi driver.

Uncle Hans's condition remained the same all those years, but I remember that one afternoon at our place Aunt Jaanne said there was a lameness that had begun in his right arm and came back regularly. It was the same year I started going to a junior high school very near the Boslowitses' apartment. The Sunday before the new school year began I went to see them. I was requested to stay for lunch.

Aunt Jaanne was telling her sister that she had put Hansie in a boarding school in Laren, because things couldn't go on the way they were. After the meal, while Uncle Hans was sitting in his study, she said, "When he has a quarrel with his father he puts his hand on the man's head. And that makes him so furious; it's horrible."

She went on to say that a neighbor woman she had talked with that morning over the garden fence had more or less reproached her for the decision, saying, "You already have one boy away from home, and now to send this son away too. . . ." "I've been lying on the sofa all morning crying," said Aunt Jaanne.

"She has her nerve to say that," her sister said. "What business is it of hers?"

I said, "Tomorrow school starts there." I pointed in the direction of the building around the corner. "Do you think I'll get homework the very first day?"

"Well, no, I don't think so," Aunt Jaanne said.

Now that Hans wasn't there I hunted through his room out of curiosity, but I didn't find anything of interest. The little dog was still there, but the writing apparatus had disappeared long since.

When Aunt Jaanne came in, I said, "I wanted to borrow a few books," and took up a position in front of the bookcase as though I were deep in reflection. "These." Without thinking, I pulled out two volumes of *Bully and Beanpole,* a children's story about a fat boy and a lean one, and *The Book of Jeremiah Called Michael.* "If Hansie doesn't mind," I said.

"If we don't mind," Aunt Jaanne said. "But you're in good with us."

"I'll bring them back before long," I said.

Three years before the war the Boslowits family moved to an apartment looking out on the river, a side-canal, and a lot that was being filled in for construction. There was a granite entryway with twenty steps to climb. From there I watched the large-scale aerial-defense exercises that were held one day, I think it was in autumn.

The Boslowitses had invited a large number of people to come and watch, and the younger generation climbed through a window at the head of the stairs above the top-floor neighbors' apartment, and onto the roof. Sitting beside the chimney, straddling the ridge, we watched the barrels of the anti-aircraft guns on the vacant sand lot spring back for a shot each time a formation of airplanes passed, a moment before we heard the sound. Fifty yards ahead of us machine-gunners were shooting from the roof of a large mansion set off from the other houses. The Willink boys were there with us, throwing pebbles they had brought along especially for the purpose. Sirens sounded the air-raid alarm and the sky grew overcast. Then new squadrons of airplanes passed over, flying through the cloudlets of the anti-aircraft explosions and discharging green, glowing balls that burned out before they reached the ground. The aerial-defense fire squad spouted water into the canal and the river to test its equipment. At the end of all the turmoil, an amphibian plane landed on the river and skimmed along the surface, then climbed again, over the big bridge connecting the southern and eastern parts of town. I was highly satisfied with the spectacle. Everyone was given tea with crisp, salty crackers.

Half a year later we moved to the center of town, no more than a ten-minute walk from the Boslowits family, on the opposite side of the river. Now we could exchange visits more frequently. Aunt Jaanne came regularly, and on the afternoons when Otto had no school—he was learning paper mat-weaving and bead-stringing somewhere—she would fetch him from the children's home and bring him along to our place for a bit of a change. Walking home from high school one Friday, I saw them approaching from the other direction, Otto hunched over more than ever, springing about like a dancing bear on a chain, so that his mother could hardly hold onto his hand. The eight-year-old neighbor girl from the second floor was jumping rope, and she had fastened one end of the cord to the iron fence around one of the narrow front yards, so she would only have to use one hand to swing the rope. When Otto's mother turned him loose so he could gallop full speed towards our house, the girl purposely stretched out her rope in his path. He stumbled but didn't fall. The girl let go of the rope and fled before Aunt Jaanne, who was so furious she could hardly make a sound.

She went upstairs in a passion, right behind Otto, and I followed them. Otto leaped into the hall with a rumble, looking forward to the few old picture postcards my mother gave him each time he came. "That anybody," said Aunt Jaanne, "that anybody could do such a thing—can you understand it? If I had been able to get my hands on her, I would have done I don't know what to her." She grew a bit calmer, but kept on blinking her eyes—a habit I noticed then for the first time.

"Let's go see if we have a postcard for you," my mother said.

"Yeah Aunt Jettie!" Otto forced out, dancing along with her to the cupboard. She dug out three of the cards from a cigar box. He sniffed at them and jumped in the air.

"Be careful, boy. There are people living downstairs," my mother said.

"Where's Otto going?" asked Aunt Jaanne.

"Yeah yeah mother!"

"Where are you going?"

"Yeah mother!"

"No, Otto, you know well enough. Where are you going?" When Otto had still not given a satisfactory answer, she said, "To Russia."

"To Russia yeah mother!" Otto shouted.

"You see, Jettie," said Aunt Jaanne, "a professor in Russia has completely cured a number of children by an operation. And ever since then, he's going to Russia." Another bit of news had to do with Uncle Hans's condition. He had collapsed and was in bed, and his right arm was paralyzed almost all the time. "And beside that there's his temper," she said. "That's something terrible."

As a more encouraging bit of information, she told us that a doctor who had treated Uncle Hans ten years before had come to visit and had said, "Man, I thought you'd died a long time ago."

That wasn't all the news. They were thinking of buying a new wheelchair for Uncle Hans so that when he had got a bit better he would be able to be outside in the air more and could go visiting here and there without it costing so much.

"But he doesn't want to," said Aunt Jaanne, "because he thinks he'll seem like an invalid then."

"But that's what he is," my mother said.

Uncle Hans did get his wheelchair, despite his opposition, but not until quite a while later. It was a three-wheeled one, propelled by levels that turned the front wheel and guided the vehicle at the same time. It had to be taken from a garage each time, and then Uncle Hans had to be carried down the high stone entryway. He hadn't had the wheelchair long before they rented a ground floor apartment. It was in the street behind ours. Though it was a dark, dank house, there were advantages to it, since the Block Committee agreed to having the wheelchair stand in the entry, and a friend who was a carpenter made a letter box in a window-pane in Uncle Hans' study so the postman could drop his letters practically on his desk. Going out in the wheelchair was an act of his own in appearance only, for someone had to push him—his thin hands, and especially the right one, had no strength at all.

One Sunday afternoon we—my parents and I—were coming back from a birthday party together with Otto, Aunt Jaanne, and Uncle Hans, and I was patiently pushing the wheelchair. We were crossing a bridge that sloped rather steeply. On the other side of the canal we had to turn left. On the downslope the wheelchair began to go faster; I held it back, but Uncle Hans ordered me to let loose. I obeyed. There was an intersection just beyond the bridge, and the presence of a traffic policeman made it impossible to turn left right away. Vehicles had to wait for the traffic signal, then cross over and line up on the right side of the street.

But Uncle Hans zoomed down the bridge and cut diagonally around the corner without waiting. "You can't do that," I called after him. Right behind the traffic policeman he veered left, but his velocity and the incline made the wheelchair topple over and hit the street with a bang. The policeman and some pedestrians came hurrying up and set the wheelchair upright, with Uncle Hans still in it. He hadn't been hurt at all, but he said nothing, and even after we got to the Boslowitses he sat at the table in silence, staring straight ahead.

Aunt Janne comforted Otto, because she thought he had seen the fall and was frightened by it. "It wasn't father that tipped over, but someone else, wasn't it, Otto; it was some other man, not father."

"Not father!" Otto shouted, and he leaned his elbow on a

teacup, which broke. It was a grey day with no rain falling, though a still sky constantly threatened it.

On my sixteenth birthday, that same spring, Hansie came along with Aunt Jaanne and Uncle Hans to visit. His mother had decided to have him come back home. "If there's going to be a war, I'd rather have him at home," she said. He was to be a salesman in an uncle's business.

"You say if there's going to be a war, as if there's nothing going on now," my father said. At that my interest in the conversation was aroused. It was true that England and France were at war with Germany, but to my dissatisfaction there had not been any military activities of importance to follow.

From time to time I went to the movies with Joost, the younger of the two Willink boys, and before the main feature there would be some insignificant news shots from the front, with camouflaged cannon standing ready or firing a shot every quarter of an hour. Once there was a favorable exception to this monotony in some shots of the grounded German battleship *Graf von Spee,* beautifully unraveled and shattered. "Horrors of the war, fine," Joost said in a comical tone as a shot from the air gave a last view of the wreckage.

"What I'd like best is short, violent street fighting here in town," I said. "From window to window, with hand grenades and white flags. But not for more than two days, because then it would be boring again."

One evening in May when I went to ask if we could borrow an electric toaster from the Boslowitses, I found Uncle Hans, Aunt Jaanne, and Hansie together in the twilight. There was a neighbor visiting them. They were so deep in conversation that they didn't notice it right away when I came in. "That means something," the neighbor said. "I say that has a significance. It means a lot more than we know." Confused, I stood waiting in the door to the sitting room for a little bit, till Aunt Jaanne caught sight of me.

"Oh, it's you," she said. "Have you heard that the furloughs are all canceled? This man's son has to be back this evening already, and be in the barracks tonight."

"No," I said, "is that so?"

"That's what they said over the radio," the neighbor said.

"Then there's something in the air anyway," I said, and I felt a deep emotion rising inside me. That same week, on Thursday night, almost everyone in the neighborhood appeared in the streets a few hours after midnight. Airplanes pushed their shafts upwards between the thin tufts of clouds.

"They're getting something to put up with again over in England," said a milkman who had concluded that they were German planes on their way to English cities and being shot at over Dutch territory by our neutral military forces. He proved to be right about the nationality of the planes, but the rest of his hypothesis was refuted when we came to realize the meaning of the deep thuds and flashes of light on the southwest horizon.

A little after seven o'clock Aunt Jaanne came upstairs. I wasn't there at the time, because the Willink boys and their sister had come for me. I had gone along to their house, and from the balcony I could see black clouds of smoke hovering above a spot that couldn't be anything but Schipohl Airport.

"It's war," said the Willink girl, whose name was Lies. We went back to my house together, elated at so many thrilling events all at one time. It was a quarter to eight.

"It's war," said my mother. "It's been on the radio already." "What did they say exactly?" I asked. "Oh, I can't repeat it all, you should have listened yourself then," she answered.

Aunt Jaanne sat in the easy chair with a black velvet cap on her head, blinking her eyes. The radio was dead, and we sat waiting impatiently for the beginning of the regular broadcasting day at eight o'clock. It was the custom to introduce the day's broadcasts with a rooster's crow.

"I wonder if they'll do cock-a-doodle-doo the same as usual this morning," said my father, coming in from the hall.

I fervently hoped that the rumor flying through the neighborhood were all true. "Really at war, wonderful," I said to myself softly.

The radio clock began the soft noise it makes before it strikes. After the sixteen notes of the chime, it struck, slow and clear. Then the rooster crowed. "That's really a shame!" said my father.

I was frightened, because everything could still be spoilt. This was probably proof that war hadn't broken out at all. I was put at ease only when it was announced that the borders of Holland, Belgium and Luxembourg had been crossed by German troops.

I went to school that morning content, while Aunt Jaanne still sat staring straight ahead without saying a word.

At school a solemn mood prevailed. The building was to be used as a hospital, and the headmaster made an announcement of the fact in the auditorium. After that we all sang the national anthem. The fact that the school was closed for the time being made the day still lighter, as though all things had been made new.

We didn't see Aunt Jaannee again until the next Tuesday afternoon. She came to visit us alone, and she looked pale. "What are you doing?" she asked. "What a smell—is there something burning? Things look pretty bad."

"Pretty bad," my mother said. "They've just capitulated."

We had begun burning books and pamphlets in the stove, and it puffed and smoked from being stuffed overfull. At the same time my brother and my father were busy filling two burlap bags and a suitcase with books. After dark they threw them in the canal.

Everywhere in the neighborhood fires glowed that evening, with new loads of things to be burned being carried up constantly, sometimes chestful at a time. Many other people threw everything in the canals. Sometimes, in the general haste, this or that was left lying on the edge. Wandering along the canal in the twilight, I found a book with a flaming red cover—I have forgotten the title—that my mother later took out of my room and refused to give back.

After the announcement of the capitulation, Aunt Jaanne let it be repeated to her once more and then suddenly went away. The following day brought two interesting events. Towards noon the first Germans rode into the city. They were men on motorcycles, dressed in spotless green capes. A few people stood along the road to watch them coming over the bridge. Aunt Jaanne had seen them too, and when she came to see us Wednesday evening she called them "frogs."

I wasn't at home, because I was busy. Hundreds of fish had come swimming to the surface of the canals, gulping for air—it was said because salt water had been let into the canals by mistake. I was catching those in front of the house with a big fishnet; they made no attempt to escape, and I took home a pail full of them.

The next day school began again, and the very first evening I went seeking consolation at a small movie-house where that week, for the last time, there was still a French film. The movie, *Hotel du Nord,* was about a suicide pact in which the boy succeeded in shooting the girl, then lacked the courage to turn his gun on himself. But the girl recovered, and it all ended with a reconciliation between them and an acceptance of life when she came to meet him at the prison after he had served his sentence. I felt satisfied with the way the problem was solved.

At home I found Aunt Jaanne sitting on the sofa and my mother pouring coffee.

It was dusky in the room, because the lights hadn't been turned on yet. Unrolling the blackout paper and fastening it with thumbtacks was a cumbersome job. And so I found them sitting by the pensive light of the tea warmer.

"You have to blackout," I said. "That light shines outside."

"You do it then, will you?" said my mother.

I remember that one window was ajar when I let down

the roll of paper. "Hans sent a letter to an aunt in Berlin, quite a while ago," Aunt Jaanne said. "It just came back, undeliverable. Moved, destination unknown, it said on it."

Just then a gust of wind lifted the blackout paper and the curtain for a few seconds, chasing a piece of paper off the table. I shut the window quickly.

Late one afternoon when there was no school I dropped by the Boslowitses. It was high summer, and Uncle Hans was sitting in front of his office-window in the sun. Almost immediately he turned the conversation to his sickness and a doctor called Witvis, who had already been there several times and wanted to try something new to cure him. "He'll have to make me run like a rabbit," he said. "You'd like to have a cigaret, wouldn't you?" he asked, and got up to look for the box. "Tell me where they are and I'll get them," I said, but he shuffled to the corner of the room and took a flat, square copper box from a table. "Are you laughing?" he asked, his back turned towards me. "No, honest," I said.

Hans came in and sat down on his father's desk. "How's it going?" I asked. "That selling, do you like it?"

"Today my turnover was near a thousand guilders," he answered.

"Is there any news?" asked Aunt Jaanne.

"News that the Germans are advancing on Brest," I answered. "They're making a terrific hullabaloo on the radio." Then I told them what a fat boy in my class had claimed. According to a prediction made by a French priest forty years before, the Germans were to be defeated near Orléans.

"He also wrote that the city on the Meuse will be destroyed," I said.

Aunt Jaanne said, "If you'll bring me the book that says that, I'll give you something."

That same afternoon, not long before dinner, I went to the Willinks for a little while to tell them the latest news from the radio. Just after I sat down in Eric's room the anti-aircraft artillery began popping restlessly. Two airplanes glistened in the sunlight, flying so high it was impossible to make out their forms, but only a glittering reflection.

A bit later we heard the rattle of machine guns and the terrifying sound of a fighter plane zooming by close overhead. From time to time when the noise grew too strong, we would hurry inside from the balcony; we could also hear the rattling of the plane's guns.

Then it was still for a moment, and we saw a black swath through the sky with a flaming star dropping rapidly at the point of it. The light was white, like the light of an acetylene torch. Then we saw a second column of smoke beside the flame: the plane had broken in two.

After a moment it all disappeared behind the houses. There were no parachutes to be seen anywhere in the sky. "May God guard those who fare on the sea and in the sky," I said solemnly. No air-raid alarm had been given.

After dinner Hans Boslowits came to our house. "Do you know what kind of a plane it was that came down?" he asked.

"No, I don't know," I said.

"It was a German," he declared.

"How do you know?" I asked. "Have you already heard where it came down?"

"Look," Hans said, polishing his glasses with his handkerchief, "we have our sources of information."

"I hope it's so," I said, "but I don't believe anyone can know anything for sure yet."

"We have our sources of information," he said, and went away.

The next day, I'm certain it was a weekday, on my way home from the movies in the afternoon I saw the announcement of the French surrender being posted as a bulletin in front of a newspaper office. When I gave a résumé at home, my mother said, "Then they're asking for an armistice. That's not the same thing. Go to Aunt Jaanne's and tell her exactly what it said.

"It may be propaganda," Aunt Jaanne said, but I could

tell she didn't doubt the announcement for an instant. That same evening she came to our place, and it was then that she told us what had happened to her all of four weeks earlier.

One afternoon two Germans in uniform had come in an automobile. "Put your hands up," one of them had said on entering Uncle Hans's room. "Don't be witty, mister," he had answered in German, "I can't even stand on my legs."

They had searched the apartment and then declared that he had to go along. Uncle Hans had gone to get dressed; once they saw him dragging himself through the house his crippled state became so completely obvious that they must have realized the foolishness of making an arrest. Then they watched Aunt Jaanne fasten a rubber flask for urinating onto his waist. "They asked if I was the only one that could do that," she went on. "I said I was the only one. Then they wrote down some more and went away again. It wasn't very pleasant though." She blinked her eyes, and a few slight quivers shot through the muscles of her face.

"How is Uncle Hans, anyway?" my mother asked.

"He's not getting any worse," Aunt Jaanne said. "Just now he's able to use that hand to write with again."

"That's something," said my mother.

Summer and fall went drably by. It was after New Year's, dull, damp spring-like weather. The second Sunday in the new year the parents of my school pal Jim had asked me to dinner, and unexpectedly I ran into Hansie there. Jim's father was a wholesale dealer in veal and had an amazingly fat belly, but he took things lightly and was a lot of fun. Although he had had three stomach operations, he didn't allow it to restrict him in any way.

"I like everything, so long as there aren't any pins in it," he said at the table. As a gesture of friendliness they had also invited my parents, whom they didn't know.

"I don't read German books any more," said a small grey-haired man when the conversation was on literature for a moment. At once the talk turned to the war and surmises of how long it would last.

"Now I'd say half a year at the outside," said Jim's father. "But actually he's not going to hold out that long."

"The way it's going now, it could last twenty-five years," my father said, smiling.

Hansie, who proved to know one of Jim's brothers, had his guitar with him, and he played a renowned tune, *Skating on the Rainbow*, with a great deal of violence. When talk of the war came up, he said, "It's going to be over this year."

"What makes you think so, Hans?" asked my mother.

He answered, "The circles who keep me informed know very well, Aunt Jettie—I repeat, very well—what's going on."

Five or six weeks later Aunt Jaanne climbed the steps to our apartment, flushed with excitement. "The greenies are catching the boys all around Waterlooplein," she said. "Can Simon go look for me? No, he had better go to Hansie's office and tell him he can't go out on the streets. But wait, I'll call him up. Have Simon wait."

"First come and sit down," my mother said. It was a Wednesday afternoon. We succeeded in calming Aunt Jaanne, "Now go call up Hansie," my mother said.

"I already have," she said.

"Oh, have you?" my mother said.

"I'm going to go around there and have a look," I declared.

"You'll be careful, won't you?" said my mother.

I cycled quickly to the neighborhood around Waterloolein and brought back a detailed report on everything. Uncle Hans puffed slowly on his stubby black pipe. "You've got a nice sweater there," he said in the middle of my account. "Is it new?"

Aunt Jaanne was busy constantly telephoning the office where Hansie worked. He was to stay there at night; I heard her promise to take him bedding and food. At her request I took the telephone, "Don't believe that what you're going to say will be of the slightest importance, high and mighty Simon," said the voice on the other end.

"Is that so," I answered, smiling, because Aunt Jaanne was keeping a close eye on me.

"That woman sure jaws a lot," he went on. "Just tell her for me that she's a horrible old jawer."

The receiver had a very clear tone, so I drummed on the floor with my left foot. "Yes, that's right," I said loudly. "I can imagine that. Fine."

"What do you mean?" he asked.

"That's it exactly," I said, "that in any case you'll be careful—but you are, so I hear. Goodbye. See you." And I put down the receiver, even though Hans had suddenly begun to shout so loudly that the telephone emitted squeaking sounds.

"Well, what did he say?" asked Aunt Jaanne.

"He says," I replied, "that we are all nervous and say crazy things to each other. But you shouldn't be at all worried, he says. Of course he'll stay inside. He says in a day everything will be over."

"You can talk on the telephone again," said Aunt Jaanne, satisfied. Then she looked out of the window and said, "Don't be worried: it's a nice theory."

Four days later Aunt Jaanne came to see my mother, who was at some friends' somewhere and might be back any moment. While Jaanne sat waiting for her, the fat magician who lived around the corner also came up the stairs. On the steps he always whistled the melody that preceded broadcasts from London. "You shouldn't whistle like that on the stairs," I said. "You don't get anywhere by it, and it's dangerous."

After he had listened to what meager news there was, he said, "I think they're going to lose, only I don't know whether it'll be before I'm dead and buried or after." He shook with laughter and went away, whistling the melody loudly on the stairs. He had barely gone when my mother came home.

Only then did Aunt Jaanne say, "Parkman's daughter is

dead." She explained how the daughter and son-in-law of a neighbor across the street from her had swallowed poison together. The man had been revived in the hospital and was recovering. "He's screaming, and they have to hold him down," Aunt Jaanne said. Whom did she mean, I thought, the father or the husband?

June was very mild, a bright, sunny early-summer month. One afternoon while my mother was sitting in front of the open window knitting, Aunt Jaanne came in with Otto. She looked pale, and the skin of her face was cracked and chalky, though she didn't use powder. "Mother mother," Otto called impatiently.

"Be quiet a little, dear, that's a sweet boy," said Aunt Jaanne.

She had to tell about something that had happened to a nephew of hers. Cycling through the heart of town, he had violated a traffic regulation and was stopped by a man in black boots, partly uniformed, partly in civilian dress. The man had grinned as he wrote down the name.

One evening a few days afterwards, a nondescript man in dark-colored clothes came to the door. He said that the nephew had to appear at an office somewhere in the center of town the next afternoon because of a traffic violation—in order, so he said, to settle the affair.

The boy went, but his mother went along. At the entrance to the office she was held back, but her son was allowed to enter. After twenty minutes he came stumbling outside, vomiting. There were several welts and bleeding gashes on his face and dirt on his clothes as though they had been dragged across the floor.

For a high fee, the two of them took a cab with rubber tires and a pony to pull it. When they got home the doctor found a slight brain concussion and a contusion of the left shoulder blade, and the collar bone on the same side was broken.

They had let him wait in a little room. The man who

had stopped him on the street came in first, then he called in some others, part of them carrying billy clubs. "This is a sassy kid that called me bastard," he explained. One of the others struck the boy under the chin and then all six or seven of them began hitting and kicking him.

"It started all at once," he had told Aunt Jaanne. One man with greasy hair kept trying to kick him in the groin. He stumbled in his attempt to avoid the man's blows and ended up lying on his back. Before he could take up a safer position, one of the men stamped on his chest. After he had turned over, someone, he thought the grey-haired man, stood on his back.

Then a bell rang or a whistle blew, in any case there was a shrill sound that made everybody stop; after that he heard all kinds of voices, but he couldn't remember anything about what happened from then on until he came outside.

"You know that Joseph's people got notice of his death?" said Aunt Jaanne.

"No," my mother said, "I didn't know."

"But they had a letter from him from camp, too, with a lot later date," Aunt Jaanne went on, "but now they don't hear any more news."

They fell silent. Aunt Jaanne looked at Otto and said, "The doctor has given him some powders. He's stayed dry for two nights already, I heard from the nurse." My mother remembered that she had neglected to give Otto any picture postcards, and she hunted out two of them from the cupboard; one was in bright colors, a view of some foreign city with a pink sky.

When I went to see Hans Boslowits one evening several weeks later, he was busy playing his guitar. He would slap the strings with his open hand and beat up and down with his foot. At my request he played *O Joseph, Joseph,* but I wasn't pleased by the performance because he followed the melody by singing "ta ta ta ta" with too much emphasis, tilting his head up so that his throat was foolishly tensed.

"It's the heartbeat of our society, this music," he said. At that moment someone tapped on the panel of the living-room door. The visitor had already come in the hall; he called out his name loudly and Aunt Jaanne answered, "Yes, come on in, neighbor."

"Mrs. Boslowits," said the neighbor, entering, "I don't suppose you've heard yet that Dr. Witvis is dead?"

"How can that be?" Aunt Jaanne asked.

"I only heard it just now," he said. "It happened last night."

Late in the evening, he went on, the doctor had taken a razor and slashed both his two small sons' wrists, holding their forearms in a basin of warm water while he did it because that prevented pain. After his wife had opened the artery on her wrist herself, he cut his the same way. The order of events was deduced from the position of the victims and the presence of a second razor in his wife's hand. The mother and the children were already dead when they were found and the father was unconscious. He was given a blood transfusion in the hospital after the wound had been closed, but he died before noon without having regained consciousness.

When I went to the Boslowitses to borrow half a loaf of bread one Sunday afternoon late in the fall, I found Otto beside the phonograph.

"Otto is going on a trip," Aunt Jaanne said. "Isn't that right, Otto?"

"Yeah, mother," he called, "Otto on trip!"

"Where under the sun is he going to?" I asked.

Aunt Jaanne's face gave the impression of being inflamed by fever. "He can't stay at the children's home or the school any more," she answered. "He has to go to Apeldoorn. I'm taking him there tomorrow."

I saw only then that the sliding doors to the back room stood open, and Uncle Hans lay there in bed. The bedstead had white iron rods, with copper globes at the four corners.

The sick man's face was thin, but even so it looked swollen, as though it was moist inside.

On a chair were bottles of medicine, a breakfast plate with a knife, and a chessboard. "I was plying chess with Hans this afternoon," he said, "but Otto was always tipping it over."

He kept to his bed the following days as well, and his situation turned serious. Winter was coming, and the new doctor said that the rooms should be kept quite warm. For a long time Uncle Hans could still go to the bathroom by himself, but eventually he had to be helped.

"He's so awfully heavy I can't do it," Aunt Jaanne said. "Actually he doesn't cooperate."

After New Year's the doctor strongly recommended his being admitted to a hospital, and he was taken there early that same week.

"He has it really fine," Aunt Jaanne told my mother after a visit, "and the doctors and nurses are all so nice."

"He doesn't have any notion of things any more," she went on soon after that. "I don't understand what's going on inside him nowadays. Hansie took him some oranges—he could buy them from someone at the office. He says, father, these cost sixty cents apiece, be sure you eat them. But he didn't eat a single one; he gave them all away. Of course you should share things, but this is enough to make you furious."

"From tomorrow on we have to be inside at eight o'clock," Aunt Jaanne said to my mother one day late in the spring. "Will you go on the evening visiting hours? I can't get back in time and what good does it do Hans if I have to go away again after three minutes? I'll just stay a little longer in the daytime then; they won't mind that."

"He looks good, he's getting fat," my mother said after she had been to visit the first time, reporting to Aunt Jaanne at her place the same evening. But Aunt Jaanne was not much interested. Hansie wasn't home yet, and she asked my mother to go somewhere and call his office, because their telephone had just been taken away.

"Have Simon go to the office and see if he's still there." My mother was at the point of going to carry out her request when Hansie came in. The streets had been cordoned off, and they had been warned at the office. He waited till everything seemed quiet again, but half-way home he had had to take refuge in a public toilet. Finally eight o'clock had come and he had finished the last section, through our neighborhood, on the run.

"We aren't allowed to go out of the city any more," Aunt Jaanne said one night when I came to tell her that my mother couldn't visit Uncle Hans the next Friday evening. "Ask your mother if she'll go see Otto this week."

The next day, a Wednesday afternoon, Aunt Jaanne came to our home. "They're taking inventory," she said. After my mother had asked her to sit down and had poured her a cup of apple tea, she said that the inventory takers had been at all the neighbors' in her building—two men, each with a briefcase. They had inspected everything and noted it all down.

They had found the first-floor neighbors' five-year-old son playing with a little dark red toy purse on the stairs. One of the two men took it away from him, opened it, and fished out a nickel five-cent piece and three small silver pieces, then gave it back. "That one isn't a quarter," the child said, "it's something that there isn't any more, my father said."

"You just be very still, little boy," the man had said then. "Very still."

It was impossible to determine whether or not she heard the knock on her door; at any rate they had disappeared without visiting her apartment.

She asked me to go along with her right away, and she had me pack a Frisian clock, some antique pottery, two carved ivory candlesticks, and the two tiles into a suitcase and take them with me. I carried them to our house and made two more trips to get old china plates, a camera, and a small, delicate mirror.

Every other week, usually on a Tuesday, my mother went to visit Otto in the big institution at Apeldoorn. The first time, Aunt Jaanne sat at our place in the afternoon waiting for her to come back. "How was it?" she asked my mother. "He looks fine," my mother answered, "and he was awfully glad to see me. The nurses are all very kind to him."

"Didn't he ask about home?" asked Aunt Jaanne.

"No, not at all," my mother said, "and he was having fun playing with the other children. When I went away he looked sad for a moment, but that he misses anything really —no, you couldn't say that."

She gave Aunt Jaanne a detailed description of how she was received by the nurse in charge of the ward and how she had given the fruit and cookies and candy to be handed out. But one part, a bag of cherries, she had given to Otto himself when they went walking in the sun along the path in the woods.

"I kept feeding him a few at a time," she said. "But he wanted to take them out of the bag himself. I was always afraid he'd slobber juice on his clothes, but it wasn't so bad." Later, after Aunt Jaanne had gone, she told me that he was sloppily dressed, with his shorts held up by a rope instead of suspenders or a belt. "And his shoes," she said. "I don't see how they can fit onto his feet in such a crazy way. There's not enough staff, but the people do their best."

She also told me that Otto had said several times, "To mother."

"Mother is at home; she'll come some other time," she had answered.

"Mother home," he had yelled out then. He had cried when she went away late in the afternoon.

A week later Aunt Jaanne came to our house one evening just after supper. "They're starting to come after them," she said. "They're coming and getting them. No more summonses, they just come and get them. They came and got the Allegro family. Do you know them?"

"No, I don't know them," my mother said.

Aunt Jaanne wanted me to go to the hospital right away and ask for a paper certifying that Uncle Hans was seriously ill. I went, and at the main entrance I was directed to one of the wings, where I handed over my note at an office. After ten minutes I was presented a white sealed envelope and took it home to Aunt Jaanne.

The next evening she appeared for a second time. She asked me if I would go again. "It says in it that he's seriously ill; that should be mortally ill," she said. "I don't know if they'll put that in," I answered, "but we'll see."

After the head nurse had taken Aunt Jaanne's note and the first certificate, I waited a quarter of an hour and was given a new letter.

"Do you know what, Simon," Aunt Jaanne said two evenings later. "You'll have to go one more time and ask if they can make a whole new paper giving the nature of the illness in it. The nature of the illness. And not in Latin; if it has to be, in German, but at any rate so it's understandable."

She gave me back the last certificate, but without any accompanying note. I set off for the hospital again.

"Mrs. Boslowits asks if the nature of the illness can be given in it," I said. "And it's better if it's not in Latin." The head nurse took the envelope and came back a little later.

"Will you wait a bit?" she asked. After some time I received a sealed envelope and came back a little later.

I went at once to deliver it, and I found Aunt Jaanne and Hansie both sitting in front of the bay window. The room was almost completely dark. The draperies were open and the curtain pushed aside, so they could see the street from the window.

"Look, that's fine," Aunt Jaanne said when she read the paper.

"Did you think that would do any good?" Hans asked.

"Of course," I answered. "He knows, he knows," I said.
"What are you saying?" asked Aunt Jaanne.
"I was humming," I said.

Not only my mother but other friends of the Boslowits family who dropped by in the evenings spoke about the situation in gloomy wonderment. "It's just like a haunted house," my mother said.

I went there regularly in the evenings, and everything was always the same. I would ring the bell, the apartment door would be unlocked, and by the time I entered the hall, Aunt Jaanne would already be back inside. When I came into the living room, Aunt Jaanne would be sitting to the left in the bay window and Hansie to the right. Once I was inside Aunt Jaanne would leave her post again for a moment to scurry into the hall and lock the door. When I went away they would follow me and lock the door after me, and by the time I was in the street I could see them already sitting like statues in front of the window again. Then I would make a motion of waving, but they never reacted.

One Tuesday morning some neighbors of theirs came to tell us that about half past eight the night before two policemen with black helmets had come. Aunt Jaanne had shown them the certificate from the hospital, and one of them threw the beam of a flashlight on it. "Who are you?" he had asked Hansie. When he had identified himself, the other man said, "He's not on the list." "Both of you have to come with us," the first one had said then.

Uncle Hans said nothing when he heard the news. They thought he hadn't heard or hadn't really understood, and they repeated it emphatically several times. He tried to raise himself up, and after they had put a pillow behind his back he sat looking out of the window. Finally the visitors, a friend of Aunt Jaanne's and her daughter, went home again.

One day some time later a neighbor came to visit. "They are emptying the Invalide," she said. She had watched while hundreds of very old people were carried down the stairs and out of the building to vehicles standing ready for them. One ninety-two-year-old man whom she thought she had known once had called out, "They're waiting on me hand and foot." "The Apeldoorn Woods were emptied yesterday too," she said.

"What did you say about Otto?" I asked my mother when she came back from her next visit to Uncle Hans.

"The truth—that everything was taken away," she said. "He only hopes he's put to death right away. The doctors and nurses stayed with the patients, did you know that?"

"No," I said, "I didn't know."

Early the following week a friend of Uncle Hans' hired a cab and took him from the hospital to an attic room he had been able to arrange for him at some friends' in the center of town. Late that night he also took the wheelchair—the tires had already been stolen from it—from the entryway of Uncle Hans' house. It was only four days until everything in the apartment was taken away, but it was agreed not to tell Uncle Hans for the time being.

He lay there alone in his new location, but a nurse came twice a day to look after him. Only a few people knew where he was.

During the summer everything went as well as could be hoped for. But when fall came, another hiding place for Uncle Hans had to be found, because a stove couldn't be used in his room.

They succeeded in obtaining a place for him in an old people's home. The papers would be taken care of.

When he was told the decision, he showed his disappointment. He explained he would rather be taken in by friends.

Sometimes he didn't seem to know what he was saying; one afternoon he said to the nurse, "Do you still remember when I was twenty-seven? No, I mean 1927. I know exactly what I mean, so—" and after that he lay lost in thought.

One Wednesday a friend, a woman who was an artist, was visiting him. "You like that atlas such a lot, don't you?" he asked. "Tell me the truth, now." He had an atlas of the world that was supposed to be very extensive and valuable, and friends had been able to rescue it from his apartment.

When the nurse came that afternoon, he said, "Take that atlas along, I've given it to Ali."

"What nonsense," she said, "it's much too nice to give away."

"Take it along," I said. Then he asked for something to drink.

The following day the daughter of Aunt Jaanne's friend came and found him asleep. "He's sleeping," she said at home. In the evening the nurse came again, found him resting, took his pulse, and left satisfied. The next morning she came back at the usual time and found his body already cold. She lifted up the head; its little tuft of hair felt damp to the touch. The thin mouth was closed, and the glasses gave the face an unreal expression.

"I didn't understand it all right away," she said later. "And I thought I heard something strange, but it was a carpet sweeper on the ground floor."

When she saw the empty box beside the glass of water, she began to comprehend. But she figured out that it couldn't have contained more than four sleeping tablets. The only conclusion was that he had regularly saved out one at a time and so built up a supply.

That night the friend who had taken him out of the hospital and the man who had given up the room for him together carried the body downstairs and noiselessly lowered it on a rope into the canal beside the house; it sank immediately, so I was told.

They both hurried back inside the house and waited together with the nurse until they could go home at four in the morning.

In the meanwhile they discussed all things: the distances of planets, the duration of the war, the existence of a god. The two men were also given a bit of information by the nurse: she was able to tell them that Uncle Hans' money could have served to maintain him for at least another year. "That wasn't the reason," she said.

# NORWAY

# Moment of Freedom

JENS BJÖRNEBOE

Translated by John Weinstock

THE COURT OFFICER in Heiligenberg relates: Part of a summer and the following fall I was up in Lappland. Mostly in the mountains, but now and then in small, thin and light birch forests—where the foliage was blond and the trunks not much over the height of a man. There weren't many mosquitoes that summer. But there was a lot of sun, and little by little I became very thin from just walking and walking, and I got brown from the sun, and my hair reached nearly to the shoulders. But I continued to walk anywhere it occurred to me. Occasionally—but not very often—I met people. The endless plateau was tremendously beautiful, and especially the thin, transparent leafy trees— they were nothing but brightness and glitter and life.

Since then I have seen a similar thin and transparent, light-green forest again—it was outside the city of Verdun, where the small bears had fought a little of their first world war against each other. On Verdun's battlefields all the trees are of the same age, and when I went there for the first time, these thousands of trees were no older than somewhere between 30 and 40 years. Therefore the whole forest was very young, it was a sort of infant of a forest, and even if it was large, it didn't have any of what makes a real forest— for a forest must have age. The trees require enormous amounts of time in order to become real trees.

And even if the soil was fertile outside of Verdun, the

trees couldn't grow so much faster for that reason. Nature needs time to rest and catch her breath. The bushes between the trees were not large either. For after the great battles of Verdun had been fought out, the whole area was transformed into pure muddy soil, so that there wasn't a green blade or leaf left for many kilometers.

At the same time, naturally, Verdun today represents an experiment of great scientific interest for forest research: the soil in that area was plowed and harrowed and turned and plowed again innumerable times, and furthermore mixed with millions of fresh corpses, boots, and on top of all that completely soaked through with rain and piss and blood. Only at the very last a new forest was sown over the hills and ridges. A few traces of trenches, fortifications and old steel helmets and weapons are still found—but one really doesn't see very many bones. The barbed wire is almost gone. Naturally in the course of the battles large quantities of excrement have gone down into the soil, in part bowel movements from three million men who disposed of their excrement in the normal or usual way—but also incredible quantities of excrement which came out through the mouth or simply through the back or stomach of the fighters; thus almost in the form of intestinal content which was more or less ready to be excreted, which naturally had great fertilizer value when it was mixed with blood and other body fluids. Another question remains unsolved, even for an otherwise optimistic biochemical science: namely which of the fighting parties had the highest protein food value—the Teutons, Anglo-Celts, or Gauls. One is tempted naturally to immediately assume that the Gauls were the most valuable, since they had far and away the most decent cuisine of all the participants in the battles. But one must not forget that at that time in War I, even the Gauls were rather scantily nourished, and moreover their people have an inherent tendency to be thin, gracious, and wiry. Also the Anglo-Celts, by and large, become sinewy, thin, often with bad teeth, even if they have beautiful manners and are very bold. The German fighters were probably on the average somewhat larger in stature, besides being more powerfully built, and they gain weight more easily, so they could have possibly become more valuable compost than their English and French brothers of the same year—but without a doubt at that time, because of persistent blockades, the Teutonic population and its armed forces were the most poorly nourished in Europe. The imperial army at that time was also thin and sinewy.

Besides one has to take age into consideration: irrespective of valor, nationality, faith and race, the major portion of the deceased were younger men, thus at an age where most of them consisted almost only of muscles and bones and sinews and a little handful of entrails. Everything considered one doesn't get the same quantity of garbage and blood from a million twenty-year-olds as from the same number of fifty-year-olds. Best would be a material made up of men in their sixties. On the other hand one should not underestimate the value of the mineral salts which in the course of time can be transmitted to the soil from bone remains, teeth, etc., and young men naturally have both more and better teeth, together with finer bone substance than older men. Another thing is that the pure meat value probably is a good deal higher per person in the case of mature men.

If one is to draw conclusions as far as agriculture is concerned, the result, mathematically speaking, will probably be that officers are more valuable in a dissolved state than enlisted men. The higher the officers are in rank, the older and fatter they will be. It is thus beyond doubt, that the best economy would be to fertilize with general staff members. The average general would according to a quick estimate supply humus of approximately 20 per cent more animal matter, than the average enlisted man.

If one computes the average enlisted man's weight as 69 kg., one would thus get 69,000 tons of high grade compost from a million corpses, while from a comparable one million

generals one would get 82,000 tons of fertilizer, to be sure
not entirely of the same quality, but in no way inferior,
either. Moreover, there is in addition rotting footwear, belts,
and excrement already produced by living participants,
which indeed amounted to quite a bit in the course of the
months that the same battles for Verdun took place: especially because of widespread diarrhea among officers as well
as enlisted men. The production of natural fertilizer must
have remained at a level of about 1,500 tons per day, of
which the largest part came from the side of the allies, who
had both more men and more food.

In the course of the entire war period this will give approximately 450,000 tons of excrement together with about
120,000 tons of cadavers. All together then one gets a sum
of not less than 570,000 tons of bodies and bowel movements, thus high grade sewer content and natural fertilizer.

If one today observes and assesses the thin, young, light
green leafy forest on the Verdun fields, one is tempted to
think that the result of the organic materials added is not
auspicious. In the meantime one must not forget the tremendous time a tree needs to grow up, compared to the time
one needs to shoot it away with dynamite.

There remains without doubt a remarkable, sacred, and
nearly celestial mood over the vast monuments which the
warring states of that time have since raised over the dead
and gone. It is an atmosphere of peace and sanctity such
as is to be found in hardly any other place in Europe.

All the same I prefer the thin leafy forest, but that may
be my own fault, and is due I suppose to my almost morbid
urge to be interested in landscape painting from different
epochs in Europe's art history.

What I ate during the first sojourn in Verdun, I don't
remember, something which in itself is remarkable, because
it is most often the only thing I remember about a place.
I suppose it was something from Strasbourg, I hope goose

liver or goose breast. But I know with certainty that I drank white Alsatian wine in large quantities.

The landscapes in Alsace are in their own way some of the finest in Europe, and the racial mixture has given rise to an unusually beautiful human type. Moreover, I like the Alsatians' temperament, and their bilingual style of life: they speak French on the surface and a Germanic dialect at heart. They are great wine makers. The Alsatian landscape is an ancient cultivated land, traversed by canals and rivers, green and gentle and noble. The soil is just as soaked up with excrement and blood as in Flanders. The architecture has a pronounced individuality, and among the high points in pictorial art must be mentioned Mathias Grünewald's enormous crucifixion and resurrection in the Isenheim shrine. Everything considered Alsace is marvelous. But one misses the light green forest at Verdun.

Totally different are the earlier battlefields at Chemin des Dames or at Hartmannswyler Kopp, of which I shall discuss only the latter. It lies directly west of Basel, on large hills, surrounded by spruce forest. The landscape is Vosgian —mountains and nordic forests.

The funny thing about the idyllic war cemeteries at Hartmannswyler Kopp is that fighting took place at the same place during both world wars, something which curiously enough led to bodies from the first war coming up again from their graves during the second war, because the shells dug up the soil several meters deep.

Here—at Hartmannswyler Kopp—I remember very well what I ate; namely a wholly excellent *truite bleu,* a delicate trout from the Vosges, cooked in lightly spiced water, with wine vinegar added which both affects the taste very favorably, and makes the skin of the trout blue. But I drank the same Alsatian white wine during the meal.

This reminds me naturally of how often I have fished and eaten trout in my earlier homeland; and while it is possible that the trout there up north in the mountain waters at an elevation of about 1000 meters is the best trout in the world, the trout in the Vosges is also of exceptional quality, and it was prepared with great art.

I lived a good while at an old inn in the vicinity of the war cemetery at Hartmannswyler Kopp—a lovely building where Napoleon Bonaparte also had spent a night, and where the house walls are provided with large iron rings to tie the travellers' horses to; I lived there partly because of the innkeeper's good kitchen, and partly because the battlefield lay so near that I could always walk over to it.

What is remarkable about the rows of graves at Hartmannswyler Kopp is that they lie in the strange tranquility of the forest. In the cemeteries there are great mounds of turned up soil, and noticable craters after the fall of the high explosives. It was here that the dead made their appearance anew, after over 20 years of silence and rest. Lower jaws, leg bones, small bones, and pelvises raised themselves anew, even uniform remnants had endured the hibernation.

Now these heroic corpses are fortunately buried a second time, and for that matter everything is fine. High spruce trees grow over the undisturbed parts of the heights, in other places the forest is naturally young. At the inn one also gets an outstanding goat cheese of local manufacture; it is fresh and mild, somewhat tart—and goes well with the white Alsatian wine. To be sure, up here one misses the large white vineyard snails which are served in garlic butter, and which are the ideal complement of wine.

There is something about the second internment which appeals to me, something in a way downright democratic. The fact is that when the grenades fell down 20 years later, and got the dead to awake and rise again, they brought vertebrae, pelvic bones, collar bones, lower jaws as well as elbows completely together so that when internment number two took place—obviously with the help of a bulldozer—the remains of the fallen from War I were merely scraped together without any real system or order, they were without uniform—and thus it happened that enlisted men, junior officers and the comparatively few officers came to rest without any difference whatsoever in rank and position. Thus in a way there is a sort of equality after death. Only 20 years later there was no longer a difference between a colonel and a corporal, between a general and an enlisted man. Fertilizer is fertilizer.

There is a sort of encouragement in this, when one has often enough observed that before a mass grave there exists no justice, but only violence.

It can be seen from this train of thought, why many years later it was important for me that I became a court officer, and through my daily presence in the court room learned to come to terms with it—with the daily sight that injustice goes—and shall go—its way.

# Music from a Blue Well

TORBORG NEDREAAS

Translated by Elizabeth Rokkan

ONLY THE NAME was blue. The well itself was black, or silver-grey, or bottle-green or bog-brown. Once there had been a blue-painted cover on it. That was why they said, "The blue well." They said, "You mustn't go to the blue well. Little Lars fell into it once." Herdis's mother said, "If you go to the blue well once more, you'll get a spanking."

Herdis felt drawn towards the old well as towards an unknown adventure. In the evening there were stars in it; she had seen them herself. But Judith and Esther and Peter and Little Lars' mother said that the Evil One was in it. Formerly she had believed them. She was afraid of the Evil One, though she was at least as much afraid of Jesus. But that had been a long time ago, certainly more than a year. It had been when she was small.

There was music down the well. She had said so once to Esther and Judith, but flushed as she did so. It was much too difficult to explain what she meant by the music. And that was how it was with very many things: it was difficult to talk about them. When they came out of people's mouths they turned to lies. Then they said, "Herdis is lying." Judith and Esther looked at each other and they looked at Herdis, and Judith said, "Now you're lying. I know you are." Then Herdis shouted, in distress, "But the brook sings. When it's been raining there's a lady who sings in the brook."

They were allowed to go *there*. Herdis took the two dis-
believing girls down to the brook, to the place where it
sprang off a little shelf into a pool. She said, "Hush," and
then they listened for a while all three of them. Herdis explained to them in a whisper that it always had to be quite
quiet for a while before you could hear the song. And as
she came to hear the voice rising and falling in a gentle
murmur above the brook, she felt great joy.

"Now you can hear for yourselves," she whispered.

At once she felt miserable right down in her stomach,
for the other two heard nothing but the rushing of the
brook.

So she said, "I'm not going to stay with you. You might
give me fleas." And left them. So they quarreled, and she was
really very sorry about it.

When they said nothing she turned away with a tight
feeling in her throat and added, "Because you have warts
on your hands."

Afterwards she cried for a bit, and the tears that came
were bitter and few, as they usually are when you have to
cry them quite alone.

But that had been a long time ago, sometime in the middle of the summer. Now the sky had grown clearer, everything had become wider and colder, there was a slight scent
of jam in the air. The evenings had begun to grow darker,
and there were stars in the sky. The land out in the fjord
was even farther away and yet at the same time more distinct. All the summer it had been lying in a blue haze or
hidden in mist. Now she could see that there were houses
there with red roofs, and amber-yellow fields of grain and
bright green meadows and trees like green shadows. The
little island where they put out the fishing nets when her
father came to visit them had moved farther out into the
fjord. But its rocks stood out clearly with their light and
shade and moss and stones and knolls and gullies.

Every day seemed to bring a brittle atmosphere of longing, and dusk followed quickly after the time of day when the kitchen side of the house lay in the red afternoon sun and was cosy with milk and sandwiches for supper on the table outside.

This part of the summer was the best. She had experienced it before; she recognized it like a friend she had not seen for a long time.

Everything was good this evening. Everything was peaceful and as it should be. Her mother had gone back to town with the black-currants and gooseberries that she was going to make into jam, and she kissed Herdis and rumpled her hair and played with it and blew into her ears and laughed and teased her before she left. She could still feel the warmth of her mother's caress; it felt like laughter inside her. All the same, she was happy that her mother had gone; she would be allowed to stay up longer, Jenny was not so particular. The feeling of freedom made her feel dizzy all over. She *owned* herself and could do whatever she liked with herself.

If she had wanted she could have gone up to the summer pasture, where Judith and Esther and Peter had gone with their mother to milk the cows in the barn far up on the mountain-side. She could hear the single cow-bell all the way down here by the sea where she had sat down to watch the dusk spreading outwards from the land. Down in the stones at the law tidemark the sea lay spitting in the seaweed and licking its lips. There was a tiny sound of bells in it, a calm little snatch of music.

And now she began to listen for something she had hidden inside herself, and which was a secret. It was songs: songs that were like no other songs she had learned, but which had come to her through the open window of a white house once that spring.

She remembered every single detail about it. At this moment she relived them over again and remembered how good the experience had tasted—but the songs would not come.

She heard only the sea plucking at the stones. There was a gentle soughing in the treetops behind her; it passed like a little shudder over the shining surface of the sea.

She shut her eyes.

. . . She had been happy long before they came to the white house. It had been one of the good days. She had gone to town with her mother and bought new sandals that she was allowed to put on at once. And material for a new dress that her mother was going to make for her. Her mother had bought herself new gloves, and a fluffy white lace affair to wear inside her jacket. It was terribly exciting to have so many new things. New sandals that danced along the sun-white pavement, making a happy clicking sound that reminded her of her mother's castanets. Herdis scurried along with her hand in her mother's. They walked home through the park, and her mother chatted to her about how they were going to the country and about all the nice things they were going to do. She was really *with* Herdis and answered all her questions, instead of just saying "Mm" and walking wrapped up in her own thoughts, as she so often did.

It was then that her mother paused in front of a fine white house and listened. The notes of a piano were pouring out from an open window, and it was not a song you could sing to, but a rippling stream of notes that frothed out into the scented air of the park. Notes, notes—and many of them at once, a thousand notes. And then there was a song just the same, far inside the thousand notes—a sad song. Terribly beautiful and terribly sad. But mostly beautiful—more beautiful and lovely than it was possible to understand. It did not much resemble the music that Herdis's piano teacher played for her when she was pleased with her, and it was strange and disturbing in quite a different way from some of the music that her mother played.

The music rose and fell inside her, giving her an almost unbearable feeling of happiness. She looked up at her mother, silent and almost a little afraid. Her mother's face seemed to be falling to pieces feature by feature. She had closed her eyes and was far away. But the hand inside the smooth glove was crushing her own, the warmth from it was passing in little spurts up through her arm. She twisted her hand out of her mother's, for she wanted to be alone. She had to be completely alone while she experienced all the loveliness that was streaming out of the open window.

Her mother began walking again, quite slowly. A slight fragrance rose out of her handbag when she opened it to find her handkerchief. She lifted her veil and dried her tears cautiously away from her eyes—but she was smiling!

Herdis hung back a little. She listened to the music getting fainter as they walked, but still heard it when it had gone completely. She was unable to speak, and she did not know whether she wanted to cry. But everything was good.

Since then she had searched for the music inside herself. Sometimes it came, but it was no longer the same. There were new notes, new songs in a rushing of notes. Sometimes they were sad songs and sometimes they were happy, yet the experience was intense and joyful every time. But she could not find them again whenever she wanted. Often other songs came and disturbed them, hymns and songs she had learned at school, and the kind of music her mother played.

Out here this summer she had heard the music only once. . . .

The well. The blue well.

Not that she had thought of going to the dangerous blue well. She had got to her feet and was standing with a small round stone in her hand. When she threw it into the sea the shining surface broke with a weak sound like shattered crystal. There was a sigh along the shore and then it was quiet again.

Her sandals crunched softly in the gravel as she walked up the slope.

Jenny had lighted the lamp in the kitchen. It shone with an orange glow, making the evening dark blue around the kitchen window. But the sky was as translucent as aquamarine; it was nowhere near dark yet.

Perhaps she could find some of the last blackcurrants; she was allowed to pick them now. The blackcurrant bushes stood on the slope behind the little potato patch and smelt bitter and slightly rancid.

The blue well lay close beside them, but she had not thought of going there.

She shut her eyes and breathed in the fresh, raw smell of the potato plants which lay scattered in shreds over the torn up earth. It was a good smell.

All the same it was too dark among the blackcurrant bushes to see any blackcurrants. There were nettles there which she could not see either. She took the path round the blue well in order to avoid the nettles.

A cover had been put over the well, an ugly, rusty piece of tin or some other metal, and stones had been placed along the edges to keep it in position. It was just as if somebody wanted to put a hand over the well's mouth so that it could not breathe.

The cover made an ugly creaking noise when she got it off, but she thought she saw a gentle glimmer from the well, like a grateful glance. Otherwise it was simply dark. It was growing dark everywhere too. That was good.

Herdis had never been afraid of the dark. It usually brought sleep with it, or pleasant thoughts, and sometimes sweet music. She thought of the dark as something cosy and familiar that wrapped itself around her like velvet and let her be at peace with herself.

She sat sideways on the coping and stared down into the well. It was like staring down into a large, black eye. She listened, and felt slightly chilled. For a moment she heard Jenny's laughter from the kitchen window. She had a friend with her, and with any luck would have forgotten that Herdis ought to be going to bed.

Herdis listened until she no longer heard the strange

little drips far down in the well, but only the music it gave her.

For the music came and stayed with her, the music came out of the silence and the half-dark and began to shine. She sat with half-open mouth and empty eyes, lost in a rapture beyond her understanding.

Then the delicate silence was pierced by the three stupidly insistent cries of a crow, and the echo revolved heavily above the tree-tops.

The music was broken. It was scattered into the half-dark like a torn string of beads.

She stared helplessly down into the well after it, and now she felt that she was sitting uncomfortably and a little painfully. She swung her feet forwards and supported them on a small projection in the well, and gave a little shudder when she felt that it was slippery. The chill from the unknown depth rose up towards her, and inside her there was an emptiness after the music that was no longer there. She started to swing her feet up onto the other side, and as she did so felt that the stone supporting her hand was loose.

It all happened so quickly and she probably did something stupid because she was frightened, but her feet slid away too soon from the jutting stone, her arms seized hold of the wrong side, crookedly and clumsily. Her body slipped slowly downwards while she hung by her arms. Fear fluttered like black birds' wings in front of her eyes. She gasped for breath and pressed her knees and her feet against the slimy rock. A scream for help turned into a useless croak; her body did not dare to lend any power to her voice. All feeling was concentrated in her trembling body that nailed itself like a terrified animal to the wall of the well. Her fingers were impaled over the coping like two dead hooks of bone; she could feel them no longer. Only with her shoulders did she know that her hands had gripped fast with skin and nails, for they had turned into stone and soil and nettles above her. Her mouth was slashed in a grimace from the scream that dared not come. Even her tears did not dare to fall. Only the stone-dead hands held her now, supported by the flayed knees impaled against the slimy rock.

The one knee had found some sort of a grip in a sharp hollow. The blood ran in a warm trickle down her leg, without her feeling any pain. She did not know how long she hung like this in cramped immobility. It could have been a year.

Then one of her feet began to move. Cold and clinging like a snail it crept millimetre by millimetre, searching in deadly terror over sharp edges, as if it had nothing to do with her at all.

It came up against pointed resistance. Herdis held her breath. Her heart was not beating, but quivering and roaring in her ears with a grey noise. She pressed her shin bone against the object stuck fast in the wall, and felt it bore viciously into her leg. The pain seemed to carry a message, the icy waves of pain through her body flickered into a weak flame of hope. Her heartbeats stumbled into life again. She released her breath so strongly that it rebounded from the rock against her face like a warm cobweb. Glued to the wall like a horse-fly, she forced her leg to cut itself slowly across the hard object, which might have been a large nail. She had to press her thigh to one side in order to lift her foot high enough without slipping from the wall for an instant. It took a thousand hours in a blind madness of fear and defiance before her foot had the hard object beneath it.

—And then it had found a hold.

And her heart began beating again. It beat in the back of her neck like a little hammer, it beat in the scratches and bleeding sores, it hammered in her throat and in the dead fingers that had turned to stone on the edge of the well. It beat with a little piping sound finally as if breaking with each blow.

The fear that had fluttered blindly inside her sank down into her stomach and lay there like a heavy sorrow. Only now did she dare to tilt her head backwards and look up.

She looked straight up into a pale green star. A strange warmth trickled down through her body, and immediately afterwards her lacerated legs were smarting shamefully. Far down in the well something dripped for a long time.

Then she leaned her head in towards the rock again. The cold, mildewed stench rose in her like nausea.

Across her shoulders she was carrying an iron weight that began to pain her like toothache. She registered it with a strange numbness. She felt no other hurt besides this torturing weight of life and death in her slender shoulders. And now she should be thinking with the foot on the bolt. It should be pushing her weight upwards. Up into the green starlight. Up into the world.

She did not move.

An empty drowsiness was stealing over her, into her thoughts and her body. She could think only in pictures, and she thought of the clock ticking on the wall at home in town, and of the colored pictures they were given when they bought new school books, and of the flower box on the balcony at home, with its rich scent of nasturtiums. They were good thoughts, but she felt more and more queasy whatever she thought about.

Time stood still. From up in the World she heard a gentle rustling like silken skirts, and felt the scent of the late summer evening as a cool caress on her forehead. It was only the evening sighing up there; then it was quiet again.

She had to press on the foot now and pull herself up. But it was as if the thought itself had become ill and nauseated, and she did not move.

And down in the well an eye was staring at her. Ice-cold giddiness whirled through her stomach. For up from the silent vortex of the well something was breathing on her, whispering sweetly and enticingly up through her exhausted limbs and into her ears. Something down there was taking hold of her and making her weak. She shut her eyes and felt how it would be to let herself slip down and down, to meet a black velvet darkness and let herself be sucked into a dizzy chasm of sweet music, of rest and warmth. . . .

It lasted for perhaps an instant. She opened her eyes wide, and gritted her teeth in a sudden uprush of anger and defiance.

Her fear had been given life again. It poured power into her powerless limbs. She wrenched her thigh with a furious croak so that her foot could get a better grip on the bolt, she forced the remnants of her strength down into the foot and felt her bowels emptying as if she were an infant. Her thigh and her leg trembled like a taut wire for a whole night and for many nights, raising her upwards, upwards. . .

Up. Back in the World.

The evening air felt lukewarm after the raw chill of the well, the air in the World was full of living scents, she drank them in with trembling mouth. And the World welcomed her with the angry smart of the nettles. Like a toad on bristling legs she moved backwards on knees and elbows until she was a good distance away from the well, which was trying to suck her back into its blackness.

Then she heard her name. Jenny was going round the house calling for her. She wanted to answer, she got up with difficulty and tried to run, but she could not call and she could not run. The terrible nausea overwhelmed her, and at once the air was full of black birds blinding her and blocking her way. The nettles rose up and whipped her over the arms.

. . . And a thousand notes and the sweetest music came rippling up from the well in a spring of blue water that lifted her up and carried her and rocked her in a crescendo of happy waltz tunes and flung her out into the whole world so that she had a tickling feeling in her stomach, and she lived nine lives in a hundred years and then something was hitting her, trying to break off her legs and whipping her on the throat and arms with nettles.

It woke her up. She was lying by the thicket of blackcurrant bushes with one of her arms in the nettles, with smarting cuts and aching limbs, her torn clothes as filthy as an infant's, and heard in blissful rapture that Jenny was calling her.

# PAKISTAN

# Grandma

## Iqbal Ahmad

AZIZ MANZIL, OLD and grey, standing by the railway tunnel, was our house. I saw "was" because it is no longer ours. After the partition of India, most of my people left the country and went to Pakistan. Those who had stayed behind followed them in two years' time, and our property was alienated by the government of India.

The passage to our house lay through a narrow, paved lane. The lane, which served as a playground for the children of the neighborhood, was flanked by two high walls that cut off the sun's rays and kept the lane in a constant shade and half-light. Twenty yards down the alley-way was an old archway; this was the entrance to our house. Along one side of the lane ran an open drain that carried black, smelly water. Once a week the municipal sweeper came on his sanitary mission, and all the children gathered round and watched him run forwards and backwards with his broom dipped in the water. This was his idea of a cleaning job. It only made the drain look dirtier than before. The dark mud that lay at the bottom would be churned up and the foul smell that always hung in the air would be intensified.

But we did not mind these things. The smell did not bother us and the muddy water was all right as far as we were concerned. A hundred times a day our ball would roll into the drain, and we retrieved it with our fingers without the least hesitation. If a grown-up person happened to be going by at that time, we waited for him to pass, or

fished out the ball with our bare toes. We did not expect anyone to find fault with that.

The lamp-lighter came at sundown to light the single
lamp in the lane, carrying a slender ladder on his shoulder
and a lantern in his hand. We children never stopped to
watch him at his work as we did the sweeper, because he
came at dusk; and the lane, quite dark by that time, held
unknown terrors for us. At the far end of the lane was an
empty house with broken walls and caved-in roofs. Heaps
of broken bricks lay in its courtyard; and in the middle
of the rubble stood a magnificent plum tree, which looked
fantastic in that setting in the daytime, but sinister at night.

It was generally believed that spirits and djinns haunted
ruins, and the wrecked house in our lane was no exception.
Every fifteen days or so, and always on a Thursday night,
some thoughtful member of our community would light a
little lamp—a tiny saucer of oil with a floating wick in it—
in honor of the spiritual creatures, and to keep them in good
humor. Also an anna's worth of sweetmeats were placed by
the lamp. This was dinner for the spirits. They fed on its
smell.

Sometimes, on a Friday morning, we would see bits of
sweetmeat in a niche of the ruin; and in the tiny saucer
would be a black stain left by the burnt-out wick. We used
to fight among ourselves for every plum that dropped from
the tree, but none of us had the courage to touch the left-
overs of the djinns. They might get offended and then sure
disaster would follow. There was at least one victim of their
wrath, or so we believed. He was a boy of fourteen, much
older than the boys of our age group. His name was Irshad.
It was said that as a child he would sometimes steal the
sweetmeats offered up to the djinns. This angered them. So
one summer's night, when it was warm and he was sleeping
on the roof, they lifted him from his bed and flung him
down. He was picked up unconscious, and with a broken
leg. His leg was now all crumpled, and he went on crutches.

So at dusk I would return home. Nasiban would be hunting for the lanterns. It was time to light the lanterns, and she could not find them. "Arif, son, please find the lanterns for me. I don't know why they can't be left at their places," she would say when she saw me. It was the easiest thing for me to find them. I would bring them to her one by one. She sat on a little platform in the courtyard with a bottle of kerosene oil, a few rags of cloth and a handful of ashes by her side. After I had brought all the lanterns I would sit down and watch her slowly detach the chimneys and polish them with rag and ash. I was absolutely forbidden to touch the chimneys for fear I should break them. Then the lanterns were filled up, and if the kerosene ran out, it was my special pleasure to go and work the suction pump and fill the bottle from the large oil can.

Nasiban was our woman servant. She did the household chores and went on errands to the market. She looked terribly old and wrinkled to me, and her dark brown skin was as tough as leather. I remember once the cholera broke out in the city, and the government innoculator came to innoculate us. When it was Nasiban's turn, the needle would not go into her skin, and the man said he would have to go and get an awl to make a hole. Although she was old, Nasiban was an indefatigable woman, and was on her feet from morning to evening.

As she polished the chimneys, she talked to me, mostly about her family. She had a married daughter at Rampur and a son working in Delhi. I listened but with half an ear. I was more interested in watching her take the lanterns to pieces and put them together again; and the special moment came when she put the light to the wick and a soft, golden flame sprang up in the crystal-clear chimney. When the lanterns had been lighted, I would dispose them about the house, swinging them back to their right places.

One lantern I took to Grandma. If she was on the point of finishing her evening prayers, she would motion to me to come to her. She would hold my face between her flabby hands, repeat a few Arabic words, and breathe a blessing on me. Then she would be free to talk: "Where have you been the whole day? You did not come to me even once."

"I was busy, Grandma."

"Oh, you were busy! I suppose you go to work like your uncle?"

I forgot to mention that I was eight years old at that time.

"No, Grandma, but I have a lot of other things to do."

"I know your things. You play the whole day in the lane." Then she would ask me to get her a jar from her cupboard, from which she gave me cookies.

I had seen Grandma for the first time a year before. My father, a law officer in Bhopal, had been killed in an accident, and my mother had come to Agra to live with her people. Now, Grandma was not my grandmother. She was my mother's grandmother. But as everybody called her Grandma, I also called her Grandma. Grandma was all white. Her hair, eyebrows, skin, and clothes were of the same color. She was terribly old. Her skin hung in loose folds from the bone. She scared me at first. When, on our arrival from Bhopal, she asked me to come to her, I refused and clung to my mother. And when my mother tried to force me to go to her, I began to cry. "Let him be," said Grandma, and my mother let me alone, feeling too weak to assert her authority after her recent bereavement.

But Grandma knew how to deal with me. She plied me with sweetmeats, and in a few days my conquest was complete. Soon I was sitting near her, playing, while she said her prayers. And when she had finished, she would always give me sweets. Sometimes my uncle remonstrated with her, saying that stale sweets were not good for me. She would become sulky and grumble to herself: "How can sweets be bad for children?" And I would be inclined to agree with her.

One day Grandma complained of some trouble in her ear. She felt as if an insect had got in it. She could hear it move, she said. She asked Nasiban to call a *singiwalla*—a professional ear-cleaner. I had never seen an ear-cleaner before. He had a turban coiled on his head, and sticking in its folds were half a dozen metal pins and a dozen swabs. In his hand was a bottle-holder with four little bottles of fragrant oils fitted in it. Round his neck was a string from which hung a hollow horn—the horn giving the man the name of *singiwalla*. Grandma told him of her complaint. The man probed the ear with a pin, put his eye to the ear, and shook his head. "What is it?" asked Nasiban, "is it wax?" "No," said the man. "It's not wax, it's ear-wigs." He peered into her ear again and said he could see them. I also took a peep, but I could see nothing. He put the cylindrical horn to Grandma's ear, and sucked. She flinched as the vacuum hurt her ear. Then he tapped out two ear-wigs on the floor from the horn. And then one more came out. After that he put two drops of oil in Grandma's ear, and charged four annas. Grandma felt much better.

The whole day I went about in fear of ear-wigs, and in the evening when my uncle returned and told me that Grandma's ailment was imaginary and that the ear-cleaner was a fraud, and that ear-wigs do not live in the ear, I did not believe him. He said that in old age the ear-drum gets a little dry, and sometimes the movement of the head shakes it and one gets that crawling sensation. All the same when I went to bed that night, I lifted my pillow to look if ear-wigs were hiding there to get into my ear. Every six months Grandma called the ear-cleaner, and he never failed to produce the ear-wigs.

Grandma was her own physician, and the most amusing of her cures was for constipation. About a month after my arrival, I was amazed one day to see her with an unlighted cigarette in her hand. She called me to come and sit next to her. She was going to smoke. It was incredible; I had never seen a woman smoke before. So I looked up in doubt at my mother and uncle, but they did not seem to mind. Later on Grandma told me the medicinal purpose behind the smoking. The idea was that if one swallowed the smoke, it would exert a pressure on the bowels and push out whatever was clogging them. So the smoke had to be swallowed and kept inside; and it was here that my help was needed. She would hold her nose and I was to keep her lips pressed together with my fingers, so as not to allow the smoke to escape. She lighted the cigarette and took a pull, but before either of us could do the holding the smoke was gone. It blew out. The next time we were quick, she clinging to the nose, I to the lips. Then it was I to the nose and she to the lips; but the greater part of the smoke always dribbled out in little threads and coils from the corners of her mouth. I enjoyed myself immensely at this game, and she would say good-naturedly: "What is there to laugh at, you little monkey?"

Sometimes an ailment would defy her diagnosis and not respond to her treatment. Then I would be sent to the apothecary's, repeating the symptoms to myself on the way. The apothecary was a very fat man, and I always felt he was another squat, big, clay jar among the innumerable jars that filled his shop.

"Raj Singh, Grandma needs medicine," I would say.

"What's the matter with her?" he would ask.

I would recount what little I remembered, and came back with some herb or dried plums twisted up in a bit of paper with "to be boiled and taken at bed-time" pencilled on it. Sometimes it would be a syrup to be taken with iced water; it strengthened the heart. Even in a serious illness Grandma never consented to see a doctor. She had a deep-rooted suspicion of everything Western.

Grandma's chief occupation was to pray, which she did day and night. In the winter, when I went to bed early and struggled to lie awake to hear the nine o'clock train go through the tunnel, I would poke my head out of the blanket and look at Grandma. She would be sitting motionless like a picture on the prayer-carpet. And in the morning, if I happened to wake before sunrise, I could hear her monotonous drone, as she read the Quran. The whole house would be asleep and plunged in darkness, but in her corner glimmered a lantern as she sat before the holy book. I asked my mother why Grandma prayed so much. She said, "Hers has been a sad life, and when one is sad one wants to pray." I always cried when I was hurt or unhappy, so I said, "Why doesn't she cry?" "She has cried a great deal," said my mother reflectively. "Even now when her sorrow revives, she cries."

I was able to understand my mother's words fully after a few months. The summer had come, and we slept in the courtyard, under the sky. One warm and oppressive night I got up for a drink of water. As I lay down again, I watched my mother and wondered how she could work the hand fan when obviously she was asleep. All of a sudden I heard a low moan as if someone was in great pain. I drew close to my mother for protection, and heard. It was Grandma crying in her sleep. As she cried she started to sing. The song penetrated me with a deep sense of fear and uneasiness. I could not follow the words as they were broken with sobs, but I noticed that Grandma's voice had turned much younger. It seemed the voice of a girl. In my panic I woke my mother. She heard for a moment and hushed me to silence. "She's dreaming, poor thing!" she said. My fear having vanished with my mother's waking up, I felt the wailing song fill my heart with sadness, and I started crying. Presently the song subsided, but the dry sobs continued after brief silences, and then they ceased.

In the morning when I got up my head was full of the night's experience. I asked my mother why Grandma cried like that. She said, "She dreamed of her married life and her husband. He left her after a year of their marriage." She stopped for a bit and then said, "Do you know how old

Grandma is?" "No," I said. "She is over ninety. She was married at sixteen, a year later my mother was born, and Grandma's husband went off with a low woman and never came back."

Grandma was married at sixteen. There were only two men in the home to which she had come, Grandma's husband and his father, Syed Aziz Ali, after whom Aziz Manzil was named. Aziz Manzil was not then what it is now. It was a two-room house with a courtyard in front. As the prosperity of the house grew, so did Aziz Manzil, till it became a planless, sprawling monster, containing within its being all the phases of its evolution. In the oldest wall, in the courtyard, were two big iron nails, driven into the wall by Aziz Ali's own hands. They were among the family heirlooms; and every year, before the rains set in they received a fresh coat of paint to prevent them from rusting.

Grandpa, so the legend went, was a very handsome man in his youth. My mother told me stories she had heard about him. He was handsome as a prince, and had an athletic build. He could run as far as Sikandra and back, which came to ten miles. He assisted his father, who was a copyist in the law court, at his work. Grandma kept house and cooked. When father and son came back in the evening, and had washed, she would serve them their dinner. As they ate, she sat with them, fanning them. When dinner was done, Aziz Ali sat in front of his house, smoking a *hookah* and talking about the day's events with friends who happened to drop in. Grandpa went out visiting friends or for just a stroll in the market-place. He returned by ten. Grandma, having eaten and finished the washing up by then, would be waiting for him. Then they would lie down and talk. I wish I knew what they said, but it must have been something pleasant, for both were young, handsome, and healthy. A girl was born to them after a year of their marriage.

One night Grandpa returned home very late. He had gone to attend a marriage in the neighborhood, where after the

feast the guests were entertained to a nautch. Sitara, the
then celebrated dancing-girl had come. She was a little brown
woman with the easy movements of a tigress and big, bold
eyes, whose power she knew. Rajahs and nawabs invited her,
and she charged the fantastic sum of five hundred rupees
for a performance. The music started, and with a stamp of
her foot, which set all the little silver bells tied to her ankle
tinkling, she released something powerful and intoxicating
into the atmosphere—the dance was under way. Grandpa
watched her spell-bound with a stupid, half-forgotten smile
on his face and fire coursing in his veins. The girl too was
struck with his appearance, as he sat there like a prince in
that crowd. With overbold movements of her body she came
towards him and receded like a tantalizing wave. It was in
a dazed condition that Grandpa came home that morning at
three o'clock. Grandma and the child were sleeping peace-
fully.

The next day he went off with the dancer, never to return. Aziz Ali was furious. He raged and fumed and swore
that he would shoot him if he ever set foot in his house.
And the poor man wept in secret over the disgrace that his
son had brought to the fair name of the family by going off
with a low woman. However, he continued to go to work,
smoked his *hookah* in the evening, but stopped seeing people.
Towards Grandma he grew infinitely tender and considerate.
Seeing her go about like a dumb, wounded animal, he would
sometimes place his hand over her head and say: "He is
dead. It's good it is so. Forget him, daughter. God has given
you a child, look after her. As long as I am alive . . . ," but
seeing Grandma's fast-flowing tears, he would stop short
and go away.

Grandma had not been prepared for this suffering. She
had been dropped in mid-air, so she found her grief insupportable. Every night she cried herself to sleep, and her
strong, healthy body became a torture to her. It was in this
condition that she turned to God, and from the age of seven-

teen to over ninety, till her death, did nothing but pray. She did not know what was going on in the world outside. She did not even know that a world existed outside the confines of our *mohallah*. Wars shook the world, India passed through a tumultuous period of her history, and Grandma did not even know who Gandhi was. The only politics she knew was that the crafty "Firangis" had stolen the throne of Delhi from a Muslim ruler, when she herself was a little child, and that there were still Muslim rulers in Bhopal and Hydrabad, where most of her grandsons served.

Seventy-five years of prayer—girlhood, womanhood, middle age, old age, all nailed to the cross! It makes me shudder now to see in my mind those vast seventy-five years stretching endlessly, and Grandma sitting motionless on the prayer-carpet, with a dim lantern burning near her, and she turning from a beautiful, rosy-cheeked girl into a wrinkled hag of over ninety. I do not believe in God myself, but sometimes I do think that there must be some small corner in this infinite universe where all the prayers can go.

Grandma believed like a child in Heaven and Hell and the Day of Judgment. "I shall demand justice from the Lord on the Day of Judgment," sometimes she would say. No, Grandma, do not demand justice from your Lord, otherwise your beloved husband for whom you cried in your sleep for seventy-five years, will be consigned to the ever-lasting flames. That will not make you happy. Make your Lord give him a beating, a most sound beating; and when he has been hurt enough and he has cried enough, ask Him to make you seventeen years old and him twenty, the age when you lost him. And although there will be no Aziz Manzil in Heaven, still find a quiet corner, and when it is night and the stars are shining, talk to each other, picking up the thread where you left off at seventeen.

# PHILIPPINES

# On the Ferry

### N. V. M. GONZALEZ

DURING THE entire two and a half hour ride from Manila to Batangas they had suffered enough. No seats had been available except those over at the rear, which was the part of the bus called Hollywood. It used to be known as the Kitchen; and, to say the least, it was hardly comfortable there. But some things just couldn't be helped—like getting to the bus station late, or being unable to raise enough money to keep your son in school. You had to accept all that —well, like Hollywood.

Except for the bus seats, Mr. Lopez had run through these things before. Now in the comparative comfort of the ferry, he could run through them again. But he didn't care to; and, hoping he could cast them out of his mind, he turned to Nilo.

"Have you checked our luggage?"

The thin bespectacled boy who sat on the wooden bench beside him replied: "Yes, pa."

"Check agin," Mr. Lopez said.

The boy got up and peeked under his seat where the *cargador* had pushed in an old suitcase, two boxes of books and magazines, and two grocery paperbags.

It was almost sailing time. During the quarter of an hour they had been on board—"Pa, let's avoid the rush," Nilo had said—a steady stream of people had, like them, arrived on passenger trucks that had raced like huge red beetles through the dust from Manila. Mr. Lopez and his son had taken one of the starboard benches, hoping they could have it all to themselves, but, presently, a big party—three elderly ladies and two young girls—occupied the other end of the bench. Tangerine-shirted *cargadores* followed after them, piling up baskets of fruit, suitcases, and grocery paperbags, too, before them and then shoving these under the seat. One of the ladies sat beside Nilo, while the two others at the far end of the bench let the two young girls sit between them. The latter were plain-looking and dressed in the uniform of St. Bridget's College and were perhaps spending the weekend with relations at Calapan.

Mr. Lopez, who had been assistant district engineer in his day, hoped he would not meet any acquaintances from Calapan. That he did not know who the women were pleased him. He was afraid he would only embarrass himself in the presence of former associates in the government service, or even with business friends. Lopez & Co., Builders, had won many a public works bid in its time, had constructed bridges and river control projects all over Mindoro. But what people would remember, Mr. Lopez feared, was the Badjao Dam. If foreign-owned timber concessions had not denuded, through indiscriminate cutting, the once heavily forested hills around Mt. Halcon, nobody would instantly see where the Dam came in. The fact was that the big flood of December 1956 had washed it away. Contracts had since then been difficult to come by.

The *cargadores* had stopped running up and down the deck. A shudder shook the ferry, accompanied by shouts from the pier, where the red busses were backing out in a steady grinding whirr. And then, finally, there was the whistle; and the boat put out toward the open sea.

It was a clear day, unusual for early July. Although Mr. Lopez had made this trip many times before, it had never quite ceased to fascinate him. Today Batangas receded slowly in the mid-morning sun, with the dome of the old church and that of the provincial capitol flashing like twin gems of a pendant in its original box of green suede that you had snapped open.

As the ferry turned toward the Mindoro coast, the view from Mr. Lopez' side of the deck was obstructed by gray canvas awnings rudely flapping in the breeze. He found himself, shortly, crossing over and leaning from the larboard rail. Hardly eighteen years ago, as a young engineer, he had married a girl from St. Bridget's, and it was on a ferry such as this one that the two of them had crossed over to Mindoro. He could not remember, though, whether the two of them had stood at the railings together, their future literally before them, and let some fragment of the Batangas skyline share, too, in their daydreaming.

Nilo had remained on the bench and had pulled out a magazine from somewhere. The bookworm, Mr. Lopez thought, as he returned to his seat, picking his way through the scattered baggages along the deck. The boy had his mother's forehead and chin; he was delicately built. The eye-glasses added two or three years to his sixteen, but he was very much a boy still. A year away from school—and hoping his luck improved, Mr. Lopez told himself—Nilo would be ready for the heavier work of a sophomore engineering student. A sudden recollection of the boy's letters the year before, in which he had described how he had scrimped on food, sometimes limiting himself to a bottle of coke for breakfast, touched in Mr. Lopez something tender and deep. The appalling fact that Lopez & Co., Builders, had been an utter failure moved him to pity for the boy, for this full year he would lose, for his having gotten himself a bankrupt father.

But Mr. Lopez caught himself, as it were; and, remarking on the magazine that Nilo was reading, he said: "Must be interesting!" He tried to sound cheerful. "What's it? A *Reader's Digest?*"

"It's theirs," Nilo said, pointing to the two St. Bridget girls. He had turned the pages up and Mr. Lopez read the title of the article that the young fellow had been reading: "My Most Unforgettable Character."

"Who's it about?" he asked.

"Go-e-thals," Nilo said. "He built the Panama Canal." He turned to the two girls and asked: "Isn't that how you pronounce it?"

"Go-thals!" the girls corrected him.

They were surprisingly not shy, and there was no avoiding introductions now. Mr. Lopez chided his son lightly: "Keeping your friends all to yourself, eh?"

The two young ones were Mary and Rose. The three elderly ladies were aunts of theirs, and the amazing thing was that they were all Miss Adevas and elementary school teachers.

"Ah," said one Miss Adeva, "What they demand of us nowadays that Science's very much in the air!"

"But we have no vocabulary for Science in the National Language," the second Miss Adeva protested. She was obviously a Tagalog teacher.

"Hmm, isn't it true that you have to be good these days in math?" asked the third Miss Adeva, the most innocent of the three apparently.

"I don't know much about these things," Mr. Lopez demurred. "I'm only a business man now."

"You're being very modest, Engineer," said the first Miss Adeva.

The three ladies were a complete surprise. Judging by their appearance, Mr. Lopez could not have guessed they were abreast with the times and were troubled in their own way by some idea of progress. It was all very heartening.

"Look, Nilo," Mr. Lopez said to his son, "there's a canteen at the other end of the boat. Why don't you run over and get some cokes?"

The ladies begged him not to bother. The second Miss Adeva tugged motherly at Nilo's sleeve, urging the boy not to leave his seat.

Meanwhile, Nilo had returned the magazine to the girl called Rose; and, pushing his eye-glasses up the bridge of his nose, he stood up and got out the coins in his pocket. He counted them unembarrassedly, the two St. Bridget girls unable to hide their amusement.

"You have enough money there, haven't you?" Mr. Lopez asked, as if ready to offer Nilo a peso of his own.

"It's all right, Pa," the boy said.

"He's such a kid, really," said Mr. Lopez after Nilo had left them. "You go wrong these days, though, if you leave boys too much pocket money."

"There's a wise father," said the first Miss Adeva.

To merit the remark, Mr. Lopez told the ladies what he surmised they needed to know about Nilo. He was an engineering student at U.P. "The highest standards, you know," he couldn't help adding.

On discovering that the ladies were very enthusiastic about engineering and that the profession was in their view getting deservedly popular, Mr. Lopez realized he had to say something similarly apposite.

"A wise choice for Nilo," the second Miss Adeva was saying.

"It used to be the law," the third Miss Adeva said with conviction.

"Oh, you school people," Mr. Lopez said, still casting about, "—well, you've certainly begun to produce a new type of student these days!"

"Thank you, thnk you," the second Miss Adeva said, flattered by the remark.

The third Miss Adeva declared that times had changed; for one thing, education had become too costly.

"Don't I know," said Mr. Lopez. This was a subject about which he had a direct and personal knowledge. "And I with only one college student in the family. . . ."

"How many do you expect to have?" the second Miss Adeva asked. "Don't tell us, if it will embarrass you. . . ."

"It's nothing to be secretive about, let me assure you, ladies," Mr. Lopez said. "I've three boys, and a little daughter. . . ."

"That's all?" said the third Miss Adeva skeptically.

Mr. Lopez whispered something to her. Lest the two others feel left out, he said: "What I said was merely that Mrs. Lopez is in the family way."

He was surprised on hearing his own words. One more moment and he could have told the ladies the whole story of his life. But he checked himself from this access of familiarity, judiciously limiting himself to his son's student career.

"He's his mother's favorite," Mr. Lopez said. He told them about Nilo's health, which had always been delicate; and he described his interview with the dean of the engineering college, who had given him a cigar and remarked: "Health's wealth, as well we know, Mr. Lopez," clapping him on the shoulder.

The ladies warmed up to the new subject. They were certain that living conditions in Manila were not particularly wholesome for young people. They complained about the dust and the noise, the crowded boarding houses, and jam-packed movies. All these must have contributed to Nilo's poor health, they decided. To which Mr. Lopez wholeheartedly agreed.

"But where else can we send our boys these days?" he added, in the tone of one used to generous doses of compassion.

The question made the ladies sad. The first Miss Adeva, in particular, flicked her long eyelids. "In any case," she said, "a boy such as yours—why, Mr. Lopez, you really ought not to work him too hard."

"That's what his mother always says," Mr. Lopez replied.

"And you must watch out," warned the second Miss Adeva. "Boys his age easily get pleurisy or something like that. I had a nephew, you know. . . ."

And they were discussing the luckless nephew when Nilo

returned with seven bottles of coke clasped together precariously, with straws already stuck into them. The deck heaved under his feet, the bench slid forward. It was all he could do to deliver the bottles safely.

As the ladies sipped their cokes quietly Mr. Lopez revealed that Nilo's mother had studied at St. Bridget's. But while this proved to be interesting in itself, especially to the two young ones, Mary and Rose—who asked Mr. Lopez: "Did Mrs. Lopez wear a different uniform from ours?"—the Adeva ladies returned to the problem of Nilo's health, expressing their great concern unequivocally. It was as if Nilo's return from the ship's canteen with the bottles of coke awoke in them feelings that had long been dormant. He ought never to prefer his studies to his health; no, Nilo shouldn't, they said. The college was right in sending him home for awhile. The first Miss Adeva said, addressing Nilo directly:

"You're only sixteen, as your father says. . . ."

It was neither a question nor a statement of fact—to judge from the tone this Miss Adeva used. Before the boy, who looked puzzled, could say anything for himself, Mr. Lopez clarified the issue of his son's age: "Next September, to be exact."

Now Nilo was blushing from being made too much of, and perhaps because Mary and Rose were blushing, too. Still on the matter of ages, the first Miss Adeva revealed that her nieces were also sixteen, both of them.

"They're twins, you see," she said, as if to explain whatever it was that might be thought of as inexplicable about youth.

The ferry was running into some rough sea, which meant they had reached the middle of Verde Island Passage. For a good half hour until the ferry came directly in the shelter of the island, it ran into the three-foot waves which occasionally caused the benches to slip again or tilt back against the railings. The Adevas were wonderful sailors, so used they were to crossing the Passage. It was Nilo who looked every inch the poor sailor. Attentively, the first Miss Adeva, who had taken it upon herself to look after him, bade the seasick boy rest his head on the bench, giving him all the room he needed.

"He'll be all right," Mr. Lopez said. "Don't be bothered by him."

"In fifteen years or so—oh, who knows?—" said the second Miss Adeva, dreamily, "there'll be a tunnel through here. We'll all be going by train."

"That's one reason we'll be needing more engineers," the third Miss Adeva said.

Now Nilo raised his head off the back of the bench, as if surprised to hear someone speak so confidently about the future. The sea had become smooth again. The sound of water like falling rain ran through the length of the ferry. It was a school of tuna, Mr. Lopez saw, caught unawares in the path of the prow. An island, one of the three that girded Calapan harbor, swung forward, and the twins cried out: "A boat!"

Mr. Lopez turned quickly to landward, and there it was: a five-ton *lanchon,* or one-masted sailboat, listing precipitously in the sheltered cove where the small island rose from a sheet of white sand into thick underbrush fringed with coconuts.

The Adevas were excited and exchanged all sorts of conjectures, their breaths quivering. One said a leak had sprung, causing the boat to list; another said that it sat on a rock right there. The third Miss Adeva averred she could see no signs of a crew. The *lanchon* had been mysteriously abandoned. Mr. Lopez wished that the ferry had come closer, although he knew it would be something of an impertinence, especially as he himself could see no signs of a crew.

Nilo remarked just about this time that the ladies had said all they had to say: "It seems, Pa," he spoke solemnly— "I can actually see it sinking!"

Mary and Rose sighed. They agreed with Nilo; and watched breathlessly clutching each other on the arm.

"Pa, isn't it sinking? Inch by inch!" Nilo said, almost begging to be believed.

"Why, that's right! Of course, it's sinking!" the three Adevas exclaimed, dramatically.

"And nobody's doing anything about it!" Nilo seemed terror-stricken. "What could have happened, Pa?"

What could he say? He could not explain this if he tried. His mind turned to Nilo, to the note of insistence in the boy's words, to the claim that he must be believed, and the little derelict explained away. But Mr. Lopez had no explanation to make here any more than for all he had made up to conceal having failed him. He knew he could not lie to him or about him any more. The time must come when he could protect him no more with excuses and fabrications. How far could he go? He would run short of college deans and cigars and Panama Canals, and the little half-truths you said about them that made each day pass sufferably. You could fashion make-believe to order; but, oh, not life, complete with its mystery and loneliness. And he had other sons to see through, to say nothing of the young girl now in grade school. A sixth lay as yet unidentifiable deep in its mother's womb, but one thing was certain: with all six of them to look after, you could grow hardened enough. And once you've developed the callousness, how dreadful it would be, Mr. Lopez thought. Thank God, he could see that.

The ferry was cutting through the channel beyond the tip of the island now: he could see that, too. The green underbrush, the white beach, the derelict itself—was it the mast that you could see above the water?—all these slipped away, and the Calapan pier emerged. The iron roofing of the buildings on the shore were garishly white in the sunshine, against the palms on the shoulder of the hill. For a moment Mr. Lopez watched his son Nilo, who stood with his two new friends, their hands on the railings, their eyes shining. A sudden beauty to his being father to this boy possessed him; and he felt that his own eyes were shining, too. The deck began to sway under him—the waves were getting just a bit frisky again—and he sat steady on the wooden bench, aware of something hard gathering at the core of his being.

"No, not yet," he prayed silently, frightened by perhaps the same terror that had seized Nilo before.

But he felt it was already there.

# Love in the Cornhusks

AIDA L. RIVERA

TINANG STOPPED before the Señora's gate and adjusted the baby's cap. The dogs that came to bark at the gate were strange dogs, big-mouthed animals with a sense of superiority. They stuck their heads through the hogfence, lolling their tongues and straining. Suddenly, from the gumamela row, a little black mongrel emerged and slithered through the fence with ease. It came to her, head down and body quivering.

"Bantay, *Ay*, Bantay!" she exclaimed as the little dog laid its paws upon her skirt to sniff the baby on her arm. The baby was afraid and cried. The big animals barked with displeasure.

Tito, the young master, had seen her and was calling to his mother. "Ma, it's Tinang. Ma, Ma, it's Tinang." He came running down to open the gate.

"*Aba,* you are so tall now, Tito."

She smiled her girl's smile as he stood by, warding the dogs off. Tinang passed quickly up the veranda stairs lined with ferns and many-colored bougainville. On the landing, she paused to wipe her shoes carefully. About her, the Señora's white and lavender butterfly orchids fluttered delicately in the sunshine. She noticed though that the purple *waling-waling* that had once been her task to shade from the hot sun with banana leaves and to water with a mixture of charcoal and eggs and water was not in bloom.

"Is no one covering the *waling-waling* now?" Tinang asked. "It will die."

"Oh, the maid will come to cover the orchids later."

The Señora called from inside. *"Ano,* Tinang, let me see your baby. Is it a boy?"

"Yes, Ma," Tito shouted from downstairs. "And the ears are huge!"

"What do you expect," replied his mother; "his father is a Bagobo. Even Tinang looks like a Bagobo now."

Tinang laughed and felt a warmness for her former mistress and the boy Tito. She sat self-consciously on the black narra sofa, for the first time a visitor. Her eyes clouded. The sight of the Señora's flaccidly plump figure, swathed in a loose waistless housedress that came down to her ankles, and the faint scent of *agua de colonia* blended with kitchen spice, seemed to her the essence of the comfortable world, and she sighed thinking of the long walk home through the mud, the baby's legs straddled to her waist, and Inggo, her husband, waiting for her, his body stinking of *tuba* and sweat, squatting on the floor, clad only in his foul undergarments.

*"Ano,* Tinang, is it not a good thing to be married?" the Señora asked, pitying Tinang because her dress gave way at the placket and pressed at her swollen breasts. It was, as a matter of fact, a dress she had given Tinang a long time ago.

"It is hard, Señora said. "Didn't I tell you what it would be like, huh? . . . that you would be a slave to your husband and that you would work with a baby eternally strapped to you. Are you not pregnant again?"

Tinang squirmed at the Señora's directness but admitted she was.

"Hala! You will have a dozen before long." The Señora got up. "Come, I will give you some dresses and an old blanket that you can cut into things for the baby."

They went into a cluttered room which looked like a huge closet and as the Señora sorted out some clothes Tinang asked, "How is Señor?"

"*Ay,* he is always losing his temper over the tractor drivers. It is not the way it was when Amado was here. You remember what a good driver he was. The tractors were always kept in working condition. But now . . . I wonder why he left all of a sudden. He said he would be gone for only two days. . . ."

"I don't know," Tinang said. The baby began to cry. Tinang shushed him with irritation.

"*Oy,* Tinang, come to the kitchen; your Bagobito is hungry."

For the next hour, Tinang sat in the kitchen with an odd feeling; she watched the girl who was now in possession of the kitchen work around with a handkerchief clutched in one hand. She had lipstick on, too, Tinang noted. The girl looked at her briefly but did not smile. She sat down a can of evaporated milk for the baby and served her coffee and cake. The Señora drank coffee with her and lectured about keeping the baby's stomach bound and training it to stay by itself so she could work. Finally, Tinang brought up, haltingly, with phrases like "if it will not offend you" and "if you are not too busy," the purpose of her visit—which was to ask Señora to be a *madrina* in baptism. The Señora readily assented and said she would provide the baptismal clothes and the fee for the priest. It was time to go.

"When are you coming again, Tinang?" the Señora asked as Tinang got the baby ready. "Don't forget the bundle of clothes and . . . oh, Tinang, you better stop by the drugstore. They asked me once whether you were still with us. You have a letter there and I was going to open it to see if there was bad news but I thought you would be coming."

A letter! Tinang's heart beat violently. Somebody is dead; I know somebody is dead, she thought. She crossed herself and after thanking the Señora profusely, she hurried down. The dogs came forward and Tito had to restrain them. "Bring me some young corn next time, Tinang," he called after her.

Tinang waited a while at the drugstore which was also the post office of the barrio. Finally, the man turned to her: "Mrs., do you want medicine for your baby or for yourself?"

"No, I came for my letter. I was told I have a letter."

"And what is your name, Mrs.?" he drawled.

"Constantina Tirol."

The man pulled a box and slowly went through the pile of envelopes, most of which were scribbled in pencil. "Tirol, Tirol, Tirol. . . ." He finally pulled out a letter and handed it to her. She stared at the unfamiliar scrawl. It was not from her sister and she could think of no one else who would write to her.

Santa Maria, she thought; maybe something has happened to my sister.

"Do you want me to read it for you?"

"No, no." She hurried from the drugstore, crushed that he should think her illiterate. With the baby on one arm and the bundle of clothes on the other and the letter clutched in her hand she found herself walking toward home.

The rains had made a deep slough of the clay road and Tinang followed the prints left by the men and the carabaos that had gone before her to keep from sinking in mud up to her knees. She was deep in the road before she became conscious of her shoes. In horror, she saw that they were coated with thick, black clay. Gingerly, she pulled off one shoe after the other with the hand still clutching the letter. When she had tied the shoes together with the laces and had slung them on an arm, the baby, the bundle, and the letter were all smeared with mud.

There must be a place to put the baby down, she thought, desperate now about the letter. She walked on until she spotted a corner of a veld where cornhusks were scattered under a *kamansi* tree. She shoved together piles of husks with her foot and laid the baby down upon it. With a sigh, she drew the letter from the envelope. She stared at the letter which was written in English.

My dearest Tinay,

Hello, how is life getting along? Are you still in good condition? As for myself, the same as usual. But you're far from my side. It is not easy to be far from our lover.

Tinay, do you still love me? I hope your kind and generous heart will never fade. Someday or somehow I'll be there again to fulfill our promise.

Many weeks and months have elapsed. Still I remember bygone days. Especially when I was suffering with the heat of the tractor under the heat of the sun. I was always in despair until I imagine your personal appearance coming forward bearing the sweetest smile that enabled me to view the distant horizon.

Finally, I could not return because I found that my mother was very ill. That is why I was not able to take you as a partner of life. Please respond to my missive at once so that I know whether you still love me or not. I hope you did not love anybody except myself.

I think I am going beyond the limit of your leisure hour so I close with best wishes to you, my friends Gonding, Serafin, Bondio, etc.

Yours forever,<br>
Amado

P.S. My mother died last month.

Address your letter: Mr. Amado Galuran<br>
Binalunan, Cotabato

It was Tinang's first love letter. A flush spread over her face and crept into her body. She read the letter again. "It is not easy to be far from our lover . . . I imagine your personal appearance coming forward . . . Someday, somehow I'll be there to fulfill our promise. . . ." Tinang was intoxicated. She pressed herself against the *kamansi* tree.

My lover is true to me. He never meant to desert me. Amado, she thought. Amado.

And she cried, remembering the young girl she was less

than two years ago when she would take food to the Señor in the field and the laborers would eye her furtively. She thought herself above them for she was always neat and clean and in her hometown, before she went away to work, she had gone to school and had reached the sixth grade. Her skin, too, was not as dark as those of the girls who worked in the fields weeding around the clumps of *abaca*. Her lower lip jutted out disdainfully when the farm hands spoke to her with many flattering words. She laughed when a Bagobo with two hectares of land asked her to marry him. It was only Amado, the tractor driver, who could look at her and make her lower her eyes. He was very dark and wore filthy and torn clothes on the farm, but on Saturdays when he came up to the house for his week's salary, his hair was slicked down and he would be dressed as well as Mr. Jacinto, the school-teacher. Once he told her that he would study in the city night-schools and take up mechanical engineering someday. He had not said much more to her, but one afternoon when she was bidden to take some bolts and tools to him in the field, a great excitement came over her. The shadows moved fitfully in the bamboo groves she passed and the cool November air edged into her nostrils sharply. He stood unmoving beside the tractor with tools and parts scattered on the ground around him. His eyes were a black glow as he watched her draw near. When she held out the bolts, he seized her wrist and said, "Come," pulling her to the screen of trees beyond. She resisted but his arms were strong. He embraced her roughly and awkwardly, and she trembled and gasped and clung to him. . . .

A little green snake slithered languidly into the tall grass a few yards from the *kamansi* tree. Tinang started violently and remembered her child. It lay motionless on the mat of husk. With a shriek she grabbed it wildly and hugged it close. The baby awoke from its sleep and cried lustily. *Ave Maria Santisima*. Do not punish me, she prayed, searching the baby's skin for marks. Among the cornhusks, the letter fell unnoticed.

# ROMANIA

# Encounter in the Fields

MARIN PREDA

IT WAS MID-SUMMER. Suddenly, two riders, each leading a second horse, emerged from the forest of tall, dark maize stalks and streaked across the plain. At first it looked as if the two riders were pursuing each other or hurrying to answer some emergency. But the two riders were only racing each other, and when they came abreast they let their horses walk. They were two young lads bringing back the horses from grazing.

"Let 'em walk, Teican's son," said one of them, lightly switching the horse he was riding over the nose. "Let 'em walk, I've something to tell you before we get home."

"Go on, say it," replied the other.

"Wait a bit, Teican's son. I've been wanting to tell you all day, whilst we were out together, but somehow I couldn't. I want to ask you something: do you know Achim, the son of Achim?"

"Achim's Achim? Sure I do. That big lout; he lives near the Mill Valley. Why d'you ask?"

"Listen, Teican's son, don't ever tell anyone what I'm going to say now."

"Don't be an ass, Dugu!"

"I don't like fighting, d'you hear, Teican's son? But if you tell anyone, I'll knock you down," said Dugu.

"Look here, if I tell you I won't say anything and you don't believe me, you better shut up. That's plain."

"All right. Well, you see, one day I went to graze the

horses in the forest. I lay down on the grass and went to sleep. When I woke up the horses were gone. I didn't worry, because I knew they'd go home, that's what they do. I got up and went after them. I was ashamed to pass through the village, the people would guess I had fallen asleep, so like a fool I followed in the horses' tracks. I skirted the village and reached the Mill Valley. That was last week, after midday, and it was sweltering hot. I said to myself that I'd like to take a dip in the mill stream, by the old willow. You know where the bend is. Hardly anyone ever thinks of bathing there. The water is too shallow. I thought, why shouldn't I bathe to get rid of my sweat? As I was getting near the bend by the willow, I heard footsteps. I stopped to see who it was. And who d'you think I saw? When I saw a skirt I hid behind the fence and didn't move. Hey, Teican's son, are you listening?"

"Go on," replied the other pulling in his horses closer to his companion.

"A girl. It was a girl, maybe you know her. It was Palici's Drina. She had come out from the back of the garden and was standing on the bank looking at the sun. You know her, don't you?"

"Of course I do. She's young, only about eighteen, I think she came to the dance for the first time this year. . . ."

"That's right. I realized that as she was near her home and it was getting towards sunset, it was likely she wanted to bathe, too. So I stayed behind the fence and what d'you think I saw? She let down her hair, then tied it on top of her. My, what beautiful hair. . . . I've never seen the like before. She's going to bathe I thought. Now don't laugh at me, my heart began to pound and I wanted to run away; I don't know why, I felt scared. . . . Well, what d'you say to that, Teican's son?"

"Nothing. And then?"

"You see, Teican's son," continued the lad slowly, "I've never been with a girl before. . . ."

"Don't worry," replied his companion quickly, "it doesn't matter. Go on."

"Then I drew back even further and watched her undress. She took off her blouse and skirt, but why the devil do girls wear so many skirts? My heart beat so fast I nearly choked. Did you ever see a girl undressed, Teican's son? For me it was the first time. She glistened in the sunlight. . . She was beautiful. Then she stepped into the water. I could see she enjoyed it. She laughed and splashed herself all over. But she seemed scared, too. Why was that?"

"Scared of whom?" asked Teican's son.

"Heaven knows . . . ! She stayed in the water a long time. When she dressed, she looked different. I stood there quite dazed. Well, then I left and went home. Father said to me: 'What's the matter with you, you muddlehead, where did you fall asleep?' I replied 'In the forest,' so he said 'You're lucky our horses are clever, otherwise you'd have got a hiding.' "

"I don't know what the matter was with me, but I felt woozy that night, so I went to bed and to sleep. But all night I dreamt of Drina as I had seen her by the stream. I woke up several times all in a sweat. My head ached. 'What's the matter with you? Did you get into a fight? Go and get a drink of water,' said my father. But do you know what I was dreaming about?"

"I know," laughed Teican's son. "No matter. Well, what did you do next?"

"That's not so good," said the lad. "You'll see. For several days after I moped around. I kept on seeing her as she had been by the stream. You know, I didn't like any girl till then. I don't know what's the matter with this one, but I liked her. I kept on thinking I would go round to her place one evening and call her to the gate to talk to her. The more I thought of her, the more I liked her. But d'you imagine I went soon? No, I somehow couldn't. I only made up my mind yesterday. If she doesn't want to talk to me, I'll see what I'll do, I told myself. So I went last night. . . . But, just wait and see, it was the devil's own mess. . . . I never thought. . . .

"I walked along slowly, whistling, and crossed the bridge in front of their house, before you get to the forest. Well, I put a finger in my mouth and whistled. My heart was beating loudly. No sound came from the house. I whistled again. Nothing. The house was dark. I waited a bit, then whistled again. I knew someone would come out, and if it was her father I would simply not answer and go away. After all I could talk to her at the dance. I was getting impatient. But her father didn't come out. She came out slowly to the gate and opened it. When she saw me she drew back, frightened:

" 'Who is there?' she called.

" 'It's me.'

" 'Is it you, Achim?' she asked, still frightened. Then she closed the gate quickly, ran back into the garden and stood on tiptoe looking over the fence.

" 'Why d'you shut the gate?' I asked her softly. My heart had stopped beating and I was no longer afraid.

" 'Who are you?' she asked from behind the gate.

" 'Dugu, Mereuță's son, from up the hill.'

She was about to say something, when a huge form suddenly loomed up beside me.

" 'Who are you?' the lout asked me. 'What d'you want?' Then he addressed the girl: 'What are you doing by the gate? I didn't whistle for you.'

"You see, Teican's son, when I heard him asking who I was I thought he was someone from the house and I felt ashamed. I was about to say goodnight and leave. But when I heard him talking to the girl like that I felt a cold shiver running down my back and I began to tremble. It wasn't fear, because you know I'm never frightened—I felt like jumping on his back. At first I kept silent, I didn't have my stick with me, but then I said:

" 'I am who I am, but who are you?'

" 'Shut up and get out,' he replied, 'or is your hide itching?'

" 'Leave him alone, Achim,' the girl said quickly.

" 'When I heard this, my anger suddenly vanished. I looked at the man and said:

" 'So you want a fight? Where do you think you are?'

" 'Get into the house, you fool,' he told the girl, but she didn't move.

"Achim turned to me and, seizing my arm, pushed me away. But I freed my arm and hit his as hard as I could.

" 'Achim,' whispered the girl from behind the fence, 'I'll call father.'

" 'I haven't my stick,' I told Achim slowly. 'I don't like fighting, but from now on I'm going to talk to Drina and if you don't like it, tell me where to find you.'

"You see, Teican's son, I realized that the girl preferred me. My heart was pounding."

"Well, and did Achim tell you where to find him?" asked Teican's son.

"He did. He said I should be by the oak tree out in the fields on Sunday morning and that he'd break every bone in my body if he saw me around there again.

" 'Go in, Drina,' I said to the girl. 'We'll meet on Sunday at Lisandru Voicu's wedding, but mind you come.'

"Listen, Teican's son, Achim and I left together. He kept muttering: 'I'll break every bone in your body,' and I replied: 'We'll see which of us will get his bones broken,' and he said, 'Don't say afterwards I didn't warn you,' and I answered, 'We'll see, Achim-Achim.' We meet tomorrow. At first I felt afraid to go alone, because I thought he'll bring somebody along. That's why I told you about it."

"We'll both go, Dugu. We'll see if he brings anyone. But tell me, what do you want to do with the girl?"

"What d'you mean?" asked Dugu. "I like her, and I liked what she said last night. She was afraid Achim would beat me. D'you see? Here we are at the well. Are you going out after supper?"

"Yes. Why?"

"I thought we might talk some more about what we'll do tomorrow," said the lad stopping the horses at the entrance to the village.

"Oh, never mind. We'll ride to the oak tree. I'll come and fetch you in the morning. Well, I'll be on my way." And Teican's son turned his horses and trotted off.

Dugu also followed the road and slowly rode home. He didn't understand what was happening to him since he had seen the girl bathing, but the days seemed long and sunny, he felt dazed, and everything around him was in a haze.

Now, too, he felt bemused. He placed one leg across the horse's neck and rode slowly along the dusty village road. On approaching the house, he heard his father's voice from the garden as in a dream:

"See you don't fall off! You seem to have dropped asleep on your horse."

"Leave me alone, father," replied Dugu, jumping down and letting the horses trot into the courtyard.

"Where have you been?" asked his father.

"To Răteasca. I went with Teican's son."

"Go and get your supper. You haven't eaten anything since morning," his father told him.

The boy sat down on the top step of the porch, then suddenly got up and walked into the house. There he threw himself on his bed and, placing his arms under his head, lay staring at the ceiling.

"Aren't you going to eat anything, Dugu?" his mother asked from the kitchen.

"No, mother, I'm not hungry," he replied.

His eyes travelled from the ceiling to the window. The sun was setting and the shadow of the apple tree in the garden stretched far out into the middle of the room.

The boy lay motionless, staring at the strange patterns formed by the tossing leaves; he watched them as they met and parted, spread apart, then clung together; now they looked like a host of fighting men, or like animals and birds, strange creatures constantly intertwined in a struggle. He turned to see better, his head leaning over the end of the bed, his hair hanging over his flushed face.

Dusk was falling.

Later, when it was quite dark and they sat at supper, Dugu heard his friend whistling at the gate, then his voice calling:

"Hi, Dugu, hi."

Dugu rose, took his stick from behind the door and walked out into the dark garden.

"I saw Achim going to Drina's," Teican's son said. "Did you tell her not to talk to him? I ask you because girls are the devil. They'll come out and talk to the man who comes first."

"She won't," replied Dugu.

"Listen to me, I know what I'm saying."

"I told her we'd meet tomorrow at Lisandru Voicu's wedding."

"But did you tell her you were coming tonight?"

"I didn't. I wanted to see what she'd do," said Dugu slowly. "We'll see. Has she been walking out with Achim-Achim for long?"

"I don't suppose so," replied Teican's son, "because Achim is only just back from the army. So you see. . . . Anyway, I think you ought to go and see if she is talking to him now."

"She isn't, I tell you. But if you like we can make a bet."

"I don't bet. How long have you known her?"

"I think I once danced next to her," answered Dugu, trying to remember. "I don't know, but I tell you she won't go out to him."

"I'm passing that way anyhow—my girl lives damned far,

near the forest—and I'll have a look and tell you tomorrow morning. Are you going to bed?"

"Yes," replied Dugu, pressing his back against the gate and stretching his muscles.

"Right, I'll be off. I'll come with the horses to fetch you tomorrow morning."

Dugu returned slowly to the house, whistling gaily to his dog. The evening was calm and the heat of the day had vanished. The sky above was studded with stars and the tall, motionless acacia trees looked huge in the darkness. After some time Dugu went to bed and fell asleep at once.

When Dugu awoke next morning, he heard flapping wings, then the long crow of a cock. The boy woke up to the joy of a new day. In a flash he remembered it was Sunday and that he would see the girl at the wedding. He leaped out of bed with a yell which shook the window panes. A hen, sitting near his bed, for he slept outside, on the porch, gave a frightened cackle, and ran away with a flutter of wings.

"Does it last long when you get that way?" asked his father, who had sat up in bed, too, and was rolling his first cigarette that morning.

But Dugu did not hear the remark. He pulled on his white drill trousers and ran barefoot out into the garden, calling to his dog.

"Ursu, come Ursu, catch him!"

The dog began to prance, looking around in surprise.

"Get him, Ursu . . . catch him!"

The boy rushed into the garden, the dog running in front. Dugu was pointing to something ahead and yelling:

"Catch him, Ursu, good boy!"

The dog jumped, looked around giving a short bark, then ran on again. Suddenly the boy stopped and, approaching the dog, picked him up by the back of his neck and flung him into the air. The dog struggled, twisted, fell, and picking himself up, was off like a shot, scattering the barnyard fowls.

"It's too early, Teican's son," shouted Dugu from the end of the courtyard, when he saw his friend on horseback in the middle of the road.

"It doesn't matter. You can't make him wait. Come on, let's go," called Teican's son.

"Who's waiting for you boys?" asked Dugu's father from the porch.

"We're going after rabbits, Uncle Tudor," answered Teican's son.

"Going after rabbits in summer? Listen to me, Teican's son, don't get into trouble wherever you're going, for I'll hold you responsible, not this young devil."

Teican's son laughed, curbing the impatient horses as they stood in the middle of the road, but did not reply. Dugu put on his shoes quickly and bringing the two horses from the stable, mounted and dashed off.

"Come on, Teican's son."

"Give him his head," replied the other, as his horse shot ahead.

"Wait, wait," shouted Dugu from behind. "Stop, or we'll knock over something! Tell me, did you pass by her house last night?"

His friend pulled up and waited for Dugu to catch up, but only replied when they rode on more slowly.

"I'll tell you. What do you expect?"

"I know, she didn't go out to him."

"You're a fool," Teican's son replied drily. "Why shouldn't she? She didn't know who was whistling, did she? What if it had been you? Well, Achim-Achim whistled for some time in vain, then he walked off a little way, sauntered around, came back and whistled again, but differently, see? The girl, who had known it was Achim the first time, hadn't come out, but she didn't think he'd come back a second time. . . ."

"And she came out?"

"Of course she did. She said good evening, but didn't open the gate. She stayed behind the fence. 'Come out here, I want to talk to you,' he said to her. 'I won't, I'm afraid you'll hit me,' she replied. But Achim, that sly devil, spoke in a honeyed voice: 'Why girl, why should I do such a thing? Don't be silly, d'you think I'm angry with you because of that boy of Mereuta's? Since when have you started talking to him?' Now just listen to what the girl replied. 'Uncle Achim, mother doesn't allow me to stay out so late, I'm going in.' When Achim heard her calling him uncle, he rushed towards the gate, swearing: 'Uncle Achim is it,' he shouted. 'Curse you, you slut. . . .' "

"Shut up," yelled Dugu, spurring on his horse. "I'll break his head open."

"Take care he doesn't break yours first," replied Teican's son, tearing after Dugu.

They had left the village behind and were galloping down the road.

"I'll let you fight it out, both of you," shouted Teican's son above the drumming of the horse's hoofs.

"You can turn back and go home if you like," yelled Dugu. "Catch me if you can."

The horses rushed on at breakneck speed, leaving behind a trail of thick white dust. After a time they turned off the road, riding across the stubble fields. Field paths drew near, intercrossed, then dropped behind, vanishing in the folds of the land.

The two riders speedily approached the tall oak trees silhouetted against the distant skyline.

"Teican's son, I'll soon be done with him!" shouted Dugu. "Look, he's not alone."

"It doesn't matter, the others are my job," yelled back Teican's son. "Make up your mind now, we're getting near."

As they approached the group of men, the two riders instinctively quickened their pace and began to circle the tree as if they were crazy. Achim-Achim and the two other men stood near the tree, leaning on their cudgels and calmly watching the antics of the two riders.

The latter suddenly reined in and leapt off their horses.

"Just watch me, Teican's son, and see what I'll do!"

Dugu threw away his stick, which had a small knob at one end, and swiftly walked towards Achim. When the latter saw Dugu approaching, he stirred and gripped his cudgel more firmly.

"You've brought along your cudgel, eh?" mocked Dugu as he approached.

When Dugu was only a few paces away, Achim-Achim stepped back and, holding the cudgel between two fingers, began twirling it lightly and calmly in front of Dugu.

Teican's son had stopped some way off and was looking at the other two men, trying to make out who they were.

"Get back or I'll hit you," said Achim-Achim grimly as he advanced, still twirling his cudgel.

Dugu did not move. He took off his hat slowly and said with a smile:

"Go on, hit me, go on," as he thrust his head forward.

Achim-Achim stopped.

"Why don't you hit me, Achim?"

"Hit him," shouted one of Achim's companions.

Dugu walked up to him.

"Go on, you hit me then. Go on."

Achim-Achim suddenly threw away his cudgel and cursed.

"So you're afraid," he said loudly. "You thought you'd find me alone and brought Teican's son along to be two against one."

"Dugu, come on, let's go," called Teican's son.

"Just a minute, I'm coming. What did you say, Achim?" asked Dugu with a smile, as he stepped nearer. "Why didn't you hit me, eh? Just tell me why!"

Achim-Achim realized that Dugu was laughing at him and saw red.

"Is that it?" he shouted and struck out swiftly aiming at Dugu's jaw.

It seemed that Dugu had been expecting this, for he avoided the blow and, knocking aside Achim's arm, leaped on to his back and with his elbow landed a blow on the back of Achim's neck. Achim stumbled and tried to hit out again. Dugu, however, was quicker and getting under him tripped him up, so that Achim fell and rolled in the stubble. Then Dugu threw himself on Achim. But, to his surprise he also found himself lying on the ground and had hardly time to avoid Achim, who had got up and was rushing at him with upraised fists. One of Achim's companions had seized Dugu by the neck and was raining blows on him.

"Teican's son," shouted Dugu, but stopped, for he saw him attacking Achim's companions, one of whom lay yelling on the ground, whilst the other was running towards the horses.

Dugu jumped up, stepped back and seized his cudgel. Achim-Achim did the same.

"My elbow is bleeding, Achim-Achim. The devil take me if I don't break your head," cried Dugu, feeling his left arm growing numb with pain.

Achim-Achim, black with rage, raised his cudgel and aimed a blow straight at Dugu's head. Dugu tried to parry the blow, but was unable to stop it. However, he took it on his shoulder instead of his head.

"Go on, Achim, hit harder, go on!" shouted Dugu.

He stepped back and tensed his muscles. He realized that he must not let Achim hit him again. Achim's cudgel was heavier and he was stronger than Dugu. So he rushed at Achim, raining blows on his head and forcing him to be on the defensive the whole time. But Achim-Achim did not heed his blows and parried them easily, twirling his cudgel to protect his head. Dugu, however, suddenly changed his

tactics and swinging his cudgel sideways, instead of aiming
it at Achim's head as before, sent the other's cudgel flying
out of his hand. Taken by surprise, Achim let it drop. Then
Dugu punched him straight on the nose and, picking up
Achim's cudgel from the ground, sent it flying to the top of
the oak tree.

Achim-Achim stumbled and held his nose, moaning.

"I've finished, Teican's son," called out Dugu.

"You got him?" asked Teican's son.

"I did, but he bruised my elbow because I was a fool
and waited for him to hit first.

"Well, another time you'll know better," Teican's son
told him.

They jumped on their horses and as they galloped off
Dugu shouted over his shoulder to Achim:

"Listen, you may be stronger, but if I catch you hanging
around her I'll break your head, so don't say I didn't warn
you. . . . Even if you bring your whole gang from Catelesti,
d'you hear, Achim's son? I'll beat you all. . . . Come on . . .
catch me, Teican's son!"

When Dugu reached home and dismounted, he remained
standing by the horses filled with wonder He felt that a
change had taken place in him. He realized that he was
standing in the middle of the courtyard, holding the two
horses by their halters; he became aware of the hot sun,
the tall green acacias, the houses, the air, the ground, and
the people talking nearby; his ear, like a sensitive shell,
caught the murmur of sounds from all around; he became
aware of his dog dying in the shade with half-closed eyes,
of the horses' hoofs sinking into the thick white dust, of
the birds and pigeons wheeling in the air above, of the vast
blue dome of the sky and deep peace; he perceived them all
suddenly, and a great, unknown joy filled his whole being.

He patted the back of one of his horses and his face
suddenly lighted, as if at last some elusive thing had unfolded and been scattered, so that he could now see it wher-

ever he looked and wherever his thoughts wandered. "Drina," he whispered and his face filled with light. "Poor Achim," he said gently, then added: "After all it's his own lookout. I saw her and fell in love, so that's that. He doesn't love her, for if he did. . . ."

"Hello, have you become rooted to that spot?" called his father from the window. "Tell me, are you thinking of getting married? For heaven's sake, don't do it today, because I won't receive you in the house, I'll kick you out."

"We'll see," replied the young man, standing near the horses. "We'll see, when it happens. Come on," he said to the horses, slapping their rumps to urge them forward. Then he turned and walked slowly, like a man with many worries, towards the gate which he had left open.

# SOVIET RUSSIA

# The Easy Life

YURI KAZAKOV

Translated by Murlin Croucher

THE NORTHBOUND TRAIN rushed on, past the sidings and small stations, not even stopping at many of the large terminals. On this trip, in the entire train, there was not a man happier than Vasily Pankov.

Vasily had not written during the five years that he had been away from home. What was there to write about? He lived easily enough; liked moving, the ever stretching road, and unknown cities. He had become used to train stations with their never-changing specific smells, to the transit ticket windows, and to the regional hotels and hostels. . . . A wanderer by nature, he seldom recalled those places where he happened to stay. He would not be going there again and so he did not even remember all of them very well. He had seen so many cities, towns, Godforsaken places—how could one remember them all!

During the past two months he worked on the installation of a power boiler, overfulfilling the work quotas, and hurrying to finish the work on time. The unfinished brick building of the electric power station could be seen on the gentle slope of a bare river bank, alongside a lumbermill with enormous piles of timber. It still had no roof, and the winches and bent boiler pipes made it resemble the skeleton of some huge prehistoric animal. There were lines of ropes and cables, logs, overhanging beams, a light-blue sky in the background, a sun that burned all day, dust, sweat, cries of workers, rush,

310

arguments, splutterings of autogenous welders, frequent howling bangs of pneumatic drills, the odor of carbide, filings, and slag stick with oil.

Finally came the time for setting the installed and welded boiler. For a long time a special committee doubted the strength of the cables and winches, but Pankov took ehe responsibility on himself. Pale, notwithstanding his swarthiness, he stood on the bridge, listening to the screeching of the block and tackle and cracking noise of the winches. Licking his dried-out lips, he watched the slowly rising cold skeleton of the boiler. Next to him stood his entire brigade of eleven men, clenching their teeth and breathing hard.

The following day they gave the brigade a diploma of good work, and in the evening he got drunk, fought with someone, kissed someone, and cried. When he woke up in the barracks the next morning he was beaten up, in a torn shirt, and had a splitting headache. For a long time he could not come to or remember anything that happened the day before.

He was going home. He was in that relaxed mood when everything seems simple and beautiful, when not even the slightest trouble clouds one's life. Pankov felt no desire aside from wishing to rest, live at home, laze on a haystack, become tipsy, play pranks, play on his concertina—in a word, he was on vacation! He thought only about the countryside. The villagers constantly came to his mind. He remembered their voices, speech manners, walks, customs, faces. . . . What he wanted was to see them all again, to chatter, boast a little, go drinking with many of them. Yes, he would gladly taste all that again. Pankov no longer thought about the boiler installation or his recent work.

2

The next day, Vasily Pankov drank a cognac at a station, and happy, constantly smiling and eyes aglow, returned to the train.

Vasily was blond-haired and oddly dark complexioned—in the village everybody called him "Smoked." His eyes were grey, happy, a bit impudent, and slightly bulging. Generally speaking, he was choosy, reserved, and dandyish. He liked clean underclothes, silk shirts, and ties. Of course he realized that he pleased the girls. He befriended them quickly and just as quickly left them. They bored him. A long time ago he decided to marry at twenty-eight, and without fail, in his own rural area. He knew that his mother had already picked out two or three brides—all good ones: healthy, beautiful, from good families which show no drunks or fools in their stock. Now it was his business to pick from these two or three. His father, grandfather, neighbors and older brothers married this way, and so would he.

In half an hour Vasily was loudly laughing and talking, turning to everyone indiscriminately: to neighbors, conductors, to young and old.

"Mamma," he said, "of course, you forgive me. Forgive me. I am completely sober. Well, I've been drinking. True. But is there a law that says you can't drink? Who am I? A constructor! Yes, Mamma, they have asked for me in Moscow at time and a half basic pay. Yes! But in my own business I can make even more! Don't you believe me, Mamma?"

For a long time he explained about earnings, types of engineers, despising their diplomas and education, generally disdaining culture, putting experience above everything, and bragging about his own importance.

In the next compartment they began to play cards and Vasily went over there, and sat down also. But, he played poorly, mixed up his turn, dropped the cards, and talked constantly. He remembered some one-armed person with whom he had once played, how this one-armed chap dealt the cards, and remembered all the turns.

A dark, heavy-set man with a rosy smooth face, gold teeth, oily bright eyes, and wearing a white smock entered the coach. He remained in the corridor in the center of the

coach and while glancing at everyone and quickly fixing a
studied cold smile said in a ringing full baritone:

"Dear friends! Our restaurant is at your disposal. What?
You can play later. . . . Cold and hot appetizers! A large
assortment of wines."

Rousing himself, Vasily Pankov went straight to the dining car, rocking at the intersections, not closing the doors
behind him, pushing and clutching at the passengers. In
the restaurant he met someone from another car, went there
with him, invited him to his country house, sang songs, interrupted everyone, tried to say something, and although wanting to appear more intelligent and educated than he actually
was, only drunken, stupid ignorance came out of him.

After about two hours, he returned to his own car, sat
down with some people playing chess, butted in and disturbed them. He then played himself, and exactly as when
playing cards, he mixed up the pieces, dropped them, slowly
looked for them under people's feet, and argued. It was impossible to play with him. Having wearied and driven the
other player out of his wits, he started walking up and
down the coach.

"Well, who wants to play with me?", he loudly asked.
"For a half pint! I'll forfeit my rook. Well, who wants to?"

No one wanted to play with him.

"Nobody wants to. Weaklings, you're all against me. Hey,
curly!" He turned to a completely bald fat man. "Let's play,
curly. I'll forfeit both my rooks. O.K.?"

The man turned to the window and acted as though he
did not hear. Blood rushed to his neck.

"Hey pops, huh? You want to play?" Vasily did not
quiet down. "For a pint, huh? You don't want to? Are you
insulted pops? Excuse me, excuse me!"

A young girl, whom Vasily apparently pleased, could not
bear it and burst out laughing. Cheered up and feeling that
everyone was paying attention to him, Vasily started clown-
ing around even worse. He was happy and thought that he

was terribly clever. He made puns, and spoke with flourishes and proverbs while telling road tales and banalities.

Nevertheless, he tired at last, quieted down, and fell asleep on his own berth. He slept with his hands dangling, his mouth agape, and snoring loudly.

In the meantime, the train rushed on further and further to the north. The day passed quickly. Beyond the windows the sky faded, fields darkened, woods became gloomy, the sunset paled and disappeared. Soon, the lights in the coach were lit. Tea was passed around, and the second night on the road began unnoticed.

### 3

How wonderful it was to travel in a train at night! The coach flinched and rocked at the rail joints, and the little dull lights shined dimly under the ceiling. Someone mumbled a word in his sleep, someone slid down from his berth, sat at the window, smoked, thought awhile, and everything was hushed at this hour. Everything was quiet, only the rails below gave a muffled sound.

Outside was a dark, moonless night. Now and then a weak light from a trackman's shack flashed past like a strange vision, or there was a small lonely station of unknown name and with its one light on the steps and the traditional birches in front. Again the window was covered with a dense impenetrable mist, and one did not know whether a forest or a field was beyond the window.

It was nice to ride in a train at night. It was nice to doze off and wake up and remember with a pounding heart the happiness or bitterness that one dreamed—nice to think that silent trees, lakes, hay stacks, lonely trackmen's shanties, and rivers known only by the sound of their bridges, were flashing past. A shimmering red spot of a bonfire appeared somewhere in the limitless black distance, stayed almost on one spot for a long time, and was then blocked out by a hillside or woods. Or, a car appeared from somewhere and traveled alongside the train. Its headlight beams jumped in front of it, and then the car, too, slowly fell behind and it was dark once again. . . .

How much land you have put behind you, how many towns and stations have rushed past while you slept and meditated! In these towns and at these stations lived people whom you have not seen and never would see, about whose life and death you would never hear, just as they would never hear about you. One's heart is rent from the thought that we will never see the great impenetrable multitude of destinies, grief, happiness, love and everything which is generally called life. The wheels clattered and you traveled on and on, towards the new, the unknowns, and that which happened yesterday is all behind and gone! How strange it was to think of all this under the even pounding of the wheels, under the hum of fast movement.

Vasily Pankov woke up at one o'clock at night. For a minute he thought dully about where and why he was traveling. Then everything came back to him and he felt a little livelier. His head ached, but it was already so late that everything was closed, and he was not able to get a drink for his hangover. Nevertheless, he became happier by the minute: his station was to come soon! Having lit a cigarette, he went out on the platform, opened the outer door, and tightly clung to the railing.

The wind blew against his face, touseled his hair, and caused his eyes to water. Yellow patches of light from the window jumped along the grass, bushes, and telegraph poles. Ahead, at the curves, he could see the twisted shaft of sparks from the steam engine quickly unwinding and melting in the darkness. Above, shone countless stars in the darkened ashy sky, the smoky Milky Way glimmered, and to the north, it looked like a bottomless abyss. There was nothing, not even a star, only lonely black space.

Pankov was happy. How many more miles yet to the

station? Three? Five? He breathed deep and hard, pushing the dense air out of his chest, but he did not want to return, did not want to go back into the coach. The black space kept moving. Now there were stars only above his head, and Vasily could not understand just what was happening. The first large drops of rain beat against his face, the wind was growing colder, and only then did he understand: what had seemed to be a black space was actually some rain clouds. He stepped back on the platform, wiped his wet face with a cold hand, and went in the coach.

Inside it was stuffy. Pankov stopped next to his berth, looked down the long dimly lit corridor where legs, some in socks, some without socks, dangled from the berths. He adjusted his suitcases and thoughtfully put on his jacket and hat.

Having slammed the door, the lady conductor went out on the platform. The train started to brake slightly. Returning, she said, "Torbeevo. Who is getting off at Torbeevo?"

Vasily stood up, straightened out his jacket, his hat, hastily grabbed his heavy suitcases, and knocking against the berths, dragged his things to the exit.

"Well, at last—here I am," he mumbled excitedly to the conductor and rushed out.

At the station blew a fresh wind of light misty rain. Pankov got off the train, set his baggage down, looked ahead, and then turned around. He saw no one. The puddles on the ground reflected squares of light from the train windows. The conductor also jumped down to the ground, quickly looked around as though she wanted to always remember these puddles, the smell of the clean wet grass, and the black telegraph poles.

"What, they haven't come to meet you?" asked the conductor gaily, expecting to hear an equally cheerful answer.

However, Vasily remained gloomily silent. He was confused and worried. A single light stood out in front, shining and blinking through the birch trees. The tall station building with lighted windows could be seen further on, while everything else faded into darkness. Not waiting for an answer, the lady conductor came out to the platform. In front, near the baggage car, someone waved a lantern. The train gave a shrill whistle and the cars started with a clank. Stretching out her hand with the lantern, and fixing her cap with the other hand, the conductor looked at Vasily and finally cried out, "Look in the station, maybe they're hiding from the rain!"

Vasily fixed his hat, breathed in deeply, grabbed his suit-cases and walked past the front yard into the station.

<br>

## 4

He entered a dark corridor, bumped against a metal thing leaning against the wall, fumbled, and opened the door. The last time he was in the station was five years ago. But, on entering, he noticed that nothing has changed in this large room. The walls were still covered with the same election posters, train schedules, and passenger rules. A large light shined in a darkened shade made from newspapers, large yellow cucumbers and bread laid on a table. . . . Only the assistant station master was new. He screamed angrily into the telephone, not even glancing at Vasily. For some reason the stove was burning. A railwayman was sprawled out on a bench, with his bag of tools under his head. His folded back arm was black and shiny with oil. A lamp smoked on the floor next to his feet. The place smelled of shag, the stove's birch-wood, and heated iron.

In the corner, someone gave a long and delicious yawn. An old man's ruddy face with a reddish beard and moist eyes looked out from behind the stove. Having noticed Vasily Pankov, the old man remembered, blinked guiltily, snatched the hat from his head, emerged from the corner, and extended his toil-hardened, rough hand.

"Greetings. I've been waiting for you!" he said uncertainly and smiled, showing yellow corroded teeth.

"Uncle Stepan!" Pankov immediately recognized his neighbor and distant relative. "But where's Mamma?"

"Who?"

"What's wrong with my mother? Is she sick or something?"

"With your mother? What's the matter with her? She's alive and healthy, waiting for you. I've come to get you. She dropped in. . . . 'Go,' she says, 'meet him.' "

"And I began to think all sorts of things," Vasily said, giving a sigh of relief. "Did you come on horse?"

"Ha-ha," laughed Stepan. "What's with you? Don't you know? We have a streetcar now. Horses! What a strange fellow you are!"

Stephan fused about, gathered up some sacks and bags in a corner, while tying and untying the ropes.

Having regained his composure, he excitedly looked Vasily over from head to foot, grunted, took a suitcase and, bent to one side, crossed the threshold, clomped along the corridor, and exited to the street. Turning to the left, he walked to the streetcar. Vasily followed him. It was drizzling as before. The birches rustled and wet leaves glistened under the street lights. The rails gave a dull shine on the place where the train had been standing just awhile ago, and a little farther, on the spare lines, were silhouetted the long platforms loaded with freight.

"For some reason we didn't hear anything from you. How are you?" asked Stepan, stopping to hoist the suitcase up on his shoulder.

"I am all right! I work as a construction engineer," said Vasily, tongue in cheek. "I earn enough. We construct everything."

"Really," wondered Stepan and spat with relish. "So you construct things? That's good work. Here, Vasily Egorich, we also had such construction going on—put the whole town in turmoil. Now we have a large factory on this bank of the river, a village, a lot of people, many are from Moscow. The girls have almost gone crazy. As soon as they started having evening balls—into the factory club, and you can't chase them out of there. And many people who work here drive our chairman nuts. There's an extirely different life in the town now!"

"Aha!" Vasily was amazed in his turn. "And how are you?"

"Who?"

"You, how are you?"

"Me? Ha!" Stepan livened up. "I'm alone. . . . Alone! The old woman, you see, died two years ago. I took her to the graveyard, gave a memorial service, all like it should be, on my word. I have daughters, you know. I gave my daughters away in marriage. Well, now they live in their own houses. So I'm alone now—oh, it's all right! Give me a free life, I'll be thankful for that! I'd like to live to my heart's content!"

They stepped over to the big streetcar.

"Is that all or is someone else dragging along?", asked the driver in a tenor voice while finishing a cigarette.

"That's all," snapped out Stepan climbing up on the step.

The driver tossed the butt in a puddle, gave a signal and listened.

"Let's go then!" he said and started the motor. "If anyone's late, too bad."

The streetcar bumped along, the headlights flared up, bringing out from darkness the road signs, shields, cross ties, and lonely bare pines. Arrows flashed past. Clattering along on the rail joints, the streetcar picked up speed and with a loud toot of its whistle, sailed into darkness. A few passengers were silent, looked out the windows, and fogged the glass with their breath.

Vasily was completely happy because he would soon see his mother and because the streetcar was warm and smelled of gasoline, grease, and suitcases. The rain was letting up. Dark violet splotches with stars began to appear on the black sky. He sat sideways, his legs spread apart, and hat pushed to the back of his head. He liked the old man Stepan, the driver, the passengers, the roar of the wheels, the speed at which they were rushing along, and the clean native air blowing in through the crack.

He bent toward the old man. "Uncle Stepan, come to our place. We'll sit around and have a drink. Today the two of us will have a hell of a good time."

The old man's beard raised a little and spread out. He reached in his pocket, bent toward his knees, fidgeted in the dark, then struck a match and smoked: it was clear, he had rolled a cigarette.

The trolley rushed on, now and then giving a whining whistle. Ahead, the lights of the factory were already glowing. Stepan fussed about, stretched his neck, and glanced ahead. He was also having happy thoughts. Soon they will be there. There will be a bustle in the Pankov home—the neighbors will come, everyone will start talking. . . .

## 5

At home in the country everything happened just as he had imagined. Every day he went for a walk, played on the concertina, renewed his acquaintance with the girls, (who blushed with pleasure), went to the factory club and to the neighboring town, boasted of his successes and of his life, and went fishing on the shoals. During these days he was happy without noticing it, satisfied. No matter what he did, no matter what he said, he felt the adoration and kindness of his mother, who missed him so much. He realized that he was handsome, young, that he pleased the girls, and was sure that almost all of them dreamed of marrying him. He needed nothing else.

But one time, when he awoke before dawn in the loft

where he usually slept, it was as though some voice was distinctly pronouncing his name, calling him somewhere. Awake, he heard a cow breathing below, and the mice scurrying in the hay. He smoked eagerly, putting the palm of his hand under the cigarette so as not to scatter the sparks.

He suddenly felt the familiar yearning for the road, the stations and hotels. . . . He was fed up. Life in his native town already seemed boring and unattractive to him. He was thinking about where to go in the remaining time. He went to the hut, drank milk, counted his money by the little dawn-lit window, listened to the sleepy breathing of his mother, and started thinking again.

At last he remembered that during the winter he had received an invitation to visit a friend who lived in a distant southern city. Having remembered this, he immediately decided not to put off his visit. He shivered with a chill of happiness and returned to the loft where he lay down in the fragrant hay and fell asleep.

During the day he packed and went around to the neighbors and relatives to say goodbye. He shook hands in a special way with the girls who happened not to work in the fields, some of whom he even hastily kissed in the dark passageways. He promised everyone to write, knowing that he would not write. His mother cried furtively, and Vasily also became sad for a moment, but happiness welled up within him, and his heart beat quickly: on the road again! On the road again!

At the station, Vasily felt oppressed. Uncle Stepan uncorked a bottle and gloomily took a drink. His mother sat propped up, blinked tearfully, and could not tear her eyes away from her son. When Vasily arrived on that happy late evening, she ran around the house not even feeling her legs beneath her, raising dust with joy and feeling quite young. And now at the station, she was an old woman again, sitting and watching her son.

"Why are you like this?" she said from time to time.

"You should have stayed longer . . . , in your native house. You'll never write to your mother—that's how you are! Where will you be? . . . You have no nest, you are a stranger to everyone."

Uncle Stepan also looked at Vasily and wanted to say something, but only groaned and took another drink.

"And now this. Where are you going?" said his mother with a feeling of lament.

Suddenly Vasily felt hot. He lowered his head and thought about his life. In fact, he felt quite bad! Everything happened by chance, no real friends, nothing—only the road, only a memory of station restaurants.

Now he felt sorry for himself, some kind of bitterness and dissatisfaction filled his heart. He felt bored and ashamed —there was nothing else to say.

Two hours later—having said goodbye to his mother, having embraced and kissed her for the last time, having felt sorry at the same time for her and for himself, having wiped his eyes—after two hours he found himself in a dining car, behind a table next to the window.

This time the train was speeding to the south. Again, towns, stations, roads, fields, and woods were flashing past the window. Sitting across from Pankov were two young lieutenants in parade dress. Both were dark-haired, with little sprouting moustaches, school insignias, and an expression of satisfaction and happiness. Neither could take his eyes off the girls sitting behind Pankov. They laughed, whispered, drank beer, made thin whisps of smoke from their cigarettes, and both blushed when the girls looked at them.

Vasily Pankov got drunk quickly; he wanted to talk, make noise, and bring attention to himself. He stood up, and swaying, with a glass in his hand, approached the neighboring table. He drank a toast with everyone, said something, laughed, and slapped everybody on the shoulder.

"You'll have to excuse me," he said. "Excuse me."

Then he returned to his table, and feeling condescension

and envy at the same time, stared at the lieutenants. He followed the waitresses with his eyes, listened to the radio, drank in this restaurant air, and excitedly thought about the city where he was going. Having forgotten about his mother, his native home, about Stepan and the girls, he is perhaps, once again the happiest person in the entire train.

The easy life! He rushes over the land, hurries, does not look back on anything, is always happy, noisy, and self-satisfied. But his happiness is empty, and his self-satisfaction is sad, for he is really not yet a man but simply a form of tumble-weed.

# SOUTH AFRICA

# The Prisoner

### Ahmed Essa

DR. THEMBA was reading the handbill when he was arrested near the bus rank at the end of Victoria Street. The boy who gave him the handbill disappeared among the row of buses, engines revved, waiting to be filled before plunging down the slope and journeying to the outskirts of Durban. The handbill, hastily composed and hurriedly printed, called on the non-Europeans to stay away from work. The dirty-blue police van screeched to a halt at his side, several police sprung out and the next moment he was pushed into the van with four other Africans and an Indian. They were charged for being in possession of propaganda advocating the overthrow of the South African government through illegal means.

At the police station, there was a feeling of camaraderie among the Africans, Coloreds and Indians—they were used to being arrested for all kinds of reasons. "Your first offense, doctor?" they asked and then reassured him, "Don't worry," one Indian kept rolling the r's. "You'll be discharged by and by." But the English judge, a phlegmatic fellow, his nose redder than his face, glanced at Dr. Themba across the courtroom for a brief moment and, as if muttering under his breath "the law is the law," sentenced Dr. Themba to four weeks, with hard labor.

The police van taking him to the central prison was closely packed, with two African policemen wedged in near the door. The airless, lightless interior was heavy with sweat.

The journey, punctuated with jolts as the van stopped or started moving again, appeared interminable. The metal rooftop of the van absorbed the heat and congealed the air inside. The stench of the sweat became unbearable.

Suddenly, the van stopped with a more forceful jolt and, almost simultaneously, the doors of the van were flung open. The air outside was hot but welcome. Two Africans clambered down behind the policeman, then an Indian, and Dr. Themba followed. He had a brief glimpse of the entrance, two enormous wooden doors with spikes above them, like arrow-heads, pointing downwards. One of the African policemen nudged him past one of the doors which stood partly open.

The entrance hall was filled with European police officers dressed in khaki shirts and shorts, standing at arrogant ease, their eyes gleaming like the butts of their revolvers protruding from shining leather holsters attached to their belts. One officer was behind a long wooden counter, collecting and putting into brown paper bags, contents from the prisoners' pockets. At the other end of the counter was another, fingerprinting the prisoners, his hands covered with black leather gloves. Dr. Themba tried to retain his handkerchief, but it was snatched out of his hands and shoved into the bag. The other officer treated him roughly, jabbing his fingers down on the fingerprint form. Grabbing Dr. Themba's right hand, he swung the doctor around. Dr. Themba caught a glimpse of the reddish-pink, hairy chest of the V of the khaki shirt collar of an officer standing next to him. The officer's eyes were making a cold survey of Dr. Themba's appearance. For the first time since he was arrested, Dr. Themba, as if looking at himself in a mirror, became highly conscious of the way he was dressed: a neatly-pressed brown suit, a white, starched shirt, and a conservative maroon tie with a tidy, small knot at the collar. Fortunately, his hair, like that of all Zulus, grew slowly, so that the stubble on his chin was hardly perceptible.

*"Is hy 'n ander verdomde politieke kaffer?"* Dr. Themba heard the man say.

The officer's eyes, the tone of his voice, the gutturalness of his Afrikaans, and the way he spit out the pejorative *kaffer,* all these increased Dr. Themba's rancor. His first impulse was to protest in some violent manner, but he decided to get away from the cold eyes. He moved hastily to catch up with the line moving down the long corridor ahead of him. He stumbled.

"Buck up, you *kaffer!"* the officer suddenly shouted into his ear.

Before Dr. Themba knew what was happening, the officer had caught him by the shoulder and swung him around. The officer's fist, the sharp knuckles jutting out, appeared in front of his face. He felt their impact. The fierce blow caught him on his lips. He lost balance. Putting out his hands to break the fall, he felt the force of the concrete floor against them first, and then against his head. A spinning numbness followed. As he came out of the sudden daze, he saw that another Afrikaner had approached and the two officers seemed to be having a heated argument. His lips were swelling and they felt as large as his face. The echo of pain continued to sing in a corner of his brain. He was conscious now of the warm, saline taste of blood. He ran his tongue along his teeth. They were all intact.

The officer who had hit him walked away and the other stood over him. Dr. Themba got up slowly. He braced himself for another blow.

"You can get back in line now." The officer's voice was subdued.

The other prisoners in the line had stopped and were waiting for him. They started moving the moment he took his first step. Without stopping, he turned around and looked at the officer who had spoken kindly to him. Their eyes met. The officer's eyes were a quiet brown. The officer remained where he was and Dr. Themba continued along the corridor.

As they approached a large room, the Zulu prisoner behind Dr. Themba leaned over and whispered into his ear.

"Do not complain," the Zulu said. "You will make it difficult for all of us."

In the large room, the prisoners were stripping, leaving their clothes in a heap on the cement floor, to be picked up by a regular jailee and stuffed into burlap sacks with labels on them. The European doctor, one hand in the pocket of his long white coat and the other playing with the stethoscope dangling from his neck, asked each prisoner, "Are you in good health?" and without waiting for an answer, passed him on.

"Had an accident?" the European said as Dr. Themba approached him. "Doesn't look too bad. Go and wash it with cold water."

After washing the blood from his face and gargling his mouth with cold water at the sink in the room, Dr. Themba stepped out into the prison yard. In the yard, a European officer, a long cane in his hand, was searching the naked bodies of the prisoners. He rapidly tapped the naked African in front of him, making him dance. He stopped the African's dancing by slapping him on the head. Using the sharp end of the cane, he searched the naked body, pushing the African's mouth open with it, prying into the nostrils, under the armpits, into the crotch and up the rectum. He whacked the African on the buttocks, a red welt appearing where the cane landed, and gestured him to move on. Dr. Themba broke away from the line of prisoners and went and stood in front of the officer. The officer raised his cane and paused, holding the cane poised over Dr. Themba's head. He remained in that position for several moments, glaring at Dr. Themba. Then, glancing over Dr. Themba's shoulder, he tapped him lightly on the shoulder, and shouted, "All right. Get dressed, all of you!" Dr. Themba turned around and found the kind Afrikaner officer behind him. The officer nodded and walked away.

In his prison clothes, a red shirt and white shorts, both oversized and with traces of sweat clinging to them, Dr. Themba was put to work immediately. An African policeman gave him a pick and ordered him to break a pile of stones. At intervals, another prisoner came by with a wheelbarrow, shoveled the broken pieces of rock into the barrow and wheeled it away. Gradually, blisters welled up in Dr. Themba's hands, broke and smarted. For dinner, he was given a zinc dish of mealie-rice with boiled beans. That evening he was put into a long narrow cell. There were forty mats and forty grimy blankets on the floor and a latrine bucket at the far end. The stench of the defecation and urine of many days, the cold of the concrete floor seeping through the mat, the bedbugs, and the burning blisters on his hands prevented him from sleeping at first. But, slowly, he succumbed to his need for sleep. The sleep was interrupted several times during the night by screaming prisoners. The first time he heard a scream, he sat up, his heart beating heavily. The Zulu on the mat next to him put out his hand and gently pushed him back.

"There is nothing you can do, doctor," he said.

"What is happening?" Dr. Themba asked.

"It must be a young man newly come in today," the other said. "Some of the men have been here for years. They have not touched a woman in all that time."

"The officers will be in the cell to stop them," Dr. Themba said.

"That is not so," the man said. "This goes on all the time."

Occasionally, during the next two days, Dr. Themba, pausing in his labor, or sitting down at meals, or on his way to the cell in the evening, looked up to see Sergeant van Schalk—all the prisoners knew the kind Afrikaner officer—and, in return, the sergeant greeted him with his customary nod. On the third morning, after finishing breakfast, Dr.

Themba got up to find Sergeant van Schalk standing in front of him.

"Come," the sergeant said.

He followed the sergeant, who led him to the non-European section of the prison hospital.

"You will work here," Sergeant van Schalk said.

The African orderly came out from his little cubby-hole office.

"Doctor," the orderly said, "I might as well get you straight on your duties. You are responsible for keeping this place clean. Each morning you will scrub the floor and clean the lavatory. You will also see to the needs of the patients here, bringing bedpans and emptying them, and washing those who are unable to do so."

He paused and the doctor looked around. There were twelve beds in the hospital. Seven were occupied. One patient had his right leg in a plaster cast suspended by pulleys. Another's head was bandaged almost up to his eyes. The orderly walked to the door and looked past Sergeant van Schalk standing close by. Seeing no one, he turned to Dr. Themba.

"Technically, you are my assistant, doctor," the orderly said. "That was the only way we could get you in here. I am at your service."

"I understand," Dr. Themba said.

"The European doctor, by the way, doesn't come in here every day," the orderly said. "He's out there seeing the prisoners come in. But he comes here on Mondays, Wednesdays, and Fridays."

Dr. Themba started work immediately. Taking a bucket of water, a scrubbing brush and a bar of brown soap, he got down on his knees in one corner of the ward. He took the brush, scraped some soap on to its sharp bristles, and scrubbed the floor. When he had a small area of the floor soaped, he took a wet rag and wiped off the soap, rinsing the rag each time to clear it of the suds. Sergeant van Schalk sometimes stood by the door. The orderly remained in his office but occasionally interrupted Dr. Themba's scrubbing and cleaning when a prisoner came in for medical attention. Whenever he had a spare moment, Dr. Themba went from bed to bed, looking at the patients. One Zulu patient, who had presumably come in after the last visit of the European doctor, had only his temperature registered on his chart. The temperature was 104°. Dr. Themba's trained ear detected that the patient's breathing sound was almost absent. Later, when the patient coughed, Dr. Themba saw flecks of blood in the sputum.

The next day the European doctor appeared with the orderly at his side. Dr. Themba was cleaning the lavatory at the time, spraying it with sheep-dip, and watched the European doctor through the partly-open door. With the orderly translating for him, the European doctor went from patient to patient. He looked at the chart of the new patient with the high temperature and asked the orderly to inquire what was wrong."

"He complains of pain in the neck and shoulders," the orderly said.

"Exhaustion," the European doctor said. "Give him some aspirin. When his temperature is back to normal, he can go back to work."

Immediately after the European doctor left, Dr. Themba, after washing his hands thoroughly with carbolic soap, approached the patient. Sergeant van Schalk, standing by the door, nodded his approval.

"Why did you not tell the white doctor of the spitting of blood?" Dr. Themba asked the patient.

The patient a drowsy look in his eyes, did not answer. Dr. Themba had the feeling that the patient had resigned himself. Dr. Themba examined him. As he suspected, the percussion note was dull on the right side of the patient's chest. The orderly came in.

"Is anything wrong?" the orderly asked.

"This patient is very ill," Dr. Themba said. "Serofibrinous pleurisy, or what is commonly known as wet pleurisy. He needs to be taken to a hospital immediately."

"Only the European doctor can give an order for removal," the orderly said. "Is there nothing we can do for him here?"

"Nothing, except see that he gets a lot of rest," Dr. Themba said. "You can do one thing when the European doctor comes by again. Let him know all the symptoms: pain in the neck and shoulders, cough and the spitting of blood, pain upon deep breath, nightsweat, and loss of weight."

On Friday morning, watching from the lavatory, Dr. Themba was happy to see everything proceed as planned. The European doctor spent some time at the patient's side. After listening to the orderly, he percussed the patient's chest, looked up and nodded his head several times. Then he called Sergeant van Schalk and asked him to make arrangements to remove the patient to a hospital. That afternoon, two Africans came into the ward with a stretcher and took the patient away.

It became customary for Dr. Themba to examine all the patients, particularly on the days when the European doctor did not visit the ward. Each time Dr. Themba turned to the patients, Sergeant van Schalk gave him the nod of approval. On Thursdays, however, Dr. Themba felt helpless. Thursday was the day set aside to carry out the sentences of lashing. All the prisoners were ordered to witness the meting out of this sentence. The strongest of the European officers tied the unfortunates securely to a triangular wooden frame and lashed them with four-feet long canes until the number of swollen, livil wales on the buttocks oozing with blood corresponded to the number requested by a judge. When the victims came to the hospital door, all Dr. Themba could do was apply some styptic lotion to the bleeding buttocks and offer them aspirin to ease the pain.

One morning a new patient was brought in and Dr.

Themba received the go-ahead signal from Sergeant van Schalk. His back toward the door, Dr. Themba leaned over the African. Hearing a movement behind him, he swung around. Sergeant van Schalk was rushing towards him. The sergeant reached him, and with a sweep of his hand, knocked the mug of water from the stand at the patient's bedside. The mug fell with a dull clink and the water spread across the concrete floor and under the bed.

"You clumsy fool," the sergeant yelled at him. "Clean up the mess you've made."

The blood rushed to Dr. Themba's face. He was about to yell at the sergeant when he glanced at the door. Two European officers had just entered. Dr. Themba understood Sergeant van Schalk's behavior. Without a word, he walked to the bathroom to get a rag to wipe the water off the floor. After the two officers left, Dr. Themba examined the patient while Sergeant van Schalk waited by the door. The patient had a yellow discoloration of the skin and eyes. It was jaundice. With an admonition that the patient explain all his symptoms to the European doctor the next day, Dr. Themba left him to rest.

Almost three weeks had passed at the hospital when Dr. Themba came in to find Sergeant van Schalk talking to an officer in Afrikaans. The officer was the one who had hit him on his first day in the prison. He was arguing with Sergeant van Schalk. Scrubbing the floor as far away from the door as he possibly could, Dr. Themba periodically glanced at the two men. The only word in the conversation he understood was *kafferboetie*—the kaffir's brother. Each time the other officer used the word, Sergeant van Schalk became angrier until, with a final tirade, he strode off, leaving the other officer watching Dr. Themba coldly.

"Come, you *skellum*," the officer said and led Dr. Themba to his old job of breaking rocks.

It took Dr. Themba a while to get used to laboring in the sun again. The blisters returned, his shoulders and back ached. During the lunch break, a prisoner whispered to him, "We are sorry that you are not in the hospital any more." The pain in his shoulders and back disappeared, but the blisters increased. Several days later, he got used to them, too.

One morning, after he had broken enough rocks to pile one wheelbarrow full, he hefted the pick high above his head and almost brought it down on an officer who stepped forward from behind him. It was Sergeant van Schalk. He led Dr. Themba across the rocky area and into the large room where the European doctor had perfunctorily examined him on the day he entered the prison. On the concrete floor was a burlap sack. Dr. Themba looked up at Sergeant van Schalk.

"Your four weeks are over," the sergeant said.

He changed from the prison uniform into his clothes, now full of creases. The blood stains on his coat and shirt and tie had dried into dark, almost black, spots. After four weeks of being barefoot, his feet felt cramped when he put on his shoes. He followed Sergeant van Schalk down the corridor. At the long desk he was given his wallet, his pen, his pencil, his notebook, his prescription pad, his handkerchief, and his loose change. He turned to find some of the officers watching him, including the senior officer, Sergeant van Schalk, and the officer who had hit him. "A prison is no place for a person like you, doctor," the senior officer said. Dr. Themba glanced at the others and said, "No, it isn't."

The entrance hall filled with light. He walked through the partly-open door into the sunshine outside. An expanse of ground stretched in front of him, reaching as far as the railway tracks leading to the Durban Central station. Most of the world was filled with a blue sky. He walked across the ground and paused. Slowly he turned around. The enormous prison door was still partly-open. In the opening stood Sergeant van Schalk. When the sergeant met the Doctor's gaze, he raised his arm. Dr. Themba raised his arm in return, adding in a whisper, "Stay well."

The two, Dr. Themba and Sergeant van Schalk, stood there for several moments, gazing at each other silently across the expanse. The sergeant lifted his hand again, paused, and then closed the enormous prison door against himself.

# TURKEY

# From "Ortadirek"[1]

Yasar Kemal

Translated from the Turkish by Edouard Roditi

THE FIRST RAYS of the sun would soon be lighting up the slopes of the mountain opposite, which seemed to be drawing a deep breath and stretching itself as it awaited the warm bright day. With its yellow, red, greenish-blue, mauve-circled, luminous-winged wild bees, its long-legged ants pressed closely against each other at the entrances to their nests, its eagles, one eye already open, nestling in their eyries, its cloud-white mountain-doves huddling together in a single hollow, its savage hawks and falcons, its ladybirds crowding in thousands in the balls of thistle seeds that are called fairy's nests, its mountain goats and timorous jackals, its foxes, their long red tails tossing like flames, its soft purple bears lying full-length in their winter sleep over the withered yellow leaves, its springing sad deer, their languid eyes like those of a love-lorn girl, its worms, its large and small birds, with all its creatures above the earth and beneath it, the mountain lay, with bared breast and open mouth, waiting for the day to strike its flanks.

Now, on the peaks, in the valleys, over the roads, there would be an awakening, a stirring, a tumult, a frightening activity, as the mountain, its stones, its earth and trees, all rose from their sleep.

The sun first lighted the space of a threshing floor on the

---

[1] *The Mainstay* (a novel).

mountain slope. Then the light crept down into the valley.
Two ants at the entrance to their nest greeted each other
lengthily with their antennae before going off in opposite
directions. The sun then touched Ali's forehead and he woke
up. For a while he could not gather his thoughts and remember where they had halted for the night. His eyes rested
on the peak of the mountain and a heavy pain settled within
him like salt water as he rose. He laid out his bedding, wet
from the night dew, to dry in the sun. A pungent odor of
sweat rose from it and disappeared in the air.

His feet ached and could scarcely bear his weight as he
limped through the fir trees. He rested his left shoulder on
a rock and relieved himself. Still leaning, he tied up the cord
of his *shavar trousers,* then sat down heavily on a stone. He
was painfully sleepy.

Elif had risen before dawn to put the dried curds soup
on the fire and now waited in vain for her husband to return.
She went after him through the trees and roused him from
his half-sleep when she found him seated on the stone.

"Your mother's still asleep. She's completely worn out,
poor thing. You'll be shocked when you see her face all
shrivelled up. She seems to have shrunk to the size of a child.
How are your feet?"

"That salt water did them no good at all. The pain's just
the same, as if they'd been flayed, and it hurts right into my
heart."

"If only you hadn't let your mother walk so long! If only
you'd taken her on your back!"

"I couldn't do otherwise. She'll walk till she hasn't an
ounce of strength left in her. Nothing can stop her. It's me
you should be thinking of, woman. Our children will starve
this year. Adil Effendi will make me pass through the eye
of a needle. Think of me, of my troubles! I'll never reach
the cotton fields in time this year. Never!"

"I just said. . . ." Elif began, then stopped.

Ali plucked the dried stalk of an autumn asphodel and

broke off its end. A tiny bee buzzed out in a flash of blue. He then slit the stalk in two. It was filled with honey which he started lapping up with his tongue. He broke another stalk, then another and another. The honey had a strange acrid taste that went to his head. It carried the smell of new fresh green herbs. Ali was drunk with sleep and honey. His feet were aching and all the scents of the mountain were flowing through his veins.

Elif was staring at him. "For heaven's sake, man! Why, you've become a veritable baby," she cried. "Come and drink your soup instead of picking at stalks like a child."

Ali paid no attention. Once, when his uncle was still alive, they had gone searching for honey together. His uncle knew every nook and cranny in these mountains and by noon had finally discovered in a valley a plane tree that was perhaps a thousand years old. Its trunk and even its long branches were hollow. Ali's uncle had lit a rag placing it in a hole in the tree's trunk and had then kindled a fire that had filled the forest with suffocating smoke. About half an hour later a hive of bees had burst out of the tree swarming into the forest in a vast cloud. "The tree's full to the brim with honey," his uncle had rejoiced. "The whole village could eat of it for a year and there'd still be more. Take out your bread son," he had added and, cutting off a chunk of honeycomb, they had sat down to eat it. Ali had become drunk. A maddening wind had blown through his head like humming bees and he had felt in his blood the scent of all the world's flowers, of cedars, firs and pine trees, and the intoxicating smell of the earth fresh with rain.

Ali broke off another stem and slit it open eagerly. It was again full of honey which he licked with his tongue. What a pity, he thought, a man should be able to eat a pound of this and forget the pain in his feet, forget everything.

"You're out of your mind, man," cried Elif, snatching the stem from his hands and throwing it down. She had begun to be afraid of Ali. She could vaguely discern on the edge of his lips a white line like that of a madman who tries to laugh but cannot and whose face somehow is frozen. "Come and drink your soup!"

Ali was smiling. Elif had never seen him like this. Only madmen laughed in this manner, all expression wiped away from their eyes. "What is it, Ali?" she murmured. "My darling, my brave one, what's the matter with you?"

Hearing Elif's pleading, Ali gathered his wits: "My children will starve this winter. I haven't been able to make it and I never will at this rate. What can I do, tell me? What the hell can I do? Adil Effendi will have me thrown into prison for my debts. And the villagers? And that rascal of a Mad Bekir and the Headman, that demon from hell?" He looked towards the spot where his mother was asleep. "And it's all because of that old pig, may she die like a dog, the old whore, and leave me free. If it weren't for her, we two and the children would have reached the plains of the Çukurova long ago. As if all she's been doing to me weren't enough, now she starts off back to the village and makes me run after her for two whole days. I've a good mind to leave her here and go. I don't care what happens to her."

Elif seized her husband's arm and shook him: "Hush," she whispered. "She's awake. If she hears you. . . ."

"Let her hear," shouted Ali. "Let her hear and croak! Why should my children starve because of her?"

Elif clapped her hand tight over Ali's mouth. "For God's sake Ali, she's your mother. Have you no fear of God? If she's heard you she'll die. She'll kill herself."

"Let her kill herself," snarled Ali from under his wife's hand. "I'll be glad if she does it! I'll celebrate it and in two days, not more, I'll be down in the cotton fields."

"We'll get there anyway. Don't be afraid. When one door closes, Allah always opens another."

"I don't care if He does," growled Ali.

Elif was horrified. "Say you're sorry," she cried. "Say it quickly! It's a sin."

"I won't," shouted Ali at the top of his voice. "Let Allah not open any door and let that house of His crumble in ruins over His head. Let it be wrecked! Wrecked! If He has eyes He can see me and if He has ears He can hear me. I won't repent."

Elif sank to the ground weeping, her hands covering her face. Ummahan and Hassan had been standing at a slight distance, trembling at their father's anger. When Ummahan saw her mother crying, she ran up and, throwing herself down beside her, started weeping too.

Meryemce had been making her way towards the fire when she heard her son's words. Her ears buzzed and her head swam as she dropped down where she stood. Gathering herself into a ball, she remained crouched here, still as the earth, not even stirring a finger.

At the sight of his wife and daughter sobbing their hearts out, Ali's anger subsided suddenly. He had released his pent-up feelings and was now hovering around his wife, not knowing what to do, how to console her. He laid his hand on her shoulder. "Get up, Elif," he murmured in a dead, weary voice. "I didn't mean anything really. Come, let's go and drink our soup. Get up, we must be on the road again. Look how high the sun is already."

Elif and Ummahan's shoulders continued to heave.

"Shut up," shouted Ali to his daughter. "Shut up, you daughter of a dog!"

Ummahan's sobbing stopped as quickly as it had begun.

"Elif," pleaded Ali, "please don't cry. Please!" He smiled bitterly. "There, I'm sorry. You see? I'm saying I'm sorry to Allah." He took his wife's hand and pulled her to her feet.

"You've killed her," murmured Elif, wiping her eyes. "Even if she lives, she'll never recover from this. Poor Mother!" She walked to the fire and looked at Meryemce: "My good mother, my lovely one, you must excuse him, he's your son. He was so blind with anger he didn't know what he was saying. Would a man in his right senses speak of God

like that? You must not worry at all. We'll get to the Çukurova anyway."

No longer angry, Ali was looking guiltily at his mother,
as his wife helped her to her feet and led her to the fire.

Elif then laid the food before Meryemce and handed her
a spoon. They all sat down to eat their soup. Throughout the
meal, Ali could not bring himself to look his mother in the
face, but Meryemce's eyes, wide open and bewildered, were
fixed on her son, as if she could not recognize him. Was this
Ali? Scenes of long ago rose before her eyes. She could not
weep or speak and something was choking within her. A
baby as small as your hand . . . Ali. . . .

You can't remember those days, can you, Long Ali? she
murmured to herself. I've seen no good from you, Longish
Ali, and, *Insallah,* you too will see no good from your children! When you suffer this same bitterness, Longish Ali,
you'll see how a bad word from your child is worse than a
bullet, yes, worse than a bullet that pierces right through your
heart!

She rose and said aloud: "I pray to God that your children will make you suffer as you've made me suffer, Longish
Ali." To conceal her tears, she ran limping into the bushes.

"See what you've done, man," cried Elif angrily.

Ali drew a deep breath: "Shall I kill myself, kill myself
right here?" His eyes fixed on Elif's he was gnawing his forefinger, almost biting into it. Then he tore at a patch in his
jacket and threw it down shouting, "Shall I kill myself?
Kill myself?"

Elif was astounded at her husband's sudden fury: "For
heaven's sake, Ali, don't! Not before the children," she
whispered.

Ali went into the bushes after his mother and found her
in tears, leaning against a sapling. He came up to her silently,
took her hand and kissed it, then came back. "Go and get my
mother, Elif," he ordered. "It's late, terribly late! What shall
I do about these feet of mine? I can hardly walk a step."

Elif went and took Meryemce by the arm and led her out of the bushes.

"I'll never be able to walk in this state. See how swollen and red my feet are? I've thought of something, Elif. . . ." His eyes were bloodshot but there was no trace of anger left in him.

"What is it?"

"We have that sack, you know, and if we cut it in two we could tie each piece around one of my feet."

"Suppose we use the horse's skin instead," whispered Elif into his ear.

Ali flared up gin: "Are you mad? Why, the horse's skin would pinch my feet and make them worse than ever."

Elif hurriedly fetched the jute sack which Ali cut into four pieces with his knife. He wrapped one piece around his right leg and tied it up with some hemp rope. It was just like a broken leg set in plaster. He carefully did the same to his left leg and then rose. It felt strange but at least it was soft. Then he went to their load, tied it up and heaved it onto his back.

"Get going, Elif," he ordered. "You too, children. Be quick about it. Mother, stay beside this warm fire and I'll be back early in the afternoon to fetch you. For God's sake, don't attempt to go back to the village once more."

Meryemce pretended not to hear. She grasped her stick and made for the road, where she stopped. "God will that none of His creatures should have to be carried on other people's backs," she prayed, lifting her hands to the sky. Then she did the ritual rubbing of her face and added: "Amen, Amen!"

Ali hastened after her: "Don't be obstinate, my beautiful mother, stay here. You'll never be able to keep up with us. Sit here. See, you can't even stand on your feet."

"Who says I can't stand," shrieked Meryemce. "My daughter, it's you I'm talking to, Elif! Look after yourselves. Just walk on and leave me. I'll go down to the Çukurova all by myself."

Ali took her arm. "Mother, please don't be obstinate," he pleaded. "Don't make things difficult for me. A little further off, I want to branch off the road in a short cut which is hard to climb but will save us a great deal of time. You'll never find your way and we'll lose each other. Please wait here!"

Meryemce propped her stick against her waist and again lifted her hands to the sky: "Allah, my beautiful, black-eyed Allah, see to it that nobody should be reduced to being carried on another's back, not even a mother by her son! "Amen!" She looked at Elif: "Walk ahead, my golden-hearted girl. I'll follow you slowly. Don't let your children go hungry this winter because of me. . . ."

Realizing that his mother had heard his former outburst, Ali became angry again. "Stay," he shouted, "or go wherever you wish. I won't have my children starve because of you. Come on," he cried to his wife and children. "Get going. Let her stay or walk on by herself. She'll see."

# Baby Born in the Field

ORHAN KEMAL

Translated from the Turkish by Talât Sait Halman

IN THE COTTON FIELD which stretched as far as the
eye could see, farm hands, fifteen or twenty in a row,
worked steadily at the weeds around the seedlings.

The temperature soared to a hundred and forty-nine in
the sun. No bird flew in the shimmering, dust-gray sky. The
sun seemed to sway. The peasants, soaked with sweat, pushed
and pulled their hoes in a steady rhythm. The sharp edges of
the hoes chopped the parched soil with a "thrush, thrush,
thrush" sound. The song the farm hands sang in unison to
the measured beat of their hoes was swallowed up in the
sun's scorching heat:

> Into what is left back they sow millet
> They sow it they reap it and they wrap it
> My darling sent me pear and pomegranate

Ferho Uzeyir wiped the sweat off his swollen hands on
his baggy black trousers and turned his bloodshot eyes on
his wife swinging her hoe beside him. He spoke in Kurdish,
"Wha? Whatsda matter?"

Gulizar was a broad-shouldered husky woman. Her dried
up face, glittering with sweat, was contorted with deep lines
and grimaces of intense pain.

She did not answer. Angered, Ferho Uzeyir jabbed his
elbow into her side: "What's up wid yo' woman?"

Gulizar gave her husband a weary glance. Her eyes had sunk with fright into their sockets. Her hoe suddenly slipped from her hands to the ground. Pressing her huge belly with her hands, she bent over, then fell to her knees on the red earth everywhere cracked by the blistering sun.

The foreman, who stood under his big black umbrella, called out: "Gulizar! Is dat it? Quit workin'! G'on, quit!"

She was writhing with pain. She stuck her shriveled yet strong fingers into a crack of the soil, squeezing them tensely. With an almost superhuman effort, she struggled to control herself. Pitch black blotches fluttered before her eyes. Suddenly she groaned, "Uggghhh!" It was a shame—a disgrace— for a woman in labor to be heard by strange men. Ferho Uzeyir cursed and swung a mighty kick into his wife's side.

The woman crouched meekly on the ground. She knew her husband would never forgive her for this. As she struggled to rise on hands pressed against the hot earth, the foreman repeated: "Gulizar! Quit, sister, quit! G'on now, quit!"

Her pains suddenly stopped, but she felt they would come back—this time more sharply. She headed for the ditch, the farm's boundary, about a thousand feet away.

Ferho Uzeyir growled after his wife, then called to his nine-year-old daughter standing barefoot beside the foreman: "Take yo' mom's place!"

The girl knew this was coming. She picked up the hoe that was as tall as she and whose handle was still covered with the sweat of her mother's hand, and fell into line.

All this was a common affair. The hoeing continued to the beat of the song sung in unison.

The sun fell full on the ditch with its slabs of dung. Green lizards glided over the red earth. Gulizar stood erect in the ditch, looked all around her, listening intently through the scorching heat. There was no one in sight. The radiant void, echoing a shrike's shrieks, stretched endlessly.

She emptied the pockets of her baggy black pants, put down a few items she had gathered when she knew her time was due: two long pieces of thread wrapped around a bit of pasteboard, a rusty razor blade, several pieces of cloth in different colors, rags, salt and a dried-up lemon. She had found these in the farm's garbage can. She would squeeze the lemon into the baby's eyes and rub the baby with salt.

She stripped below the waist, folded the baby pants under a big piece of rock, spread the rags on the ground, unraveled the thread and cut the lemon in two. About to kneel, she heard something move behind her. She covered herself below the waist, turned around. It was a huge dog! She picked up a stone and flung it. Frightened, the dog fled, but did not disappear. It waited, sniffing the air with its wet nose.

Gulizar was worried. What if she delivered the baby right now and fainted—the dog might tear her child to pieces! She remembered Ferice, the Kurdish girl. Ferice too had given birth in a ditch like this and, after placing the baby beside her, had fainted. When she came to, she had looked around—the baby was gone. She had searched high and low. . . . At last, far away beneath a shrub, she had found her baby being torn to pieces by a huge dog!

Gulizar took another look at the dog, studying it closely. The dog stared back at her—it had a strange look. . . .

"Saffron," she said, "Dat look o' yo's ain't no good, Saffron." She wondered how she might call her daughter who was about a thousand feet away. "G'on, beat it! Yo' goddam dirty dog!"

Reluctantly, the dog backed away about thirty feet, stopped, sat on its haunches and, with a blue gleam in its eyes, waited.

At that moment Gulizar felt another pang, the sharpest yet. Groaning, she fell to her naked knees, resting her body on her hands gripping the ground. The vein on her neck, thick as a finger, throbbed. Now came pain after pain, each sharper than the one before. Suddenly a gush of warm blood.

. . . Her face took on a terrified expression. The whole world collapsed before her eyes.

"Ferho, man," the foreman said. "Go take a look at dat dame. . . . She may die or somepin'."

Ferho Uzeyir glanced in the direction of the ditch where his wife was in labor, shook his head, cursed and went on working. Anger at his wife swelled inside. Cold sweat poured from his forehead, trickling through his thick bushy eyebrows.

"Look here, son," the foreman repeated. "Go see whatsa what wid dat dame. Yo' never can tell!"

Ferho Uzeyir threw his hoe aside and walked over. He would give her a kick and another kick. . . . He just couldn't get over the way that good-for-nothing woman had made a monkey of him.

He stopped by the ditch, stared down. Gulizar had fallen on the ground sideways. In the midst of blood-stained rags, the baby—purple all over—was twitching and a huge dog was pulling at it.

He jumped into the ditch. The dog leaped away, licking its blood-covered mouth. Ferho Uzeyir brushed away the green-winged flies gathered on his baby's face. The infant, its eyes closed, kept making motions. Ferho opened the pieces of cloth. The baby was a boy!

A boy!

Ferho changed instantly. He lifted his head to the sky. A smile filled his harsh face. He picked the baby and the bloody rags from the ground.

"Ma son!" he shouted.

He was nearly insane with joy. After four girls—a boy!

Gulizar, sensing the presence of her man beside her, opened her eyes and, in spite of her condition, tried to get up.

"Good fo' yo'," Ferho Uzeyir said. "Good fo' yo', woman!"

He dashed out of the ditch with his boy in his arms. The

foreman saw him coming across the cracked red soil. "Dere, dere . . ." he said, "dat's Ferho comin' dis-a-way!"

Hoeing stopped. The farm hands, leaning on their hoes, stared. Ferho came up panting, out of breath, shouting: "Ma son! Ah gat me a son!"

He pressed his baby, still purple all over inside the blood-drenched rags, to his bosom.

"Hey, careful, man," the foreman said. "Take care, man! Quit pressin' like dat—yo gonna choke 'im. . . . Now get down to de farm-house. Tell de cook Ah sends yo'. Tell 'im he oughta give yo' some oil and molasses. Let's make 'er drink some. G'on!"

Ferho Uzeyir no longer felt tired, the heat no longer bothered him. Now he was as young as a twenty-year-old boy, as light as a bird.

He headed for the farm's mud-baked huts whose thatched roofs loomed ahead.

# There Is a Nut on the Roof

Aziz Nesin

Translated from the Turkish by Gönül Suveren

THE WHOLE NEIGHBORHOOD was in a state of excitement. "There is a nut on the roof."

The street from one end to the other was full of people curious to see the lunatic.

First from the local station, then from police headquarters, cops came in cars. Fire engines followed them. The mother of the nut was imploring her son, "Come down, my boy. Please come down, son."

The lunatic was saying that if he was not made sheriff he would throw himself down.

The firemen opened their nets in case he did. Nine firemen were bathed in sweat while running around the building holding out the net. In a half-imploring, half-threatening tone the police sergeant was trying to lure the nut down.

"Make me sheriff and I'll come down, or else I will throw myself down."

All the imploring and threats were of no use.

"Come on, friend. . . . Why don't you come down!"

"Hey, look. . . Instead of making me come down, why don't you come up!"

Someone from the crowd had a suggestion. "Let's tell him that we made him sheriff."

Another one contradicted him. "How is that possible? Can you get a sheriff from a looney?"

"Good God! We are not really going to make him sheriff."

An old man leaning on his cane said, "That's impossible. In jest or otherwise, that's impossible."

"But maybe he'll come down."

"No, he won't. I know these people. Once they go up, they never come down."

"If he would only come down. . . . The rest is easy."

"He won't come down."

Someone down below shouted, "Hey, we made you sheriff. Come down."

The nut started dancing and shouting. "I won't come down! If you won't make me a member of the City council, I won't come down."

The old man said, "You see, didn't I tell you."

"Let's do what he says."

"He won't come down no matter what you do. Once a person goes nutty enough to climb on the roof he will never come."

The sergeant shouted, "All right. We made you a member of the City Council. Don't keep all of us waiting down here. Come down."

The nut just kept on dancing. "I won't come down. . . . Make me the mayor, then I'll come down."

The old man said, "You see, it's too late. Now he will never come down."

The first chief, who was sweating profusely, said, "What if we said we made him Mayor." Then he cupped his hands to his mouth and shouted, "O.K., son, come down. We made you Mayor, come down and take over your office."

The nut, dancing like mad, shouted back: "I won't come down. What am I to do among people who elect a nut for Mayor? . . . I won't come down."

"All right, then. What do you want?"

"I will come down only if you make me a cabinet member."

After a short discussion the people down below shouted:

"All right, we made you a cabinet member. Now come down. You see, you're holding everybody up."

The nut thumbed his nose at them. "I won't come down among people who make a cabinet member of a nut."

"Come on, brother. Don't be so difficult. You see, we made you a cabinet member and all the other cabinet members are waiting for you. Come on down."

"Who are you kidding? I'll come down and you'll put me in the nuthouse. I won't come down."

The old man said: "Don't make yourself hoarse. I know these nuts well. If you were made a cabinet member, you wouldn't want to come down either."

By now the nut was shouting frantically: "If you don't make me the Prime Minister, I will throw myself down."

"All right," they shouted back, "we made you Prime Minister."

The old man said, "He won't come down."

The nut started to dance again. After a while he shouted: "Make me the King. Otherwise I'll throw myself down."

What the old man said was coming true. They consulted him. "What do you think? Shall we make him King?"

The old man said, "It's too late now. You have to do what he tells you. He was made the Prime Minister already."

"All right," they shouted, "we made you King. Come down now."

The dancing nut shouted back. "I won't."

"Well, what else do you want? We made you King, too."

"I won't come down. Make me the Emperor or else I jump."

They asked the old man, "Would he really jump?"

The old man told them he would.

"All right," they shouted, "We made you Emperor. Now come down."

The nut answered right back. "What has an Emperor like me to do among stupid jerks like you?"

"Well, what is it that you want, then? Tell us, we'll do it. Why don't you come down?"

"Am I the Emperor?" the nut asked.

"You are the Emperor!" they shouted from below.

"If I am the Emperor, I come down when I like. I am not coming down."

The police sergeant was getting mad. "Let him jump," he thought. There will be one nut less. That was true, but it would have caused him problems later. . . . The Fire Chief turned to the old man.

"What are we to do now?" he asked. "Won't this nut come down ever?"

"He will."

"How?"

"Let me bring him down."

"Everyone was curious as to how the old man was going to bring the nut down. The old man addressed the nut, who was on the seventh floor: "Your Highness, the Emperor. Would you like to go up to the sixth floor?"

The nut answered in all seriousness. "All right." He then went through the roof opening, came down the steps to the sixth floor and looked out the sixth floor window to the crowd below.

The old man asked again, "Would your Highness like to go up to the fifth floor?"

The nut answered that he would.

Everyone was dumbfounded. The old man addressed the nut, who this time was looking out of the fourth floor window: "Would My Reverend Emperor like to go up to the third floor?"

The nut answered, "Certainly."

He was now looking out of the third floor window. He was no longer dancing madly as he had on the roof. He had assumed the seriousness of a Real King.

"Would His Excellency like to go up to the second floor?"

"I would."

He had come down to the second floor.

"Would Your Excellency come up to the first floor?"

The nut had come down to the street; he was among the crowd. He went directly to the old man and put his hand on his shoulder: "God, it is only too evident you are a nut too. Only a nut understands a nut," he said, and then turning to the police sergeant addressed him: "All right, now you tie me up and send me to the nut house. . . . But did you learn something about how to treat a nut?"

While the nut was taken away the crowd gathered around the old man: "Hey, pop," they asked, "how did you do it?"

The old man shook his head "It is not easy to be in politics for forty years," he said, and added yearningly: "If only my legs had the strength, I also would climb up on the roof, and no one could bring me down."

# UNITED STATES OF AMERICA

# Lilli

KAATJE HURLBUT

I STILL KEEP the clay figure Chase King was engaged on when he died. By now the clay is dry and hard, and since I have never wanted to cover it or enclose it in any way, it has collected dust and looks like something petrified: something caught in sudden catastrophe and fixed in an attitude of final struggle, still rendering its stark appeal for life even after an endless age in death.

In spite of the dryness and the dust, it is much as it was, one of the arms may be somewhat bent. The lead tubing of the armature bends easily and I was in a hurry the morning I unbolted it from the turntable and took it away before the police came. Not that the police would have had any special interest in it; they wouldn't have known what it was, nor would anyone but me. That was why I wanted it: I knew what it was. But under the circumstances they might have objected to my removing it from the studio.

I shall make no attempt to describe it for one cannot reproduce in adjectives the product of creative intelligence, of individual perception and personal concept. I can only say of this breath-taking little figure that it has arms and they are of spirit and they are glorious.

Even if this piece had been completed it could never be associated with the rest of Chase King's work. (And you could no more say it is a finished piece of work than you could say an exquisite little fetus suspended in alcohol is a child: it has about it, as a statement, as a product of passion and skill, the same tragedy of arrested expectancy, the perpetual mute insistence of possibility.)

The thing I best remember as a vivid exmple of his work was a male figure, cast in bronze, about eight feet high. Standing with the head thrust forward and the arms dangling, it presented an aspect of dumb waiting: waiting for some impetus to release into action the senseless, headlong might contained there. It was the most menacing thing I have ever seen. It made you shrink from it, not physically, but morally, and slam the door of your instinct against its suggestion.

I recall that after Chase died some old idiot of incredible insensitivity purchased it from a gallery and stood it in her garden. I haven't the faintest doubt that she planted forget-me-nots at its feet. People took a morbid interest in his work because of what happened, or rather, because of what little they ever knew.

I met Chase during our student days at the Academy. He hadn't two cents above his tuition and meagre living expenses which it had taken him four years to earn and save after he had left high-school; and he paid for his art supplies by doing odd jobs at night. His parents, living on his father's pension (he was a retired engraver, commercial) could not afford to help him. At the time I was tossing away an expensive education on bad paintings and what I considered Bohemian love affairs. (They were all bad little girls with dirty necks.) I was strictly "taking up art" but at the time thought myself the Left Bank on wheels. I admired Chase tremendously, being what I was, and never ceased to wonder why he accepted me unless it was my very innocuousness. But in all the years I knew him I was his only close friend, to apply the word rather curiously. For we never had a conversation in our lives. I would talk and he would listen with a detachment that precluded any possibility of boredom. He would listen, massive, angular, hollow-eyed, still, with a faint smile that went no further than his lips but which was oddly arresting: because for all the power and restrained motion of his immense arms and shoulders, for all the assured determination of his jaw, his mouth when he smiled had (and there is no other word for it) a sweetness about it: the smile released his aspect of sustained resolution, if only tentatively. And then, after a long silence which emphasized the distance between our levels of thinking, he would begin to talk. He had a quiet voice and he spoke briefly, scarcely articulating a thought, as though speech were too idle a matter on which to exert effort, as though words were merely the debris floating on the surface of his mind. He would speak of a rock formation: its mass, its weight, its tortured balance, the potentialities of its force. (He spoke continually of force. He did not recognize the inanimate: presence implied force, and everything lived through its force, whether manifest or potential, and eventually submitted to a greater force. I didn't discuss this with him for I could only do so by argument and he didn't argue.) I don't recall that he ever spoke at any length on a general topic or ever discussed a personality. He spoke almost entirely of the things he watched. And he never ceased to watch.

He watched with the continuousness of breathing; it was as though his eyes lived an independent life of their own. He did not comprehend a thing at once. His comprehension was a labor, canny and methodical; but once it was accomplished it was as though he had established a vital kinship with the object.

He would watch construction crews with their bulldozers and steam shovels and cranes; he would stand on the subway platform and watch the express come swaying and plunging through the tunnel as though nothing would ever stop it; he would walk down to the water-front and watch the dockhands at work; his eyes, alert, expectant, would follow a boom as it lifted its great swaying burden.

I observed from the first a curious thing about him which I did not understand until I studied his work. With equal intensity he watched the rippling back of a stevedore and the triumphant hoist of a cargo boom; a bulldozer slicing through a hill-side drew from him the same hungry scrutiny as a drunk in a street fight taking a savage swing at an opponent. For it was the force, the might, the power which compelled his attention and not its medium and even a casual study revealed its domination in his work.

In his work he produced effect by almost imperceptible implication, but the result was immediate, and was that of tremendous indiscriminate force: in the curve of an arm he implied the shattering might of a wrecker's skull-crusher; in a figure whose head and shoulders inclined to a slight forward angle, he implied the slow gathering power of a locomotive. But the intent of this force, this might, was missing: it seemed to have no purpose. The movement implied was never of intention, but of impulse; and where no movement was implied, the implication was not of repose, but of instant readiness, as the readiness of a powerful coiled spring momentarily restrained. And so with this appalling absence of defined intent, there remained only force: blind, head-long and senseless.

After I left the Academy I didn't see Chase again for three or four years. I had consented to be towed around Europe by a stern but loving old aunt of mine who had given up trying to educate me but sought to at least immunize me from total ignorance by exposing me to the world's finest art and worst plumbing. During that time Chase left the Academy: his parents had died within a short time of each other in the dim coal-mining town from which Chase had come and had left him the princely sum of six hundred dollars which he spent on equipment. He got a job as a stevedore and rented the top floor of an old brick-front house on East Tenth Street which had long ago been converted to a studio of sorts. From

time to time a heavy, sullen Lithuanian girl, who lived somewhere in the neighborhood, came to stay with him for a few
days to pose and clean and cook. It was during that period
that he turned out what was to be considered some of his
best work. He began to exhibit now and then and to get an
occasional commission.

When I got back from Europe I had no idea where he
was but we ran into each other on Bleecker Street one evening. We walked thirty or forty blocks (he was on one of his
walks and I tagged along) catching up on this and that. I
remember how glad I was to see him and what a relief it was
to me that he hadn't changed. Before I left him I asked if I
might bring some people down to see him.

"They're pretty grotesque," I warned him. "Particularly
an old pal of Auntie's who has violent reactions to things."
I didn't tell him that Auntie's old pal, Emmaline, when not
pub-crawling on four continents, indulged in devouring
young artists and spending small fortunes on their promo-
tion. It wouldn't have interested him but he might have
shied.

"Bring them. Come at night," he said.

A week later I did. I had rather passively acquired a collection of people whose aim from day to day was discovering
bigger and better things to be bored by. I suspected them of
a canny knack for selecting only those things whose magni-
tude would readily succumb to their contempt. They were
not prepared for Chase King.

We wound up at his studio after a rambling party in the
Village. Lilli was with us, though she was not one of us. She
had started out with a painter named Henry whom we abandoned along the way because he was too drunk. But Lilli was
too pretty to abandon with him so we made her come along
with us.

After climbing the two flights of stairs to the top floor we
collapsed on an inhospitable array of boxes and buckets in
which clay comes packed and on Chase's sagging studio couch.

For the first few minutes everyone sat and stared, murmuring abstractedly when I introduced Chase who bowed briefly but did not speak.

The place was dirty and disorderly and gloomy, except for a powerful light hanging from the ceiling above a turntable, and yet it was the most impressive place I've ever been in. There was an immensity about the room which had nothing to do with its dimensions, and a bleak austerity that was coldly inspiring. There was an air of intense activity, as though something vital were taking place through the entire room, as though space and object, light and shadow, were coordinated to bring about a single objective.

The walls were hung from floor to ceiling with hundreds of sketches in charcoal, chalk and pencil; there were figures, animal and human, in every conceivable attitude; there were photographs of figures, of details, of groups, torn from magazines, and pages ripped from anatomy books.

Other than a couple of tables and Chase's big sagging couch the only other furniture in the room was an easel and two turntables, one beneath the light and one in the corner, both in use, the work covered with dirty damp rags.

In any other man this kind of room might have been an affectation; this kind of living might have been a brief period of experiment, or a passionately extravagant gesture designed to blot out some unbearable inadequacy. But I thought as I watched him that night standing quietly, rolling a piece of chalk between forefinger and thumb, the strong, round-topped thumb of the sculptor so coordinated with the eye as to be an instrument of sight, I thought: this is all of his life; there is nothing more than this: Only these crowding shadows held at bay by a glaring light; only what takes place in light and shadow, a sustained activity; a sketch here, there, a dozen places, where a single line has frozen the motion and energy of mass and form, a line of such knowledge and purity that the unschooled eye wavers in comprehension; only an unborn thing on a turntable huddled beneath wet rags, clinging for life to the lead tubing of an armature. There is only this and his physical needs: a couch, a gas ring where coffee bubbles strongly, a kitchen somewhere, a bathroom, and clothes closet.

Auntie's old pal, Emmaline, was the first to break the silence. I had one eye cocked for her reaction to Chase. Her latest protégé who was with us was beginning to fade from favor. I recalled the morning my aunt dragged her from bed to see the Sphinx at sunrise: she had regarded it coldly and murmured in withering reproach: "Really!" No mortal woman save Emmaline would have called Chase King "pet."

"Oh pet, you intimidate me so! Do say something gay."

Her nonsense defined something for the others to accept and the spontaneous shout of laughter broke the ice. Emmaline's all-but-devoured young artist, a mildly talented painter who wore purple sandals, pulled a bottle from his pocket and we all had a drink.

While Emmaline stalked Chase and the others drifted around the studio (except purple-sandals who took the bottle into a corner and sulked) I shared a box with Lilli. It was the first time I had met her. She hadn't been in New York very long. She had come from Vermont where she lived with some cousins after her parents died and had a job now with a model agency. As we talked she kept looking at Chase, her eyes wide and quiet. I was asking her careful questions so that her answers would match her loveliness and accomplish my private fancy.

She gave me a patchwork portrait of herself which was the brighter for her obvious inner reserve. She said that she had posed all that day for a jeweler's ad, decked in fiery opals, that she was reading Trollope again, that she had spent a month's clothes allowance on a wonderful glass bowl that morning, that she had never learned anything well but cribbage and that she didn't see why sculptors never looked like their work: Mozart, she said, looked much like his music, and so did Beethoven and certainly Bach did; seeing portraits of Rembrandt and Sargent you would quite expect them to paint as they did. But sculptors, she had observed, looked like anything but their work: men with faces like cows did such gloriously incomprehensible abstractions; and puffy little men with sick eyes produced Olympians.

"Look at that poor driven neurotic, Michelangelo," she said. "And goodness only knows what was behind Rodin's beard!"

I suppressed a chuckle and said: "We're looking now at Chase King." I was curious to know what this stately child-like creature thought of Chase and his work. She was obviously the kind of person who did considerable thinking about things if she did little else about them.

"Yes," she said, nodding, "I admit it: there is a similarity. But the similarity isn't an important one."

"Isn't it?"

"I meant it isn't an essential one. The likeness is only physical. People in families can look alike and yet have no essential common trait. The spirit is not the same."

"But that's hardly the same thing. What have you seen of his?"

"The pieces that were exhibited uptown. What I meant was," she said, going back, "that these figures of his are mighty, as he is. But there is a blindness about them: they grope in their might. And he sees so much. Look at his eyes. They are wonderful."

Presently, after gazing at Chase with that wide, quiet gaze of hers, she laughed and turned to me.

"You know, sculpture refuses to be art to me. The pieces that have arms and legs and stomachs, I privately think of them as people. That's why I can't say anything intelligent. I'm a sort of kindergarten member of the I-only-know-what-I-like school. I'm just beginning to graduate to the apologetic class."

"I utterly approve of you, Lilli," I said, thinking of wrapping her in cloth-of-gold and carrying her off forever.

Just then someone across the room called her and she rose with a swift light movement and as she did Chase caught her in his glance. Stately, fragile, curiously elusive, she moved across the room and he watched her. We stayed perhaps an hour longer and until we departed his eyes never left her.

I knew Chase at that time as well as I had ever known another man. But to my own justification I must say that as well as I knew him, to estimate him was beyond my capacity.

I have observed that quality of Lilli's in other people now and then. The first I remember was a grandmother of mine, though my recollection of her is dim (I was six when she died) and is only that of the infinitely light touch of her hand and its cool fragrance, and of a compelling inner quietness that made me want to climb into her lap and whisper. I have often observed the quality in certain children. In the minds of these people you are aware of both wisdom and innocence; in their bodies you are more aware of spirit, alive and clean and quick, than of bone and flesh. You are a little amused to find them quite human, touched by their faults and whims and sorrows. You are charmed by them, but you do not quite take them seriously, as though they held no permanent place in the world but had only been lent for a touch of enchantment.

Such was Lilli with her child-like stateliness, her elusiveness and her grace, with the quietness of her eyes and her unrooted spirit. At a casual glance Lilli did not strike you as remarkable in any way, but merely lovely. The only reason you looked twice was to be sure of what you had seen.

As Chase watched her that night I was arrested by the shift of expression in his eyes. I was so thoroughly familiar with those eyes of his in which operated an uncanny touch-consciousness: it was as though the senses were transposed, for it was the skillful labor of the thumb which did the automatic work of seeing that which took shape beneath it; and it was the eye whose visual touch knew instantly the aspects of form. This faculty was his chief medium of comprehension.

And it was, I think now, this touch-consciousness with its inherent instinct for form which failed him when he looked at Lilli.

I shall never forget his first startled glance. He lifted his head as an animal does when encountered by something curious, and gazed at her, puzzled and guarded. As she strolled about the room with an even, unpracticed grace highlighted by a quick movement of her hand or the turn of her head, I wondered why he watched her at all. She was a lovely girl, but I knew that had nothing to do with it; he wasn't simply looking at her as I or another man would look at her. He was watching her with the same measured intensity with which he watched a giant crane's shovel grab a ton of earth in its jaws and swing it aloft.

I watched her too, wondering what there was in her of the thing he sought to comprehend and record: force, might, unreasoning and unyielding. Slowly, as I watched her, remote perceptions came into focus and sharpened and I recognized the thing in her that was not any kind of power or force, or even strength in the usual sense; something that was not so much indomitable as indestructible. But more than anything, whatever else it might be, it was something unquenchable, like a light beyond reach. It had its own astonishing reality: once you sensed it you were keenly aware of it, even though it was far beyond sight.

Not only on that night but always afterward when I saw them together, his eyes, in unwilling fascination, followed her every movement. And in their watching there was always the hungry scrutiny, the perplexity, and at last, just for an instant, a flicker of baffled hostility.

Emmaline reacted as I had suspected she might. Chase, unlike the Sphinx, stopped her in her tracks: he was too big a mouthful even to consider devouring.

"Not a bit sweet," she said, "but superb!" And she was determined to drag him into the limelight. Giddy and grotesque as she was she was exceptionally able at executing her notions. The fellow in purple sandals was soon going about in conservative oxfords looking for a job and Chase was engaged in as much work as he could handle.

Whether people like his work or not, or better to say, whether they accepted or rejected his idea, it arrested their attention and created a minor fad. A piece representing two figures engaged in a mauling struggle and called "The Dancers" by someone (not Chase) was given the social-significance treatment by a critical review and reproductions were in demand. A gross figure crouched in uneasy sleep for which the Lithuanian girl had posed became a conversation piece for it so simply stated the popular symbology of the slumbering soul or the slumbering beast or anything that suited the moment or the mentality. A glib thought-splitting controversy made the rounds over a portrait bust of a well-known educator: a sensitive likeness of the man's delicately estethic face lay but thinly over an imperative suggestion of the brutal menace that so characterized Chase's work. The result was a hideous mockery and was assumed by many to be intentional. Such was the circle of Emmaline's influence. Chase, presumably the center, remained aloof and only accepted commissions in which he was interested. By spring he was able to give up his job.

He allowed himself, however, one rather odd extravagance, although any extravagance would have been odd considering Chase. He purchased a dozen and a half white shirts and wore them, sometimes as many as three a day, unbuttoned, shirt-tails hanging or buttoned to the neck and neatly tucked in. I asked him why and he said he liked them. I accused him of a vulgar display of riches and he smiled his nearly transforming smile and said:

"I grew up in a coal-mining town. You should have seen what passed for a white shirt."

"Would you have known white if you saw it?"

"Clouds were white," he said musingly. "My mother used

to hang a white shirt I had on the clothesline inside a flour-sack. Then it was only half as gray as the sack."

Emmaline didn't like them at all. "He's so surpassingly shocking," she said. "They spoil the effect. He might as well go about in a satin waistcoat." But she consoled herself: "As long as he keeps that pachydermous female around we shan't really have lost him." She referred to the Lithuanian girl who had become a fantastic joke among the circle of people who lionized Chase. At the time no one knew her name: she was a refugee peasant, somewhere between sixteen and forty; she had been the model for some of his most impressive work. She was a broad muscular creature who complied with his request to keep her clothes off even in the bitterest weather when the studio was cold as a tomb and that when possible she performed the simple household chores unclad. I was always popping in and out of his studio and at first, unless she was posing, she would resignedly lumber across the floor, take a dirty kimono off a hook behind the door and put it on. But as time went on she didn't bother.

Looking idly one day at the magnificent brutish strength of her, the powerful thighs, the flat hard stomach, the tight sloping breasts with their black nipples and the receding chin and forehead, I said to Chase:

"Do you sleep with this creature?" She didn't understand enough English to know what I said.

Chase, absorbed in studying some photographs, murmured, "Hell, no." Then he glanced up and looked at her quizzically. "Yes," he said, "now and then. God, she's dirty."

I saw Lilli occasionally. Idly I strolled into the circle of her enchantment and tried to buy her a pearl or hold hands with her, but in vain. If she wasn't about to take the train to Vermont to visit her cousins, she had to spend the evening mending a petticoat or washing all her gloves, or she had to be in bed early to be up betimes for an appointment. She was friendly and she was sincere, but she was preoccupied.

As the months passed she began to go about looking fearful and holding her breath, as though she had suddenly found herself halfway up a ladder of cobwebs.

I said to her one day when I had ambushed her at the door of the agency where she worked, "What has happened to you, Lilli? I love you so warmly. Won't you talk to me?"

She slipped her arm through mine, smiling, and said: "Will your goodness go to waste if I don't use it?"

"It certainly will. I shall become embittered and take to drink. Now talk to me."

"All right," she said and stopped smiling. We walked a block or so in silence. Presently she turned to me in a kind of pensive alarm.

"You know him awfully well, don't you?"

"Who?" I asked, laughing. She looked so absurdly grave.

"Chase," she said. "I'm so in love with him."

I was aware that I remained smiling because it involved so much effort.

"Lilli," I said drily, closing a forward door in my mind against a chill that was rising in the depths, "don't be a damned fool."

She quickly turned her face away from me and her breast rose as she took a deep breath.

"I will if I want to," she said stiffly. "It's a free country."

I took her small gloved hand and held it tightly for a moment and then kissed it.

"All right, lily maid, but talk to me."

Lilli always talked as though words were her own invention and she had not discovered sentences. Her speaking produced immediate experience: you saw and felt and understood things from her viewpoint alone. Certain words danced with inflection, a half-phrase halted with sorrow, a barely spoken implication came riding out on a laugh.

"Remember that night," she said, "that you led us to him? And terrible Emmaline was there. And that latest boy of hers with the brown mind: so earnest and so limited. Are all her protégés like that? She's so colorful. I suppose she keeps them for contrast. What a pygmy he was beside Chase. (Can't you just *see* him painting nudes with skirts on and still-lifes full of stone jugs and cat-tails?) What a man Chase is. How much of a man and how without nonsense.

"He was so alone that night. With great dark and great light around him. And steadfast. What a frightening thing steadfastness is. And he didn't talk. Did you ever know a man who talked so little? What do you suppose words are to him? Just a necessary inconvenience like money?

"And isolated he was, but with an austere contentment: like a desert plant, flourishing where others die.

"At first, when that tautness broke in me and I understood that I loved him, I wanted to. . . . Oh you know women: I wanted to comfort him: sweep the floor and kiss his eyelids. Think of it! But soon I realized that he didn't even know what comfort was: I've seen how he lives. I go there all the time."

"You do?" I said. "So do I. Why haven't we met?"

"Well," she said, with a rueful smile, "I go early in the morning because no one else is there then. Except the refugee girl sometimes. But she's hardly human, poor thing."

"Lilli," I said, trying to elude her enveloping viewpoint, "I keep waiting for you to make sense. Are you going to?"

She sighed. "I guess not. Oh, don't think I haven't tried to find an apt reason for this. Far, far in the back of my mind there is something horribly like pity, or sorrow: too often when I contemplate him I want only to weep. But as for a reason," she shrugged, "I think a reason would only get in my way. Most reasons for loving are for appearances, anyway.

"I only know that he is to be loved and it is I who love him."

I shook myself mentally in order to shed her viewpoint and spoke briskly trying to establish my own:

"Lilli, how well do you know Chase?"

"Well enough to love.".

"Talk sense, Lilli."

"We're talking love."

"Lilli, darling, please. . . ."

"You are wonderfully sweet to me."

"I love you."

"Talk sense," she said.

"Dammit, Lilli, answer my question. How well do you really know Chase?"

"How well does anyone know him? How well do you? He doesn't talk and say what he is. If you mean how often do I see him, I told you I go there all the time. As for his coming to see me, I'm sure he doesn't even know where I live."

"What do you do when you go there if you don't talk?"

"Sit on a box and stare at him."

"That must be intriguing."

"I am intrigued and he doesn't mind. I asked him and he said he didn't."

"Oh he didn't, did he?"

"At first I went there only with Emmaline and those frights of hers. Or are they yours?"

"She can have them."

"Oh. Well, one day I went by myself. Early in the morning. He starts work as soon as it's light, you know. I asked if he minded my being there and he said no and he asked if I minded if he worked and I said no. So there you are. He hardly notices me unless I move and then he looks suddenly at me and stares for a long time. Not at me, but around me or through me, as though I were something else."

"We never talk. Although sometimes we speak." She laughed suddenly, tipping her head back in complete surrender to whatever possessed her. People passing on the street glanced at her and smiled.

"What's the matter with you, Lilli?" I asked, laughing helplessly with her.

"I don't suppose you'll think it's funny," she said, "but one day after the customary gales of silence, he asked me if I were married." She shook her head and laughed again. "There I was, so in love I felt spun out of light, and for the first time in my whole pointless silly life, and he asks me if I'm *married!* I got into such a fit of laughing I couldn't answer him. He looked at me as though he had never seen laughing before, and as though it might be dangerous."

We walked along in silence for a while. She smiled to herself now and then. Presently she said:

"Why do you sigh?"

"Did I? Look here, Lilli, you're rather given to thinking, after a fashion. Try to think: what is the point of this?"

Now it was she who sighed.

"Well, he lets me sit and love him; he lets me make sandwiches for him and coffee, when the refugee girl isn't there. I don't think I can conjure much of a point out of that, do you?"

"No, and I doubt you will ever have any more to work with. Chase isn't for you. You know that. You *know* that. Just back away now and head in another direction and you'll forget it." I was trying to draw a straight black line through the whole thing. But she only shook her head slowly.

"I'm not altogether as silly as I sound to you. I'm not the little girl having a case of flip-flops. I'm positive that you know that. Otherwise I couldn't talk to you."

"All right, lily maid. What are you going to do? Those boxes are damned uncomfortable to spend your life on."

"I don't know," she laughed with a broken sound. "I could just go up to him and put my arms around him and say: 'I love you with the most awful tenderness. Please marry me and I'll make coffee and sandwiches and never bother you'."

"Yes, you could do that," I said, thinking that indeed she could and indeed she might, and what beautiful arms she had.

About ten days after my talk with Lilli, Emmaline telephoned me in hysterical excitement to tell me that Chase and Lilli were married. I didn't believe it and said so. She indignantly assured me that I was mistaken and that she had engineered the whole thing. I didn't believe that either.

"Now you've got to help me with them," she said. "I've arranged a perfect blast of a party and you've simply got to make them come to it. Promise me you will."

"I can't promise anything of the kind," I said cautiously. "You'd better let me talk to Chase or Lilli first."

I tried to telephone Lilli at her apartment but was told that the telephone had been disconnected. Chase had no 'phone so I left word at Lilli's agency to call me. She called me next morning and we spoke briefly.

She was willing to confide to me alone, she said, that she and Chase were not married. But living in sin, she said, embarrassed her, so she told people they were married.

"Which is a preposterous reason for telling people we are married because we're not even living in sin!" She laughed gaily. "We're just living. In a living room! You know that room behind the studio that was full of junk? Well, it's still full of junk, only it's lovely second-hand store junk: a strip of gold carpet and a deep chair that sighs, oh, and a wondrous glass bowl of mine which was all I had to move. When? Oh, almost a week ago. Now, please come soon. You're our best person." Then she added, lowering her voice to a sober pitch: "And do pretend we're married, just to be polite."

Very solemnly I promised her that I would be as polite as my elevated ideals permitted, and that I would indeed come soon.

Emmaline's reaction, it seems, had been one of her finest. She had stormed into Chase's studio as soon as she heard about it. (Lilli had told her friend, Henry, the painter and Henry had told an acquaintance who had told Emmaline.) It was early in the morning: Chase was working, the Lithuanian girl was posing and Lilli was stacking discarded sketches in a neat pile. Emmaline furiously upbraided them, shouting, swearing, threatening, with much "after-all-I've-done-for-you" and fist shaking and bracelet jangling. When at last she had exhausted herself into puffing speechlessness, Chase, smiling faintly, had turned his back and gone on working; the Lithuanian girl, understanding little English, had paid her no attention at all; and Lilli had put both thumbs to her ears and wiggled her fingers before she calmly went on stacking sketches. Emmaline had then exploded into shrieking laughter and embraced them both, declaring that they were impossible and that she forgave them. Before she left she asked Lilli how she could bring herself to marry a beast like Chase King. Lilli told her that she had done it to save his honor.

I went to see them often. Chase's living habits remained unchanged. Even though he had given up his dock job he had put in a twelve and fourteen hour day too long to break the habit, if he had wished to, which he did not. If he wasn't working in his studio he was out walking, alone and absorbed. But Lilli, though she worked as steadily as ever at her job, seemed to leave her old life behind her in the midtown apartment she had "fled," as she said. ("There's something 'institutional' about furnished places; they make you homesick even if you haven't any home.") She no longer went about evenings with her "few slight friends" and ceased going to Vermont weekends, and except in business, she seemed to want to avoid people.

Whenever I went there I sensed an urgency in their welcome. They were like strangers at a party who have run dry of conversation and grasp at a mutual friend to rescue them from embarrassment.

Now and then on a weekend morning I would find Lilli alone in the room behind the studio to which, with odds and ends and scraps, she had given an illusion of airy elegance. But Lilli never seemed lonely. She kept company with some

inner delight and I would find her gazing serenely out the
window on whose sill a handful of black twigs rose in a
dancing tangle from a glass bowl, catching at the gauze curtains as they stirred in ghostly motion in the summer wind.
That was how I found her the first day I called on them.

"Well, lily maid, how's the spell progressing?"

"You promised," she said reproachfully, kissing my
cheek, "to pretend we are married."

"Why, Mrs. Lilli, I'm pretending with all my heart!"

"Then don't call me a maid."

I held her at arm's length and looked at her. "If I ever
beheld a maid!"

"I suppose your vast experience makes you unfailingly
discerning," she said wryly.

"Oh, unfailingly! Though anyone who would put you
in the category of mere experience should be shot dead."

I sat beside her on a long divan covered with an India
print of brown and amber and looked at her. The fearful
expression of holding her breath had almost left her; it was
almost overcome by a contemplative sweetness which was of
a definitive quality: she seemed more herself than ever
before.

"What," I asked her in genuine curiosity, "do you do
besides make sandwiches?"

"I love," she said gravely, "and wait."

"What are you waiting for?"

She looked at me guardedly for a moment as though
she reserved some melancholy secret and presently she
shrugged without answering.

"Are you waiting for Chase to build you a vine-covered
cottage and say 'yes, dear' to you?"

She tipped back her head and let forth a gay shout of
laughter. A sudden breath of wind caught the curtains and
billowed them out into the room as if in a quick happy response to her laugh.

She rose from the divan and said: "I'm waiting until

Chase wants me to pose, if I must be waiting for something definable. Why else do you suppose he allowed me to come here?"

"Allowed you! Good God, Lilli."

"After one of his rather frightening staring spells one day he said to me: 'I want you to pose for me. Will you?' And I said, 'Yes, if you will let me come live with you.' He said in the most surprised manner: 'Why do you want to live with me?' And I said: 'Because I love you so much.' I think he thought I was insane. He didn't say any more about it for days. Then he asked me again if I would pose for him. And I said the same thing. More silence for days. Then he asked me again and I said the same thing again. At last he shook his head and sighed. 'All right,' he said. 'What will your friends think of you?' 'I'll tell them we're married,' I said. He just shrugged and said, 'I think you'll be sorry.' Isn't it funny? But I couldn't bring myself to ask him to marry me. It seemed . . ." she broke down in a fit of breathless laughing . . . "it seemed so immodest!"

Presently I asked where Chase was.

"Out staring at things, I suppose. He should be back soon. Come on in the studio and have some coffee."

There was a faint smell of gas when I opened the door to the studio. The coffee pot on the gas ring had boiled over and put out the flame.

"How I fuss with Chase about that and now I've done it myself." She went over and turned off the gas.

"You sound very domestic, Lilli."

"Clutching at straws," she said. "Look, I washed the cups."

She pointed to the three cups which had served Chase and his guests since I could remember and which had always been lined with black coffee stain.

"Did you use acid?"

"No, just steel wool. Marie used to rinse them sometimes."

"Who?"

"Marie. The Lithuanian girl."

"Oh. Is she still posing for Chase?"

"Yes. No. I mean she comes here, though he doesn't really need her any more. But she just comes and stands around, poor soul. So I put her to work. She never raises her eyes and she turns a dark red whenever I speak to her. You should see her scrub a floor: it's almost frightening."

She poured coffee into a clean cup and handed it to me with a little bow.

"Thank you, Mrs. Lilli," I said.

Chase came in a few minutes later. It was the first time I had seen him since Lilli came to live with him. I glanced at Lilli who was regarding me sternly and said to Chase:

"Congratulations, Chase."

He disconcerted me with a penetrating stare. I moved my hands in a helpless gesture. He shifted his stare to Lilli and slowly shook his head. She grinned at him and winked. And Chase, as he so rarely did, laughed aloud.

A month or so later she began posing for him. Some of the preliminary sketches he made were a complete and interesting departure from his usual superbly correct anatomical drawings.

I came upon him one morning in the midst of one of his cleaning up frenzies which marked the beginning of a new piece of work. Cleaning up consisted of retrieving his tools, letters and bills, his watch, his razor, a necktie and a toothbrush from the general litter of the room and laying them neatly on a table which had been cleared for that purpose by tipping one up and sliding its contents to the floor. Lilli, to his concern, was sweeping and thereby endangering certain items he might have overlooked.

He stood and watched her for a moment and then passed his usual comment to me which was to shake his head. Presently he said:

"Have you any plans for this morning beyond this performance with the broom?"

"No," she said, "it's Saturday. I'm just going to wash the windows."

"Good God," he said quietly. And then: "May I ask why?"

"Why? Because you can't see out of them. That's why."

"Marie can do that, then. I want to do some sketches."

"But she's cleaning the back room."

"Undress."

I didn't know until later that was the first time he had asked her to pose. He turned to rummage through a pile of sketch pads. Lilli looked uncertainly at him and then glanced at me.

"Chase?" she said.

"Well?"

"I don't . . . it would embarrass me, I'm afraid," she said, glancing at me again.

"I'm just leaving, Lilli," I said.

"No," Chase said sharply turning to me. "You stay. Please," he added courteously.

Lilli looked sideways at him and stubbornly shook her head.

"All right," he said impatiently, "just go and put on something light. Silk. Dip it in water first. That thing you sleep in."

Lilli stared at him in astonishment. I heard her as clearly as if she had spoken: "How do you know what I sleep in?" She glanced at me, flushed, and left the room.

Chase turned to me: "I want you to talk to her," he said. "Keep her animated, so she'll be herself, whatever the hell that is. Otherwise she'll just sit and stare at me." He rummaged in a box, found a piece of charcoal, threw it on the floor, picked it up and looked at it, and threw it down again; he looked in the box again and found a stub of pencil. "You don't mind, do you?" he asked when I didn't answer.

"Not at all," I said quickly. Something in the timbre of

his voice had arrested my attention; something too in his expression and the way he was using his hands. I couldn't define it: there was a quickness and at the same time a hesitancy I had never observed in him before.

The door opened and Marie lumbered into the room carrying the battered old coffee pot.

I said: "Good morning, Marie." Chase ignored her. She stopped and stared at me. The dirty garment that hung on her thick powerful body might have been a sack except that it was covered with vivid red flowers and the material was sleazy; that and a pair of men's tennis shoes were obviously all she wore.

"Good morning," I repeated, nodding to indicate a greeting as she continued to stare at me. She ducked her head at me and went over to the gas ring and set the coffee pot down. She fumbled with a book of matches trying to light the gas. She struck one after another and presently Chase swung around and snapped: "For God's sake, Marie!"

Slowly she flushed a dark red and stood still with her head lowered. I looked at the gas ring and saw that the burner was encrusted with burned coffee grounds. I took a piece of newspaper from the floor, removed the pot, scrubbed off the burner and took the matches from her. "Allow me," I said, trying to smile at her, and lit the gas. When I handed the matches back to her she grinned widely at me. The grin was so sudden and so ghastly that I stepped back. I turned away and walked to the window when it occurred to me that she was being coy. I shuddered and didn't turn around again until she had left the room.

When Lilli returned she was draped in pale wet China silk that clung caressingly to her body. She reminded me of the lithe children in a Sorolla painting, bathing in thin wet garments in a sunlit pool: bathing and idling and being children.

Chase glanced at her briefly. "Walk," he said.

She grinned. "Yes, boss."

As she idly paced around the room I talked to her about one thing and another, mostly nonsense. Whenever she laughed she stood still, tipped back her head and gave herself completely to laughing. Chase leaned against the wall rolling a piece of chalk between his thumb and finger and watched her in silence. Presently he secured a sketch pad in an easel and began to draw swiftly. In the space of half an hour he made twenty sketches or more, tore them from the pad and dropped them on the floor. As they sideslipped to the floor, half curling among the trash, I glanced at them. There were merely faintly curving lines intersecting one another, now and then cut through with a heavy slashing stroke. They were all much alike, as though they were a subtle variation on some elusive theme. Now and then he would stop and lean against the wall and watch her, alert and expectant. After a moment a puzzled expression would come into his eyes, followed by an intense, hungry scrutiny and then, as always, before he withdrew his eyes from her, there came that fleeting glint of hostility.

A sudden shattering of glass sounded in the next room. Lilli turned quickly to face the door and stood without moving.

"What was that?" I asked when Lilli didn't move.

"Marie," she said quietly. "She's broken something, poor thing. I'll let her sweep it up and hide the pieces. Maybe it's something I won't even miss." She returned to pacing up and down the room.

Chase went on sketching for a minute or two and then, without the slightest warning, kicked a wooden box lying near his foot and set it smashing against the opposite wall.

"That will be all now," he said curtly to Lilli.

She stood wide-eyed and motionless, looking from Chase to the splintered box. She drew her breath and said in a shaky voice: "It's a good thing I wasn't in the path of that box."

He glanced at her coldly and turned away. She looked at me uncertainly and left the room.

I sat where I was, too astonished to say anything, while my mind uneasily digested the fact that what I had thought, in all the years I had known Chase, was a cold and calculating detachment was nothing of the kind, but was an almost inhuman control of passions whose intensity and depth were beyond my measuring; and that control had broken, if only for a moment. I glanced again at the splintered box and realized suddenly that I was sweating.

Lilli opened the door and stood with her hand on the knob. There were tears in her eyes.

"My bowl," she said softly, "my wondrous glass bowl. She has broken it."

By the end of summer Emmaline was calling me every day or two to bawl me out for not making Chase and Lilli behave themselves: they refused to attend parties and to fall in with her extravagant plans. She accused me of selfishly keeping them to myself and of encouraging Chase in what she termed his romantic nonsense. For Lilli, at Chase's request, had given up her job and continued to pose for him, and he was ignoring all other work as thoroughly as he was ignoring Emmaline. His simple expedient of locking the door and refusing to open it to the most persistent hammering drove Emmaline to a frenzy which she indirectly vented on Lilli, rendering a description of her evil influence on Chase which made the Gorgon Medusa look like Pollyanna.

Chase and Lilli still continued to accord me the same urgent welcome: for their curious relationship had advanced to some sort of mutual focus, though it was tentative and strained; they were more sensitively aware of each other and at the same time, more like strangers, cautious and restrained. And I was more than ever a vital medium of communication for them: they spoke to me as they could not speak to each other and enjoyed the lack of constraint my presence induced. And yet when I left them and closed the door behind me, I sensed the profound unity of some essential spirit.

I loved Lilli. I had loved her from the first moment I knew her. But for Chase I had never felt any more than admiration, even as great as it was. For his passive acceptance was not in any way flattering, merely compelling, and it was based chiefly on the fact that I did not question his work or object to it, but understood its stark subjectivity. (For unless you understood the simplicity of his concepts and their direct expression in his work, a fundamental sense of morality rose unbidden to question the result.) But of late, as there had come into his manner toward me a certain warmth, as though of belated recognition, I began to feel not only a genuine fondness for him, but anxiety.

For his work, it seemed to me, was not a conviction to be argued with, but a simple statement of the plane of being on which he existed. Consequently, no intellectual challenge was valid. But Lilli, simply by being what she was, so boldly, so exquisitely what she was, constituted a challenge that could not be ignored. And he had not sought her: she had come to him herself, even though she did not intentionally engage him any more than a sparrow engages a stalking cat. I could never fasten on a conclusion but I would always emerge from my speculation with a raw pity for Chase, while Lilli, elusive even in thought, escaped with but a touch of sorrow.

I was in the studio one stifling day in September. The noon sun came roaring through the skylight overhead. Traffic noises rose clamoring from the street and were comically punctuated by Marie's outrageous snoring in the outside hall. Having worked for Chase for three or four years she continued to come now every few days as a matter of course although there was no longer anything for her to do. If Lilli didn't invent some task for her, she either just stood around or slept. Chase, with his shirt unbuttoned to the waist stood

resting his elbows on a turntable, watching Lilli as she languidly paced up and down and talked to me. She had overcome her shyness and was undressed. The stateliness of her
child-like figure was even more commanding without clothes.
She ignored Chase, long accustomed now to his periods of
silent watching when only his eyes seemed alive.

"Heat," Lilli sighed. "Turbulent heat. Volcanic. In a
moment I suppose we'll erupt through the skylight and boil
down on 10th Street. We'll cool to ashes and be blown away
by the wind. Wouldn't it be splendid to be blown away by
the wind?"

"You easily could be," I said.

"But not Chase." As she glanced at him he stirred. "He
would turn into one of those lumps of lava. He'd be dug up
5000 years later and end up in a museum with a tag on him,
right beside one of his sculptures and nobody would know
which was which."

She rose on the ball of her foot, turning as she did, and
walked slowly toward him, smiling gravely.

"All but his wonderful eyes," she said. "And they would
burn away into smoke and drift through the atmosphere
where they could watch forever: watch and touch, surrounding things with sight, getting inside things and seeing, knowing utterly the infinitude of form. It would take him eternity
and he would be as happy as God."

She was standing close to him. He was no longer watching her, but looking at her, listening to her, absorbing her:
she had his total attention. Neither was aware of anything
but the other. I might not have been there. Their rapt attention to each other seemed to compel silence: Marie, for a
moment, ceased to snore; there was a lull in the noise from
the street; the only sound was the faint singing of the heat.

With startling swiftness Lilli laid her palms on his breast
and whispered: "Chase, I love you."

He remained still for a moment. Then with painful slow-
ness as though he fumbled in sleep, he found her hands and

pulled them from his breast and turned away to face the turntable, where the clay model, covered with a wet cloth, huddled before him like a dirty cowering little ghost.

Stepping in front of it so that I was unable to see it, and still moving as though in sleep, he removed the cloth and turned his head to look at Lilli. His expression was one of bitterness and futility.

I looked long and curiously at the figure. It was the first time I had seen it uncovered. At a glance it gave the impression of a creature caught in flight, being slowly pulled down even as it struggled aloft. The base was a heavy sinuous mass which rose into an arching frenzy of motion. Even at the distance at which I observed it (an obscure sense of intrusion prevented me from examining it closely) and even in its undefined, groping stage of progress, its effect was one of stark violation.

Deliberately I turned my eyes from it. I didn't want to look at it any more or think about it. I wanted to get away from it and from the tension and the singeing heat. "Volcanic," Lilli had said.

Lilli had not moved. Her eyes were oddly brilliant and she looked at Chase as though she willed some silent communication that he would not receive. Presently she turned from him and sighed. She drew the back of her hand across her brow and sighed: "Ice."

"I'll get it, Lilli," I said, rising.

"No, I'll get it," she said and added, frowning crossly, close to tears: "I have to cry for a minute, anyway."

She walked over and took a piece of silk from a nail on the wall, pulled it around her and left the room without looking at Chase who, when she passed him, turned his back.

He thrust his hands deep into his pockets and moved restlessly around the room, coming to stand again before the turntable where he looked at the figure through narrowed eyes: he was not so much looking at it as watching it, quizzically, as though he expected it to execute a subtle change beneath his gaze.

Only his eyes moved when Lilli kicked open the door and entered carrying a tray of ice-filled glasses. She had tied the piece of silk around her middle and it trailed the dusty floor behind her; she had swept her hair up from her neck and fastened it on top with a tortoise-shell comb; she had also wept, regained her composure and fortified it with just a touch of impudence. She carried the tray high before her, its weight in her hands tightening her muscles so that her small breasts tipped up before they sloped away into the hollows of her armpits.

Enchanted, I must have smiled, for she grinned at me as she set the tray on the table beside the gas ring. I glanced at Chase. The same narrow gaze, quizzical and expectant, with which he had regarded the clay model, remained on her as she poured coffee over the ice in the glasses. Only his eyes moved, following her, when she walked toward him with the glass. She held it out to him and he slowly removed his hand from his pocket. Then he reached out, but, instead of taking the glass from her hand, he caught her suddenly by the wrist.

She gasped and drew back as the glass smashed on the floor. Still holding her by the wrist, without a flicker in his intent gaze, he seemed for a moment not to realize what had happened.

Lilli relaxed and smiled at him. "Let me go," she said softly. "I'll sweep up the glass and get you more coffee." He released her and looked down at the glass. He glanced up at her again and then at me. Then he said: "Move away. You'll cut your feet." And he stooped down and began to pick up the splinters. He looked up at her once more and said: "I'm very sorry." In reply she laid her hand lightly on his head for a moment and left the room to get another glass. When she returned she filled the glass with coffee and set it down on the edge of the turntable beside him.

For an hour I had tried to summon the energy to get to

my feet and leave but the heat stifled my effort. At last I extended an invitation to an air-conditioned bar. I was turned down but on the strength of contemplating it I managed to get up and put on my coat.

As I walked toward the hall door and murmured good-bye to Chase he came over and held out his hand. It was one of those things that spotlight a gesture so obscured by habit you've never given it a thought before: in all the years I had known Chase it had always been I who had held out my hand to him.

I looked once more at Lilli, just for the sake of seeing her in her trailing silk, her tortoise-shell comb and the heat-damp curls at her tembles.

"Good-bye, lily maid," I said out of habit, but she didn't notice. She only smiled and said: "Come back soon."

When I went past Marie, still sleeping in the hall beside the bannister, she stirred but didn't wake.

It was with considerable relief that I heard Emmaline had taken on a new protégé. ("A ghastly little boy with a vicious red beard who designs the maddest furuiture! You'll *adore* him!") But she still kept after me to exert my influence on Chase in the matter of turning out some promised work. "Think of what I've *done* for him!" she said. It was impossible to make her admit (undoubtedly because she knew it was true) that Chase had merely allowed her to do what she had done and that his cooperation had ceased as indifferently as it had begun. I told her vaguely that I would see what could be done.

But I put off going there. Through the summer I had fatuously assured myself that the fantastic relationship between Chase and Lilli would by the simple force of life-long habit and daily circumstance terminate of its own accord; that Chase would complete this phase of his work and go on to something else; and that Lilli, with her warmth and fastidiousness, would tire of isolation and harsh living and return to her normal life. But I had only to go there to know that this was not likely and I resisted the inevitable frustration of witnessing the grotesque comedy in which they sought each other up and down a treacherous spiral which forever gave the illusion of a circle.

It was Lilli's nature to love without wisdom, without design, but with gentleness and enduring kindness, with nonsense and deadly earnestness. And it was her instinct to enchant. While Chase was like the hawk, whose telescopic eye is intent upon its prey and who ducks the persistent little bird that flutters around its head.

And yet her loving was infinitely involved with the thing he searched for: the invincible; and it was at the same time a flat contradiction to his concept of it. And as her enchantment increased, so increased his helplessness and his hostility.

The heat wave held until the end of September. October was poetically bright. I slipped into old habits as you slip into old shoes, expecting familiar comfort, but found only tedium. I was too aware of Chase and more of Lilli, too anxious, to be free of them. I could only maintain a physical distance.

November came with cold that stabbed and held like a spike. I felt the primitive urge to close the door and build a fire: to be alone and warm. On a Friday I bought a stack of new books and had firewood sent up to my apartment and prepared for a long weekend of reading. But after twenty minutes of the first night and a chapter of a new novel, Lilli came wrapped to the ears in a blue coat.

I knew the coat: I had seen her in it the winter before. It was the color of the summer sky and she had sparkled in it as though it had been the color of her spirit. But that night she seemed to wear the coat as a kind of mockery, so scarcely was she there. Her name came to my lips in a whisper.

"Lilli."

Her eyes were enormous with some compelling preoccupation. Her face was drawn and strangely composed. When

I reached out to touch her, her lips twitched as if to smile.

Hello, best friend," she said at last when I put my arms around her and held her close for a moment. She was shivering.

"Come to the fire," I said, "and keep your coat on until you're warm. This is a hell of a night to be out." I wanted to talk, to chatter, in order to dispel a feeling of dread and establish a tangible matter of warmth and comfort. I led her to a deep chair beside the hearth and knelt down and took off her shoes. Her feet were icy. She tucked them under her and leaned back, drawing her coat close around her. I went into the dining room and poured a big drink of brandy and took it to her.

"Drink this. All of it," I said. She sipped the brandy slowly at first and then drank it down. She gave a little shudder, swallowed at the heat of a couple of times and then she looked at me and smiled slowly.

"Don't look like that," she said. "I'm all right. I'm just cold, that's all."

I felt oddly reassured to hear her speak and see her smile, even though her voice was quiet and tired and her smile stopped at her lips.

"It's a wonder you haven't frozen to death in that goddamned barn of a place," I said furiously. My sudden anger astonished me but not Lilli. I was sitting on the floor beside her chair. She only shook her head and placed an icy hand on mine and said:

"It's not so bad really. The top floor gets most of the heat and anyway we've tightened up the windows with strips of paper. It's just that I got a bad chill yesterday and I haven't been really warm since."

"If it's so damned warm and cozy, how did you get a chill?"

She laughed faintly at my continued anger and her eyes fell away from me to the fire. She looked into the fire for a long time. I wondered if she were going to answer.

She shrugged presently and sighed. "Something frightened me. I suppose that was it."

Something frightened her. Fear. That was it. A taut band of resistance broke within my mind, releasing a blind dread that staggered and groped, seeking identity with some known reason.

"What frightened you, Lilli?" I asked quietly.

She shrugged helplessly. "Nothing. Literally. And that's the truth."

You're not making sense."

"There's no sense to be made. It was childish. Too silly to talk about." She looked down into the empty brandy glass. I went into the dining room and brought the decanter back and poured her another drink. I set the decanter on the hearth and took my place at her feet again. She sipped brandy for a while and we did not talk. Gradually a faint brightness crept into her eyes and a flush came to her cheeks.

"Indulge me, Lilli," I said at length, "and tell me what frightened you."

She laughed and shook her head. "When you were little didn't you ever pass a dark room whose door was open and think something was going to reach out and grab you? Or going up a dark stairs, think you were being followed? And nearly *die* of fear?"

"Yes. Is that all it was?"

"That's all. And the final absurdity was that I *was* being followed." She laughed again and the bright brandy flush on her face was oddly like a mask.

I filled her glass again and touched her hand. It was warmer. She turned her hand over and her fingers closed gently around mine.

"I was coming in from the delicatessen with something for supper last night, poking along up the stairs and all of a sudden that feeling of being followed seized me and I really panicked. I couldn't move for a minute. And then it was all over . . ." she frowned into the fire and added hesitantly . . . "except that I had that icy, chopped-off feeling that something had happened and it was too late." She paused again and a slight tremor shook her. "At the top of the stairs I turned and looked down," she laughed, "and there was poor old Marie trudging up behind me in her everlasting tennis-shoes. I felt so silly. I told her she could fix supper for us. She has a factory job now, but she still comes up every few nights and tidies things up. Chase hates having her there but she adores him so, poor thing, and I've become rather fond of her.

"I told her to start supper and I went into my room to lie down because I still felt shaky. And then the chill began. It's a deadly thing, a chill: it's as though your body were trying to shake loose from your soul.

"I called Chase," she smiled, remembering, "and he was like an old grandma. He wrapped me up in blankets and carried me into the studio where it's warmer and put me in his bed. I couldn't stop shaking so he lay beside me and held me. Marie fixed supper and brought it in but he didn't leave me. I went to sleep after awhile. When I woke up it was almost light and he was still there. Awake."

Her voice had gradually dropped until she was whispering. She leaned her head against the back of the chair and I thought that with the warmth of the fire and the brandy she had fallen asleep. I sat looking at her still face: with her eyes closed and the faint bluish tinge of her lids she looked exhausted. Suddenly, to my astonishment, tears rolled down her cheeks, though she didn't move.

Then she whispered: "He loves me."

She slept then for a little while: the tears dried on her face and her fingers uncurled from my hand.

Why did she come? I kept asking myself. Why, when it was too late? Why? Maybe she didn't know it was too late. I longed to be able to speak to her in another language: the dark familiar language that lies behind the wall of words and speaks comprehension as it disdains knowledge.

During the silence of her sleep it was less like time passing than distance widening. Suddenly the fire set about crack-
ling and sputtering and she woke.

"Why did you come?" I asked her presently.

"I came to see why you stayed away and to ask you to
come back. Why did you stay away?"

Aching, I answered: "Because I wanted so much to help
you and I couldn't."

"If you only knew," she sighed. "You did what no one
else could do: you made us remember we were people."

Her words were like echoes: she seemed to be speaking
from the bottom of some deep shaft of thought. I reflected
that when I had first known Lilli, her thinking had been so
clear and light, as though she juggled crystal bubbles: a
pretty aimless trick of mind. And it occurred to me that now
she had gone inward and had encountered fear at the bottom
of some plunging shaft. And I could no longer reach her.
She was gone from my world.

In a little while I put her in a taxi. She made me promise
that I would come soon. Tomorrow, the next day. I didn't
want to promise, but I did. I promised and kissed her good-
bye.

"Good-bye, lily maid," I said.

When I saw her again she lay on the floor beside her bed:
in a little white heap she lay, like a handful of petals, and
she was dead.

The next night the cold relented and toward evening it
began to snow. The tender silence that comes with snow, the
mood of forgiveness, softened a bitter anger I had felt all day.
As I stood at the window and watched the snow feathering
the sill and veiling the street lights, I decided to go to the
studio once more. Lilli's phrase came back to me: "You made
us remember we were people." It struck me as hollow now,
its meaning gone, but I wanted something to hold fast to. I

thought, I'll go and take a bottle of champagne and make them remember they are people.

With the champagne tucked under my arm I took a taxi to 10th Street. When I got out of the cab I realized all at once how late it was: all the houses were dark. I looked up to see if the lights were on in the studio. They shone like a beacon through the snow.

I climbed the two flights and, turning up the hall, I noticed that the door to the back room was ajar, but I went on and knocked at the studio door as usual. There was no answer. I knocked again and waited a moment and then tried the door. It was unlocked and I went in.

Chase was alone in the room, sitting backwards in a chair, with his arms and head resting on the chair back. He was asleep.

"Chase?"

He raised his head slowly, not knowing what had awakened him and looked up before him at the turntable where the little figure stood uncovered. It wasn't until then that I noticed it, and looking at it, I couldn't take my eyes from it, so compelling it was and so much had it changed.

The raving little arms that rose out of the sinuous, twisting torso were no longer like a separate entity, captured, violated, in a frenzied struggle to pull free; but raised in triumphant flight, as if the gross mass of the torso were nothing. I kept looking at it, hypnotized, expecting something to happen.

Then Chase turned his head and saw me. He moved so quickly that I was startled. He jumped up from the chair and strode across the room, smiling.

"My God, it's good to see you," he said, clapping his hands on my shoulders. "Where the hell have you been? I thought you were dead."

His sincerity and warmth were as astonishing and as moving as anything I've ever known. "It's good to see you,, too, Chase. How have you been? You look awfully tired."

He did. He was thin and a certain brilliance in his eyes emphasized the pallor of his face, even though it matched the quickness in his voice and movement.

"I've put in a couple of tough days." He nodded at the figure. "This thing is beginning to take shape."

"I think you've hit your stride," I said.

"Damned near." He went over to the gas ring and lit the fire under the coffee pot.

"How about champagne for a change? I brought a bottle."

"The hell you did! Let's have a party."

"Where's Lilli?"

"In the back room. I'll wake her up."

"Don't on my account. She didn't seem well when I saw her last night. Is she better?"

"Yes. She's a lot better. She'll be glad you're here. Anyway, she's slept for hours, the lazy little witch."

He went to the door of the back room and stopped. He turned around and looked at me, about to say something, but hesitated. He put his hands in his pockets and took them out again and finally shrugged his immense shoulders in a helpless gesture.

At last he said with a quiet diffidence: "Lilli and I are going to be married. I thought you'd like to know that." He turned abruptly and opened the door to the back room and switched on the lights.

As light flooded the room he took one step into the room and stopped still. He stood so long without moving that I stepped to where I could look past him.

I saw Lilli. I knew at once by the angle of her head that her neck was broken. She was on the floor beside her couch, without any clothes on, one foot tangled in the sheet. Though the angle of her head was unnatural, it was not grotesque: she was altogether lovely.

All at once Chase moved through the room like a whirlwind: it was amply furnished with tables, chairs, floor lamps, hassocks; but he moved in a straight line, kicking, flinging furniture aside; with a quick turn of his wrist he flung a huge wing chair out of his path and sent it smashing against the wall six feet away. When he came to where she lay he stopped and stood looking down on her. He stood so for a long time and his entire body trembled. Gradually the trembling ceased and I said to him very quietly:

"Don't touch her, Chase."

He seemed not to have heard me for he still remained as he was: motionless.

"Chase . . ."

He slowly turned his head and stared at me. His eyes held the blind expression of a mortally injured animal: he was completely dazed. Slowly he turned back and looked at her again and stooped down.

The first thing he did was to take the sheet and cover her to the shoulders.

"Chase," I said, "don't touch her. Her neck has been broken."

But he only shook his head and said in a thick muted voice: "She's cold. She'll get a chill lying here. It's warmer in the studio." He got up and unfolded a blanket that lay on the foot of the bed and then carefully lifted her onto the blanket and folded it around her. He picked her up once more and carried her into the studio. He laid her gently on his bed and then he lay down beside her and held her in his arms.

I looked once more into the back room and snapped out the lights and closed the door. I went over to his couch and looked closely at him. His eyes were closed and his lips were pressed against her temple.

"Chase. Try to understand me: she's dead. I've got to call the police and it's better not to wait. For God's sake, talk to me. Did you . . . did you . . ." I couldn't say it.

He opened his eyes presently but he didn't look at me. I saw that they were glazed and expressionless and I turned away. I went out of the studio and into the hall and closed the door behind me. And for some reason when I passed the hall door to the back room I closed that too.

With the bottle of champagne still under my arm I walked downstairs, not knowing what I was going to do and not caring: nothing seemed to have any importance. On the last flight down, I became aware that someone was moving in the hall below.

Then the hair on the back of my neck stood out and I looked down into the brutal terrified face of Marie as she tried to flatten her bulk against the wall.

As I stared down at her, the terror broke into panic and she ran for the front door and out into the street. I went out after her but I didn't even look to see which way she went. I turned west and walked through the snow, numb with the knowledge I had borne too long.

I wasn't aware of where I went or how long I walked. I remember that somewhere I dropped the champagne into an ashcan. It was almost daylight when I found myself back at 10th Street. I remember thinking that presently I would call the police, but first I would go up and see what I could do for Chase.

I was stiff with cold as I climbed the stairs. I smelled gas at the second floor and tried to run but my frozen feet, as in a nightmare, refused to hurry.

When I opened the door to the studio I fell back, covering my face against the poisonous onslaught of the gas. In a moment I took out my handkerchief, covered my nose and mouth and ran in and pulled the chain that opened the skylight, and then stumbled back into the hall again choking.

My eyes stung and watered but I could see Chase lying as I had left him, holding Lilli. After a few minutes I went over to them. He was dead.

In the profound stillness of the early morning the only sound was the faint hiss of the gas ring where the battered old coffee pot had boiled over again and put out the flame.

# From My Notes About My Mother

WILLIAM CARLOS WILLIAMS

HER FATHER DEAD when she was eight, her mother when she was fifteen or so, without other relatives than her one brother, no one to turn to—she must have had a struggle with herself those years to keep heads up.

This was her training for the future with which to do what battle might be necessary. The whole world of modern ideas was far and away beyond her. Never shall I forget my astonishment to hear her say that the moths, always present in our attic, must have been spontaneously generated out of the natural dust there. That's where her mind was, in the fourteenth or fifteenth century as far as the mechanics of her life were concerned.

Her greatest traits were her moral integrity, her desire to know and to survive, her curiosity—and the necessity which drove her. Her mind seems to have been free as the air and as unfooled—as far as her limitations permitted and that went pretty far. She wanted to recapture the past—as who has not?—the past of a happy childhood of sounds and colors, of fruit and happy faces, gentleness, a guitar strumming and young women laughing together with gleeful faces, inventing as they progressed and the world growing up around them to a mysterious future of success and sensual, if mild, delights. She never lost that desire. To live. Not to die.

How best to tell of her childhood? It begins with her life in Mayaguez: the ocean, the sky, the mountains, the flowers, the birds, the house, the servants. Herself! intensely, egotistically, as in the case of all children, taking possession of that world where to the end of her life she continued to see herself at a great distance.

Sometimes at Easter or Christmas a flowering plant would come to us reminding her of her childhood:

"That takes me back. A rose red verbena when I was eight years old. I had a little plant in a box just like that. How I loved that plant and how I took care of it! It was one of the first things I had that was entirely my own."

"You were born on Christmas Day, weren't you?" I asked her.

"Yes. Not Christmas. On the twenty-third or the twenty-fourth. I don't know."

"In 1850?"

She ignored the question and continued: "Now I remember. My mother told me I was born between Saturday and Sunday. Or Sunday and Monday, I don't know which. Halfway between, in the middle of the night."

I don't know what she meant, precisely, by that, but it may have been she meant to imply something about the course of her life, that it had remained indeterminate, nightbound.

My brother Ed who is an architect brought some books to the house to show to her—Le Corbusier and his newfangled house on stilts in one of them.

"It makes me think of the house where I was born," she said. "It was not in the city. I suppose like a little farm. Under it there was nothing. It stood on stilts and had stone steps in front that went up very easy. No, there was nothing under it, just fresh air. I remember when I was a little girl I used to go there in my bare feet to get *anuelos,* because they would make me itch and I used to love to scratch them."

As far as I can tell she can't have lived there long after her birth. It was no doubt on some later date, after they were living in Mayaguez, that she remembered going back to the old farm to wander about, out of the sun, with the chickens and black children to enjoy being flea-bitten.

For her substantial memories certainly centered about the Mayaguez house where the family knew whatever prosperity—and it seemed to be fairly substantial—it ever knew. This is how she described it to me:

"The street was here, one house next to the other. There was a big parlor, a balcony in front with french windows that opened to it. It was close to the street, almost no front yard. There was an upright piano and the little organ that my brother played. When Patti began to sing she sang in that room; my father brought her, with Gottschalk; she was a very young girl. To this side, if you sit at the piano, was my mother's room and my crib was there—I suppose you call it a crib. It had high sides."

The description of the house went on, from room to room, from the scrubbed bare boards of the floor to the steep staircase, to the barrel of molasses in the pantry and back to the visit of Gottschalk and Patti, one of the high spots of her life:

"The piano, I remember, had two silver chandlelabras on each side, which were taken out for Gottschalk to play—to give him more room. Patti was flying about and called my father 'Uncle.' "

Trying to remember the house where she had lived as a child was, in her own words, "giving myself a mental exercise—anything to pass the time." She was a wonder at that.

A tune, maddening her to deprivation, had been running in her head for weeks. She had done everything she knew to get rid of it but unsuccessfully. She had joked about it, saying she had once seen Coquelin enacting the part of a man so bedevilled:

"A little song I used to sing when I was a young girl—it has been running in my head all day. I am saying something but I hear it there all the time. It makes me crazy! It makes me think of Coquelin, the only time I saw him. He had a song in his head and he couldn't get rid of it. But you would have to see him to understand. Nobody could be so funny. Finally he jumped into the water to drown himself, to forget his obsession. When he came up vomiting the water out of his mouth—the song was still there."

Perhaps my way of telling this isn't exactly what you might prefer or expect, but in this family you are expected to understand what is said and interpret, as essential to the telling, the way in which it is told—for some reason which you will know is of the matter itself. That is to picture it. "Figure to yourself," as my mother would often say—obviously translated directly from the French.

The overtones of her way of speaking would, thus, often come from three languages—and quite unconsciously—so that one had to listen and interpret to perceive exactly what her meaning was. It was never a perfunctory language or a formal one but highly descriptive.

Poor soul, when sometimes I'd be tired and short with her, exasperated at her continual complaining about her "pains" which were eternally worse than any she had ever had in the past, she'd say, "If I don't speak to you, then I don't speak at all." She would get her way and I'd say no more. So that, rather than see her sit wooden-faced and silent at table, I'd deliberately give her a small glass of vermouth or anything we had, if she'd take it. It was like fishing, was fishing in fact, for more often than not she'd come up with a story.

"I should say I have been frightened. I remember when my mother would go out. They would leave me with a colored woman. It was a two-story house near the town with a sugar plantation next to it, a big field. One night she was telling me how the Devil would come across the field and take little childrens up! I was listening with my very eyes. Then she told be to go upstairs to bed. I started up the stairs and the wind came across the sugar cane. Whoo! I don't know how I got up the rest of the way. I fell to the top. I thought the Devil had me sure."

Listening to a blue jay in the garden, Bee bee! Bee bee! in a strident voice: "There is a bird there, in Puerto Rico," she said. "I don't know what they call it, that says, *Julia achivivo!* very fast *Julia achivivo! Julia achivivo!* The Christi sugar estate was next to our house and when I was a little girl I used to go there without any shoes and sit under a guava tree. I would gather my skirt full of fruit and eat them. I would eat the green ones first and save the best. Then when I came to them I couldn't eat any more. They say when you plant an apple seed in the tropics it comes up a guava. I don't know if it is true."

And like the rooms in the house, the varieties of fruit along the roadside would be described: "The *mango* they plant in yards like our apple-trees. Then there is the *caimito*. It is round like an apple and bright green but inside it is pure white, like milk. Toledo always called me *cara de caimito* because when I was young my face was round like that. The *nispero* is about the same size only it is brown and soft inside—fluffy. Then there is the *corazón,* red and shaped like a heart and the *quenepas,* small like a plum and green, it comes in bunches and you bite it and open it, tac! and suck the inside. There is a bean too, the *guama,* that, when you open it, has little things like cotton and inside of each is the seed. It is very sweet. You take each one out and suck it. There is, too, a grape that grows by the sea, a seaside grape. There is a kind of orange which I have never seen here. It is half orange, half grapefruit, a sort of bitter sweet. It has a rough skin, like big pores. They call it *toronja.* And there is another orange, like an orange only much smaller and it is always green. Green, green, green! It never gets yellow. The taste is just sugar and water, no taste at all but very sweet. Or perhaps just the least taste of orange. They call it *lima.* They have a little plant they call *nuribibi*—dead alive. If you touch it, it looks as if it were dead, it collapses. Then after a little while it is alive again. The sensitive plant, yes."

Her observation seems to have been minute and dispassionate and, so far as her condition and surroundings were concerned, comprehensive, if not philosophical or profound, as the meanderings of a childish intelligence sometimes will be. She saw and tasted everything with relish at least, and respected the truth.

As Mayaguez, the tropic island, dominated her childhood, with its human drift, its loyalties and aspirations, so France, especially Paris, dominated her young womanhood.

"That rose!" she said to me one day when I brought a rose in to her from the garden. "It seems to me that is the smell of the roses in that circle there in France—the first summer that I went, the real rose smell."

There had been a broken engagement and her brother offered to send her away. "Where do you want to go?" he asked. "To the United States or to France?"

She chose France, a correct choice. There is no place in which to get over a love affair like Paris. She got over it quick—or never. It is usually the intelligence which rallies first. Something is killed but the person we know, ourselves, is witnessed proceeding quite unaffected to the various points of vantage invented by the day—table and bed and in among the furniture and plants. Finally we are impressed and follow ourselves about, at first wanly, indifferent, but finally with a different kind of interest. The world comes up new. We begin to see it for the first time. It gets itself impressed on us. She found release in painting, in study, in the great world of Paris.

This should really be known as a fashion essay, the varying clothes of the ideal. The ideal was her constant companion. Not religion, certainly not that. But something spotless and heavenly—surrounded by its clothes of her world. As a child, fruit and flowers, as a Parisian, Paris. Her reactions to it all were Catholic, that is, untouched by prejudice.

She saw what she saw, she heard what she heard; that must not be falsified, like it or not like it, that was the truth. So, her memories of the doings about Paris at the time, the people going about in the petty salons, in the school and at home, reveal the period more than they reveal her.

What did she mean by "the truth"? That's what her story is. For what does any man care about the truth, in her sense, especially what does a writer care, an artist, compared with his convictions? Nothing. Perhaps that's why she never got very far with painting. She wanted to be a portraitist. The truth for her was curiously at war with her sensibilities. One had to report the world according to one's perceptions of it, willy nilly. But this meant serious denials. There was another truth, the truth of self, of angry demands, of satisfaction, of love. She had rejected love for truth's sake. But she had denied herself in that crises. What truth could there be in that?

She saw faces in the fringes of rugs and curtains as she sat with unfocused eyes in contemplation which, when you went to look directly at them, disappeared. Everywhere, faces, beautiful and grotesque made by a stray thread in a given fabric, in a pattern of wall paper—faces, staring, in contemplation—children, madonnas. Lions also and dogs.

The mind would be lost in the distances of thought when suddenly a face would begin to appear to call her back. She had no theories of the world or of the arts. The truth was, to her, the truth—and she remained unsatisfied, seeking to follow and to learn.

She worked hard at the Institute and won honorable mention. She played the piano. She sang. M—— was her teacher. "He always gave me the emotional roles. *L'adieu de Marie Stuart.*"

"*Allez mon enfant! Allez! Allez,*" he would say to encourage her. "Out with it. Come on, come on!"

One day when she was very old she began to sing unannounced, in her shaky old voice, *Pieu per voi che por me!*

A duet from *Traviata*. Then he answers her . . . Let me see
. . . But she could not remember it—"More for thee than for
me"—the truth, the bitter truth.

Isn't memory a kind of automatic intelligence? One day I
was eating an orange at table and happened to take up my
half empty glass to pour a little water over my fingers into
my empty tea cup. "How one thing makes you think of something else," my mother said. "When you did that it made me
think of one of my old friends—Mme. Givry. She was a little
old woman. One day when she had finished eating she took
her glass of water and did just what you did. It made such a
funny impression on me."

When she left Paris it was to join her brother and his
family in Puerto Plata, Santo Domingo. There her fate
awaited her among those low tin roofed and thatched houses
in the person of her future husband, a young Englishman
who left the Island to go to the United States.

So she came to America and was married. Before the
ceremony, she lived for a time with a professor's family in
Jersey City. I once had a card of hers, though I cannot find
it now, on which was printed: *Instruction in Spanish, French,
Piano, Singing and Painting*. I couldn't help smiling. Poor
mother. I suppose by sheer weight of potentialities she hoped
to make a go of it—in Jersey City, 1881. I wonder if she ever
had a pupil.

She went with her husband to live in a little house in the
suburbs on the Erie Railroad—Rutherford Park. So the
clock of the years began to tick, slowly and relentlessly for
her among the torn up streets, the kerosene lamps, the water
tank in the attic, the kitchen pump, the hot air furnace and
wooden sidewalks; the mosquitoes, the hot summers and
bitter cold winter nights. Pop began his steady daily march
to the Railroad Station a mile from the house, and back at
night—stopping each night on his return from the city to
 see if he could hear the baby scream across the woods and
the fields.

Who shall define the love between a man and woman or limit it in the imagination? It may be slender or robust, it may be intermittent and yet of purest quality. Between a man and a woman of different races it will have another character than that between a man and woman of the same race. The age of the two will have a strong determining character upon it. So long as it lasts and continues to be rewarding to them, so long as it bears some sort of fruit or even stands as a windbreak for them it may be authentic. She enjoyed the love of her husband, I am sure. She gave him her love, I am sure of that also. But what each held to himself and to herself within the memory differed greatly. The house in which they lived together was built out of disappointed hopes but it was a good house. It didn't fall down. It didn't even leak. It didn't even seem to shake in the wind, as far as the children could see. There are as many kinds of love as there are trees—or ferns—or things that grow. We judge too hastily when we think only of the magnificent (if they are magnificent) branches of some romantic love. We are jealous. Everybody wants to be rich. Most would rather have an imitation of it made out of green paper than enjoy the actuality of a common weed. They loved each other—which didn't prevent them from a feeling of loss.

So I say, in a life that continues there is a part that lives as there may be a part that dies. In her, though the part that was dying filled her with dread and resentment, for all that —call it cowardice if you care to—there was a part that refused to die. She never had in her any element of the suicide. That may be the female of it, I don't know. It was strong in her. She lived.

Ten miles deep inside, a little boy—preordained by chance, free to run now that it was April—ran. His legs seemed to bounce by themselves under him, he scarcely knew how they could go so fast—or that they were legs. He desired and, riding his pleasure, he arrived and took.

It was all in a great yard with a painted wooden fence of

boards, cut out into a scroll design and painted green and red that stood above his head—but he could peek through and see the people passing.

Behind him his smaller brother, six or less, came following while the mother leaned upon the balustrade of the balcony that encircled the house and watched them play.

There above them as they played leaned nothing of America but Puerto Rico, a foreign island in a tropical sea of earlier year—and Paris of the later seventies.

The spring, the great black cherry trees in blossom and . . .

# The Steamer

CHARLES ANGOFF

I DIDN'T LEARN HER real name till I was in my early teens. For years I thought she was called Mrs. Steamer, and I assumed that when she was referred to as The Steamer, the definite article was only an affectionate form of Mrs. Her real name was Mrs. Sophie Marushek, but she was so enormous in size that someone in our family at once dubbed her The Steamer, and so she has been called for some fifty years. At first she was called The Steamer behind her back, but gradually she began to be called that openly, and since she didn't seem to mind, people have called her that ever since. She must be well over ninety now, and when I see her— which, unfortunately, is not very often—I greet her as Steamer or Mrs. Steamer, and she is not in the slightest offended. Indeed, if I called her by her right name, Mrs. Marushek, she would probably feel I was behaving not like a relative but like a "stranger."

Actually, I am a very distant relative. She is the mother of a cousin's wife, which makes me, as my great-grandmother, Alte Bobbe, would have said, "a favorite nephew of the Sultan of Turkey's youngest daughter." But in our big family, there are no "distant" relatives. A relative is a relative, with all the prerogatives and rights that go with that status—including the right to have a meal on short notice or no notice at all, the right to sleep over at one another's home ("An extra bed, frankly, we haven't got, but we'll manage somehow, don't worry. After all, what are chairs made for? Bring

402

them together and you have a bed"), and the right to partici-
pate in family fights, discussions and friendly arguments. My
uncle's marriage to Frances, The Steamer's daughter, her only
child, was cause for much celebration in the family, for she
was about his own age—and till then he had shown a strange
and bewildering predilection for older women, especially
widows with children.

Not that the family didn't like Frances; she was pretty
and obviously was in love with Aaron, but she did seem to
talk too much about "nature." This, however, like nearly all
her other attributes, she got from her mother. Leah, Aaron's
mother, and Alte Bobbe, Leah's mother, were simple folk
who worked hard and knew no new-fangled notions, and
The Steamer mystified them. For The Steamer was a
"worldly" woman, completely unlike all the other women
that my grandmother and great-grandmother had ever
known. The Steamer, shortly after entering the family, asked
the two older women to take a long walk with her. Leah
and Alte Bobbe excused themselves: they were tired. But
The Steamer asked them again and again. They consented
to walk two, three hundred yards with her to the park. The
Steamer laughed at them. "Is this a walk?" she asked.

"We walk enough in the house," said Leah.

"It's no *mitzvah* just to walk," said Alte Bobbe. "You
should forgive me, only loafers walk just for walking. God
gave us feet to walk somewhere—not nowhere."

"But it's good evercise," said The Steamer.

"In Russia I knew many peasants who live to be 100,
and they never did exercise," said Alte Bobbe. "This twisting
and turning for no reason can't bring any good."

The Steamer thus had to do her own walking. How she
managed to drag her huge bulk—she was short and weighed
well over 350 pounds—puzzled the other two women. The
Steamer then began a campaign to educate Leah and Alte
Bobbe about the beauties of nature. She talked at great length
about the wonders of the sun and the moon and the trees

and the flowers and the clouds and the rain and the snow. Leah and Alte Bobbe would look at each other in wonderment when they were bombarded with such talk. They were fond of flowers and trees and so on, but they made no *tsimess* (literally, a delicacy) out of them. "A flower is a flower, and a tree is a tree," said Leah, "and what more is there to say?"

"Yes, but they're nature," said The Steamer. "And nature is so beautiful."

"Who said it isn't?" asked Alte Bobbe.

But there were other things about The Steamer that seemed even stranger to Leah and Alte Bobbe—and, indeed, to the family at large, including my father and mother. The family had deep emotional roots in Russia, whence they all came. Their ancestors had lived there for generations, and they were buried there. They were also nostalgic about the neighbors, both Jewish and non-Jewish, they had left behind. They couldn't get the various smells and sights of the old home out of their systems. But they realized, at the same time, that America was a better country in every way. There were free education, freedom of worship, equality of citizenship, abundant opportunity, and "in general, good things for the Jews," whereas Russia was a despotism that seemed to specialize in anti-Semitism. The Steamer agreed that Russia was a despotism, but she didn't "see any angels running around the streets of America." She had come from an old Jewish-Russian revolutionary family, and thus could spout considerable Marxist terminology, though she clearly had little notion of the full meaning of the terms. One of Leah's children, Chashel, at first secretly and then not so secretly, laughed at the Steamer's Marxist pretensions—never, of course, in front of The Steamer. Chashel herself was active in the Socialist-Zionist movement, but she didn't like pretenders. She told her mother and grandmother to pay no attention to The Steamer. "She's only a babbler," she told them. "She doesn't know any more than you do, and you know more. Marxism is a very profound learning, and The

Steamer, like I say, is only a *pluppler.*" Leah and Alte Bobbe
listened to Chashel and thought to themselves how wonderful it would be if she, too, knew nothing about Marxism,
and if she forgot about it all and concentrated on getting
a husband.

The Steamer, who had no idea when, where or how to
spout her "learning," insisted upon enlightening Leah and
Alte Bobbe. She denounced America for being "the worst
capitalistic country in the world," for "stealing bread from
children and miners' wives," for "permitting sweatshops,"
and for "permitting big companies to sell bad food, especially
meat."

To all such talk Leah had one answer: "What you say
may be so, but at least here people can complain, and where
people can complain, things will be better, and from what
I read in the *Forward,* the little time I have to read, I see
that they are improving slowly. Poor Jews have become rich
here, my children go to free schools, and a Jew has been
appointed to the biggest and most important court in the
whole country. Who said this was *Gan Eden?* But people can
breathe here, Jews can walk on the sidewalk; they don't have
to get off the sidewalk and bend their heads when a Christian
policeman passes by."

"Ah, but Russia!" exclaimed The Steamer.

"May Russia sink a thousand miles into the ocean," said
Alte Bobbe. "What pleasures did we ever have there?"

"But Russia is Russia," said The Steamer. "Ah! Russian
music, Russian books, dancing, everything—there are no such
things, there cannot be such things, in America. Russia is
Russia, and America is America."

Leah and Alte Bobbe wanted to know why she ever came
here, if she loved Russia so much, but they didn't want to
offend Aaron's mother-in-law, though they began to be sorry
for Aaron, since he undoubtedly had to hear a lot of The
Steamer's foolish gabble, and they also suspected that Frances

believed as her mother did. Alte Bobbe was sure that Frances talked like her mother. She said, "The Steamer has been a widow for many years, and she had the sole upbringing of her daughter. That's bad. When there is a husband he forces a silly wife to keep her mouth shut, and the daughter learns some sense from him. But when a foolish woman also carries the pants, then only God can help the daughter. With a son, in such a situation, it's a little better. He's out in the world more, and can learn how silly his mother is. But a daughter is home much more. Nu, we can't do anything. When a man marries or is related to a curse, he must learn to live with it."

The Steamer disdained to read Jewish papers. She read only Russian papers and Russian books, or so she claimed. Aaron said that she really did little reading of any kind, though she made a great show of her interest in Russian newspapers and magazines and books. "Even if she did I don't think she would understand," he said.

Sometimes The Steamer would bring a Russian paper to Leah's home and leave it there for her and Alte Bobbe to read. They thanked her but asked her to take it back with her. "We have little enough time to read, and the time we have we'd much rather spend with the *Jewish Daily Forward*."

The Steamer accepted her defeat in this regard, but she obviously felt superior to them and she hoped that Leah and Alte Bobbe would realize how sorry she was for them. Alte Bobbe, who now understood The Steamer much better, said, "Nu, we are simple people here. We are not as well-read as you. In our simple way, we are satisfied with the *Forward*. And perhaps we should be ashamed to say it, but we really are not so ashamed of being Jewish and running a Jewish house."

Alte Bobbe, with her last pointed remark, wanted to let The Steamer know that she and Leah preferred not be annoyed by her on another and far more serious matter, that of religion. The Steamer went to synagogue only twice a year, on Rosh Hashonnoh and Yom Kippur, and she didn't serve pork in her own home; she wouldn't have dared to flout the prevalent opinion of the Jewish community by staying home on the High Holidays or by serving pork. But otherwise she was, as Alte Bobbe said, "not much better than a *goy*." She was not too careful about keeping *flaishing* and *milchig* dishes apart, and there was grave doubt that she waited the mandatory six hours after a *flaishig* meal before eating a *milchig* meal. The Steamer did not take too much pains to hide her opinions about the "childishness" of most Jewish religious observances, even to Alte Bobbe and Leah, who were very strict in such matters. "After all," she said, "many nice people eat ham and pork, very nice people. I don't eat it myself, but maybe I'm foolish, too. But President Wilson can't be a pig because he eats pork."

"Who said President Wilson is a pig?" said Leah. "He's a very fine man, may he live long. For appointing so many Jews to big offices in the government we Jews should always be grateful. And there are Jews, too, who eat pork, I guess. What the Reform Jews do, I don't know, but I can imagine. But we live our own life here, as we think Jews should. Other people live the way they want to. After all, it's not a shameful thing to observe Jewish laws."

The Steamer still would not be offended. "Shameful? I didn't say shameful," she said. "But I thought you like America so much. Then why not be more like Americans?"

"We do like America," said Alte Bobbe. "But we can love it and be Jews as the same time. Why not?"

"Nu," said The Steamer. "I still think that we Jews have clung to all sorts of *narishkeiten* (foolishness) ."

Leah couldn't contain herself any longer. She didn't want to cause trouble in Aaron's home by saying anything unkind to his mother-in-law, but The Steamer was being grossly impolite, and in Leah's house, too. Leah said, "Nu, by you it may be *narishkeiten,* but by us it's Judaism, and we intend to do as we have been doing."

For a while The Steamer desisted from propagandizing her ideas, especially those concerning religion, but then she began again. This time both Leah and Alte Bobbe told her plainly that they preferred not to be annoyed with her talk any more. "Let us be friends, as *mechootonim* should be, and let's not argue. You won't change us," said Leah, "we'll end our days as we began them. Perhaps we're foolish, but we are what we are. And we shall certainly not ask you to change your views." The Steamer "behaved" herself thereafter, but she visited her son-in-law's family much less often. After Alte Bobbe died, she barely ever came to Lea's house at all.

In time Leah—who was not as observant as her mother—learned that Alte Bobbe was entirely right about the influence of The Steamer on Frances. For, much to her horror, she discovered, almost by accident, that Aaron and Frances had decided not to send their children to Hebrew school, and planned not to teach them Jewish ways at all. "We have come to the conclusion," said Frances to her mother-in-law, with the same disregard for other people's feelings as her mother revealed, "that it's unfair to impose superstitious ideas upon young children."

"But who said superstition?" asked Leah. "They're Jews, they should know what Judaism, is, of course they should know about Jewish holidays. What sort of nonsense is this, Aaron? Tell me."

Aaron, unfortunately and much to the surprise of his mother, had completely surrendered to the "enemy," so to speak. "But you can't mean this, Aaron," pleaded Leah. "You're my son. I know you. I know your upbringing. Think of your father *olav hasholem*. He raised you up to be a Jew. Your wife is a Jew. Your children should be Jewish. Not teach them anything about the Torah, about Passover, about Rosh Hashonnoh—how can you talk this way, both of you?

Do you want to make animals of your children? God in Heaven, what is this?"

But Aaron and Frances would not change their decision, no matter how much Leah pleaded. The Steamer, of course, sided with them, but all she would say to Leah was, "It's their children, and it's for them to do with their education as they wish. I want to keep out of this." But Leah knew, and everybody else knew that The Steamer had originally put the idea into Frances' head, and that the two of them had swayed Aaron. What especially broke Leah's heart was that the boy was not even *bar-mitzvah*. Both the boy and the girl didn't know the significance of Yom Kippur or the whole story of Passover.

In time the boy and the girl married. They both married Gentiles, and they both were divorced shortly after their marriages. The girl married a second time, also to a Gentile, and they seem to be getting along. But they observe no religious holidays of any sort. Just before her recent death, Leah said of the girl's home, "I don't, and I never will, understand a home without holidays. Such a home is empty. Nu, I'm only glad that Alte Bobbe, *olav hasholem*, didn't have to see such a home. Even for a wonderful country like America we Jews have to pay a price. Maybe we older people are the foolish ones. I don't think so."

YUGOSLAVIA

# Twilight Is Falling on the Earth

Lojze Kovačič

Translated by Donald Davenport

THE EMPTY beer bottles bounced and clanked in the cases in the cart as the chestnut horses galloped around the corner toward the Church of the Sacred Heart of Jesus. The red belfry above the trees, resembling hands folded in prayer, just then released a flock of grey pigeons.

"Tell my wife," the driver shouted to Munda, who was standing behind him leaning against the staff of a flag, "tell her that I'll be home in two hours." His sweaty hair fluttered in the wind like little tails, around the edge of his over-sized cap.

"I will—in two hours," Munda shouted back.

"Give her this, too, so that I don't lose it." The driver thrust a small green box of new razor blades in his hand. "Only be careful, my boy. I paid a damn fancy price for them."

"Don't worry, old man—so long," Munda shouted. He picked up the flag and jumped out of the cart onto the ground. The clattering of the cart was muffled after the first corner.

On a secondary street in front of the inn where vats of copper sulfate stood, a group of barefoot boys gathered around a red Italian Lambretta. A boy with a beardless face, resembling the beak of a hawk, squatted on the curb and expertly inspected the engine.

"It's a good one," Munda thought. "It's Šibe's and, I hope,

410

it's not locked." The boys moved aside on the sidewalk when he approached them.

"Good evening, Mr. Munda!"

Munda silently lifted a boy from the ground, shoved the flag into his hand, and tried out the engine. The motor started, snarling, and flapped its Indian red mud guards. He shut it off immediately.

"Just as I thought, who else but Munda."

Against the door of the inn leaned a small, stout man in a checkered shirt and grey trousers, with motorcycle goggles casually tucked under his belt. Munda approached him slowly, stern and slim in his white gym shirt, arrogant, with his red ascot twisted around his neck.

"So what, Šibe."

"Nothing, absolutely nothing," the man said quietly, almost tenderly, without looking at him. "Just come with me for five minutes. Over here in the garden." He was thirty, eleven years older than Munda.

"Just as the gentleman wishes," retorted Munda with the acid smile of a drowned man.

Šibe turned and walked ahead of him. The children became restless. They stared quietly, cat-like, after them, rubbing their elbows and biting their fingernails.

"Scram, devil's brood!" shouted the man when he approached the wattle fence of the garden, and picked up a stone from the sand. The children stopped at the corner.

In the tall, quiet garden grass, Šibe turned to Munda. His cheeks were sagging and bluish like a frozen juniper.

"You know, you bastard, what happens to someone who plays with my motorcycle."

"A jackass," thought Munda. "I've known him since I was a small boy, and he has always been such a selfish swine. He always had a loud mouth and had everything the others did not have, and never will have either." He pulled his hands out of his pockets.

"Well, come on."

In a flash a broad hairy fist with a chain swinging on the wrist knocked him on his back.

"That's what happens!" said Šibe and stood beside his legs. "And that's not all that might happen, either."

Munda moistened his sore lips which had turned white with his tongue.

"All right," he mumbled in a hoarse voice. "All right."

"Sure, it's all right," Šibe grimaced, took the goggles from under his belt and calmly began to clean them.

"The ape. Look how he dresses," Munda said to himself, looking closely at Šibe's shirt hanging over his belt and grey pants, which at the bottom dipped softly and tenderly in the bright green grass, like in a fashion magazine. Then, lying as he was, Munda cautiously eased his own feet closer to Šibe's, quickly pressed them tight, pulled them to him and threw Šibe on his back onto the grass. Immediately Munda was on his feet, on him, and began to hit him rapidly about the face from right to left and again from left to right. He clenched his teeth from hatred. "Take this, you devil, you lost soul!" His hand was hot, as if his knuckles were on fire. "Break his balls, Munda!" shouted the boys behind the fence. "Bash his snout in!"

"Even better, punch him in the kidneys," said a youth with glasses.

Munda got up. His hands were bloody. . . .

"You bastard," groaned Šibe. "Bastard." He pulled out a thick black bolt from under his back and threw it at Munda. Munda jumped aside with wildly ruffled hair, like an eave over his eyebrows, and walked toward the garden gate.

"Bastard," Munda repeated icily. And then with a satanic face, he said, "Bastard! And what kind of word is that? I've never heard it before. Come on, explain it to me, you who always think only with your ass. Bastard! No! If he could, he would kill me with his damn eyes," thought Munda. "He would have killed me in no time. I knew it," he said when he closed the gate. "I knew you never understood what you say."

The boy with the flag waited for him in front of the inn, like a good pupil awaits his teacher. He had not moved from the spot all this time.

"You really fixed him, huh?" he asked confidently, in a friendly fashion, because he had waited so long and faithfully.

"Yeah," Munda nodded and took the flag from him.

"Your wife is in the shop," the boy said, embarrassed and empty handed. The children appeared at the corner.

"You really gave it to him, Munda," they shouted.

"Yeah."

A slender young woman in a red polka-dotted skirt with a fancy hairdo and a turned up nose said goodbye loudly to the customers on the doorstep of the shop.

"Damn chatterbox." Munda threw a small pebble at her. It rolled into the shop. The woman turned and ran up to him.

"Let's hurry up. I left the child at home alone," she said curtly and fished out a key from her handbag. They walked across the small empty square on which there was neither a monument nor greenery.

"For heaven's sake, why are you carrying a flag?" she asked.

"Should I take it back to Saturnus? I'll take it back in the morning when I go to work. Boy, did we ever yell about Trieste. Do you hear how hoarse I am?" He was pleased that his voice was so hoarse.

"I hear." She looked at him. "You took my kerchief again. How many times do I have to tell you it's the only one I have."

"Shut up."

He arranged the kerchief. He was handsome with it in his white sport shirt. All the boys of his age were similarly dressed.

"You think you'll turn some girl's head?" she asked caustically.

Standing on the steps, she opened the door of the house, while he walked past her and cautiously stuck the staff of the flag into the darkness of the hallway, crowded with tenants' bicycles, cages, and the lockers of the concierge.

"You're repulsive!"

She tossed her head back and laughed to herself, as if she were alone.

"Slut."

"Ha ha! Of course, now I'm repulsive, now I'm a slut. I'm everything."

She pushed a stone under the door, it remained open, and it was bright in the hall. She was still laughing.

"But you'll never get my kerchief again. So that you don't charm anyone," she said.

He grabbed her by the elbow and twisted her arm behind her back. She screamed, crouched as if to leap, and worked herself loose.

"She disgusts me, my god, how she disgusts me," he said to himself. The concierge opened the door. Small, with a face round and smooth like a plate, she stood in the snowy brightness of her kitchen.

"Ah, it's you! Don't bother. I'll close the door." She kept smiling at him with a healthy maliciousness and envy, the way she did with all young married couples. When she passed by them, she brushed Munda, and he felt on his thigh the garters of her girdle, which creaked as she walked.

"You disgust me," he said to his wife as they climbed the stairway. "And if you don't shut up, I'll break every bone in your body when we get upstairs. Maybe you remember that 'game' from Wednesday."

She walked in front of him down the wooden hallway which was stinking of damp laundry, linden blossoms and mice. At every step her rosy heels slipped out from her bathing sandals.

"You know what you are?" she stopped and said, "A brute—a big brute."

Their room, small and gloomy, was heated and lit by an electric hot plate on which rattled an aluminum pot with boiling water. It smelled of rags and patches which lay on chairs and hung from them, and of the freshness of yellow roses, from the commode, which had begun to wither.

They closed the door behind them.

"Daddy!" The happy voice of a child was heard from the corner.

"What is it, Janko?" Munda leaned the flag against the wall, lifted the child from the crib, and stretched out with him on the bed.

The boy was a year and a half old, with dark hair and eyes bright as a birch tree. Munda watched as the child crawled awkwardly toward him as if he had fins instead of legs.

"Today I met the priest Grozd," he said and lifted the child by the legs with his head upside down. "Ukh ukh," he shouted with joy.

"Look at this ham." Below, on the house door was affixed before the war a tin plate with an ad for Westphalia ham. "He's as skinny as a bean pole. And how stupidly he looks at me. Magpie! I would like best of all to knock his teeth out." The child began to scream.

"Leave him alone, you idiot!" Fani shouted, shifting from one foot to the other in front of the glowing hotplate, silent and slender, like a ballerina in her short silk slip. Munda tossed the child back onto the bed.

"All of us have a few screws loose," she muttered, stopping in the middle of the room, "and with you, everything is all right, huh?"

"Oh, my little lark," he embraced her. She slipped out the very same moment, touching him with a tuft of stiff hair. "You think so?" She stuck out her tongue.

He made a funny and stupid face, as people do when

they are alone, convinced that no one is looking. "The priest was walking like this." He bent over, clutching his breast with his hands as if he had a golden cross there. He took a small step and hugged her. She pushed him away.

"You, you!" she said angrily in a voice rude from crying. "Now I'm pregnant again. You know that? And how will we live? Just tell me that! Just tell me!"

"Oh, we'll manage somehow. You'll have to have an abortion."

"The hell I will. I've tried everything. I took a bath every night. Nothing helped."

She stirred some kind of soup with a spoon. A mound of peas lay on a small board beside her, as if they had been counted out, and some unevenly chopped parsley.

"We'll find a doctor. He'll help us."

"ZZZ," she made a circle with her finger in front of her forehead.

"Not one doctor would do it. And even if he would, he'll ask for a lot of money. Do you have it? No! Watch out, the child will fall down."

Janko crawled along the edge of the bed toward the bright spot of sunlight which was lying like a dead butterfly fastened to the blanket.

Munda placed the child on the floor.

"I can borrow money," he said.

"Who will you borrow it from?"

"I don't know yet."

"No one will lend it to you. No one you know has that much money. All of them put together don't have that much. What then?"

"We'll talk about that later. But now be quiet."

"When will we talk about it—when? You think, young as I am, I will again parade around with the belly. Oh, no. You're wrong. And one kid is enough for me already."

With a finger she wiped bitter tears from the corners of her eyes. She was married when she was sixteen and a half.

She was a child, just a child, to whom her father—he was a waiter—gave some money the first of every month. On Saturdays she would wait in front of the photo studio for the girls who lived around the corner, to go to the dance in the sports palace together. Every Saturday she was the first to come and on the way, with an enormous appetite, she ate bread crumbs from a bag in her purse, so that passers-by would think what marvelous sweets she could afford, or that she was taking pills because she was sick. She especially liked to be sick like that girl in the castle in the Scottish film. She imagined how wonderful it would be to be sick and be wrapped up in a checked blanket on the porch of some sanatorium abroad, where no one knew her, and yet everyone knew about her. And she would like very much to have a boy friend like Metka from Mencinger Street: an older, unhappy, and disillusioned man who already had greyish hair at the temples, and water in the lungs, or some other illness. Fani dreamed about such a boy friend at that time: she would visit him every day at the hospital and, instead of regular food, she would cook only violets for him.

For this reason she could not stand Munda, although he flew around her like a butterfly. He wasn't serious enough and too much of a ruffian for her. Many times she was told about how such boys ruin girls and leave them in the gutter. And what's more, she had known Munda since he was a child, and she would always consider him a child and herself a child when she was with him. And that she simply could not accept. After two years, they began to meet at dances. By that time, his mother had already died. He had grown up very little, but wherever there was a fight, he, too, was there with his fists and his insolent, inquisitive snout. He would walk stealthily behind her like a greedy beast, and at the dances he put almost all the other dancers to shame. He never said anything to her, but, when they would dance he would pinch her so much that the next day she was black and blue all over. One evening after the dance, she and

Boris Nedog went to the park. Suddenly on the bench he
began to squeeze her and, just as he was unsnapping her
bra, Munda appeared and hit him over the head with a
briefcase, knocking him out, and he took her away. After
that, Nedog was never seen again at the Mosti. He got stuck
on some she-goat by the name of Pika who was supposedly
a sales girl in the People's Store. Fani fell head over heels
in love with Munda. She whistled at Nedog; he meant about
as much to her as empty space. She loved Munda more and
more. He was very dear to her, she was pleased that every
one feared him, and she was not in the least bit afraid of him
when they were together. Later, when she became pregnant,
she moved into his room. He still had his box with two
hundred and seventy pictures of locomotives, ships, and
planes, which they played with together as children in front
of the gate. When the baby was born, she left the position
of messenger at the city plant, Koža. Now she was eighteen,
and he nineteen. In the fall, he would have to go into the
army.

"I don't want a child. I don't wish a child!" she shouted.
Munda embraced her, lifted and carried her, wiggling like
a bundle of wildcats, to the bed.

"I don't feel like it, not now," she shouted. Munda put
the child in the crib and covered the crib with a blanket.

"It's just you and me, dear Fani," he said and patted
her on the arms.

"I still want to sweep the room," she whispered. Broken
buttons from her sweater were in front of her lips. "Then
I will come."

"Nothing doing. I'm in the mood now."

The evening sun soaked the linen curtain on the window
and dripped into the purple murkiness of the room. Melting
into each other, they felt the objects in the room closing in
on them, as in a dream, while the floor lifted itself like a
raft on a slow white river. The raft floated into the turbulent water. The raft was sinking deeper.

"Finish quickly," Fani whispered. "I still have to clean up the room."

They were looking at each other. The bottoms of their eyes receded into the distance, as if they were looking at each other from two ends of an endless, flat road. Then they were lying beside each other, tired and empty, as if they had emerged from the deep black water. Munda turned away. He no longer felt anything toward her. He heard her get up, look for her slippers under the bed, pour water in the hall, and then wash his marks and bruises on her shoulder.

"Damn! How empty the world is," he thought and then dozed off. Fani's voice woke him. She was standing by the open window watering the vegetables in the window box.

"The last few months, I thought I'd buy so many things," she said.

"Stop that," he hissed and in wild anger clenched his fists under the pillow.

"I was planning to buy some linen for two sheets. We only have three. But nothing will come of that. We can't buy anything. And look, I wrote that a year ago."

He tightened his fists in a rage. "Damn it, again there's no peace. There's still no peace here."

"Here!" She tossed a knife at him on the bed and looked at him with a dark flashing in her eyes, as if a bird had flown in front of her glance and left a shadow of his wings in them. "Here, kill me. You think I don't see you clenching your fists under the pillow. Oh, how you clench them."

He drew out his red, tightly closed fists like some kind of sick animal.

"Slut, slut." Twice he stuck the knife into the floor. He looked at her as if she had been his greatest enemy all his life, and as if in wild joy he was afraid to believe that he had indeed found him.

The child began to cry.

"Janko, Janko," she stuttered. Terror seized her from his look. She hung a small incense burner in the old place, beneath the calendar of the Workers' Union with a picture across the whole page of a miner's family with ruddy cheeks in the dining room.

"Kill me," she whispered and sat down next to the hot-plate with the child in her arms.

"I'll kill you. You bet I'll kill you."

He felt the desire to beat her. He would beat her senseless until she became nothing, so he would not have to feel her presence next to him. He walked to the window. In all the doorways, people stood talking. From the candy shop, Orient, where a blue light bulb was burning in the window, children came out with ice cream. Someone was playing on the saxophone on the upper floor behind the door of the wooden porch.

He said, "I'm going to the movies."

Fani got up and stood behind him. "You really intend to go?"

He turned around and began to kick a light, empty box by the wall. "Yes, I do."

Janko grabbed the box. Munda took it out of his hand and continued to kick it around the room. Janko followed him with his eyes. He saw only two restless, alive pant legs and heels which appeared beneath him.

"Will you take me, too?" Fani asked, walking slowly after him. He nodded.

"Really," she shouted joyfully. She kissed him on the neck and hurried to the hotplate.

When they had finished supper, Fani put the child to bed: in his tea, she had already mixed a solution of poppy seeds to make him fall asleep sooner. They dressed. In a white skirt, which had a wide red sash with a big bow on the side—she had sewn it herself—she wore a blue bolero and he a windbreaker. (On his windbreaker, he still had three shock workers' emblems of the Youth Railroad Brigade.)

The street was empty and grey, only a light was burning

in the butcher shop, illuminating the pavement. They walked quickly. She held onto his elbow, arranging her hair and stumbling over the stones in her black high-heeled shoes. They stopped at the corner. The clock in the bell tower struck seven-thirty and from behind a house in front of them, a bicycle wheel was flung, wobbling across the street.

"I'll run ahead and get the tickets," he said nervously. He pushed her hand away from his elbow and ran off. She walked after him slowly in the darkness, like a little girl, along the high white fence above which swayed small heart-shaped leaves.

Munda ran down the middle of the street because there were too many people on the sidewalks, clambering over piles of sand and stones which the strollers slowly passed. Once again he descended quickly from those piles like an airplane—as a boy he used to imitate the motor-raa-rraa—jumped across puddles, and ran along the Ljubljanica River on the soft grass. He cut across the road, evading some bicycle riders who were humming with a silken noise in the middle of the street and, in the falling darkness, resembled spinning wheels with huge grasshoppers sitting on top.

"If I could just get those tickets," he repeated to himself. He ran without stopping, out of breath, as if he had a sack of rocks around his neck.

He stopped. In front of the lighted entrance of the theater mulled a black, dense mass of people. "What if it's already sold out? What if it's already sold out?" That thought stuck in his mind like a round stone. He flew through the crowd. Angry faces followed him, and he elbowed his way to the long line in front of the cashier's window. Munda, slyly, stepped in behind a woman in the line.

"Where did that one come from," several people said.

A tall man in a round hat leaned toward him. A gold tooth flashed in the corner of his mouth when he opened it.

"What do you want? What? Get out of here and wait at the end of the line, my friend. At the end of the line." The giant pronounced these words, syllable by syllable, slowly, as if he were typing them.

"I was here the whole time," Munda said, not raising his eyes, peering into the cashier's window and clutching the money in his hand.

"Out with him. Throw him out of line. We've already waited a whole hour," shouted a woman in the crowd who was standing next to the red step.

"Don't tell me any stories," the giant said angrily. "I saw how you slipped into the line and I'm telling you—get out!"

The man pushed him so that he flew out of the line into the people who were standing near the cashier's window.

"You conceited brat. And you're too young to go to the movies this late, anyway."

Munda shoved his hands into his pockets so that the people would not notice his wedding ring.

"I've been standing here the whole hour," he said. "The whole time."

The room was saturated with smoke, the scent of perfume, and shaving soap. A bright light from the ceiling sparkled on the pins, pocket handkerchiefs, and shawls of the women, on the small chains around their necks, and on the display windows with pictures; the blackness of the dark suits swallowed it.

Munda looked at the people and, angry as he was, he saw only the lips and moustaches under the blinding light. He was stepping forward when two men grabbed him from behind. One of his emblems came loose, fell on the floor, and disappeared in the maze of feet.

"I stood in line the whole time," he repeated in a hollow voice, talking from his stomach. He waited until the two released him and then jumped to the ticket window, next to someone who was just putting his money and ticket into his pocket. Those behind crowded him to push him out like a cork from a bottle.

"Leave him alone," someone said. With elbows sticking

into his sides, with noise and curses in his ears, Munda stood firmly on spread legs, leaned through the window into the blinding light, and handed his money to a woman in a purple shawl.

"Two tickets, please, near the screen. Two tickets." He rushed outside, followed by threats and blows on the back.

"Did you get the tickets?" The face of Fani swam before him in the crowd.

"Yes, I got them."

In the corner, behind a high counter with display windows, a dark-haired man with a knife in his hands was selling halvah, candy, and pretzels. In front of the counter, beside the entrance in the hall, stood an empty chair. Munda sat down.

"Here, sit down on my knees," he said.

"I'll wrinkle my bow."

"It doesn't matter, sit down."

She pulled the bow to the side and sat down. They lit cigarettes. The people stood in front of them and the smoke floated above their heads in countless spirals, but the two of them were in the shadows of their backs.

"Maybe I'll get the money for the doctor," Munda said suddenly.

She lifted her head, exhaled the smoke, holding the cigarette like something magic between her fingers and looked at him.

"Where?"

"It isn't far," he said whispering.

"Roman asked me the last time if I could get some fenders from the factory for his cars and motorcycles. People say that he has connections. . . ."

"Don't you dare!" she said frightenedly.

"Don't blabber. I know where some fenders are and even some tin which the very black devil knows nothing about. Under the building, in a shed. They have forgotten about them. And if I don't take them, someone else will, and then there goes our chance. Only. . . ."

"And if they catch you and lock you up?"

"Me? You're crazy, girl! They'll never catch me. God, that's all I need. I'm working my head off. After all, some of that belongs to me, too. If everybody lived on his salary. . . . The devil of it is, how to carry them out."

"Let's forget about it. Better look. It's Rita Hayworth," said Fani, and pointed with a cigarette to a large green placard on the wall.

"What movie was she in before?" Munda asked with a cigarette in his lips.

They were among the first to enter the aisle and sit down on the smooth, warm seats at the end of the row. The loudspeaker was playing "Hora Staccato," and then "When the Apple Trees Blossom in Normandy."

"No one else will come," Fani said looking at the filled row of seats: nervous hands and calm knees, purses and faces, pale yellow and red women's hats, and unbuttoned men's shirts. The lights went out. The screen lit up in the darkness, began to flicker, and went out, as if an avalanche of white, blinding snow slid next to a great window and disappeared in the depths beneath the stage. The lights came on again.

"How would we look on the screen?" Fani asked laughing, squinting from the unexpected brightness. "Wouldn't the people laugh!"

In her lap she held an open purse. They took candy from a small bag inside it and ate. The auxiliary seats creaked.

"In Hollywood, we would be a flop, girl," he said. "They measure everything there. The nose, so many centimeters, the head, so many, the lips, then the eyes, and waist. That's the way Rita Hayworth is. Otherwise she couldn't be in the movies." The lights went out. He helped her take off her bolero, and put it on his knees.

They held hands, and clung to each other as did the people in front of them, behind them, and around them. The movie began.

# CONTRIBUTORS

*Foreign titles of publications are Anglicized*

## AUTHORS

S. J. AGNON (1888-1970) has been described as "a brilliant portrayer of Polish Jewry in recent generations. . . . His narrative manner is pure art: a calm, epic manner that flows quietly like the waters of a crystal brook with no unnatural surprises or disturbances. Agnon has a unique style: the style of the Midrashim and the Chassidic tales, the scholarly Talmudic style brought to a rare consistency and perfection" (Joseph Klausner). Agnon was generally acknowledged as the greatest living Hebrew writer of his time. He was awarded the Nobel Prize for Literature in 1968. Some of his fiction has been translated into many languages, but unhappily most of his work remains the preserve of those who know Hebrew.

IQBAL AHMAD (1922-    ) teaches English at the University of Waterloo, Ontario. His work has appeared in *Canadian Form* and *The Atlantic*.

MULK RAJ ANAND (1905-    ), internationally known novelist, edits India's premier art magazine, *Marg*. The second volume of his autobiographical novel, *Morning Face,* will be published soon. He was recently appointed the first Tagore Professor of Art and Literature in the University of Punjab. He writes that his work "is marked by humanistic tendencies and a radical outlook." He concluded a recent letter with these words: "The late spring flowers flare here and I wish you much creative work, as, indeed, I wish myself, in this time when the forces of death are working overtime to render everything meaningless."

PULGIS ANDRIUŠIS (1907-1970). Acclaimed in Lithuania before 1944 for his humorous sketches and for the definitive Lithuanian version of *Don Quixote,* he had enhanced his stature in Germany and Australia with his novels of wit and his lyrical evocations of Lithuanian landscape and character.

CHARLES ANGOFF—see note about editors.

ASHER BARASH (1889-1952)—Polish-born writer of short stories, novels and poetry—lived in Palestine after 1914. In his Eastern Galicia year, his fiction dealt with the stable and more tranquil pre-World War I period, when there was a place even for Jews in the scheme of things. In his Palestine-Israel years, he portrayed the slow, laborious building of the Jewish homeland. His work also includes seven novellas covering three thousand years of Jewish history, from the early Hebrew monarchy *(Saul and the Asses)* to Nazi Germany *(In Marburg)* .

JENS BJÖRNEBOE (1920-    ) is a controversial poet, novelist and playwright. *Lease of These,* a novel exposing Norway's educational system, was translated into English; another novel, *Without a Thread,* was confiscated by the police. A play, *The Bird Lovers,* has been received with enthusiasm by critics all over Scandinavia.

DINO BUZZATI (1906-    ) has published more than ten books of fiction, including novels and collections of short stories, which have been widely translated, and thirteen plays, several produced successfully in Italy, Germany and France. *Sixty Short Stories* (1959) won the Strega award. Buzzati is also a painter, a stage designer for La Scala, a skiier, and a fancier of boxer dogs.

FRANCSICO A. COLOANE (1910-    ) —son of a whaling captain—knows first hand the life he describes in his fiction. Seaman, whaler, seal hunter, and sheepherder, he writes with sympathy for the humble rancher of Patagonia, the seal hunter of inland streams, the fisherman and the Yagan Indian. His stories in *Cape Horn, Tierra del Fuego, The Gulf of Trouble* and two books for children are laid in the transition from early pioneer to near-pioneer period reaching our era. Coloane has described Tierra del Fuego as a "land of surprises, unforgettable, beloved! The man who has been awed by her mysteries will be anchored there forever in his memories. She and her men are like icebergs. When ice has torn away the blue base, the mass suddenly turns over and once again, white and solids, sails on!"

DHUMKETU (1892-    ) —nom-de-plume of Gaurishanker Goverdhanram Joshi—is a leading Indian short story writer and one of the veterans of Gujerati literature. His more than forty-five published works include novels, travel books, autobiography, satires, plays, life sketches, and four volumes of short stories. He is a member of the Sahitya Akademi, New Delhi.

HEIMITO VON DODERER (1896-    ) found his talent as a writer while a prisoner in Siberia during World War I. Although he published poetry and fiction in the early twenties, his greatest work came much later: *The Illuminated Windows* (1950), *The Strudhofstiege* (1951), *The Demons* (1956) —all novels—and *The Torturing of the Leather Pouches* (1959) —a book of short stories. "The Magician's Art" is the first example of this important Austrian author's prose in English.

AHMED ESSA is a professor of English at the University of Nevada, Reno. Besides writing he is a distinguished photographer.

ENDRE FEJES (1923-    ) began publishing short stories in Hungary. His novel *Rusty Graveyard* was successfully dramatized. He has also written film scripts.

ENNIO FLAIANO (1910-    ) began his career as a film and drama critic. From 1945 to 1953 he was editor of *Il Mondo*. He is the author of several one-act plays and of many film scenarios. One of his novels has been translated into English under the title *Miriam*.

MARIN FREDA (1922-    ) is one of Rumania's most eminent writers of short stories, novellas, and novels. *The Marometes* (1955), depicting a village in the Danube plain on the eve of the second world war, is considered his greatest work.

OLIVER ST. JOHN GOGARTY (1878-1957) —Irish poet, novelist, essayist, surgeon, and Senator of the Irish Free State —was a tough fighter in politics, a licensed airplane pilot, a motorcycle racer, a skilled archer, and a writer of more than twenty books. He was described by his friend, "A. E.," as "the wildest wit in Ireland." The day of his death in New York City, he mailed the following poem to the editors of this anthology:

### HIS EPITAPH

*Don't let death confuse you all:*
*Death is not unusual.*

N. V. M. GONZALEZ is the author of several novels, including *The Winds of April* (1941), a prizewinner in the Commonwealth Literary Contest, *A Season of Grace* (1956) and *The Bamboo Dancers* (1959) ; and two story collections, *Seven Hills Away* (1947) and *Children of the Ash-Covered Loam* (1954). He received the first Republic Award of Merit, as well as Rockefeller study and travel grants to the

United States and the Far East. *The Bamboo Dancers*, which received the Republic Cultural Heritage Award in 1960, was published last year in the U.S. (Allan Swallow). In the Philippines, Gonzalez is represented in many anthologies. In the U.S., he is included in *Span*, edited by Lionel Wigmore, and in *Stanford Short Stories 1950*, edited by Wallace Stegner. He was the first president of the Philippine Writers Association.

KAATJE HURLBUT'S stories appear in many magazines: *The Literary Review, Red Book, Good Housekeeping, Ladies Home Journal, Saturday Evening Post;* and anthologies: *Best American Short Stories of 1961, 40 Best Stories from Mademoiselle* (1961), and *Science Fiction Annual* (1962). She is currently working on a novel in her home in Guilford, Connecticut, U.S.A.

ORHAN BEMAL (1914-    ), wholly without formal education, has published twelve books of socially realistic short stories and novels concerned with "the village-born workers in new urban industrial centers, the underprivileged little man of Istanbul, and the Anatolian migrants . . . [His work] presents a deeply moving and wonderfully exact picture of the social evolution of the masses in modern Turkey" (Kemal H. Karpat).

YURI KAZAKOV (1927-    ) has published several short-story collections since 1953. Many regard him as the best contemporary Russian short-story writer.

YASAR KEMAL (1922-    ) ended his formal education in the last year of secondary school, worked at a variety of jobs, and now is a reporter for the newspaper *Cumhuriyet* in Istanbul. He has published a volume of short stories, three novels, and several books of folklore. "He writes from personal experience, with intimate knowledge of his material and compassion for his subjects—the peasant left to the mercy of landlords, petty officials and money lenders" (Kemal H. Karpat).

LOJZE KOVACIC (1928-    ) was active as a librarian and now is a theater director in Ljubljana. One of the best from the middle generation of the Slovenian writers, he is known chiefly for his volume of stories, *Picture Postcards of Ljubljana*. He also writes for children.

MARGARITA KOVALEVSKA (1910-    ) graduated from the Latvian Academy of Art during the years of Latvian independence (1918-1939), and gained recognition as painter and book illustrator. Now living near Washington, D. C., she divides her time between painting and writing. Her first novel, *The Flower of Disaster* (1962), has been acclaimed by critics as an outstanding work of Latvian literature.

VEIJO MERI (1928-    ) is the best known of the younger Finnish novelists and short story writers.

ELSA MORANTE (1915-    ), wife of the writer Alberto Moravi, is the author, among other works, of two novels, *Deceit and Sorcery* (1948) and *Island of Arthur* (1958), which have been widely translated. "Behind the scaffolding of a discursive and extremely diluted rational style, embellished by a singing tone, one quickly discovers the painful authenticity of a warm and obsessive emotion, an emotion which could be expressed only by a person well acquainted with the Southern soul" (Giacinto Spagnoletti).

ADRIAAN MORRIËN (1912-    ) edits the magazine, *Literary Passport*, the only Dutch review entirely devoted to foreign literature. Chief works: *The Fatherland* (1946), poems; *A Slovenly Person* (1951), stories; and *Friendship for a Tree* (1954), poems.

Torborg Nedreaas (1906-    ) has published two books of verses, in 1962 and 1964.

Aziz Nesin (1915-    ) began his career as an army officer, resigning at age thirty to write. At first he earned his living variously as a grocer, counter clerk, book seller, photographer. . . . His published books include six novels, two plays, three newspaper columns, two satires, and twenty-four volumes of short stories, several of which have been translated into various European languages. In Italy his stories won first prizes in 1956 and 1957 in the international humor contest. In Turkey they provoked thirty prosecutions, resulting in various jail sentences totalling almost six years.

Hiroshi Noma (1915-    ), banner-bearer of postwar Japanese literature, served in north China and the Philippines during World War II. His massive novel depicting the inhumanity of Japanese army life, *Zone of Emptiness,* has been translated into French (1954) and English (1956). The Japanese original of "A Red Moon in Her Face" was published in 1947.

Kostes Palamas (1859-1943), noted Greek poet, published a book of short stories in which the two parables appear. In the prologue, Palamas wrote "that he has felt his highest obligation to be that of giving of himself to others without hesitation and without restraint. His theme in both 'A Man from Afar' and 'Digging for a Statue' is the artist's struggle for this superhuman goal. In the latter, he crystallizes the mature artist's insight. He realizes he will never reach the goal, but peace comes to him with the grateful acknowledgement of a people whose lives he has enriched by giving of himself in terms of their needs and understanding" (Helen E. Farmakis).

Gerard Kornelis van het Reve (1923-    ) published his long realistic short story, "The Decline and Fall of the

Boslowits Family," in 1946. The year following, a controversial novel, *The Evenings,* appeared. *The Acrobat* (1956)
is a volume of short stories written in English.

AIDA L. RIVERA won the 1954 Hopwood award for fiction,
at the University of Michigan, for her collected stories, *Now
and At the Hour.* "She has managed to create women of the
Filipino middle-class . . . (until recently, sociologists have
denied that the Philippines possess more than an upper,
landed class and a submerged tenant farmer-proletarian class).
She seems to prefer the 'observational eye'" (Manuel A.
Viray). Miss Rivera lives on a south Mindanoa farm.

KARL RISTIKIVI (1912-    ). Novelist. In most of his
work he is a sensitive realist, broad in scope and quietly intimate in approach. He has published a historical trilogy
dealing with the period of the Hohenstaufen emperors.
Lives in Stockholm.

SIMON VESTDIJK (1898-    ), a highly original and pro-
lific writer in contemporary Holland, has published seven
volumes of short stories, including translations of Poe and
Conan Doyle; scores of novels; twenty-one books of poetry,
including translations of Emily Dickinson; many volumes of
essays; and a work on the future of religion.

VLADIMIR VONDRA has written numerous short stories
and is on the staff of the literary magazine *Plamen.* He has
published two books: *Ballad of an Outlaw* (1956) and *Two-
Faced* (1960).

BEB VUYK, of Dutch-Indonesian descent, was born and
bred in Rotterdam, moved to Indonesia in 1929, and became
the wife of an Eurasian, whose family had lived for more
than 150 years in the Moluccas. Her life on a tea plantation
is described in her novel, *Thousand Islands* (1937). Another

novel, *The Word of Bara* (1948), was partly written while she was interned with her two sons during the Japanese occupation. At this time, her husband worked as a P.O.W. with the Burma Thailand railroad. Emotionally and politically involved in Indonesia life, she and her husband chose Indonesian nationality after Independence. In 1958 political circumstances forced exile to Holland, but they remain Indonesian nationality after Independence. In 1958 political circumstances forced exile to Holland, but they remain Indonesian citizens who hope to return to their country "when the shouting and shooting have died down." *Full of Sound and Fury* (1960), a volume of short stories, depicts the life and fate of individuals during the Japanese occupation and the Indonesian revolution.

WILLIAM CARLOS WILLIAMS (1883-1968) practiced medicine and wrote most of his thirty-eight published volumes of poetry, fiction, plays, sketches, criticism, and autobiography in Rutherford, New Jersey, which is also the home of the first of Fairleigh Dickinson University's three major campuses. Among his many distinguished services, including his generosity to promising young writers, Dr. Williams gave strong support to the launching of *The Literary Review,* which featured him in its first number (Autumn 1957). Concerning his story, "From My Notes About My Mother," he wrote: "The manuscript has never left my family."

STEPAS ZOBARSKAS (1911-    ), twice honored with literary prizes for his short stories by the Lithuanian Red Cross, now lives in Woodhaven, N. Y., where he devotes his time and energies to promulgating the literatures of those countries whose writings are not readily available to the English-speaking reader. He edited and in part translated *Selected Lithuanian Short Stories, Lithuanian Folk Tales,* and *Lithuanian Quartet.* His latest collection of short stories, *Young Love and Other Infidelities,* was published in 1971.

# EDITORS

Dr. Clarence R. Decker, co-founder and co-editor with Charles Angoff of *The Literary Review*, was academic vice president and professor of Comparative Literature at Fairleigh Dickinson University. From 1938-1953 he was president of the University of Kansas City, where he founded and edited that University's *Literary Review*. In 1949 he was awarded the Order of the Aztec Eagle by the government of Mexico for his "outstanding contribution to the diffusion of knowledge of Mexican art and culture in the Middle West." In 1952 he served as Assistant Director for the Far East of the Mutual Security Agency, in which capacity he took an active interest in international cultural exchange. For four years (1957-1960) he was president of the Poetry Society of America. He died in 1969.

Dr. Charles Angoff has had a many-sided career as fiction writer, lecturer, editor, and teacher. Educated at Harvard University, he began his literary apprenticeship as a newspaperman in Boston. In 1925 he was an assistant to H. L. Mencken on the *American Mercury*, eventually became managing editor and then, in 1935, editor. He subsequently worked for the *Nation, Scribner's, The American Spectator, North American Review*, and *Living Age*. Author or editor of more than thirty-five books, Dr. Angoff has had two plays produced, and has contributed poems, stories, essays, one-act plays, and reviews to one hundred magazines and newspapers both in the United States and abroad. His most recent books are *Winter Twilight* and *Season of Mists* (novels), *H. L. Mencken: A Portrait From Memory*, and *Prayers at Midnight*, his third book of poems. He is Professor of English at Fairleigh Dickinson University, editor of the *Literary Review*, chief editor of the Fairleigh Dickinson University Press, and President of the Poetry Society of America (second term).

LIBRARY
OKALOOSA - WALTON JUNIOR COLLEGE

DISCARDED

OKALOOSA-WALTON COLLEGE
1000024183